MW00559621

Dead Man's Hand

DEAD MAN'S HAND

The Saga of Doc Holliday

Book Three

A Novel

VICTORIA WILCOX

TWODOT®

GUILFORD, CONNECTICUT
HELENA, MONTANA

For
Jennifer, Heather, Ashley, and Ross
My best creations.

A · TWODOT® · BOOK

An imprint and registered trademark of The Rowman & Littlefield Publishing Group, Inc.
4501 Forbes Blvd., Ste. 200
Lanham, MD 20706
www.rowman.com

Distributed by NATIONAL BOOK NETWORK

Copyright © 2015 Victoria Wilcox
Previously published as *The Last Decision*

All rights reserved. No part of this book may be reproduced in any form or by any electronic or mechanical means, including information storage and retrieval systems, without written permission from the publisher, except by a reviewer who may quote passages in a review.

British Library Cataloguing in Publication Information available

Library of Congress Cataloging-in-Publication Data available
Names: Wilcox, Victoria, author.
Title: Dead man's hand : the saga of Doc Holliday / Victoria Wilcox.
Other titles: Last decision | Saga of Doc Holliday
Description: Guilford, Connecticut ; Helena, Montana : TwoDot ; Distributed
  by National Book Network 2019. | Previously titled The last decision,
  published by Knox Robinson (London), 2015. The third volume in the Doc
  Holliday trilogy. |
Identifiers: LCCN 2019018109 (print) | LCCN 2019018842 (ebook) | ISBN
  9781493044740 (e-book) | ISBN 9781493044733 (pbk.)
Subjects: LCSH: Holliday, John Henry, 1851-1887—Fiction. | GSAFD:
  Biographical fiction. | Western stories. | Historical fiction.
Classification: LCC PS3623.I5327 (ebook) | LCC PS3623.I5327 L37 2019 (print)
  | DDC 813/.6—dc23
LC record available at https://lccn.loc.gov/2019018109

∞™ The paper used in this publication meets the minimum requirements of American National Standard for Information Sciences—Permanence of Paper for Printed Library Materials, ANSI/ NISO Z39.48-1992.

CONTENTS

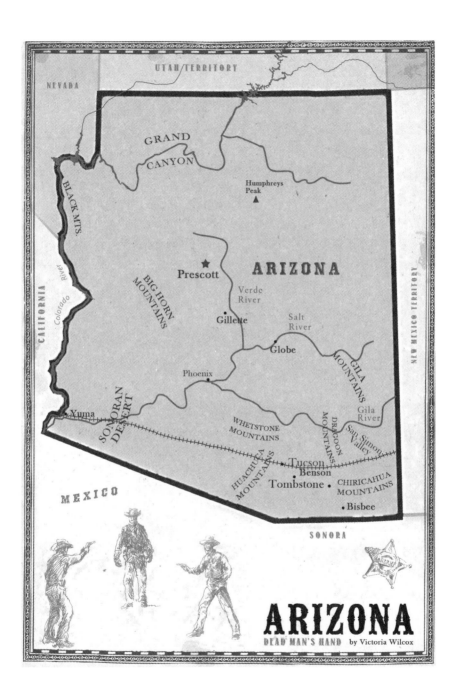

ARIZONA
DEAD MAN'S HAND by Victoria Wilcox

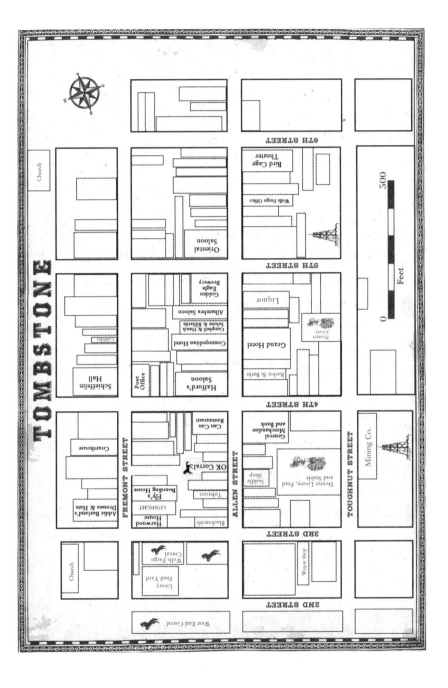

TOMBSTONE

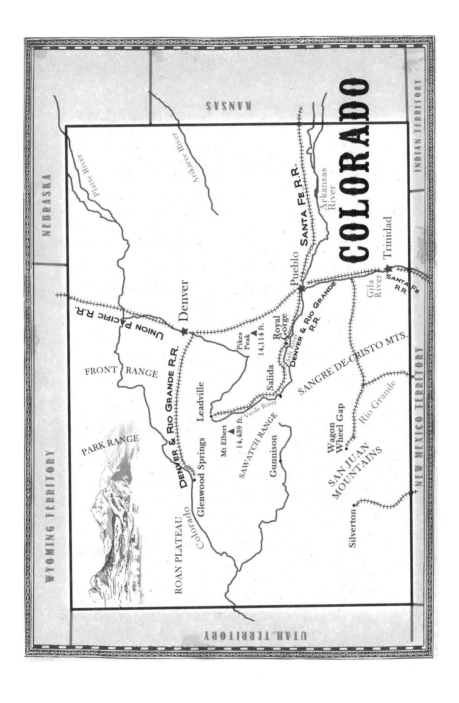

COLORADO

NEBRASKA

KANSAS

WYOMING TERRITORY

UTAH TERRITORY

NEW MEXICO TERRITORY

INDIAN TERRITORY

Platte River

Arikaree River

Arkansas River

SANTA FE R.R.

Trinidad

Pueblo

Denver

UNION PACIFIC R.R.

DENVER & RIO GRANDE R.R.

FRONT RANGE

PARK RANGE

ROAN PLATEAU

Colorado

Glenwood Springs

Leadville

Mt Elbert
▲ 14,439 ft.

SAWATCH RANGE

Gunnison

Verde River

Salida

Pikes Peak
▲ 14,114 ft.

Salt River

Royal Gorge

DENVER & RIO GRANDE R.R.

Gila River

SANTA FE R.R.

SANGRE DE CRISTO MTS.

Rio Grande

Wagon Wheel Gap

SAN JUAN MOUNTAINS

Silverton

Chapter One

ARIZONA TERRITORY, 1879

KATE ELDER DESPISED WYATT EARP. THERE WAS NO OTHER WORD TO describe it. She hated him with the kind of passion that some women reserved for a romantic rival. And in some ways, he was a rival, being John Henry Holliday's most admired friend and recipient of some of the time and attention that Kate thought was owed to her as a wife. Except that Kate Elder wasn't Mrs. Holliday, just Doc Holliday's mistress, a fact that never ceased to rankle her. She was always bringing it up, as though he might have simply forgotten the lapse and just needed reminding to rectify it. But his memory was fine, especially in the matter of why he hadn't, and wouldn't, make Kate his wife.

Problem was, Kate didn't just hate his friend Wyatt—she'd tried to have him killed, back in Dodge City, a sin which John Henry could neither forgive nor forget. But he also couldn't forget how Kate had saved his own life once, taking him over the mountains from Colorado to the New Mexico Territory and the miraculous Montezuma Hot Springs. He wouldn't be alive, and healed, without Kate. So he owed her his life, if not his legal name.

So they'd arrived in the Arizona Territory as something of a common-law couple, and he hadn't objected when she signed the register at the Prescott Hotel as "Dr. and Mrs. J.H. Holliday." The register wasn't a legal document anyhow, much less a marriage license, and for a time, Kate had seemed happy enough. She was happy anywhere Wyatt wasn't, and he'd only stayed in town a few weeks, just long enough to restock his

Conestoga before traveling on to try his luck in the silver boom camp of Tombstone, south by the Mexican border.

But John Henry's fortunes were doing just fine in the Territorial capital of Prescott, nestled in the cool highlands of central Arizona, and he declined Wyatt's invitation to ride along to Tombstone. Although Prescott was still so new that it was mostly a string of sawmills along Lynx Creek and a half-finished wooden courthouse on a half-built town square, there were already enough big-stakes gambling games in the saloons on Montezuma Street to make things interesting. Besides, he'd had enough of sitting a horse and breathing in trail dust for one season, after traveling in Wyatt's wagon train across the high desert from New Mexico, and he intended to enjoy the brisk pine-scented air of Prescott for awhile. So he sold the horses he'd bought in Las Vegas and used the money to rent rooms at the Prescott Hotel, and settled down to his accustomed routine of sleeping late before dressing for an evening of gambling halls and saloons. It was pleasant enough, and profitable enough, that when Wyatt wrote letters from Tombstone to say that the town was even more than he'd imagined and that John Henry should join him there, Kate protested loudly. She liked Prescott, she said, with its boisterous newness and its busyness as Territorial capital—though what she meant was that she liked having John Henry all to herself without Wyatt Earp around as competition.

But when Wyatt wrote yet again, saying that there was no dentist in Tombstone, and that a man who could pull teeth and pull fast cards as well was sure to make a comfortable living, John Henry was finally per-suaded. The truth was, it was Kate's protestations that made up his mind to go. He didn't like the idea of doing what a woman wanted just because she wanted him to do it, especially when she acted like she had some right to make such demands. She wasn't really Mrs. Holliday, after all, in spite of that hotel register signature, and taking Wyatt up on his offer seemed like a good way of telling her so without saying it right out loud.

Although Kate wasn't pleased at the news that John Henry was pack-ing up for Tombstone, she went along without objecting too much—at least as far as Gillette, a two days' stagecoach ride away. That was where the Prescott-to-Phoenix stage laid over for the night, though the town was nothing much more than the headquarters for the Tip Top Mine, without a proper hotel or anywhere else for passengers to sleep. And maybe it was the discomfort of their accommodations—a narrow cot in the office of the mine superintendent and a paltry plate of supper served up from the mine's general store—but Gillette was as far as she could force herself to go.

"I don't know why he has such hold over you," she complained as she and John Henry lay together on the comfortless cot, trying to find some sleep. "We were doing just fine in Prescott. You were set to make a fortune on those government men, the way the poker was going. And Prescott is full of government men to play."

"Government men don't have fortunes to lose," he commented, and turned his face away from hers to cough. As always when he took to traveling, the dust of the road brought the coughing back on, though his lungs weren't near as bad as they had been before his stay at the Montezuma Hot Springs in Las Vegas. He was healed, the doctors there had told him, though he'd need to be careful of himself. Which meant that he ought to be getting some sleep instead of listening to Kate go on about Wyatt Earp.

But Kate didn't seem inclined to let him sleep, even if he could find a position that would let him rest on that hard little cot. The superintendent surely never meant for it to be used as a real bed, and probably kept it for short solitary naps in the middle of long summer days. For two tired bodies, it was barely enough room to stretch out with one arm underneath and one flung out overhead. Still, he was willing to try, if Kate would just stop talking and let him drift into dreams.

"And now look where we are!" she said, "sleeping on a rail in a shack! We could have been back at the Planter's Hotel in St. Louis by now, if you'd listened to me and not followed after Wyatt and his pandering family!"

"Pandering? That's hardly a term that seems fittin' for the former law of Dodge City. And Virgil's a U.S. Marshal now, you know. They're more likely to arrest a whore than barter for her."

"You don't know them like you think you do," she said, turning away from him and nearly pushing him off the cot with her cold shoulder.

"And do you know them any better?" he asked. "Seems to me you spent the whole ride from New Mexico avoidin' havin' any conversation with them at all, keepin' your distance like a regular princess. I reckon the other ladies thought you were actin' too good for them."

"I am too good for them," she said haughtily, "and so are you. And both of us are too good to be spending the night in a place like this!"

"There was a time you didn't mind where we spent the night, as long as we spent it together. Used to be, you had better things to do with a bed than complain about it."

"I still do, if you'd pay less attention to Wyatt and a little more to me," she said as she turned herself back toward him. Kate's solution to every fight was always the same: turning her temper into temptation and trying to make him forget anything but her.

He was willing to forget for awhile, at least long enough to wear himself into sleep for a few crowded hours. That was supposed to be the benefit of having a mistress, after all. But Kate was acting less like a mistress and more like a wife all the time, and even her lovemaking was losing its charm. Come dawn, they'd just be bickering again.

But as they rose early the next morning to be out of the superintendent's office before the workday began, Kate was uncharacteristically quiet. He'd expected a continued tirade, with stinging criticisms of his friendship with Wyatt Earp and pleadings for them to return to Prescott instead of going on to Tombstone. That was, after all, what her lovemaking of the night before was meant to have done, persuading him to come away with her instead of following after Wyatt. But John Henry didn't see why he had to choose one way or the other, and was prepared to listen with tolerant but deaf ears to her demands. What he wasn't prepared for was her silence, or the words that finally came with cool detachment as they left the mine office and headed to meet the stage.

"Have you heard anything of Globe?" she said, and he had to consider a moment before answering.

"Seems like I have. It's another Arizona silver minin' camp, isn't it? About a hundred miles from nowhere, as I recall."

"All of this country is nowhere, as far as I'm concerned," she replied with an air of resignation he hadn't heard before. If he didn't know her better, he'd think she was finally giving up on her dreams of St. Louis and New York and a grand career on the stage. But it was something else she was giving up on. "They say Globe is going to boom bigger than Tombstone, and I'm thinking about going there."

She stopped then, looking at him and waiting for his response. And all he could think to say was, "But Wyatt's invited us to Tombstone. Why would we go to Globe?"

"Not *us*," she said, "me. I'm going there alone, without you or Wyatt or anyone else. I'm leaving you, Doc."

If she'd expected her declaration to bring him to his knees, begging her to stay or maybe offering his hand in marriage as a desperate attempt to keep her with him, she'd bet on the wrong cards. For what he felt was more anger at her ingratitude than anything. Though he had never made her his wife, he'd treated her like one most of the time, keeping a roof over her head and paying for her pricey gowns and things. He'd allowed for her tempers and stood up to her passions, but she couldn't allow herself to share him with the only real friend he had in the world. He didn't want to choose between her and Wyatt, but she was giving him no choice.

"And what are you going to do for a livin', my dear?" he asked coldly. "I doubt there's a theater grand enough for your likin' in any of these mine camps."

"I have other talents besides acting, you know." And when he raised a sarcastic eyebrow and was about to say that he did indeed know of her other gifts, she added, "I can cook a little, and sew as well. Or hire myself out as a nurse to some sporting man with a consumptive cough. At least I'm not afraid of getting sick or working too hard."

"Leave then, if that's what you want!" he said angrily. "Take yourself off to Globe or Tucson, or hell for all I care!" And before she could look into his eyes and see that he did indeed care, he turned away and pulled his hat down low over his face, Wyatt style. "I suppose there's another stage leavin' out of here for Globe. I'll be happy to buy your ticket on it, Miss Elder."

Kate was nothing if not haughty, and though her arrogance had once been an attraction to him, now it was a wall that shut him out.

"No need," she said. "I already took what I wanted out of your pockets last night. I figured you owed me that much for the coupling."

And before he could stop himself, the words came out of his mouth almost unbidden. "Ah, so you finally admit to being what everyone else already thinks you are—a whore."

He didn't even try to move his head away from the stinging slap of her hand, but took it with some satisfaction. He could, at least, still make her angry if nothing else, and the thought of it almost made him smile.

If Kate had waited around awhile, instead of making a dramatic exit on the first stage out of town, she would have had a surprise. For when John Henry boarded his own stage, it wasn't headed on to Tombstone after all, but back to Prescott. Her unexpected desertion had left him shaken and suddenly tired, and he didn't think he could manage the long desert journey alone. Besides, on the road back to Prescott was the Castle Hot Springs, which the stage driver had advertised as being a fine resort for consumptives and other invalids. And though John Henry wasn't feeling like an invalid anymore, he wasn't feeling like his best self either, and the thought of chasing the January chill away in a hot mineral bath was mightily appealing. Luckily, Kate hadn't cleaned out his pockets entirely.

He could have returned to the Prescott Hotel, but decided to make himself a more permanent member of the community by renting a room in the home of a local mine superintendent. The fact that the acting governor of the Arizona Territory, an ambitious man by the name of John Jay Gosper, had rooms there as well gave the place a certain prestigious air, and if it were good enough lodgings for the governor, it was good enough for Dr. John Henry Holliday. It didn't matter to him that the governor hadn't been elected to his high position, but had been moved up from his own office of Secretary of the Territory to sit in for Governor Frémont when the famous explorer made a prolonged visit to Washington, D.C. Political power, however it came, was still powerful.

Secretary Gosper didn't seem inclined to elaborate on the legendary career of the absent executive, but John Henry already knew something of it. For what child growing up in nineteenth-century America hadn't heard of the Great Pathfinder, John C. Frémont? He was nearly as famous all by himself as Lewis and Clark were put together, his maps of the Oregon Trail and the Sierra Nevada as important to the expansion of the American west as was the Lewis and Clark Expedition that had gone exploring for a northwest passage to the Pacific Ocean. Without his maps to mark the way for the thousands of wagon trains that crossed the continent, there might not have been a western expansion at all. His fame had even garnered him a nomination to the United States Presidency, a position he might have won, if a backwoods Illinois lawyer by the name of Abraham Lincoln hadn't beat him out in the election. Though Frémont had failed in politics, his success as an explorer was fittingly rewarded with an appointment as Governor of the newly-made Arizona Territory that stretched from Utah clear to the Mexican border. But even Frémont, with all his exploring expertise, couldn't seem to keep things in Arizona under control. Which was why, according to Gosper, the governor had left the Territory and returned to Washington with his wife and family. John Frémont's adventure days were over, and Arizona needed a younger, braver hand to take care of the challenges of the modern West.

At least, that was the impression one got from talking to John Gosper, who seemed a man of energy and imagination, intent on making a good showing of himself as long as he occupied the Governor's seat—though even Gosper didn't know how long that would be. Although Governor Frémont had left the Territory with a wife who disliked the desert climate and enough luggage to keep her and the rest of the Frémont family well-dressed for years in Washington, there was no telling when he might decide to return and resume his position. What Gosper did know was that as long as he had the Territorial Seal in his hand, the fate of Arizona was in his hands as well.

Although John Henry didn't hear from Kate after their parting in Gillette and his return to Prescott, he did continue to hear from Wyatt Earp in letters as spare as the lawman's lean and sinewy frame; all fact and no fancy at all. But the facts Wyatt had to tell were often interesting enough to make his letters almost good reading.

Like the way his proposed express business had ended before it began, being crowded out of the running by the several other express businesses already operating in Tombstone. *"The roads are full of wagons,"* was the way he put it, and John Henry could imagine the trail to Tombstone like a day at the Roman races, with chariots jostling and careening out of control, horses whipped to a lather as the drivers vied for first place and the silver reward at the end. *"I've taken a position with Wells, Fargo & Co."* Wyatt wrote, and John Henry could picture him riding shotgun on a treasure coach, rifle laid ready across his lap, solemn eyes searching the horizon for the sudden danger of road agents. *"I have a Faro game at the Oriental Saloon,"* Wyatt said, and John Henry envisioned green baize and crimson carpets and blue clouds of cigar smoke lit by the undulating glow of oil lamps. And though John Henry had to make most of it up himself, adding to those letters what Wyatt left out, he still liked to think that whatever Wyatt Earp did was somehow a step above the ordinary, an adventure about to happen.

But he wasn't quite ready yet for new adventures himself, as he was still enjoying the unexpected benefit of Kate's desertion—namely, the opportunity to make acquaintance with the likes of John Gosper. For if Kate had been living with him, flouncing her stagey self around like a theater demimonde, John Henry would never have been considered good enough company for the acting chief executive of a United States Territory. Sporting men and their mistresses, while common enough in the New West, were not yet accepted as polite society. The single and available Dr. Holliday, on the other hand, was not only acceptable, but soon sought after by the polite ladies of the town. It only added to his suddenly proper-again reputation that he shared lodgings with the also-single and eminently marriageable Mr. Gosper. So within weeks of seeing his mistress off on the stage to Globe, John Henry attained a status he thought he'd left behind forever in Atlanta: eligible bachelor and popular supper guest.

He and Gosper made a fine looking duo as they accepted the many invitations that came their way: Dr. Holliday with his sandy hair and mustache and his china blue eyes that the ladies still swooned over; the honorable Secretary Gosper with his chestnut curls and neat dark beard and his eyes that seemed so solemn and thoughtful. As their favorite hostess liked to say, together the two of them looked like a set of china salt and pepper shakers.

The observant hostess was Mrs. Rebecca Buffum, Prescott's leading society lady and wife of wealthy mercantile owner, William Mansfield Buffum. The Buffums' fine new brick home was next door to Richard Elliott's house where the bachelors resided, but it wasn't just convenience that made having supper with them so appealing. In addition to being one of the leading merchants in the Arizona Territory, William Buffum was also both a member of the Territorial Legislature and a member of the Territorial Prison Committee, which were being faced with the same problems that were plaguing Secretary Gosper's newly-formed Territorial Stock Raisers Association.

"Rustlers!" William Buffum said with disdain over the after-supper sherry Mrs. Buffum served to her guests in the parlor, his angry tone in sharp contrast to an almost cherubic countenance. For with his halo of curly blonde hair and a curly blonde beard on his full rosy cheeks, Buffum looked more like a Christmas angel than a middle-aged merchant. But there was nothing childlike about his words. "Rustlers!" he said again, "and these useless county laws have made it nearly impossible to stop them! Most stock brands are only registered in the county of the ranch they come from. So all a cow-thief has to do to steal his neighbor's cattle is register the same brand in another county, then herd the cows over the county line and claim they're his. And there's nothing we can do to stop them, at least not the way the law is written now. And if we could stop them, what would we do with them? The jails are already overfull with road agents and stage robbers. And hanging's losing its respectability as a deterrent to crime, more's the pity."

"Maybe we could ship them all off to someplace where there's more jail room available," John Gosper replied, as he took the glass of sherry Mrs. Buffum offered to him, giving her a dark-eyed smile and a "Thank you, Ma'am!" that made the older woman's cheeks turn pink. Gosper's reputation as a ladies' man seemed well enough earned, if he could so easily charm such a proper matron as Mrs. Buffum.

"And just where might we find this righteous place with so little crime that the jail cells are advertising for occupants?" Buffum asked.

"Well, I don't know how righteous it is, but I hear Michigan is willing to take inmates, for a price. Or so says Crawley Dake, our United States Marshal. He hails from that direction and still has some connections there. I suppose the cold climate might cool down a few of our desert hot-heads."

"For a price," William Buffum repeated, "always for a price. Sounds like even Marshal Dake is on the take."

"As long as he's on our side, I don't mind if he makes a little extra income through his efforts. Surely you as a business man ought to understand that."

William Buffum took a slow sip of his sherry, then settled himself comfortably into his leather wing chair, looking the very picture of pioneer prosperity.

"Oh, I understand the blessings of business success, all right. It was, after all, the call of cash that brought me across from California when Arizona first became a Territory, back in '71. Came over the desert from Yuma on a wagon train and settled here in Prescott, as it was headed to being the Territorial capital. Seemed like an opportune place to open a general store and help outfit all the new folks moving this way. And it did, indeed, turn out to be opportune. Why, in eight years, I went from being a Los Angeles saloon keeper to a member of the Territorial Legislature, assigned by Governor Frémont himself." He took another sip of his expensive sherry, congratulating himself. "And how is our famous Governor doing? Do you hear much from the Frémonts?"

"Too much," Gosper replied with an edge to his voice. "It seems he disapproves of the bounty offer on stage robbers, and is threating to come back and put an end to it."

"And what bounty is that?" John Henry asked, as ever finding talk of money interesting.

"I made a proclamation last summer, in the governor's absence. After the legislature turned down our request to fund a special police force to hunt down road agents, I decided to turn to the citizens themselves to do the policing. I made an offer of three-hundred dollars reward for the capture and conviction of anyone connected with the robbing of express coaches—and five hundred dollars for killing of the same."

"Seems like a more profitable venture to shoot the robbers, rather than tryin' to bring them in," John Henry commented, "and safer as well. Highwaymen aren't known for goin' to jail willingly. A passenger could lose more than his purse makin' the attempt."

"Precisely my thoughts," Gosper agreed. "The old rule of a three-hundred dollar reward for capture and conviction has never delivered us any results. So I upped the ante to five-hundred dollars as added incentive. Better for the territory to pay a little more and save the expense of jail and a trial, I reasoned. Let the stage passengers shoot the villains down and the roads will be safer to travel."

"And have you made any payments on the offer?"

Gosper's eyes grew darker. "Governor Frémont doesn't deem it civilized to have the citizens shooting down outlaws in his new-made territory. A territory his own wife is afraid to settle in, because of ruffians like these."

Which brought the conversation back to rustlers again, but this time William Buffum invited his own wife to leave the room and instructed her to keep the parlor door closed to anyone else.

"Such talk is too rough for women," Buffum explained. "Makes them afraid to travel the countryside, as well it should. Which is one of the reasons we've got to do something about these robbers and cow-thieves. Can't have hooligans getting in the way of civilization."

"Nor in the way of business," Gosper added. "When the rustlers steal from the big cattle ranchers, the ranchers don't make their fair share of profit. And one can't run a big ranch without profit to pay for it. Without profit, the ranchers don't spend any money elsewhere, making rustling a crime against the entire economy, not just the ranchers. I suppose that you, as a Southern man, understand what happens when the big farms go bust and get broken up."

John Henry nodded. He did indeed know, having watched the South slowly dissolve as the plantations were divided up after the War and given away to the former plantation slaves. Where there had been a smoothly-managed society before, there was chaos after.

"So what do you propose to do about the rustlin'?" he asked. "Seems like a vast piece of country you've got to consider down there."

"It is," Gosper agreed. "Which is why I organized the ranchers last year and formed the Territorial Stock Raisers' Association. You can't fight a war without an army. Problem is, we're not quite sure who the enemy is."

"I thought you said it was rustlers. Can't you just go after them? Back home, when the Yankees were breakin' up the plantations, the Klan went after the troublemakers easy enough."

"And therein lies our trouble," William Buffum said. "Where you came from, it was Yankees versus Rebs, or whites against colored. There wasn't much question which side a man was on. But things are different here. The rustlers aren't from one part of the country or another, or even of one color. Some are outlaws from Texas or New Mexico, moved on to devil us here. Some are small ranchers themselves, come here to settle and make a little profit on the side. Some claim to be miners or laborers, just looking to make a living. But none of them comes wearing a scarlet letter so we know what they are and can protect ourselves. And the Association is having a hard time making a capture."

Gosper nodded. "And once the Governor returns, he'll no doubt try to hobble the Stock Raisers' Association like he's planning to end the road agent bounty."

"But what about the local law enforcement?" John Henry asked. "Surely there's police in those parts."

"Not nearly enough," William Buffum said. "And none too willing to keep the peace. Outside of their own town interests, they turn a blind eye to the trouble on the roads and ranches."

"So how does Governor Frémont propose to solve the situation?" John Henry asked. "Seems like, with no police and no citizen army there's really no law at all. How does he aim to handle it?"

"Diplomacy!" Gosper said with disdain. "John Frémont has a religious faith in the goodness of mankind. He thinks he can set things straight by talking things out. And while he keeps talking, the Territory gets more dangerous."

"And yet the people love him," William Buffum said with a sigh. "The streets will be strewn with flowers when he arrives."

"And when might that be?" John Henry asked.

"Too soon," Gosper said, and added heavily, "You won't miss it."

John Gosper was right, for only a man half-dead or all the way drunk would not have noticed John C. Frémont's triumphal return to his territorial capital. He came in on the morning stage, accompanied by his wife, Jessie, and a coterie of Arizona politicians all playing courtier for the governor's attention, and accompanied by Fiorella LaGuardia's Prescott Brass Band playing anthems and schoolchildren strewing the flowers Buffum had promised. It seemed that the entire county had come out to crowd the streets of Prescott, even the ladies of the demimonde in bright satins and bold décolleté and giving the governor, and all the other men in town, an eyeful. In fact, the only person in Prescott who didn't seem jubilant at the governor's festive return was Acting Governor John Gosper. For in a swirl of stagecoach dust, he'd gone from being the most powerful man in the Territory to a paper-pushing secretary, and the demotion didn't rest easy on him.

But other than Gosper's brooding expression at the ceremony of returning the Territorial Seal to its original custodian, the governor's return seemed a generally festive occasion. It was a show that Kate would have loved, John Henry thought, and almost wished that she had been there to see it with him. But Kate was gone and he wasn't going to let her absence ruin him for a perfectly good party. So he attended the governor's welcome home ball along with the other unattached gentlemen of Prescott, squiring the single ladies of town around the dance floor and politely returning their hopeful flirtations. Then he stayed up late, writing a long letter describing the festivities to Mattie, who would be impressed by his new social status and the fine company he was keeping. But as he sanded the letter and sealed it into an envelope, he thought how little company there really was in his life, when both of the women he cared for were too far away to offer any real companionship. And the curse of his new social life was that he couldn't even pleasure himself with any of those willing women of the demimonde who looked so fetching in their décolleté. Respectability, he thought, was a hard burden to carry.

He couldn't quite say what it was that decided him on finally making a visit to Tombstone. Maybe it was the newspaper stories he kept reading about the boom there, bragging how the mining camp had finally gotten a real water system and how grand the new Grand Hotel would be. Maybe it was the weather, now cooling into autumn in the mountains of northern Arizona and taking the heat off the deserts to the south. Maybe it was his housemate's sudden demotion to Secretary of the Territory, which brought with it melancholy moods from Gosper and fewer invitations to dine. Or maybe it was his own growing realization that respectability, at least the kind that Prescott political society offered, wasn't enough to satisfy him anymore. All he knew for sure was that he felt dissatisfied somehow, and that he needed to do something about it.

It wasn't until later, when he was on the road again with Prescott behind him and who knew what lying ahead, that it occurred to him that he might even consider paying a call on Kate.

Chapter Two

TOMBSTONE, 1880

THE ONLY PLACE HE COULD REMEMBER THAT SMELLED AS NEW AS Tombstone was Valdosta when it first emerged from its virgin piney woods, all sawdust and raw timber and freshly turned topsoil. For Tombstone was still more mining camp than settled city, its newly surveyed town blocks scattered with tents and lean-tos between the shiny new saloons and the bustling new merchant shops, and everything seemed to be under construction all at once. But unlike Valdosta, built of fear and desperation, Tombstone was being built of hope and greed, and the combination gave a kind of feverish polish to the unfinished look of the place. The streets might be dirt and dust, but Tombstone had big city dreams.

The town lay along a windswept ridge at the edge of the shallow San Pedro River valley, thirty miles north of the Mexican border. To the west were the Whetstone and the Huachuca Mountains, to the east were the Dragoon Mountains where Spanish explorers had gone searching for the Seven Cities of Gold, and farther to the east were the Chiricahua Mountains where fierce Apache warriors guarded what the Spanish had never discovered. If there were precious metals in those mountains, only the Apache would ever know of it—or so the soldiers at Fort Huachuca had told prospector Ed Schieffelin when he went digging around those borderland hills. All he'd find in those Indian-infested wilds would be his own grave.

But Ed did find treasure, two rich silver strike claims he named the *Tombstone* and the *Graveyard* in honor of the soldiers' predictions. When others followed his lead in prospecting the area, even richer veins were discovered—and the *Lucky Cuss*, the *Tough Nut*, the *Grand Central*, and the *Contention* claims were quickly filed. At fifteen-thousand dollars and more to the ton, the Tombstone strikes made southern Arizona the silver capital of the whole country. So rich was the future of the area that General William T. Sherman, who had once advised Congress to *"Get Mexico to take back all of it!"* now called the Tombstone mountains, *"A permanent mine of silver to the United States."*

In a matter of months, Tombstone's population went from one stubborn prospector to three-thousand adventurers, and the silver boom had begun. Where only a year before a dirt-floored tent saloon had been the one watering hole, now there were thirty saloons and three hotels and enough gambling halls and bawdy houses to keep all of hell happily occupied. If the boom kept up, Tombstone would be bigger than San Francisco by the turn of the century—or so said the bartender in the saloon at the Grand Hotel, where John Henry registered for his first few nights in town.

The Grand Hotel had a pompous air about it, all decked out in Brussels carpets and silk upholstered furnishings and real silver service in the dining room. Even the fancy men's saloon off the lobby had a high opinion of itself—as did the bartender who refilled John Henry's silver traveling flask with whiskey.

"Don't aim to keep pouring drinks for long," the barkeep said, "and won't need to, the way this boomtown is booming. Why, by this time next year, Tombstone will be in need of some real political leadership, and that's what I have to offer. Name's Johnny Behan," he said, putting out his hand like a practiced campaigner, "just arrived in Tombstone and ready to serve the people of this fine community. Elections are coming up soon and sure would like to have your vote."

Though he was slight of build and short on looks, with thinning hair and a too-thick mustache, his dark eyes had the same intensity that made John Gosper such a favorite with the ladies. Passion, Mrs. Buffum would have called it, and found him admirable enough.

"I appreciate the invitation," John Henry said, taking the flask but ignoring the handshake, "but I'm not registered to vote in this county."

"And who is? Most folks are new here, or just passing through. But I can assure you that once you sign the voter roll, you won't find a better candidate than me."

"Seems like a bold statement for a bartender."

"Oh, bartending is just my sideline. Public service is my career. I aim to be Sheriff here, like I was up in Prescott. Soon as the legislature names this new county, my name is going on the ballot: Johnny Behan," he said again, flashing that campaigner's smile. "You won't forget it."

"You may be right," John Henry said pleasantly. "Though if it were such a memorable moniker, I think I'd have remembered it by now, seein' as I just came from Prescott and I don't recall ever hearin' the name of Behan before."

The bartender's bravado seemed to falter a bit at that, and he changed his story in mid-telling, like a practiced politician. "Did I say I was just in Prescott? No sir, that was a few years' back. My most recent travels took me to Gillette, where I had a saloon near the Tip Top mine. Don't suppose you've ever heard of that, either."

"Actually, I have," John Henry said, remembering too well his last uncomfortable night with Kate, sharing a bunk and angry words in the mine superintendent's office. And before he started into reminiscing, he said cheerily, "And now here we both are in Tombstone." Then he raised his newly-filled flask like a toast to the future. "May it be filled with good fortune for us, like it was for Ed Schieffelin!"

"And votes," Johnny Behan added, spoken like a real politician.

"So who's the girl?" John Henry asked, nodding toward a gilt-framed photograph of a dark-eyed lovely proudly displayed above the bar.

"That's my fiancée," Behan said with a smile. "Miss Josephine Sara Marcus of San Francisco—Josie to her friends. She'll be joining me here as soon as I get settled."

"Congratulations," John Henry said, tipping his flask again. "Though it seems a shame to waste such a wide-open town as this on married life."

And once again, the bartender turned his story around. "Did I say I was getting married? No, sir! I only proposed so her parents would let her leave San Francisco—respectability is a big thing to the Jews, you know. But I don't have a mind to marry again, not after my first wife left in a huff over some nonsense. Holy or not, I am through with matrimony!"

"And what does Miss Josie say about that?" John Henry asked, remembering well Kate's many tears over his own opposition to entering the wedded state.

"Haven't told her yet," Johnny Behan said with a shrug and a smile. "One thing public service teaches you—let the people believe what they want."

John Henry had a feeling Behan would do just fine in politics.

Across Allen Street from the Grand Hotel were the Cosmopolitan Hotel and the Maison Doree Restaurant, with Hafford's Saloon to one side and the Occidental Saloon to the other. In fact, most of Allen Street was saloons, with the Alhambra Saloon, Hatch's Saloon, Melgren's Saloon, and the Crystal Palace Saloon rounding out that block alone. And one block down at the corner of Allen and Fifth Street was the Oriental, where Wyatt had his Faro game—or so he'd said in his typically economic letter on the subject. *"The Oriental is a fine house,"* he had written, *"owned by an Irishman named Milt Joyce. The bar is from a hotel in San Francisco. The floors are covered."*

What Wyatt hadn't said was that the covered floors were thick with Brussels carpeting, the gaming room lit by crystal chandeliers, the reading room supplied with books and newspapers and writing materials for the patrons. Nor did he mention that the usual saloon noise was softened by music from a piano and a violin that carried out through the swinging doors and into the desert night, calling like a siren song. And by the look of the crowd in the saloon that evening, nobody was working very hard to resist the call.

Even in that crowd, Wyatt was easy enough to spot. He was head-and-shoulders taller than most of the men around him, his dark hat worn even indoors and pulled low over his face as if to shade the non-existent sunlight. But as John Henry pushed his way through the patrons, headed toward the back bar where Wyatt stood smoking a cigar, he felt a hand clap him on the shoulder and spin him roughly around.

"Well, I'll be damned!" Morgan Earp said brightly, his words coming out in a rush of whiskey breath. "If it ain't Doc Holliday! You never can tell who you'll meet up with in this town. I thought you were off in Prescott living the fine life, or so Wyatt's been saying."

"And I thought you were up in Montana chasin' Sam Houston's granddaughter."

"Louisa? Hell, I don't have to chase her anymore. She's my wife now. Been my wife for two years. If I want her, I just roll over to the other side of the bed. Married life is a fine thing, Doc, a mighty fine thing! But then, you should know about that, after all this time with Kate."

"Kate's not with me anymore," he said with a shrug, as if it meant nothing much to him. "She decided to try her hand in Globe instead. So I suppose you could say I'm single again."

"Which makes you a lucky cuss in a town like this. A Lucky Cuss!" Morgan said with a laugh. "Why, that's the name of one of Schieffelin's mines, so I guess I just made a joke!" And being pleased with himself for his unwitting humor, he laughed heartily and slapped John Henry on the shoulder again.

"You haven't changed any, have you Morg?"

"What's to change? I started out smart and good-lookin'. And I'm already on my way to being rich. So what else should I be?"

"Nothin', Morg, nothin' at all. You're so near perfect already I wouldn't be surprised to see you lifted up, like Enoch when the Lord took his town to heaven."

"Are you preaching me a sermon?" Morgan asked, looking quizzical. "When did you get religion?"

"I've been God-fearin' all my life," John Henry answered, with at least some degree of truth. He had *feared* God, even if he hadn't always obeyed him. "But I'm not preachin' to you, Morg. That would be a Biblical waste of breath."

"Just like Doc," Morgan said with a laugh, "talking in circles and making my head spin! But it sure is good to see you again. Wyatt hasn't been much fun at all since he started chasing asses."

John Henry grinned. "I never figured Wyatt for a womanizer! The ladies of Tombstone must be especially appealin'."

"Not that kind of ass, Doc! I mean the mules that got stole from over at Fort Rucker. They chased 'em, then stopped chasing, then said there was no mules to chase in the first place. Wyatt's been perturbed ever since."

As always, Morgan couldn't tell a story straight if his life depended on it.

"Morg, what the hell are you talkin' about?"

"You haven't heard? I'm talkin' about those Army mules that got stole awhile back. A Lieutenant from the camp comes here saying the mules might be on Frank McLaury's ranch. Wanted some men from the town to ride along and show him where the McLaury's live, so Wyatt and Virg and me went with him down to the Babocamari."

"And what's the Babocamari?"

"That's a river near here where the McLaury brothers have their ranch. So off we go like a regular posse, and what do we find?"

"Mules?"

"Nothing. At least nothing that ain't supposed to be there. Just a branding iron that could have been used for changing the government mark. But no mules, and only a suspicion of who it was that stole them."

"But no proof, so no way to find the mules."

Morgan nodded. "But you know Wyatt. Can't leave well enough alone, and now he's bound and determined to find the mules and the mule-thieves as well. Which is more or less ruining his enjoyment of this fine party town."

John Henry glanced back at Wyatt who was still standing at the bar with his cigar in hand. If Wyatt were enjoying the party, how would anyone know? And if he weren't enjoying it, how would anyone know that, either? Wyatt's emotions existed, but they were so well trained that they all looked about the same to an outside observer.

But John Henry wasn't on the outside, and he could tell just by the way the shadow of chandelier light fell across Wyatt's wide-brimmed hat and darkened his face that he was not happy with the outcome of things.

"So what's he plannin' to do about the situation?" he asked, and Morgan answered with a shrug.

"Not much he can do. The Army's stopped looking, so that means there's no money in it. But it irks him nonetheless, especially since Frank McLaury put a card in the paper saying how he was wrongly accused and everyone knows it was really the Army that stole their own mules, and any man who says otherwise is a coward and a liar. Wyatt's just waiting for McLaury to make a real fight of it, and they can have at it."

"But for now he's here dealin' Faro," John Henry commented.

"And making plenty of money doing it, especially now he's bought an interest in the saloon as well. He makes money every time somebody pours a drink, and that's all the time. And hell, that'd be enough for me! But you know Wyatt. Nothing's ever enough."

Morgan spoke affectionately, so the remark came as more of an observation than a criticism. But John Henry had to agree that it did seem to sum up Wyatt well. Nothing was ever enough for him as long as there was more that he could do—the same spirit, no doubt, that had sent Wyatt's father back and forth across the Santa Fe Trail four times, moving his family from Illinois to California and back again as if the thousand mile wagon train trek were just a stroll in the park. And like him, Wyatt seemed to be always looking for something more.

"And what about you, Morg? What are you up to these days?"

"You're lookin' at it! I know how to enjoy a party, even if Wyatt don't! And in between the partying and the pool hall, I work a little here and there. Gotta make enough gambling money to keep Louisa in silks and satins. And now she's talking about wanting a baby. Guess I'll have to get a serious line of employment to pay for that—or a bigger stake at the gaming tables!"

It was just like Morgan to make light of something as life-changing as fatherhood, yet there was something in his face when he said it that looked like it wasn't such a light thing, after all. And it occurred to John Henry that maybe Morgan was more than in love with Louisa—maybe he loved her, as well.

"Wonders never cease," he said by way of comment, then turned his attention back to Wyatt. "So how did he entice you down here? I heard you were rollin' in Deadwood."

"Oh, it wasn't Wyatt that enticed me. It was you, Doc, with that letter of yours about streets of gold and silver veins like a whore's breast. That was some fine writing, even if it was a lie."

"And what makes you think I was lyin'?"

Morgan grinned over his drink. "Take a look around. See any gold in the streets?"

"But what about the whores?"

"Hell, I'm a married man!" Morgan said with mock indignation. "I can't be looking at other women!"

John Henry smiled at the reply. Wonders really did never cease.

"But Wyatt's not just dealing cards," Morgan said, his conversation as always looping back on itself. "He's wearing a badge again, deputy sheriff to Charlie Shibell of Pima County. Charlie takes care of Tucson and leaves Tombstone and the mountains to Wyatt. That's why him and Virg were out looking for those mules. With Virg being Deputy U.S. Marshal and Wyatt being Deputy County Sheriff, they pretty much have the law covered around here."

"That'll come as a blow to Johnny Behan, I'm afraid," John Henry commented, remembering the bartender's pretensions at a County Sheriff seat himself.

"You know Behan?" Morg asked, seemingly surprised.

"Only by way of acquaintance. He filled my whiskey flask over at the Grand Hotel and we had a nice chat. He has big plans for himself, evidently."

"And who doesn't, in Tombstone!" Morgan said with a laugh. "But Tombstone is still up-and-coming, and full of chances for a man to start again. Even Behan."

"What do you mean, start again? I understand he had quite the illustrious career, awhile back."

"Awhile back is right. From what I hear, he left his illustrious days in Prescott when he got run out of town for philandering. Talk about chasing ass!"

"I hope we're not still talking about mules."

"Hell, no! At least, from the looks of her."

"Morgan, you are the world's worst storyteller! What are you talkin' about?"

"I'm talking about Behan's lady friend, the one he brags about to anyone who'll listen. Miss Josie something-or-other. You must have seen her picture over the bar. She's the reason he got run out of town instead of re-elected sheriff in Prescott. Josie was working there in a brothel which he used to visit on a regular basis."

"There's nothin' wrong with a man visitin' a whorehouse, as long as he pays for what he gets. It's the whores who are breakin' the law, anyhow."

"Except that Behan was married and Josie was a teenager, and that makes it wrong in the sight of God and the law. Which didn't impress the people of Prescott next time he came up for election. They run him out of town like a pestilence."

"And his wife divorced him," John Henry added. Behan had called it all nonsense, but that was just more politicking, saying what he thought people wanted to hear.

"That's right. But Tombstone isn't so particular about a man's past. Tombstone's about tomorrow and what's coming up next."

"Why, Morg, that was practically poetic," John Henry said with a smile. "I believe marriage has turned you into a romantic after all." And when Morgan gave him a flustered look in reply, he laughed to himself and turned his attention toward Wyatt instead.

"So now that big brother's a lawman again, are you gettin' a chance to chase bad men?"

"More than in Dodge, anyway. These mountains are full of robbers and such, and only a few officers altogether, so Wyatt can't tell me to stay home like he used to. He has to deputize me, now and then. Like last month, when me and Virg went after a horse thief over in Contention City. And what do you think we found along the way?"

"Sagebrush?"

"A bunch of Army asses!"

"You mean soldiers?"

"I mean mules, Doc! You sure do keep getting confused."

"I can't imagine why."

"We ran right into a gang of rustlers driving a pack of stolen mules. Army mules, by the brand on 'em. So Virg shows 'em his badge, him being Deputy U.S. Marshal and them being U.S. Army mules, and says to hand over that stolen property. Which they don't do, being rustlers."

"I reckon not."

"They just stood there laughing, like he was telling a good joke. But Virg don't joke much more than Wyatt, so while the rustlers were laughing I pulled my pistol and ran it up under the nose of the one closest beside me. They stopped laughing after that, but I laughed all the way back to Tombstone!"

"Sounds like a lark," John Henry said, amused as always by Morgan's exuberant enjoyment of life—even when outnumbered by outlaws. And while he had been intently listening to the tale he hadn't noticed Wyatt move away from the back bar of the saloon and make his way through the crowd.

"That's right. Everything's a lark to Morgan," Wyatt said, putting his hand on his brother's shoulder. "Even when he loses the treasure he's supposed to be guarding. Tell him how funny that was, little brother."

Morgan looked up sheepishly. "Ah, Wyatt! Why'd you have to bring that up?"

"Go ahead, Morg," John Henry said, siding himself with Wyatt, "I like a good treasure tale."

Morgan shrugged, his face reddening. "It's not the treasure Wyatt's talking about, but the way it got lost. Which wasn't really my fault. Could I help it if the boot was broken?"

"You kept the treasure in your boots?" John Henry asked, and noticed that Wyatt almost broke something like a smile.

"Hell, no!" Morgan replied vehemently. "It was in the boot of the wagon, of course. There was eight bars of silver bullion onboard the Benson stage and two more in the boot, which I was riding shotgun on. But when we stopped at Contention, we saw the boot was broken and the two bars were gone."

"Robbers?"

"Rough roads," Wyatt put in before Morgan could answer. "The bars fell out of the boot and the driver had to turn the stage around and go hunting for his treasure. 'Course, if the guard had been guarding instead of socializing, he might have noticed a couple of fifty-pound bars of silver falling off the wagon. All of Tombstone was laughing when they heard about it. I don't know that Morg will ever get hired to ride shotgun again."

Morgan grimaced. "You see how it is, Doc? Wyatt uses every little mistake to prove I'm not man enough to wear a badge."

"Oh, I don't doubt your manhood," Wyatt said, "just your manner. If you had half a mind to do law work, I'd back you in it. But you don't even think to disarm a known outlaw when you see one."

"Like who?"

"Like Doc Holliday here, who must surely still have a warrant out for him somewhere or other. You think he's walking around unheeled?"

"I will not give up my pistol!" John Henry said, affronted.

"That's the law," Wyatt said. "Firearms stay behind the bar, Doc. But you can have it back again, as soon as you need it. Just like in Dodge."

No one else would have noticed the smile in Wyatt's somber eyes, or would have understood why John Henry answered by politely pulling his Colt's Navy from his coat pocket and handing it over. But then, no one else had stood with them on the streets of Dodge City, staring down a gang of angry cowboys. That kind of adventure made for strong associations—and real friends. And that was worth even more than the safety of a six-shooter.

The Earp brothers and their families had taken up residence in three adjoining adobe cottages on Fremont and First Streets—a convenient enclave, with Wyatt and Celia, Virgil and Allie, and Jim and Bessie and their children all close enough to gossip over the garden fence. Or so said Morgan, explaining why he had chosen to take bachelor's quarters instead, away from the rest of the family, then stayed on in the cramped little cabin even after Louisa came to join him.

"Bad enough having my own wife know my business without having other women know it too!" was the way he put it, which sounded like surprisingly good sense coming from Morg. Women were trouble, mostly.

Yet John Henry found himself wishing that Kate had come along to Tombstone with him after all, and even wrote her a letter inviting her to make a visit there. It was her kind of town, he told her, playing up the place and describing the elegant saloons with their chandeliers and show stages, the streets crowded with shops and restaurants, the music halls and fancy-dress dances. Kate would have loved it all.

While the Earps went about their daily domestic business, John Henry took a boarding house room and bought into the gambling at the Alhambra Saloon, near to Wyatt's Oriental. As he'd only come to Tombstone for a visit, not planning to take up permanent residency until he'd appraised the situation, he'd left his dental equipment behind in Prescott and would have to rely on his other profession to support himself for the duration. Luckily Tombstone was, as Wyatt had described it, a wide-open town with an insatiable thirst for the games. So for only a minor investment, John Henry was able to take a share in a Faro bank, then take over the game completely and hire his own dealer. And by the end of his first month in town, he was raking in a nice profit every night and spending enough of it to satisfy his own gambling habit. But though he wrote to Kate again, telling her how well he was doing and that Tombstone's theater would be even more entertaining with her talents there, she still did not come. She didn't even reply.

Mattie wrote, however, her usual long and chatty letters that kept him up on family matters at home. Cousin Robert's dental career was doing well, she said, citing his new position as Secretary of the Georgia Dental Association and publisher of the *Southern Dental Journal*. What a shame it was that John Henry couldn't receive a regular subscription to the publication, with his transient life and too many moves—all a gentle reminder that he shouldn't have moved away at all. And how sad it was when her Grandfather Phillip Fitzgerald finally passed on at the grand old age of eighty-two, the last Irish-born link in the family. John Henry would have been impressed by the funeral celebration, with its wake and whiskey drinking and a burial ceremony fitting a king of Tara, if only he'd been there to see it. And how amazed he'd be to see the way Atlanta was progressing, with over fifty telephones in town already and the first public hospital newly opened by the Sisters of Mercy of Savannah. The good Catholic sisters had invited charity-minded citizens to volunteer time to the hospital, and Mattie was hoping to spend some hours there herself. And so her letters went, always sharing the news of home; always wondering when he was going to come home again. But home seemed like a lifetime away from Tombstone, and a place he had only dreamed of once.

Every town had its troublemakers, and in Tombstone the trouble came from a gang of west-coast gamblers who called themselves "Slopers," since most of them came from the western slopes of the Rocky Mountains. The ringleader was a tough named Johnny Tyler, who'd come from Texas by way of San Francisco. And though that should have made him more respectful of the better class of San Franciscans who'd come to run the saloons and gambling halls of Tombstone, it didn't. He treated everyone with the same democratic insolence, insulting anyone he pleased and aiming to intimidate himself into the top spot in Tombstone's sporting society. And here and there, his plan was working. When Johnny Tyler and his unsociable Slopers sat down at a game, the rest of the players suddenly seemed to lose interest and moved on to another saloon with more companionable company—unless the owner was willing to pay Johnny a portion of the evening's take to keep his boys at bay. And if the owners didn't pay up as promised, Johnny Tyler's insults would turn into threats.

It was a racket, all right, but the smaller saloons in town found it easier to pay off the Slopers than to fight them. But the Alhambra, where John Henry had his Faro game, was not one of those lower-class establishments. It was owned by a trio of San Francisco businessmen and run in businesslike order, and they approved when Faro-dealing Dr. Holliday made a showy display of his pistol to make the point to Tyler and his gang. If the Slopers thought the Alhambra was going to start paying protection money, they were dangerously mistaken, and John Henry found the whole episode laughable.

The laughter was what started the real trouble. For when the other saloon owners heard how easily the Alhambra had run off Johnny Tyler, they tried the same solution, simply refusing to be intimidated. It was a response the Slopers hadn't expected, and at first it put them off. But it wasn't long before they learned who had started the rebellion and blamed Doc Holliday for ruining their racket—and narrowed their broad threats against the saloons to more specific threats against him in particular.

John Henry wasn't worried about the threats, since from what he could see the Slopers were mostly talk and not much action. They weren't real criminals, after all, just sporting men looking for an angle to play and finding that the town wasn't willing to play along. So as long as they stayed away from the Alhambra and his Faro game, John Henry didn't have any grudge against them. But when Johnny Tyler tried to take a seat at his poker game at the Oriental one Sunday in October, matters took another turn.

Sundays in other communities were for Church meetings and picnics in the park; Sundays in Tombstone were for poker. It wasn't so much that the men in town lacked a proper devotion to deity but that the mines made payroll on Saturday and the boys didn't want to waste a chance to magnify their earnings. So Sunday worship for most anyone affiliated with the mines meant a wash and a shave and a day in the saloons. And

John Henry, being himself a religiously trained person and a respecter of a man's right to worship according to his own conscience, was happy to help in the oblations.

His three partners in that Sunday evening's poker game were all trying to make their fortunes in the Tombstone mines, though only one was a real miner by profession. J.B. Robinson had already tried his hand at Lynx Creek and the Big Bug Mine near Prescott before coming to Tombstone, and had high hopes that, this time, his efforts would pay off. Young William Porterfield had only become a miner in the past few months since leaving his family's California valley farm to follow the call of the silver boom. And Frank Mitchell was more interested in mining shares than in mine work itself, being a watchmaker by profession and a business associate of John Henry's old friend, Billy Leonard. But poker had a way of making all men equals once the bets were placed, and only the cards could determine the winner—the cards and a clever mind, which John Henry certainly possessed. And finding himself with such non-professionals as those three silver boomers, he felt confident in winning the pot and their week's wages for himself. Call it the collection plate, he thought with a smile, and a worthy way to spend the Sabbath Day.

But Johnny Tyler's arrival spoiled the spirit of the game. For in spite of Tyler's unsociable ways he was still a real sporting man, and real competition in a game that had been just exercise before, and John Henry was less than enthusiastic about letting him join in.

"I thought you Slopers had already been slid out of town," John Henry said in irritation. "To what do we owe the displeasure of your continued company in Tombstone, and at this game in particular?"

Johnny Tyler, looking as dandy as any sport in a cutaway coat and a brocade vest instead of looking like the Texas tough he really was, replied with a frown.

"I'm just here to play cards, like everybody else. I hear it's a double eagle to get into this poker game and five bits to see the first raise," he said, as he pulled a gold piece from his vest pocket and tossed it onto the green baize.

"Five bits for a real gambler," John Henry replied. "Which is four bits more than it would take to tame a sorry piece of horseflesh like yourself."

"I don't follow your drift."

"He means you're a mare," William Porterfield offered by way of explanation and with a scarcely concealed laugh. Being recently from the farm, he was more familiar with horse work than poker games. "He means you'd be easy to break, Mr. Tyler. A one bit horse ain't much of a fighter."

"Is that right?"

"That's right," John Henry said. "From what I've seen so far, you're all words and no action. And I can beat you at both. But right now I'm busy winnin' this poker game, and I don't feel like wastin' my energies on you. Gentlemen?" he said, turning his attention to the miners, "Shall we deal this hand?"

"You can't keep me out of a game that I just anted into!" Johnny Tyler said, his face growing red above his white silk cravat.

"You anted in?" John Henry said as he tossed another double eagle into the pot. "Why, all I see is my own two gold pieces, and nothin' else. And this hand is startin' without you."

He didn't consider it stealing, really, to take money a man was so willing to be parted with. Tyler would probably lose it in the end anyhow, and more to go along with it. Why not save him the disgrace, and relieve him of it early?

And even with all that, things might not have turned out too badly, if only John Henry could have kept himself from laughing. But seeing red-faced Johnny Tyler standing there huffing and puffing and not knowing what to say made him suddenly feel quite hilarious. And that was when Johnny Tyler finally made good on his threats, springing on John Henry with fists flying.

It could have been worse if firearms were allowed in the Oriental Saloon. But Johnny Tyler, like everyone else, had put his pistol behind the bar before entering the gaming room. But the fisticuffs had attracted the attention of Milt Joyce, owner of the Oriental, who hustled himself over to settle things down.

"You makin' trouble again, Tyler? I thought you knew better than to play your Sloper game in my saloon."

"The only game I'm playing is poker, if this thief here hadn't stole my money."

But Milt Joyce wasn't interested in explanations, and gave him a ruddy-faced scowl. "Get out of my place, Tyler, before I call the law. See the sign over the bar? No guns—No brawls. Now get out."

Words alone wouldn't have sent Johnny Tyler whimpering to the door, but Joyce's big blacksmith hand on his collar and a swift kick to go with it did the job.

Then Joyce turned to John Henry and caught him smiling at the scene.

"What's so funny, Holliday?" Joyce said. "And what did he mean about someone stealing his money? You up to some trick?"

"No trick, Mr. Joyce. I just refused to honor an uninvited wager. It's a gentleman's right to turn down an unacceptable player."

"Turned down and kept his money!" William Porterfield put in, his youthful enthusiasm overcoming whatever common sense he might have had. "Doc dropped his own double eagle on top of Mr. Tyler's and acted like it was his own. I never seen such a smart play!"

"And you won't be seeing it again," Milt Joyce said, clearly not sharing the farm boy's amusement. "I want you out of here, too, Holliday. Stealing poker bets! You're giving my saloon a bad reputation."

And without so much as a please, Milt Joyce gave him the same treatment he'd given Johnny Tyler, grabbing him with one rough hand on his neck and booting him out the door.

John Henry had never been handled with so little respect for so little cause. He stood on the board sidewalk in front of the Oriental, burning with embarrassment and anger. How dare Milt Joyce treat him so! And instinctively, his hand went to his pistol pocket—and found it empty. His pistol, like everyone else's in the saloon, was behind the bar.

"I would like my pistol, please," he said as he walked back into the saloon, showing Milt Joyce more respect than he deserved.

"Go to hell," was Joyce's impolite reply.

"I'm not goin' anywhere without my property!"

"Consider it lost in a poker game, like Tyler's wager. Consider it payment for the trouble you've caused me. Now get out."

And with that, Joyce pulled John Henry's pistol from behind the bar, cocked it, and took aim at its owner.

"Nice balance," he said. "Shall we have a little target practice to test it out?"

Even angry, John Henry wasn't fool enough to dare a bullet unarmed. Without another word, he turned on his heel and walked out of the saloon.

He remembered as if it were yesterday the summer afternoon when that particular revolver had come into his possession. It was his twenty-first birthday, and his Uncle John had given him the 1851 Colts' Navy Conversion as a coming-of-age gift. It was part of a matched set that was his shared inheritance with his cousin Robert, each of them receiving one of the pistols. And he remembered, even more clearly than his Uncle's presenting the pistol to him, what had followed after and how he and Robert had used the revolvers in a shooting match for the prize of a kiss from Cousin Mattie. And thinking of her now and remembering that day made him hate Milt Joyce for taking away his only memento of it.

He had other pistols, of course, like any well-heeled sporting man, and they were waiting for him in his boarding house room. And before the anger of the moment could cool in him, he was on his way back to the Oriental with a Colt's Thunderer in his pocket and a little Remington Derringer in his vest, both loaded up and ready to go to work. The Derringer had been a gift from Kate, given to him one Christmas when they were on better terms, and she'd had the butt inscribed with a pretty sentiment—though as it was bought with his own money, slipped from his purse before she'd gone Christmas shopping, it didn't seem like much of a gift. The Thunderer he had bought for himself when it was new and all the rage and before it was commonly known to be a fragile handgun. Samuel Colt and Company was still perfecting the self-cocking revolver, and the Thunderer had some problems in aim and balance, but it did just fine short range. The nickel-plated, pearl-handled revolver that had been a gift from Bat Masterson he left in his room, respecting Bat's request that he not do anything with it that might cause trouble for Wyatt.

"I thought I told you to get out," Joyce said, looking up to see him coming back through the swinging saloon doors.

"I did," John Henry replied coolly, "and now I've returned. And this time, I've brought a friend." Then, smooth as silk, he pulled the Thunderer from his pistol pocket and drew a bead. "Hand over my pistol, Milt, and nobody gets hurt. Or rather, you don't get hurt." And to make his point, he added a barrage of obscenities that would have made even Kate blush.

But instead of looking threatened, Milt Joyce just laughed.

"Now, there's no need for theatrics, Doc! You can put that pistol away. I aim to give you what's rightfully yours." And so saying, he dried his hands on a towel and pulled the prized Colt's from under the counter, smiling amiably as he walked around the bar. Then without warning, he raised the pistol and slammed the heavy barrel against John Henry's head.

The pain seared into his brain, his body clenched in response, and somewhere in the sudden darkness two gunshots exploded. Had he fired, or was he fired upon? All he knew, as he sank down into the darkness, was that he felt like he was dying.

There was a smell of something old and sweet in the darkness, like leaves burning in an autumn harvest, and he drew a slow breath and let his mind ponder on it. And suddenly he was back in Georgia again, a boy in his father's home—a home filled with the aroma of cut leaf and tobacco smoke. But it was Wyatt's voice, not his Father's, that came to him out of that smoky memory.

"Thought we'd lost you," Wyatt said, "the way you bled all over the Oriental's carpet. Milt's going to be out some money, replacing that. But you got your pistol back at least, which is what I hear caused all the commotion."

John Henry gave a groan that turned into a cough, and opened his eyes painfully. His left eyelid was too heavy, his vision a narrow window where there should have been light. "Am I blind?" he asked, more for confirmation than consolation.

"Just swelled up," said Wyatt. "Doc Goodfellow says you'll be back to your old card tricks soon enough. Or once you get out of jail. Milt's pressing charges today."

"For what? I'm the one who got hit!"

"You're the one who got buffaloed. Milt took a pistol ball in his hand from those wild shots you got off. You got his barman Parker too, in the big toe. Nice shooting for a man who was going down unconscious."

"My father always said I had a talent for target practice."

"Did he tell you your temper needs reining in?"

"Upon occasion."

"Well, count this as one of those occasions," Wyatt said. "Milt Joyce is not a man you want to cross, friendly as he is with the politicians in this town. As long as he keeps their liquor glasses filled, he can fill their minds as well."

"Why Wyatt, how very philosophical of you."

"It's just a fact, Doc. Milt Joyce has plenty of friends."

"Meaning that I don't?"

"Meaning that you ought to be more careful in the future. I'll do what I can with the charge and try to get you off light. But I don't know if I can do it again. Like I said, Joyce has friends, and this town is all about whose side you're on."

"Then I'm glad you're on mine," John Henry said, more gratitude in his heart than his voice would allow.

Wyatt shrugged. "I stand up for the men who stand up for me. I haven't forgot Dodge City."

"And I'll try to remember not to cross Milt Joyce."

"And while you're at it, try to remember to watch your mouth as well. I doubt Tombstone has never heard such beautiful swearing as what you said to Milt last night, and that's going some. The morning paper didn't dare print a word of it, but it's getting around."

John Henry took that as a compliment.

Later, when the swelling in his eye was down some and his head had stopped spinning, he tried to write a letter to Mattie about his ordeal and how he'd almost lost their Uncle's prized pistol. But somehow, he couldn't get the words to come, for how could he trouble her with a tale like that? Even though Wyatt had gotten the charges reduced from assault with a deadly weapon to assault and battery and he'd paid his token fine instead of jail time, the story would worry her needlessly. Once his head wound had healed that would be the end of the whole affair—and he'd be careful to leave his Colt's Navy tucked away in his room for safekeeping and carry one of his other pistols for protection.

So he didn't write to Mattie after all, and decided to write a letter to Kate in Globe instead, knowing she'd appreciate the blood and thunder theatricality of his weekend. But after he'd written it and was pleased by the dramatic way it read, he tore up the letter and threw it away. Kate never answered any of his letters anyhow, and this one surely wouldn't encourage her to pay a visit to Tombstone.

In the end it was his old Prescott housemate, John Gosper, to whom he wrote about the injustices at the Oriental. Gosper had an interest in the political maneuverings of the Territory and the nature of things in Tombstone in particular, and had asked to be kept informed. And within a week, he had a letter back. Gosper wrote that he was happily busier than before as Secretary of the Territory, since Governor Frémont seemed inclined to continue his celebrity life and leave the political work of Arizona to more fit men like himself. So he thanked John Henry for the interesting letter and asked for more of the same, and in particular for a close accounting of the political situation in the town. Though Wyatt had warned him to keep a wide berth of Milt Joyce, John Gosper asked him to ingratiate himself wherever he could in order to obtain whatever information might be had.

And before the month had ended, there was plenty more to tell.

Late October brought disagreeable weather—dark clouds mounting above the Huachucas, storms along the San Pedro river valley, torrents of rain and blinding lightning flashes on Goose Flats. At Blynn's lumber yard a man was struck and killed by an electric bolt that lit up all of Tombstone, causing excited talk that there must be a huge mineral deposit nearby. No one much cared about the dead lumberman. When the rain stopped and the streets turned from muddy rivers back to dirty roads, packs of coyotes came out to assess the possibilities. So it wasn't unexpected that when the bad weather finally passed and the first fine moonlit night arrived, the town would be in a mood for celebrating. Which was what a gang of cowboys set out to do, following a night of cards and liquor, and it was only when their revelry turned lawless, shooting at the moon, that the law stepped in.

John Henry was at the Bank Exchange Saloon that night, deep into a poker game with Wyatt, when they heard the first gunshots.

"Down Allen Street," Wyatt said. "I'm out."

"I'm with you," John Henry said, and folded what had been looking like a promising hand. And though he was inclined to get his gun from behind the bar in case he had cause again to back up Wyatt like he had in Dodge, he decided to go unarmed. He was still recovering from his head wound and those assault charges, and needed to keep a quiet reputation for awhile. But he couldn't stay back in the saloon when there was shooting going on.

They found the shooters two blocks down at the corner of Sixth Street, with young City Marshal Fred White holding them off. There were eight of them, all drunk and laughing, but only one whom John Henry recognized: Billy Brocious, his poker partner from Fort Griffin. He hadn't known Curly Bill was in the country but wasn't surprised to see him either, boomtowns tending to attract all kinds of riffraff. But eight of such men against one marshal was bad odds.

The odds changed when he and Wyatt arrived, and changed again a moment later when Morgan and his friend Fred Dodge showed up.

"Throw me a pistol!" Wyatt hollered to his brother, and Fred Dodge quickly obeyed—Wyatt had that kind of commanding effect on all men, evidently.

But before Wyatt could put the gun into play, Curly Bill pulled his own pistol and pointed it at Marshal White, saying in a liquor thick voice, "I'm just corralling this crowd, Marshal. No need to arrest 'em. I'll be takin' these boys back home. Come along, boys." And with an unsteady hand, he waved his pistol over his head like he was calling to a herd of cattle.

"Put the pistol down, Bill," Marshal White ordered, "and I'll let you all go. But I can't allow firearms in city limits." The marshal wasn't much older than the cowboys he was trying to control, and he understood that they were just in high spirits. So it was only a warning he was giving as he reached out to steady Curly Bill's pistol and keep him from accidentally shooting someone. But as his hands closed around the barrel, Curly stumbled and the sudden movement made the hair-trigger mechanism discharge in a cloud of black smoke, sending a blast into the marshal's groin.

For one agonizing moment of silence Curly Bill and the marshal stared at each other over the barrel of the smoking gun before both men started screaming. Fred White's belly was torn open and gushing blood, his shirt front on fire, while Curly Bill, his swarthy face gone ghastly white, was hollering his defense.

"I didn't shoot him!" the cowboy cried. "I didn't shoot him!"

Then both men went down at once, as Wyatt buffaloed Curly Bill over the head, and Marshal White fell forward into John Henry's arms.

Too late, Virgil arrived, and could do nothing but arrest the cowboys who stood dumbfounded and docile, watching as the city marshal of Tombstone bled to death in the street.

It seemed somehow appropriate that having died such a ghoulish death, Fred White should go to his final resting place on Halloween. His funeral at Gird Hall was attended by everyone in town and followed by a cortege that wound its way through the streets to the mournful sounds of the Tombstone brass band, with his grief-stricken young wife weeping as she walked beside the casket. The cortege stopped at the hillside cemetery just south of town, where the marshal was buried amid sage brush and cactus, fulfilling the old prophecy that all there was to be found in that country was a tombstone.

John Henry wrote to Gosper of the death of Tombstone's marshal, and how Curly Bill Brocious had been sent to Tucson for a trial in a less prejudiced venue. Even with Fred White's dying testimony that the shooting was accidental along with the word of a local gunsmith who knew that pistol and said it was defective and often fired at half-cock, the townspeople would not believe that Curly Bill hadn't meant to murder their marshal. After too many stage robberies and too many heads of cattle rustled in the unpopulated desert lands, they feared the cowboy threat had come to stay.

Gosper didn't wait for the mails to make a reply, but wired back that John Henry was to keep an even closer watch over doings in that country, expanding his interest beyond the political situation in Tombstone to the activities of the cowboys, as well. Then he followed the wire with a letter explaining that with the results of the recent election for Sheriff of Pima County with jurisdiction over the rich Tombstone hill country, there were fears that the cowboy element had already influenced the political process. And if the cowboys could sway the elections, they could as easily take over the territory.

What he didn't mention, but John Henry already knew, was that the hotly contested County Sheriff race between incumbent Democrat Charley Shibell and Republican Bob Paul had already been swayed. When the first results came in from the San Simon voting district where the cowboys were headquartered, Shibell appeared to have been reelected by a slim margin of 42 votes. But when the final results from San Simon were tallied, his lead had grown to 101 votes with only one vote for Bob Paul. The fact that the vacillating vote count came out of polls located in the ranch house of cowboy Joe Hill and with cowboy sympathizers as poll officials, made it seem a clear case of voter fraud.

What was even clearer to John Henry was that the cowboy situation was taking on an unexpectedly personal aspect. For as he answered Gosper's request to take a closer look into the cowboy's dealings, he learned that among the poll officials who'd helped to upset the voting results was a recently arrived outlaw from Texas, a former Shackleford County cattle rustler by the name of Johnny Ringo. And if he'd had any question that Ringo was one and the same with the man he'd known back in Fort Griffin, all doubt was dispelled when the mail brought a letter from Kate, as well, announcing her visit to Tombstone for the upcoming Christmas holiday.

The timing couldn't be mere coincidence, nor could Ringo's sudden arrival and association with Curly Bill. They had been partners in Fort Griffin too, working for John Larn, the king of cattle rustling in that country along with being county sheriff. And if any two cowboys knew how to walk both sides of the line between law and lawlessness, it was Johnny Ringo and Curly Bill Brocious—and the Arizona Territory was in for trouble. Even a military post on a hill overlooking Fort Griffin hadn't been able to keep that town under control, and Tombstone had no fort at all to protect it from the likes of Johnny Ringo and Curly Bill.

But the cowboys couldn't take over a town without a cooperative lawman to lead the way, tipping them off to opportunities and taking a cut of the proceeds when those tips paid off. Which was why they wanted to rig the election for county sheriff, John Henry reckoned, putting their own man in office—or at least someone with sympathies leaning in their direction. And though Charley Shibell probably wasn't their ideal choice for a legal link, he was certain to be more sympathetic than former lawman and Wells Fargo detective Bob Paul. But Paul did not take his Election Day loss lightly and sued for another vote, and Wyatt, who had supported him in the first contest, resigned his own post as deputy to Charley Shibell to back his favorite again.

If Wyatt had known that his resignation would lead to Shibell's appointing Johnny Behan to take his place, he might have saved his resignation for awhile—or so he told John Henry. For Behan was just what the cowboys wanted, seemingly custom made to suit their lifestyle. He was more politician than lawman, eager to please whomever would vote for him and not above bending the rules to his own advantage. And with a move afoot in Prescott to split Pima County and make Tombstone the seat of newly-devised Cochise County, Behan was in prime position to be made the new county sheriff. It was no wonder the cowboys treated him so well and Behan seemed to bask in the political limelight.

As for Kate, she arrived on the stage from Globe looking rested and radiant, like she was out to catch an old lover. It only remained to be seen which one that would be.

"I enjoyed your letters," she said, as she settled her things into his boarding house room, making him think that if she meant to stay awhile he'd have to find larger accommodations. Kate had never been one to pack lightly, and she'd brought along enough gowns and shoes and accessories to fill a whole lady's store. Her hats alone could keep a milliner in business for weeks.

"I wish I could say the same about your letters," he replied, watching her unpack into his already arranged dressing table and wardrobe, pushing his things aside as if they didn't belong there. "But you're a poor correspondent, Miss Elder."

"I was a good correspondent once," she said coolly, "but that didn't seem to impress you. But I did write to tell you I was coming to Tombstone. Would you rather I'd have just arrived unannounced, and have you not be ready for me?"

"I am never ready for you," he replied, enjoying the old banter. No one could answer him back like Kate.

"But there'd have been no need for letters at all," she went on, "if we'd stayed put in Las Vegas. And think how well we'd be doing by now, with our saloon and your dental practice."

"I think I'd be dead by now, or in jail at least, if we'd stayed put. You forget about Hoodoo Brown, the reason for our hasty departure."

"Too hasty, so it seems. Mr. Brown left soon after we did, running from the law himself. You recall that he was romancing the sheriff's wife?"

"I remember you gossiping about it."

"It wasn't just gossip. So when Sheriff Carson turned up dead, people got suspicious. The gossip now is that although Mr. Brown and Mrs. Carson left town separately, they've run into each other again in Houston, an extremely affectionate reunion. I doubt very much that Hoodoo Brown will be around to bother you anymore. So you see, we could have stayed put and made a nice living for ourselves, instead of following the damned Earps."

He wasn't going to make a fight so soon after her return, so he said lightly, "And how did you gather all this wonderful news? Globe seems a little isolated for Las Vegas gossip."

"Just because I wasn't writing you doesn't mean I wasn't writing at all." Then she turned to him with a pouting smile, her moods as changeable as ever. "But let's not quarrel over the past, shall we? What's done is done. And you are happy to see me again, aren't you?"

He couldn't deny that he was, in spite of the anger he'd felt when she'd left. But it was only her leaving that had irritated him so. If she'd stayed with him instead of deserting him in Gillette, he'd have been content enough. And it occurred to him that a man could put up with a lot from a woman, as long as she was willing to be a comfort when he needed her to be. In truth, it was only her unfounded feelings against Wyatt that had made them quarrel at all—and those must have been abated for her to be willing to join him in Tombstone at last. He didn't want to ponder long on the thought that it might be less a tolerance of Wyatt and more a need to see someone else that brought her back after being so long estranged.

"Come, Kate," he said, taking from her hands the velvet skirt she was trying to crowd into the already overflowing wardrobe. "It will take you all night to finish this, and we've better things to do with our time. And yes, I am happy to see you again."

It had been far too long since he'd made love to a woman he actually cared for.

If Kate had meant to resurrect her old romance with Ringo, she made no mention of it. As far as John Henry could tell, she really had come to see him in answer to his many letters asking her to pay him a visit. And she was surprisingly civil, as well, even nodding her prettily hatted head when Wyatt passed by them on the street.

But he didn't know everything that she did while in Tombstone, since he had his own business to attend to. He still had his Faro game to run, though as Kate had long since tired of watching him pull Faro cards from the silver dealer's box she declined his invitation to join him there. She was more interested in poker, where she could watch his hand and offer advice in her own feminine ways. But most of her time in Tombstone was spent shopping, being fitted for new frocks to join the ones she'd brought with her, then turning her attention to selecting jewelry to go along with the frocks. And it did cross his mind, once or twice, to wonder if she might be visiting more for the shopping and less to share his company again—a question worth asking, as it was mostly his money that was paying for her purchases.

But he was content to have her shop and keep herself occupied, especially when he had other business to attend to, like riding out to the mill town of Charleston with Wyatt, looking for a missing horse. That was the story they gave, anyhow, to cover the tracks of their real mission, which was to make sure cowboy Ike Clanton did not testify concerning the voting fraud in the San Simon. Ike was to be subpoenaed as Charlie Shibell's lead witness in the contested election results case, and Wyatt wanted to make sure that his lies wouldn't work to Charlie's advantage. So when Wyatt heard that Johnny Behan was riding out to Charleston with a subpoena looking for Ike, he asked John Henry to go along with him and put a stop to it. Of course, they couldn't interfere with the legal delivery of a court document, but they could make it hard for Behan to find Ike, and harder for Ike to tell his tale under threat of repercussions. Looking for a lost horse was a good excuse, especially since Wyatt could claim that the Clantons had stolen it even if they hadn't. He didn't need to actually bring charges to put the fear of the law into Ike.

So John Henry rode along with Wyatt, racing their horses like it was a contest, passing Behan along the way and having a good laugh about it when they reached Charleston ahead of him. And before Behan could get there, they had already found Ike at a poker game and threatened to have him arrested if he didn't turn over the missing horse immediately. Ike, not having the horse, decided to leave his poker and get out of town before they could make good on their threats, which made him unavailable when Johnny Behan finally arrived, and gave John Henry another laugh and cause for a drink in celebration. It was just a shame that he couldn't tell Kate of the lark when he returned to Tombstone that night, flushed from exercise and a winning poker hand. But after carefully not mentioning Wyatt in his letters to her, he didn't want to mar their reunion by bringing him up now.

He and Kate passed the holiday pleasantly enough, attending the opening of the new varieties theater called "The Bird Cage," and even toying with the idea of taking in a Christmas morning church service to hear some carols, if they could have decided which Church to attend. With Kate's lapsed Catholicism and John Henry's lapsed Protestantism, there wasn't much left except the Chinese congregation that worshipped Buddha instead of Baby Jesus and didn't have a Christmas service at all.

So instead, they went to the races at the Tombstone Driving Park just outside of town, where both Virgil and Wyatt had horses entered in the trotting match. The course was a mile around the ring and back, with a purse of $100 to the winner, and as there were only four entrants, the

Earps had combined odds of 50/50—worth betting on even for someone who didn't bet on horse races. And with those odds and out of loyalty to Wyatt, John Henry broke his usual rule of saving his money for something over which he had more control, and put down fifty dollars on Wyatt's pony, Sorrel Reuben.

The pony lost, but the entertainment of a day at the races was worth the investment, even though Kate refused to cheer Wyatt's horse and put her own money on Jim Vogan's horse instead. But since both she and John Henry lost their bets, there wasn't much for them to fight about, and he did enjoy showing her off in all her newly acquired splendor. She was still striking after these three years of their on-again, off-again affair, with her honey-colored skin and eyes that flashed with Gypsy passion. And as long as she kept that passion for him instead of turning it vocally against his friends, she could be quite pleasing company.

Tombstone celebrated the New Year with a fancy dress ball at the new adobe schoolhouse, and which Kate demanded that they attend—a difficult demand to answer, as the ball was by invitation only and John Henry had not been invited. That honor was reserved for the more respectable citizens of the town, like mine company owners and political figures, and as he had left his dental tools in Prescott and was relying on gambling to make a living he wasn't considered quite proper company. But when he paid a call on the lady chairman of the event and mentioned that he was a close associate of both Deputy U.S. Marshal Virgil Earp and his brother, former Deputy County Sheriff Wyatt Earp, the invitation was quickly forthcoming. Had Kate known what names he had to drop to get her to the ball, she wouldn't have wanted to go.

But not knowing, she enjoyed it immensely, especially since she was without question the most overdressed woman there. When Kate heard the words "fancy dress" she took them seriously. Though she'd already spent a small fortune of John Henry's Faro money on new gowns, she decided she needed something newer for the New Year, and made her entrance in purple silk moiré and Spanish lace and the biggest bustle anyone had ever seen. Or so she claimed, as she congratulated herself on being such a social success.

John Henry enjoyed the show and laughed to himself over her arrogant insecurity. Surely only someone doubtful of her place in the world would worry so much about it. But the music from the five-piece band was pleasant and the dancing invigorating, and the presence of some little colored boys hired to play darky servants amusing. And when one of the ball committee members, hearing that the doctor was from Georgia, wanted to know if this party bore a favorable resemblance to such events in the Southern states, he could only smile and say that imitation was the highest form of flattery and the Old South would have blushed scarlet at the compliment. But Kate found something lacking.

"It's a shame there's no fireworks," she said, when midnight brought a final waltz and the end of the ball, but no noisy celebration in the sky. "In San Francisco, they'll have fireworks at midnight."

There was something almost wistful about the way she hung onto her unfulfilled dreams, still longing for that better life she had only imagined. With all the things his money had bought for her, he still hadn't been able to give her what she really wanted. But how could he, when he still had unfulfilled dreams of his own?

He could have offered her a trip to San Francisco, at least, to make part of her dreams come true. But he had no desire to leave Tombstone just then when things were getting interesting and Gosper was waiting on his information. So instead, he tucked her arm into his and said soothingly: "We'll make our own fireworks tonight, darlin'. But first we've got to stop into the Alhambra so I can check on my Faro game. It's gonna take a good night at the tables to pay the bill for that gown, I reckon."

But there were fireworks, though not in the way that Kate had asked for them. For the cowboys, who had spent their New Year's Eve raising the devil in Charleston and chasing the minister out of his church, somehow got an idea that the celebration would be better with a visit to Tombstone—and somehow chose the Alhambra as their partying place.

They arrived just as John Henry had settled in at the Faro table, with their horses making a clatter on the board sidewalk. The fact that city ordinance prohibited animals from mounting onto the boardwalk didn't seem to bother the cowboys anymore than the ordinance against carrying a gun in town, as they jumped from their mounts and strode into the saloon, pistols brandished.

"Drinks for my friends!" one of the cowboys commanded, then turned amiably and gestured toward the rest of the patrons, "and drinks for these fine folks, as well! Then we'll be off and no hard feelings. And a happy anum to all!"

The voice was familiar—musical, resonant, redolent of bad memories. But the face was hard to place, hidden behind a calico scarf tied bandit-style.

But Kate knew him in an instant, her eyes growing wide and her painted lips taking a quick breath—

"Ringo . . ." she whispered, and smiled.

The cowboy hadn't heard her and she made no move to attract his attention as he and his friends took their drinks and left, true to their word. But there was no mistaking the look in her eyes as she watched him walk away. Whether or not she had known he was in Arizona, she was glad to be seeing him again.

Not knowing what to say to her about Ringo, John Henry said nothing at all, nor did she bring up the encounter. And within days there were more pressing things for him to worry about than an ex-lover's ex-lover come back around.

Charleston had spawned more trouble, this time with a gambler nicknamed Johnny-Behind-the Deuce who'd shot an engineer from the Tombstone Mill and Mining Company over a disputed hand of cards. The miners of the town didn't take the killing lightly and aimed to lynch Johnny before a real trial could hang him, forcing the town constable to hustle him into a buggy bound for the supposed safety of Tombstone. So with an angry mob behind him and a tiring draft horse in front of him, the constable was relieved to come across U.S. Marshal Virgil Earp out on the road, exercising one of Wyatt's racehorses. Virgil pulled Johnny up onto the horse behind him and galloped on toward Tombstone, where he handed the gambler over to Wyatt for safekeeping while he rushed off to send a wire to the marshal's office in Tucson for instructions. And Wyatt, hearing of the coming crowd of lynching-minded miners, sent for his brother Morgan and Doc Holliday to back him up.

John Henry had been eating supper with Kate when the message came from Wyatt, carried by a breathless Fred Dodge.

"Wyatt wants you," was all Fred said, not taking the time to explain the situation, and John Henry put down his fork and excused himself from the table.

"You're not leaving in the middle of your meal?" Kate said, more command than question. "You don't even know what's going on."

"I don't need to," John Henry said. "Wyatt wouldn't call if there weren't trouble."

"Always Wyatt!" Kate said angrily. "He calls and you obey, like some dancing puppet on a string!"

"I don't have time for this," he said, putting on his coat and wondering whether he'd need his pistol or something with more firepower.

"Then neither do I," Kate replied, throwing her linen napkin onto the table. "Don't think you'll see me here when you return. Or ever again."

She still had the impeccable timing of a stage actress, knowing how to throw a tantrum at the most dramatic moment, and her anger forced him to stop and try to explain.

"Kate, please understand. A man has to stand up for the men who stand up for him."

"I don't understand, and I don't want to! I thought when you wrote and didn't mention Wyatt that things were done between you. I thought you'd gotten over your idol worship of him at last. But you're as blinded by him now as ever. And I won't stand to be second in your affections. If you want me to stay with you, then stay with me now!"

He didn't know, as he took his hat and headed for the door, if she'd be there when he returned or not.

Wyatt was in Jim Vogan's bowling alley, covering Johnny-Behind-the-Deuce with his pistol and issuing commands to his quickly-gathered guards.

"No one do any talking but me," he ordered, and gestured to the men to take positions around the prisoner. "Keep your pistols out and ready, but no one shoots unless I say so. We're going to move this man through the crowd and take him to Tucson and let the law there deal with him. Though if it was me judging, I'd let the mob have him." The last was said by way of warning to the prisoner, who whimpered when Wyatt pushed a gun against his ribs. He didn't know, as John Henry did, that Wyatt was more known for buffaloing than shooting, so the threat worked. "Doc, I want you covering me from the right, in case any of those miners gets an idea to shoot this man and gets me instead. Morg, you cover my left. Virg, you go on out ahead of us and make a passage through the crowd."

It was one of the longest speeches John Henry had ever heard Wyatt make, and the first time that he had ever seen him issue orders to both his younger and older brothers. But neither Morgan nor Virgil questioned his authority, and moved quickly into their places. And though Wyatt had no badge to demand allegiance, the rest of the guards did the same, following his orders without comment. Only Johnny-Behind-the-Deuce made any sound, his whimpering turning to tears as Wyatt strong-armed him into a kind of human shield, protecting the men who had come to protect him.

"We'll do our best to get you safely to Tucson, but if anyone takes a bullet, it won't be my men. You're the criminal, O'Roarke," he said, calling the man by his less-colorful legal name, "so you'll be the one to pay."

Then on Wyatt's signal, the guards pulled their pistols and followed Virgil out into the street, with Wyatt holding O'Roarke in a bone-breaking grip.

"Stand back!" Virgil said, and the closest of the men moved aside to see what was coming behind him. Then a roar went up from the crowd when O'Roarke was pushed into the street ahead of Wyatt.

"Stand back and make passage!" Wyatt commanded, his deep voice carrying out over the mob in the street. "I am taking this man to jail in Tucson! And anyone else who wants to go to jail with him, commence to shooting now. We're ready for you."

John Henry held his pistol steady, staring down the forty or so angry miners who had followed O'Roarke from Charleston with intentions to hang him. He knew that on Wyatt's left side, Morgan was ready as well. But as Wyatt's words echoed in the cold desert air, not one of the miners moved forward, seeming almost entranced. What was it about a man that could command such obedience, even from men who didn't know him?

And as Wyatt had ordered, the crowd parted and made a passage and Johnny-Behind-the-Deuce was escorted peaceably to where Fred Dodge was waiting with a wagon and a team of fresh horses. Like Moses parting the Red Sea, John Henry thought as they walked through the now-silent mob. Like some old-time prophet, leading the way to the promised-land safety of Tucson, it was something like a miracle.

And Kate wondered why he'd follow Wyatt into hell and back.

Chapter Three

FEBRUARY CAME WITH FRIGID COLD AND HIGH WINDS SWEEPING ACROSS the desert. In Tombstone, the wind blew the dirt streets into swirls of dust that sifted and settled into every crack of wood and wall. The miners' shacks, not much sturdier than tents, threatened to blow away completely.

Kate had blown away, as well, being packed and gone as she had threatened, though as she'd left and come back again two times already, John Henry wasn't so sure she was gone for good. He was beginning to think that her desertions were more for dramatic effect than to be really rid of him—like a cliffhanger at the end of a Ned Buntline story. It was too bad her dime-novel dramatics only served to make their relationship seem even cheaper than it already was.

But it was just as well she was gone off, for if his friendship with Wyatt displeased her, their new business venture together would make her livid—although it might make him a millionaire if he lived long enough to see the venture pan out. Though that wasn't quite the right phrase to describe it, according to Wyatt.

"*Pan out* is a gold rush term," Wyatt told him, as they sat together in a back corner of the Oriental, having drinks with a businessman by the name of William Allen. "You don't pan silver; you crush it out of the rock in a stamp mill. Which is why we also need to make a water claim, for the steam power. There's going to be a lot of ore to mill, if this vein assays like Allen here says it should."

"So what does the ass say?" John Henry quipped, though the play on words was so common around Tombstone that neither Wyatt nor William

Allen laughed. The Assayer was the man who measured the amount of precious metal in a sample of rock—and got lots of complaints if he didn't find what a miner was hoping for.

"There's good springs up Mormon Canyon and Ramsey Canyon," Allen said, ignoring the old joke, "and maybe up Hayes and Tanner too. And what water we don't need, we can sell off to another mining company."

"Why not just use the San Pedro," Wyatt asked, "with the river so close by?"

"Not enough of it, at least where we could get to it," Allen replied. "The San Pedro looks like something now with all the rain we've had this year, but come summer it'll hardly be a trickle—just enough to keep the leopard frogs and the flycatchers happy. Without the cottonwoods along the banks to mark the riverbed you'd never even know it was there."

"Like the silver," John Henry remarked, having his doubts about the deal. Although a big Eastern outfit had already done some prospecting on the claim, they hadn't found what William Allen supposedly had: a rich vein of precious ore running through twelve-hundred feet of quartz rock in a claim he called The Last Decision.

"Oh the silver's there, all right," William Allen said confidently. "I've seen it with my own eyes, sparkling like heaven itself. Don't know how the Intervenor Company missed it when they did their digging. Maybe they started at the wrong end of the claim. Maybe, being as the owners are in Philadelphia and the miners are here, they didn't supervise things very well. In any case, their bad luck is good luck for us, if you're interested in buying in."

"I'm interested," Wyatt said, "just want to make sure we're not doing anything shady. Some folks might call it claim-jumping, locating a new mine right on top of an old one."

"But that's just the point," Allen said, gesturing to the map laid out on the table between them. "The Last Decision's not actually on top of the Intervenor. It just shares a section of it, as there's two veins that run together partway. This new claim runs crossways of the Intervenor. The Mining Act calls it a Relocation. I assure you, gentlemen, it's completely legal."

"So if there's really two veins down there," John Henry said, "why hasn't the Intervenor Company filed on both of them?"

"I can't answer that," William Allen said with a shrug. "For obvious reasons I haven't been inclined to discuss it with them."

"And how do you propose to get the silver out of the ground without their learnin' of it?" John Henry asked. "Mining's not exactly a quiet industry."

And as if to underscore his argument, the floor of the Oriental gave a groan and the glassware on the long bar trembled. Being as the town of Tombstone was built on top of some of the original mine sites, the ground sometimes answered back to the sound of the subterranean blasting, dynamite having a way of shaking things up. It was bothersome enough that John Henry didn't think he could do any dentistry while he was staying there, with his nerves and his hands jumpy all the time. But blessedly, the constant pounding of the stamp mills was farther off, at Charleston and Contention City.

"A very apt question," William Allen replied, "and the reason for the urgency of this endeavor. For once we start our own excavations, the Intervenor Company is sure to take notice and start scouting around, and then it's a race to see who can get to the silver first. But if we can beat them to it . . ." He paused, looking around him to make sure no one was listening in, then said in a lowered voice. "It's only fifty dollars in gold for a share, if you gentlemen are interested in buying in. If not, I'm sure there's plenty of other smart investors in this town, looking to make themselves rich . . ."

"And all we have to do is believe you," John Henry said.

"I've got the samples right here," Allen insisted, pulling a handkerchief from his pocket. "You can take them over to the Assay office yourself and have them weighed. Just don't let on where you got them from, or that hill will be crawling with prospectors."

John Henry ignored the handkerchief Allen was offering him, and said with a laugh, "Mr. Allen, you read too much! That's the oldest bait and switch in the book. Why, I made up a better scheme than that myself before I ever set foot in a boomtown!"

"But it's true!" William Allen said, laying the open handkerchief on the table. "There's the silver shavings I took from the outcropping! See for yourself!"

"That's just what I'd like to do," John Henry said doubtfully, "assumin' you can remember where this highly unlikely silver is to be found. And if I find out that you've been lyin' to us . . ."

"Now hold on, Doc," Wyatt said, sweeping up the silver shavings to take a closer look. "William Allen's got a good reputation in this town. We've got no reason to disbelieve him. Just because you tried to run a blazer on Ned Buntline doesn't mean every miner you meet is dishonest. There's not many men as nimble-minded as you, making up schemes right and left."

It was the closest thing to a compliment he'd ever received from Wyatt, and it took the sarcasm out of him for a moment. "So you're really thinkin' of dealin' yourself in?" he asked.

Wyatt nodded, "I'm thinking on it. I didn't come all this way to Tombstone just to enjoy the scenery. If there's a fortune out there for the taking, I don't mind being the one to take it."

John Henry sighed, "Then I reckon I'm gonna have to take a look at this mine claim myself. Can't have you throwin' good gamblin' money away on a dream."

"All gambling's a dream, Doc. That's why we like it so much."

Wyatt didn't often have much to say, but when he did it generally made sense.

The Tombstone hills were covered with a patchwork quilt of sage brush and mine claims. There was the Toughnut and the Gilded Age, the Grand Central and the Contention, the Lucky Cuss and the Goodenough, the Graveyard and the Way Up and the Owl's Last Hoot, along with dozens of other colorfully named locations, each marked by monuments of stone at their four corners. None of the claims was larger than fifteen-hundred feet by six-hundred feet, the legal limit of a filing, and some were far smaller, sneaking in where a careless surveyor had left out a foot or two in his mapping. But even a small plot of ground above could yield a fortune down below, as the silver veins spread out like the roots of an ancient and overgrown garden.

The Intervenor was one of the larger claims, being one of the first locations in that mining district, though for some reason the owners had never done much to develop it. There were no hoisting works to lift the ore out of the mine shaft, no pumps to clear ground water out of the tunnels, no rail cars or mule-drawn wagons to carry the ore to mill. There was nothing but sagebrush and a partially excavated cave in a slope of land overlooking the town.

"Worthless as desert dust," William Allen said, when he and John Henry had hiked the quarter-mile south from Tombstone to the mine site and explored what there was to see, which was nothing much. "My guess is, the owners started looking here, then got distracted by richer finds. This claim was filed just before they bought the Contention off of Ed Schieffelin."

"That could be a little distractin'," John Henry remarked. For the Contention, as everyone knew, was one of the best producing mines in all of Arizona Territory, having already paid its stockholders nearly one million dollars in dividends.

"Too bad for them they stopped digging this site where they did," Allen said. "If they'd just gone a little farther . . ."

Though it was just after noon on a cloudless February day, Allen had brought along a miner's caged oil lamp. Now he swung it into the mouth of the shallow cave, and said, "Follow me, and I'll show you what they missed."

It was no wonder that the soldiers at Fort Huachuca had warned Ed Schieffelin about finding his tombstone in those hills, for there was nothing more resembling a newly dug grave than a newly started mine. When a prospector saw a tilt of land that he thought looked promising, he went to digging, hoping to find ore bearing rock. When he did, he kept on digging, hoping to find the vein. And when he found that, the real excavating began. But crouching in that damp darkness in a tunnel too small for a man to stand erect, John Henry's only inclination was to get out. Time would bring his own grave soon enough, without his crawling into one in a Tombstone mine.

He was just about to say as much and head back out into the sunshine, when Allen swung the lamp sharply to the right, exposing another chamber cut into the rock.

"This is the vein I was telling you about," he said. "It runs crossways of the Intervenor claim, which makes it a whole new location."

And as he steadied the lamp, the light hit on something that reflected back and made the blackness come alive—a chunk of white quartz crystal embedded in the dark rock wall, and in it a streak of silver.

"Well, I'll be damned . . ." John Henry said.

And that was all it took for him to catch the silver fever.

He wrote to Mattie about his new investment, eager to share his excitement, and received in return a letter so full of questions about the mining industry that he had to do some studying before he could reply. And while he was reading up on the subject in the daily reports of the two local newspapers, the *Tombstone Epitaph* and the *Nugget*, he received a letter from John Gosper, as well, asking for information of another kind.

His old housemate was Acting Governor of the Territory again and trying to deal with ever escalating trouble in the border country, and his frustration showed in heavy black ink strokes across the official stationery. The problem was that Governor Frémont, under orders from Washington to quell disturbances along the border, had asked the Territorial Legislature for funding for increased police presence, only to be turned down again and again on the basis that border issues were a Federal, not a Territorial, concern. The Legislature had decreed that if the United States government wanted to patrol the border, they could send in troops from Camp Rucker or Fort Bowie; the Territory would not fund such an expense. So in the end, Governor Frémont had given up his seemingly impossible task and taken himself and his family back to Washington where he could enjoy the status of his station without having to do the real work. A work that still needed to be done, and which was left weighing heavily on John Gosper's shoulders. It was, as he wrote of it, *"a most inopportune time to be Acting Governor."* Then he added a plea for John Henry to keep his ears open and share whatever intelligence he might discover relating to disturbances in the southern country—anything at all that could help the Territory control that wild section.

It wasn't long before John Henry learned something that he hoped Gosper would never hear about.

One of the interesting things about living in a boomtown was that you never knew who was going to step off the stage when it arrived. One day it was Billy Leonard, his watchmaker friend from Otero, New Mexico, still looking for adventure. One day it was yet another Earp, Wyatt's youngest brother Warren, come to join the family and try his luck at whatever Tombstone could offer him. And one day it was Kate, come to pick up a dress she'd ordered before her hasty departure, then moving into John Henry's rooms like she meant to stay awhile.

Kate could have picked a better time for traveling, with the roads more full of road agents than ever and the weather turning from frigid cold to snow. But things were dull in Globe, she said, though she was still so angry at John Henry that she considered dull preferable to visiting Tombstone again. But there she was, nonetheless, proving that a woman didn't always mean what she said.

She did, however, intend to go shopping again, which was actually good news for John Henry. At least while she was spending his money at Addie Bourland's dressmaker shop or Heintzelman's Jewelry, she didn't question how he spent his time. Which was, of late, meeting with his mining partners or visiting with Billy Leonard, whom Kate disliked almost as much as she did Wyatt—though ironically, it was through Kate that he and Billy had become reacquainted, when she saw him on Allen Street and commented that he looked even more delicate than he had when she'd called him a Nancy-boy and had questioned his proclivities.

The truth was, Billy had lived a hard life since leaving New Mexico looking for something more adventurous than mending broken watches, and it showed on him. Where he'd been slender of frame before, with pretty features and girlish curls, he was downright frail now, and his current living conditions weren't helping what was probably an advanced case of the consumption. Instead of staying in a warm boarding house room, sleeping and eating at regular hours like John Henry did, Billy lived in a drafty shack at an old watering hole called the Wells, two miles north of Tombstone, along with a couple of disreputable types by the names of Harry Head and Jim Crane. But the shack was only temporary quarters, Billy assured John Henry when he rode out for a visit, as his real home would soon be a piece of land in New Mexico that he'd won in a poker game. Billy called it his "ranch" though there was no herd of cattle or even a cabin on it, and he talked about someday building it up into a real outfit. Though sick as he was, someday wasn't likely to ever come.

If Harry Head and Jim Crane had shown half as much initiative as Billy in spite of his illness, they could have made some money on the side hauling water from the Wells into town for folks who didn't want to pay the high prices being charged by the new Tombstone Water Company. But Harry and Jim were as useless as they were lazy, in John Henry's opinion—until the day when they got an idea and turned dangerous, as well.

The idea started in the mind of Harry's friend Luther King, who was variously known as a road agent and cattle rustler and boasted an arrest record several states long. The fact that his ideas rarely worked out didn't dissuade Harry and Jim, once Luther explained his idea to them. For Luther's scheme promised instant wealth with very little work, and a rise from being ne'er-do-wells to well-offs almost overnight, and all it would take was a little careful planning and some clever preparation. The proof that they were neither clever nor careful came in their sharing the idea with John Henry on one of his visits to the Wells. But they were so full of enthusiasm for the answer to their financial difficulties that they couldn't contain themselves, making John Henry a sort of accessory before the fact without any intention of becoming one.

Luther King's plan was to rob the Kinnear Company Stage on one of its runs from the Tombstone mines down to the railhead at Benson. Depending on the day they chose to do the deed, the stage could be loaded with as much as $50,000 worth of silver bullion, enough to steal and split and still payoff whatever law wanted to interfere. All they had to do was stop the stage where it slowed at a draw near Drew's Station, then take the money from the Wells Fargo agent on board, and they would all be rich. They laughed at the simplicity of the plan, even though Billy Leonard was smarter than the rest of them and should have known better.

But with the pain of the consumption, Billy had taken to using morphine and the narcotic had clouded his mind until he too thought Luther King's plan would work, in spite of John Henry's warnings—although John Henry had given him more than just warnings, trying to help him out by slipping him winning poker cards when he could do it and not offend Billy's sense of squareness, and offering to pay off his debts when he wouldn't take the cards. But in Billy's drug confused mind, it seemed better to rob a stage full of strangers than to take money from a friend.

John Henry tried to explain to the would-be robbers that there were too many problem points with their plan. True, the horses did have to slow coming up the rise on the far side of the draw, but that's just where a good Wells Fargo guard would be most wary. Drew's Station might seem like the middle of nowhere, but it was too close to Contention City in one direction and Benson in the other for a robbery to go unnoticed long. And if they actually did get away with the treasure, they'd quickly have the whole of Wells Fargo and Company after them. They wouldn't get far if they did get the money, and would pay for it with their lives. Surely, there was some less dangerous way for them to make a living.

But once having made the plan, the boys grew increasingly eager to try it, and John Henry's logic and persuasion couldn't change their minds. All they wanted was news that a big shipment of silver was coming out of the mines—news that was easily obtained, as the whole of Tombstone counted the take on a daily basis and the newspapers eagerly printed the reports. Still, John Henry hoped his warnings would be heeded by his friend, at least, and that Billy Leonard would leave stage robbery to his less intelligent partners.

It was mid-March when John Henry heard that a load of $26,000 in silver bullion was being sent down to Benson, which he feared was more than enough to set the plan into motion. But when he heard that the guard on that stage would be Wyatt's friend Bob Paul, his fear turned into action. With Paul's contested election case still to be decided, the former lawman was back at work as a Wells Fargo detective and one of the grittiest treasure guards on the road. If the boys went up against Bob Paul, they were sure to come out the hard way.

He hired a saddle horse at Dunbar's stable and rode out toward Charleston, in the opposite direction of the Wells and the long way around to pay a visit on Billy Leonard. But as he'd heard there was a big poker game going on in Charleston, he reckoned that his stopping by would give him a good alibi later, should he need one—and something in his bones told him that he would. Then he turned north and followed the San Pedro until the trail to the Wells cut off to the east.

It was a hard ride, over rugged terrain tangled with mesquite and with a stiff cold wind blowing across the hills, and by the time he reached Billy's cabin a light snow had begun to fall. And as he'd feared, the boys were busy getting their gear together for a late night run at the Benson stage. They welcomed him heartily, excitement flushing their stupid faces, and offered him a drink to warm himself.

"I'm not here for hospitality," he said. "I'm here to stop this lunacy before it happens. You will not get away with the treasure tonight, boys."

"And what makes you so sure?" said Luther King, polishing his pistol.

"Because I know the guard who's goin' out with the stage. It's Bob Paul, and you won't find a worse adversary. He'll shoot you down the minute he sees you, without askin' your business."

Jim Crane laughed. "But he ain't gonna see us! We're wearing disguises," he said, drawing out the word with delight. "Harry here's been making us beards out of rope, which he learned to do when he was a rangler. They'll never guess it's us!"

Harry Head displayed his handiwork, a mess of frayed and braided hemp rope tied onto a red calico bandana. It looked laughable and nothing at all like a real beard.

"You know there's a full moon tonight?" John Henry asked. "Might as well be on stage with gaslights to illuminate this little show of yours. And you'll have plenty of audience, with Bob Paul drawin' a bead."

"It's no show, Doc," Billy Leonard put in, barely getting the words out between coughs.

"And you ought to be in bed, not ridin' out in this wild weather," John Henry replied.

"No choice, the way I see it," Billy said. "Might as well make my fortune or die trying. Hell, I'm dying anyways."

"You talk too much, Leonard," Luther King said. "Ought to save your strength for standing watch. You need to be steady if the guard gives us trouble."

And hearing that, John Henry knew his friend's place in the holdup. While the more vigorous men would be riding down on the stage and hauling off the treasure, their frail partner would be left to watch and aim—meaning that Billy Leonard was to be the shooter.

"Don't do this thing, Bill!" John Henry said with urgency. "Let these boys hang themselves if they want, but don't you get involved."

"I'm already involved," he replied with resignation, "but you don't need to be. Get on back to Tombstone, Doc, and forget you ever heard of this."

"Why don't you come with me? Kate's in town again and she'd enjoy showin' off for you."

Billy smiled wanly. "Kate never much liked me, you know that. Kate doesn't like anyone who takes your attention away from her."

"I said you talk too much, Leonard," cautioned Luther King darkly. "It's time to say goodbye to your friend, unless he wants to join in with us."

"I'll pass," John Henry said, "like you boys need to do, as well. Let this stage go. There'll be others less guarded." If he couldn't dissuade them, he might at least be able to postpone their plans until he could get Billy out of the gang.

But Luther King took his words as a challenge. "Sounds like maybe you've got an eye on that treasure wagon yourself," he said, swinging his pistol around to take a warning aim at John Henry.

He could have pulled his Colt's right then and put an end to Luther King's suicidal insanity. But Head and Crane had weapons too, and the odds of one against three, or one against four, weren't appealing. Instead, he laughed.

"I've got enough trouble handling my mistress without taking on Wells Fargo, too! She is the most damnably difficult woman you ever met!"

Luther ruminated for a moment, then gave a stupid smile. "You mean Katie Elder? I've heard tell of her. A regular desert dust storm, that's what Ringo calls her, a certified virago. Whatever that means."

John Henry knew what it meant, and wondered if Ringo were talking about the woman he used to know or the one he was getting reacquainted with now. Either way, he didn't much like hearing about it. But any link between him and Ringo would give him respect from a cowboy like Luther King, and mean his safe ticket out of the Wells.

"I've got to be gettin' back," he said, putting on his hat. "So are you comin' with me, Billy?"

But Billy Leonard answered heavily, "You have a good ride, Doc. Tell Kate I said hello."

The snow was still falling lightly when he left the Wells, dusting the trail. It was a pretty sight, but he was too worn out from one long worried ride and the prospect of another to care much about the scenery. Would Billy Leonard heed his advice and stay out of the stage holdup? Would he be able to talk the others into not going through with the plans at all? John Henry's mind was a swirl of questions, and he was wearing himself out looking for the answers. So when he overtook Old Man Fuller, headed back from the Wells to Tombstone with a team of horses and a wagonload of water, he hitched his horse to the back of the wagon and climbed up on the buckboard, dozing his way back into town.

"You smell of horse," Kate said by way of greeting when he returned to his room. "Where have you been?"

"To Charleston," he said truthfully, glad already to have that alibi in place. "There was a big poker game going on over there."

"Charleston? Did you see anyone we know?"

"I couldn't count all the people you know, Kate. But Ringo wasn't there, if that's what you're askin' about," he said, not bothering to watch her face for a reaction. "Now draw me a bath, darlin'. I've got to get ready for work."

By work, he meant his Faro game, which seemed like a good place to spend such an evening as this one might prove to be. The more people who saw him around town, he hoped, the less likely they would be to link him with trouble away from town—like a foiled stage robbery and a hunt for the robbers after. For there was little chance, in his opinion, that the gang would pull off a successful holdup, or get away with the treasure if they did. And if it were known that he had learned of the robbery in advance and not warned the law, things could be as bad for him as for them. But how could he give warning without endangering the life of his friend?

So he passed the evening nervously, making a show of his usual nonchalance but inwardly jumping at every sudden sound, then ordering a double whiskey when he heard the heavy hoofbeats of Kinnear's stage leaving from in front of the Wells Fargo office two doors down the street. And still, Billy Leonard had not come back to Tombstone.

He was still at cards hours later when word came racing through town that there had been a stage holdup near Drew's Station. Bob Paul had wired the news from Benson, then took a fast horse back to town to gather a posse and spread what he knew of the story.

The stage had left Tombstone, bound for the railhead at Benson, with Paul riding shotgun. At Watervale, two miles outside of town, the stage stopped to pick up more passengers—among them, a young miner who had to sit on top instead of inside the crowded wagon. From there, the coach drove on past Contention City toward Benson, thirty miles to the north.

It was nearing ten o'clock that night under a bright clear moon, when the coach slowed as it drove through the willow draw and went up the incline on the other side.

"Hold!" a voice commanded, and a man with a shotgun stepped into the moonlit road.

"I hold for no one!" shouted Bob Paul, as he lowered his Winchester and watched two more men appear out of the willows. Then without waiting for more conversation, he fired on the robbers and ordered the driver to hasten on.

The coach lurched ahead in a volley of shotgun blasts as the robbers returned fire, and the driver slumped forward and fell, shot through the heart. For a moment his body lay on the traces, the reins still clenched in his dying hands, until he tumbled to the road beneath the horses' thundering hooves. On top of the coach, there was a groaning from the unfortunate young miner, shot by a blast in the chest.

Two men were wounded or dead and the driverless coach was careening wildly, passing Drew's Station in a whirl of snow and dust, but Bob Paul was not going to let the robbers steal his treasure box. Dropping his shotgun, he slid to the right of the box and grabbed for the heavy metal brake, pulling back hard and slowing the coach until he could gather the reins and get the team under control. He didn't look back to see if the robbers were following him, but drove on at a gallop toward Benson.

Back at Drew's Station, the wranglers had heard a team of horses thunder on past about the time they were expecting the Benson stage, and ran out to find the driver dead in the road. Now the holdup was murder, and the law would be hot on the trail come daybreak.

The posse was made up of Sheriff Behan and U.S. Deputy Marshal Virgil Earp, along with Wyatt and Morgan and the local Wells Fargo agent, Marsh Williams. And though John Henry had been invited by Wyatt to come along, he claimed a sudden illness and went home to await the news that came back with frustrating slowness.

The posse had started out by riding to the scene of the holdup, where they found shell casings and wigs and homemade rope beards, along with enough blood to show that Bob Paul's shots had taken some effect. Following the tracks of the assailants' horses for three more days, they came to a ranch where they discovered Luther King heavily armed and hiding behind a milking cow. He went along with only a whimper, they said.

While Sheriff Behan and Marsh Williams rode back to Tombstone with the captured robber, the posse traveled on. But after six days in the mesquite and the mountains, Bob Paul's horse gave out and he and Wyatt walked back to Tombstone, eighteen miles across the desert.

They'd been gone more than a week when they returned exhausted to town. But Wyatt didn't wait until morning before sending his younger brother Warren with a message for John Henry, waking him with a knock at the door, which was answered with irritation by Kate.

"Wyatt wants to see the Doc," Warren said, then remembered to tip his hat to Kate, and added, "Ma'am."

"And what does your brother want with my husband at this hour? Dr. Holliday is gone to bed."

But John Henry was already pulling on his linen shirt and reaching for his trousers. "Tell him I'll be right there," he called sleepily, and Warren nodded in reply.

"Then you can go, Mr. Earp," Kate said haughtily. "My husband will be along presently."

"No, Ma'am," Warren said, looking abashed in the face of her dismissal. "Wyatt says I'm to bring the Doc back with me right now."

"Then you can take us both," Kate said unreasonably.

"No, Ma'am," Warren repeated. "Wyatt says I'm to bring no one but the Doc, Ma'am. Especially yourself, Ma'am."

Kate's anger came out at him in a rush. "I will not stand here and be insulted in my own home! Wherever my husband can go, I can go!"

But before Warren could answer her, John Henry grabbed her arm and pulled her away from the door.

"It's my home, Kate. You're just a visitor, remember? Now be a gracious hostess and get Mr. Earp somethin' to drink while he waits on me." And without thinking, he tightened his grip on her arm until she winced and pulled away.

"Get your own drink!" she said to Warren, spitting out the words, "there's whiskey in the wardrobe." Then she turned on John Henry and said angrily, "I'm going out!" and pushed past him through the door.

Warren waited in embarrassed silence until she left. "I'm sorry, Doc," he said when she was gone. "I didn't mean to make trouble for you."

But John Henry replied with a sigh. "Don't fret, Warren. You haven't made any trouble I don't already have. She'll be back in a little while, anyhow. She's left her purse behind."

By the time he returned from talking with Wyatt, Kate was back and packing to leave again, but still demanded to know what was going on. But all he could tell her, or ever tell anyone, was, "The damned fool. I did not think it of him."

For though Bob Paul hadn't been able to guess the identities of the robbers behind their wigs and homemade rope beards, Luther King was willing to tell all to save his own hide. His partners, he said with only the least bit of coercion, were Harry Head and Jim Crane—and Doc Holliday's friend, Billy Leonard.

If Luther King had had other information to share, he didn't stay around long enough to share it. For just days after his arrest, he slipped from the city jail after signing his horse over to the jailer, who claimed that the prisoner disappeared so fast that he couldn't be found. Wyatt was righteously angry over the escape, saying that if he'd been on the job he would have kept Luther King behind bars, and that it seemed Behan was in cahoots with the cowboys to allow such an important arrest to be thwarted. But a week later, the newspaper reported that Luther King had been hanged in the Huachucas by the very cowboys who had helped him to escape, they likely considering it proper justice for giving away his accomplices.

But the accomplices were not easy to find, once King was arrested and they went into hiding, and after two weeks of trailing, Virgil and Morgan and a second posse put together by Behan finally gave up the search. The Dragoon Mountains, full of Apache legends and Mexican ghosts, seemed to have spirited them away as well. Or so John Henry hoped, as he stayed close in Tombstone and listened to the rumors, wondering if his own name would soon be part of them.

But worse than rumors were the lies of Milt Joyce, who took the opportunity to accost him as he walked into the Oriental one night, looking for Wyatt.

"Well, here comes the stage robber," Milt said accusingly, and the rest of the patrons turned to stare.

"If I'd pulled that job, I'd have got the money!" John Henry said as lightly as he could manage. "Whoever shot that driver was a rank amateur. If he'd downed the horse, he'd have got the bullion." Then he ordered a whiskey like he hadn't a care in the world, and ignored Milt Joyce for the rest of the evening.

But later, when he ran into Joyce again in the street, he made a point to tell him what would become of a man who made such false accusations. And he was almost glad when Milt Joyce swore out a warrant for his arrest for Threats Against Life. Milt had gotten the message, anyhow.

Still, rumors had a way of spreading on their own, so he wasn't surprised when he got a letter from John Gosper in Prescott, asking for answers to hard questions about the Benson stage holdup. What did surprise him was that Gosper added an invitation to a small party at the Prescott home of Mr. and Mrs. William Buffum, where the conversation was always about more than just supper.

He left Kate in Tombstone, but took Gosper's letter with him on the long ride north—one day by stagecoach to the railhead at Benson, another day on the Southern Pacific Railroad to Tucson and Maricopa, and two more days by coach to Prescott. And as he traveled and pondered on Gosper's words, the view around him changed slowly from the Mesquite and cottonwoods of the San Pedro country to the Saguaro and Cholla cactus of the central desert to the pine scented coolness of the Prescott Mountains, and he began to see Tombstone as only a small part of a grander panorama.

The outlaws of southern Arizona weren't just trouble for the local law. They were causing an international situation that could turn into war if not quelled soon. For according to Gosper, the Mexican government was threatening military action if the United States didn't put a stop to the outlawry along the border, especially the theft of Mexican cattle by American cowboys. But the United States was refusing to take action, invoking the Posse Comitatus Act that forbade the military from taking over for local law unless the law requested it. And as of yet, the local law enforcement wasn't asking for any help.

Gosper didn't mention the local lawmen by name, but John Henry knew who they were, and wasn't surprised at their reluctance to call on Federal support to stop the rustling. Sheriff Behan had hired rustler associates Frank Stillwell and Pete Spence as deputies, making the local authorities more outlaw than law themselves, and the fact that Behan and his men had let Luther King walk out of Tombstone's jail more than proved the point. If they were so willing to let a criminal go free, they were probably even more willing to take a cut of whatever booty the criminals might gain. And John Gosper, as Acting Governor, had his hands full and tied at the same time.

The center of Prescott's political society was still, as it had been, William and Rebecca Buffum's comfortable brick home, and John Henry was still a welcome supper guest there—especially since his former housemate was once again the leading man in the Arizona Territory. Though it wasn't Governor Gosper who was the center of attention on this evening, but a man by the name of Thomas Fitch, whose greater fame had Mrs. Buffum all aflutter.

"Oh, my dears!" she exclaimed to John Henry and John Gosper as she welcomed them at her door and bustled them through the parlor and into the dining room, "What a treat we have for you tonight! Mr. Thomas Fitch here at our very own table, and such a celebrity! Of course, I've known him for some time, as he and Mr. Buffum have been friends since their days together in the Territorial Legislature. But it's always a special evening when he joins us. Such a mannerly gentleman! And so talented, as well! Did you know he's an actor as well as a lawyer, besides holding seats in both the Congress and the Senate? Why, he's even written a play! Mr. Buffum calls him *the leading legal light in all the Western Territories.* Imagine!"

"I imagine you are falling in love with Mr. Fitch," said John Gosper with an injured tone. "I thought I was your favorite, and here you are fawning over another man. Why, if I weren't so looking forward to your famous cobbler, I'd have to leave right now in protest!"

"Shame on you for saying such things!" Mrs. Buffum replied with matronly propriety, though her cheeks turned a girlish pink at the tease. "You know that Mr. Fitch is one of Mr. Buffum's dearest friends! But of course you must, since it was Mr. Fitch himself who asked us to invite the both of you to supper tonight."

"The both of us?" John Henry asked.

"Why, yes," she said with a smile. "And you especially, Dr. Holliday. Mr. Fitch was very particular that we have you here as well. I had no idea you were such a favorite of his."

"Nor had I," he replied, throwing a questioning glance at Gosper. For not ever having had the pleasure of meeting the esteemed Mr. Fitch, he couldn't imagine why the gentleman would ask for his company.

But Gosper was too busy making flatteries to Mrs. Buffum to offer any explanation, and John Henry followed them into the dining room wondering what it was he'd gotten himself into.

The answer came, but slowly, after a long lingering over the bounteous table and a conversation that centered mostly on Thomas Fitch's many career exploits. For the Senator, as he preferred to be called, had tried almost everything to make his fame and fortune in the Western Territories, and told of his adventures with a flair that was more actor than attorney. With a generous waistline bound in a rich brocade vest, a mane of silver hair curling over his shirt collar, and a resonant baritone voice, he seemed more suited to a stage than a supper table, and as he spoke, he laid one well-manicured hand on his gold pocket watch and used the other to gesture dramatically.

"Virginia City, Nevada, gentlemen! The Comstock silver lode! And I was there to take part in the excitement, giving my humble efforts to the editorship of one of the two newspapers in town—the leading paper, I am proud to say, which was called *The Union* for good reason. For though we were abiding in the territories, we still considered ourselves staunch supporters of the Federal government and looked forward to a successful conclusion to the great conflict between the states. We had, after all, just won a terrible victory at Gettysburg and another at Vicksburg, and it looked like the end of the rebellion was to be soon at hand. But not all of the citizens of Virginia City agreed with my editorial opinion, and the editor of the *Enterprise*, our meager competitor, wrote a personally insulting rebuttal to my views. What else could I do, but challenge him to a duel to prove the worth of his words and my own integrity? And so a duel was organized and drew much attention, as such matters usually do, with reporters from both papers hoping that there would be enough blood spilled to open up new job opportunities for themselves, along with giving them something thrilling to write about. For as one of them wrote of it afterward, they felt it their duty to *keep the public mind in a healthy state of excitement, and experience has taught us that blood alone can do this.* Those particular words being written by a young reporter from the other paper, a chap named Clemens, who had come to the territory tagging along after a brother who had taken a position as secretary to the Governor of Nevada. Orien Clemens was the secretary's name and as restrained and cautious a mind as his brother's was fanciful. But it was the brother, not Orien, who made a real career of telling stories. In fact, that was how my own name first became popularly known, when this young Clemens turned me into a character in a story he was writing. He even had the audacity to call me by name in the work—*Mr. Fitch.* This being in the days before I became a Senator, of course."

"And what of the duel?" John Henry asked. "Since you're standin' here tellin' us about it, I reckon you won."

The Senator sighed dramatically. "The duel was called off, more's the pity. And the worst that came of it was Clemens calling me an arrogant newspaper editor. I wrote an editorial in response advising him to leave reporting behind and stick to storytelling, as he seemed to have more flair for fabrication than for fact. To which he replied with an editorial saying that I should get out of reporting, as well, and find a career devoid of facts entirely, like politics perhaps. Well, I couldn't very well expect him to follow my advice without my being willing to follow his. So I left the newspaper and turned my talents to the law, which is how I became a Nevada State congressman, the beginning of my public career. And he took my advice, as well, and went on to write a book you may have heard of: *Tom Sawyer*. Clemens was the way I knew him, but when he left Virginia City he started using the pen name *Mark Twain*."

John Henry had, of course, heard of both Mark Twain and *Tom Sawyer*, the recently published and wildly popular story of a boy growing up along the Mississippi River, though he hadn't yet taken the time to read it. His own reading of late had been mostly the mining reports and the local papers.

"Mark Twain calls the Senator arrogant," William Buffum said, "but I call him accomplished and rightfully proud. He should be telling you how he helped turn the Territory of Nevada into a State by drafting the new state constitution, though it was his oratory, more than his writing, which won him the most acclaim."

"And the most disdain," the Senator said with a wag of his silver-haired head.

"And how's that?" John Henry asked.

"What the Senator means is that the speech he gave in our neighboring Territory of Utah brought him a certain ill-repute. The speech being a defense of the Mormons against the Cullom Bill which threatened to outlaw their practice of polygamy."

"Polygamy?" John Henry asked. "You mean havin' more than one wife? But that's against the law, isn't it?"

"Only in particular states," John Gosper said, "but not all. And not at all in the territories."

Senator Fitch nodded in agreement. "It probably never occurred to our founding fathers to specify the number of wives a man might take, assuming most men wouldn't know what to do with more than one wife at a time, anyway. Most the men I know have a hard time handling a first wife, without adding a second or third—though some men of my acquaintance seem pleased enough to keep an extra woman handy without considering her as family. Which tends to blur the line between polygamy and plain old-fashioned adultery, and made me question which was worse: claiming to be married to an extra woman, or claiming not to have the extra woman with whom one was behaving married. So when the legislators of the country proposed a bill to outlaw polygamy, I had to wonder why they found the practice so suddenly offensive. The only conclusion I could make was that the Mormons might prove such a powerful political force if allowed citizenship, gathered in strength as they are in their mountain valleys and answering to their prophet for guidance in temporal as well as spiritual things, that the legislators felt compelled to break them somehow. Polygamy, they seemed to declare, would be the rock upon which the Latter-day Saints would be broken."

"Mr. Fitch had the courage of conviction to speak against the legislation," William Buffum put in, "which earned him enemies in political circles, as you might imagine, though it earned him a goodly number of friends in the Utah Territory, including a close association with their prophet, Brigham Young. I suppose you can quote a bit from your speech before the Utah congressional congress. As I recall, excerpts of it were printed in all the papers that year."

"I remember some of it," Senator Fitch replied, "at least, the part I think you would like to have me recite tonight, calling the Mormons to fight against the government's unrighteous interference in their religious affairs. While the Saints were mostly living a Godly life, the local law was ignoring the more worldly elements around them, and I spoke to encourage them to action." And with that, he took what looked like an orator's stance in the center of the smoky parlor, one hand in his vest and the other gesticulating the finer points of his message. Like a little Napoleon, John Henry thought, readying for a revolution.

"Your magistrates are successfully defied, your local laws are disregarded, your municipal ordinances are trampled into the mire. Theft and murder walk through your streets without detection, drunkards howl their orgies in the shadow of your altars. The glare and turmoil of drinking saloons, the glitter of gambling hells, and the painted flaunt of the bawd plying her trade, now vex the repose of the streets which beforetime heard no sound to disturb their quiet save the busy hum of industry, the clatter of trade, and the musical tinkle of mountain streams."

And though it seemed there should be a round of applause after such a performance, both Gosper and William Buffum sat silent and thoughtful as the Senator went on.

"And that, gentlemen, is how I see things in this Territory as well. For our magistrates are also defied and our local laws are disregarded. Do not theft and murder walk our streets and threaten our roads?"

"True, true," William Buffum replied. "Which is precisely why we are meeting here tonight." Then he turned his attention to John Henry. "And why we have asked you to join us, as well, Dr. Holliday."

"I don't understand."

"You understand better than most," John Gosper said, "being in the thick of the trouble. In fact, it's your understanding of the situation that offers a solution to it. Surely, you must have guessed the import of my many questions regarding the troubles in the Tombstone district?"

"I reckoned you had somethin' up your sleeve."

"A good way to phrase it," Gosper said, "considering the clandestine nature of our plans."

"Clandestine," the Senator added, "because these plans are also somewhat outside the scope of the law, if not altogether illegal. Though as Machiavelli wrote, sometimes the end justifies the means. For if we don't have control of the border, we don't have control of anything."

"I appreciate the philosophy lesson," John Henry said, "but I still don't know what y'all are talkin' about. What ends? What means? And what do they have to do me, anyhow?"

"A great deal," William Buffum replied, "but only if you are willing to join with us in this endeavor, an endeavor which, without you, will be most difficult to accomplish. That endeavor being the eradication of the criminal element from our border with Mexico, thereby preserving the peace between our two countries and preventing what seems to be an almost certain war."

"Sounds like a worthy cause."

"But one which has been frustrated time and again," Gosper said, "lost in a confusion of red tape and regulations. Even the military seems unable to handle the matter, as this telegram indicates." Then, pulling a paper from his suit coat pocket, he unfolded it and held it before him, saying, "I received this just last week, a copy of a letter from the Major General here in Prescott for the Adjutant General in San Francisco:

"Sir: In reply to your dispatch of the 17th instant, on the subject, I have the honor to state for the information of the Division Commander, that 'Cow-boys' are a gang of desperadoes, originally cattle lifters from Texas. They appeared in such force in New Mexico, that in Lincoln County, they defied the constituted authorities for a considerable time. They have committed many murders, and have stolen cattle, horses, and mules in Arizona and Sonora, escaping across the boundary lines. Our Government, being called upon by Mexico to stop these intrusions, murders, and robberies on Mexican soil, referred the subject to Governor Frémont, who sent a message to the Arizona Legislature for authority and money to call out the militia; but the Legislature refused, many of the members considering it the duty of the General Government to redress the grievances complained of by Mexico. It strikes me that we have international obligations that ought not to fall on Arizona.

Cannot something be done to relieve the people on both sides of the border, alike terrorized, plundered, and murdered by these outlaws?

Enclosed please find extract from Legislative Journal of 12th instant, which seems to point out a remedy, if it can be applied, namely for the Attorney General to arrest the 'Cow-boys' through the U. S. Marshal by allowing him a sufficient number of deputies."

"So it sounds like you have your solution," John Henry commented, still unsure of what it all had to do with him.

"We would have," the Senator said, "if there were any funds available to pay for this force of deputies to the U.S. Marshal. But allowing and allocating are two different matters, and neither the Federal nor the Territorial government will make the allocation. So no money, no deputies, and no cow-boys under arrest."

Then William Buffum spoke. "There are, however, other ways to fund such an endeavor. I pride myself on being a man of business, and having as my close acquaintances other men of business, both in this territory and elsewhere. In particular, I have professional associations with certain of the wealthier cattlemen in the southern regions of Arizona whom I supply with goods from California for their little fiefdoms down there. And they are, of course, intimately aware of the problems these border ruffians can cause. Because of the outlaws, the roads are dangerous to ride. Because of the outlaws, supply lines are threatened. Because of the outlaws, their cattle are stolen and sold away. So they are, as much or more than the Mexican government, interested in seeing these disturbances abated. So interested, in fact, that some of them have offered to pay the expenses of a private police force that would finally rid them of these problems."

"But the payments must be discreetly made," the Senator added, "and all done in a manner which doesn't put them at odds with the official work of the Territory. It cannot be known that certain citizens have joined together with certain members of the Territorial legislature and, without the sanction of the whole, created an independent organization to enforce the laws."

"The whole scheme is a legal impossibility, of course," said John Gosper, "planning search and seizure without warrants. Which is why I wanted Senator Fitch here to advise. He is, as you have heard tonight, one of the brightest legal minds in all the western territories, with a history of maneuvering through treacherous waters. For this plan to succeed, we will need to chart a careful course so that neither the drafters nor the funders of its execution will ever be known to have had anything to do with it. In fact, the very existence of a plan must never be made public. Beyond these four walls," he said, glancing up at the finely appointed and smoke-filled parlor, "there is no plan. Only troublemakers on the border who will soon be finding themselves in trouble."

It was a daring plan, all right, mounting a private police force answerable only to a shadowy group of men who had no right to do such a thing. Yet, it just might work.

"So now that you have a plan and a way to pay for it," John Henry said, "all you need is some hired guns to carry it out."

"We prefer to think of them as a posse," the Senator said, "with the special jurisdiction of cleaning out those mountain passes."

John Henry nodded. "Like the Vigilantes, back home," he said, remembering when a gang of young hotheads tried to chase the Yankees out of their county and were almost hung for their efforts. "But who do you think would be willing to take on such a dangerous assignment? Vigilantes usually fight for their own cause, not the safety of a border, unless there's money in it."

But as soon as he said the words, he knew who would take on such a job. There was one man he knew who didn't mind putting himself in harm's way for the sake of peace in the community, and who was always looking for a way to make some money as well.

"That's why we asked you here," Gosper replied. "You know better than any of us here in Prescott how things work in the Tombstone district. We were hoping you'd have some names for us."

The three men looked at him solemnly, and John Henry felt a sudden sense of responsibility come over him. These men, having taken him into their confidence, now put their careers and perhaps their lives into his hands, putting him into an uncomfortable position of power.

"I know someone," he said slowly. "He's been a lawman from time to time, as well as a teamster, a railroader, a buffalo hunter, a gambler—and most importantly, a private detective discovering the whereabouts of cattle thieves."

"Sounds like our man," William Buffum said with a nod. "But one man alone can't do this work. It will take a whole force to go against these outlaws."

"Which point I was just coming to," John Henry said. "For in addition to all of the above qualifications, the man I suggest brings his own devoted force along with him. A force bound by blood. He has brothers who'd be willing to stand at his side in whatever scheme he proposed— for a price, of course."

"And where might we find this family of outlaw hunters?" asked Senator Fitch.

"That's the beauty of it, gentlemen. They happen to be down on the border already, in Tombstone, looking to make their fortune."

"A fortuitous circumstance," William Buffum said. "But can these brothers be trusted to keep our confidence? Are they careful with their conversation?"

"Oh, they're careful, all right," John Henry answered. For of any man he knew, Wyatt Earp was the least conversational. And Morgan, if they could encourage him to join the endeavor, talked so much that no one much bothered to listen to him. As for Virgil, his oath as a U.S. Deputy Marshal might preclude him from joining whole-heartedly in the plans. And there was yet one possible problem with the plan—the U.S. Marshal for whom Virgil worked. "And what about Crawley Dake?" he asked. "Does he know of this scheme?"

Gosper glanced at Buffum and Fitch, then answered. "Our good United States Marshal has been made aware of our intent to offer assistance beyond the Legislature's approval. He has, in fact, been asking for such assistance ever since taking office himself. But he only knows what we choose to tell him, for his own protection. He is, after all, a Federal employee and under different constraints than the rest of us."

Constraints that both pulled and pushed him, John Henry thought, being under orders to keep the peace while being charged with upholding the law, which two commissions seemed contrary in this case. And it was the very contrariness of the situation that caught his own imagination.

"So what you need, gentlemen, is a connection," he said, "someone who can stand between you and your agents to help you keep your hands clean. Someone who can mix in with the outlaws or play cards with the lawmen, without really being a part of either world, and whom no one would suspect of having any interests but his own. Someone who is neither law nor outlaw, but something else entirely. And I reckon it wouldn't hurt if that someone had played the part before, usin' his station to ask questions others can't ask and gettin' answers others can't get."

"That's right," said the Senator approvingly. "And do you happen to know such a man?"

He could have said no and saved himself from whatever trouble might come of it. But if he were going to get Wyatt and his brothers involved in the scheme, he couldn't very well stay out of it himself. So he took a long look at each of the men in the room, measuring their dedication to the cause, and nodded an answer.

"What you need, gentlemen," he said, "is me."

Chapter Four

Sierra Bonita, 1881

Between the Dragoon Mountains east of Tombstone and the Chiricahuas east of the Dragoons lay the hundred-mile long Sulfur Springs Valley, the richest ranching land in the Arizona Territory. It was a high cienega lush with gramma grass and watered by an endless underground river, with stands of cottonwood trees where the underground springs seeped up through the sod. It was also the ancestral home of the fierce Apache, but when the Army built Fort Grant at the head of the valley and scattered the Indians into the mountains, the valley opened up to opportunity. All a cattleman had to do was buy a claim to one of the watering holes and five miles of public domain grazing land around it was his for the using. And if a man was smart enough to file a series of such claims, he could build a whole ranch for the price of the water alone.

That was the way Henry Clay Hooker had established his empire in the Sulfur Springs Valley, turning one homestead into a ranch of three hundred-thousand acres. The cowboys who worked the land said that if a rider left from ranch headquarters and rode forty-five miles a day, it would take him four days to make a circle of the place. And with a thousand acres of the land fenced for raising corn, barley, and alfalfa as cattle feed, Henry Hooker counted his herd at thirty-thousand head of prime beeves—the biggest ranch in the Territory.

But he hadn't started out as a rich man, or even as a cattleman, with his first herd being more of a flock. Hooker had begun his career as a merchant in the California gold mining town of Placerville, nicknamed Hangtown for its wild ways. And if it hadn't been for a fire that swept through Hangtown and destroyed his store along with most of Main Street, he might have stayed in the mercantile business. But with no goods left to sell and only a few hundred dollars to his name, Henry Hooker was forced to make a fast career change. So he bought a flock of five-hundred turkeys for $1.50 a head, and proposed to drive them over the mountains like cattle and sell them for a profit to the hungry miners of the Nevada silver fields.

But turkeys don't herd like cattle, as Hooker soon discovered, even with a hired drover and two shepherd dogs worrying at them, so the men spent more time chasing the big birds around than leading them to market. And when something spooked the flock and they all took off running and disappeared over a ridge, Hooker figured he'd lost his investment for good. Then he and the drover crested the height and found the turkeys flocked together down below in a stand of aspen trees, contentedly pecking for food. So although the whole adventure had seemed absurd at the outset, Hooker got the birds all the way to Carson City and sold them for a neat profit of $5 a head.

Having made one successful drive, Henry Hooker decided to try his hand at another, and invested his turkey profits in a business supplying beef to the military posts and Indian agencies of the Arizona Territory. Along the way, he learned how to appease the Apache, made friends with Chief Cochise, and became so expert in the cattle trade that he eventually bought out his partners and took over the business for himself.

But it was no cowboy that John Henry met, when he arrived at the Sierra Bonita Ranch bearing a letter of introduction from Governor Gosper and information too sensitive to be sent by wire. Instead, the man who offered a firm handshake at the hacienda door was the very picture of a prosperous Yankee banker—dressed in a black cutaway coat and stiff white shirt, his gray beard trimmed close, his northern voice clipped and hurried.

"I'm Hooker," he said, though it came out more like *Hookah*, with the "It's a pleasure to meet you, Dr. Holliday," sounding like *Dactah Halliday*.

"And you, Sir," John Henry replied, thinking that it was probably useless to try to correct the speaking habits in a man of mature years, like Hooker. But the sharp New Hampshire accent didn't stop Hooker from being a genial host, welcoming a stranger into his home like any good Southerner.

"We live comfortably here at the ranch," Hooker said as he showed the way through the well-appointed parlor with its brocaded settees and square Steinway piano, an interesting contrast to the fort-like façade of the house. The place was built with adobe walls twenty inches thick, the windows all facing toward an inner courtyard, making it impregnable in case of an Indian attack. But the Indians had left the Sierra Bonita alone so far, and the thick adobe served mostly to keep the house cool in the hot Arizona summers.

"This valley, and the mountains around it, were Chiricahua Apache land," Hooker said, as he ushered John Henry into the ranch office—three walls of bookcases surrounding a rolltop desk, its pigeonholes stuffed with papers. "It wasn't until the government sent the Apache to San Carlos that the valley opened up to settlers. That was when Cochise was Chief of the Chokonen Chiricahua, and he did his best to keep things peaceful. He'd already lost enough of his kinsmen to the Apache Wars, and didn't care to lose anymore."

"You speak of him as a friend," John Henry commented, having heard something of the story.

"I was," Hooker said, "and honored to call myself so. Our acquaintance began quite by accident, when I was supplying beef to the Army posts, and traveling from one post to another. It happened that I had to pass through the Dragoons, and came upon a narrow gorge where I discovered myself surrounded by Apache on the high ledges of rock above. I didn't see any way out but through, so I kept riding, and was met on the other side by none other than Chief Cochise himself. He told me that he was impressed by a man who wouldn't run from danger, and invited me to his camp for the night. It was at his campfire that I learned he had been watching me for some time, and was glad that I had brought cattle into the country, as his people were hungry. I knew, of course, that some of my herds were being stolen, and assumed it was Indians who were doing it, but now felt a certain compassion for them. So Cochise and I agreed that if I would let his people have what beef they needed, he would vow to never molest me or my family. Which vow he kept until his dying day, and I was singularly protected from the atrocities other cattlemen suffered."

Then he nodded toward a blood red Indian blanket, hanging like a tapestry on the wall of the office and woven with the letter C intertwined with Hooker's Broken H brand.

"That blanket was given to me by Cochise in token of our friendship. I consider it the greatest treasure of the Sierra Bonita."

"Which makes it a very great treasure indeed," John Henry said, "if what I have heard of the Sierra Bonita is true. They say this is the richest ranch in all the Arizona Territory, and you one of the richest men in it."

Although good manners would usually forbid him commenting on a man's financial situation, it was Hooker's money that had brought him on this mission, and he was eager to get to the point of the conversation. He'd been several days on the road since leaving Prescott, traveling by stagecoach and rail and then by stagecoach again, and he was already feeling weary and ill-tempered. But Hooker seemed inclined to talk about his ranch, and good manners decreed that John Henry should listen.

"Things changed when Cochise died and Geronimo and Victorio became leaders of the Apache. They didn't understand, as Cochise had, that it was useless to fight the White Man. So they fought. When Victorio escaped from the San Carlos Reservation and went on a rampage, killing and mutilating whites, I determined to remove my family from this valley and put the ranch up for sale, stock and all. That was two years back, and not a buyer was interested in this Apache land, rich as it was. Wealth isn't much good if you're not alive to enjoy it. So I sent my family back to California and I stayed here on the ranch, protecting my investment that nobody wanted to buy."

And that was the first time that John Henry realized what was missing from Hooker's well-appointed surroundings: people. Other than a few ranch hands and a Mexican who'd answered the door, he'd seen no one else on the property. The hacienda with its protective adobe walls and stylish furnishings, its carpeted tile floors and expensive piano, was silent and still as a tomb. Except for Hooker, who kept talking.

"Last fall, the Army found Victorio down on the border and killed him. But Geronimo is still a force to be reckoned with. It may be a hopeless fight for the Apache, but they will fight it to the end. Thus, my hacienda has thick walls and no windows to the outside, for protection. I may have come to this property by Providence, but I am obliged to look after it myself."

"You came to it by Providence?" John Henry asked, noting the odd way Hooker had put the thought. "I thought you bought it up, one well at a time."

"I did, but first I had to find it. Remember, this valley was Apache land, with no white men in it but the soldiers at Fort Grant, north toward Mount Graham. Even after the Apache were driven out it still seemed a dangerous place, with Indians loose up in the mountains. No one even thought of looking at it. That's why I say it was Providence that brought me to it, or I would never have thought to settle here—Providence and a cattle stampede."

"A stampede?" John Henry said with polite attentiveness, though he thought Hooker would need little encouragement to go on with his tale.

"Back in '72. That was the year the Apache were sent to the San Carlos Reservation, and when I was holding my Army contract cattle in the Galiuro Mountains. One night my herd stampeded, and I followed the trail down to a stretch of wet meadow in the Sulfur Springs Valley. It was the best cattle grazing land I had ever seen, and empty of settlers for a hundred miles. So I took over where the Apache left off, and have made a good living in this place. But I would never have thought of it if the cattle hadn't shown me the way."

"I thought you said it was Providence, not cows," John Henry said, with the start of an irreverent laugh that was quickly quieted by Hooker's solemn reply.

"I believe in Providence, the same as my Puritan forefathers believed, even if I don't hold with much else. When you're descended from the founder of Hartford, Connecticut, you can't help but have some staunch old religion in you somewhere. So yes, I do believe in Providence, and I believe I was led to this valley just like those beeves were, finding a promised land. Truth is I was glad when the place didn't sell. I hope it stays in the Hooker family for a hundred years after me."

"And what if Providence had led you into an Indian attack?" John Henry asked, more to understand than to argue the point.

Hooker shrugged. "I didn't say Providence is always kind. But I do believe that there's a plan and a road ahead of us, if we just open our eyes to it. Nothing happens by chance."

And feeling uncomfortable with the serious turn of the conversation, John Henry took advantage of the moment to bring up the point of his visit.

"And when a plan is revealed, what then?"

"Then we follow it," Hooker replied pragmatically.

And just as John Henry was about to share Gosper's plan and how it was to be financed, Hooker said:

"And how much does the governor think he'll need to put down the cowboys?"

John Henry was stunned into silence for a moment before asking, "You knew why I was here?"

"I know what's on the governor's mind," Hooker said, "what's on all our minds. No sooner do we get the Indians halfway under control, than these Texas cowboys move in to steal our stock. I've lost more beeves to rustlers than I ever did to the Apache, and with less reason for it. At least the Indians ate the meat; the cowboys just change the brand and sell it as their own. And it's not just the rustlers we have to deal with. I have it on some authority that there's a ranch on the White River, down at the south end of the valley, where the cowboys are welcomed to do their branding and graze their stolen cattle, for a price. So even some of the cattlemen are in league."

"Do you know the names of these cattlemen?" John Henry asked, thinking any information he could glean would make Wyatt's job easier—assuming Wyatt was willing to take the job.

"I do," Hooker replied. "It's the McLaury brothers, Frank and Tom. Moved over here from the Babocamari River a few months past. I wouldn't go so far as to accuse them of rustling themselves, but they're mighty easy in their dealings with the ones I do suspect. Like Old Man Clanton and his sons, over on the San Pedro."

John Henry knew the men Hooker was talking about. The McLaurys were often in Tombstone, dealing with their butcher or taking a hand in the high stakes poker games. Frank, the elder brother, black haired and vain, considered himself a ladies man, and had even made advances to Kate when he thought John Henry wasn't watching. Tom, the younger brother, was more reserved and circumspect, and Kate thought him the better looking of the two. They'd been known for raising Cain along with the cowboys, and had both been in the crowd arrested in the fracas following the shooting of Marshal White. As for Old Man Clanton, John Henry had never met him or heard of his coming into Tombstone, as he left his sons Ike and Billy to take care of town business on his behalf. But if the sons were any reflection of the father, then Clanton was petty and mean-tempered and didn't hold his liquor well.

"So you know what it is that Gosper wants from you?" John Henry asked.

"Money, of course. He knows I have enough. And he knows I'm willing to make an investment to protect my property."

"Which Providence led you to," John Henry said with a smile, his respect for the man growing.

"That's right. And I'm not about to let a gang of thieving cutthroats come down here and ruin what I worked for. I'll fight like the Apache to keep my land, and I'll win."

And with his Yankee determination—and his financial resources—he probably would. Then John Henry remembered something.

"So if you knew from the first what I came here for, why did you wait so long to say it?"

Hooker smiled. "We don't get much company, this far out from civilization. I was glad to have someone to talk to."

Hooker wanted the particulars, of course—how much money was needed, how it would be passed from him to the vigilantes, who those vigilantes would be. All of which John Henry answered as best he could, except for assuring him of Wyatt's assistance. That much remained to be seen. But the plan was complete enough and came with enough authority that Henry Hooker readily agreed to it. When John Henry left the ranch, he would carry with him a draft to be held by a cashier at the Safford, Hudson & Company Bank in Tombstone, and dispersed as necessary to pay the expenses of Gosper's secret posse.

But Hooker would not know the details of how the money was used, so that he could truthfully say, if ever asked, that he had merely advanced it at the request of certain business associates in Prescott. And those associates, if ever asked, would only say that Mr. Hooker was a generous man with his money and often made investments in the business ventures of others. And if there were more questions than that, the answers would be carefully constructed by Senator Fitch to cover the truth, using his background in law and newspaper writing to say only what needed to be said, and nothing more. But John Henry knew all.

And now all he had left to do was travel back to Tombstone and sell the plan to Wyatt—the hardest part of the job. But first he accepted Hooker's invitation to stay to supper and spend the night at the Sierra Bonita, resting up from one journey before starting another. There was, after all, plenty of room in the big empty ranch house.

It was a rest that he needed, having made one long trip to Prescott and then another to Tucson and across the Dragoon mountains into the Sulfur Springs Valley, breathing coal dust and road dirt and missing too many hours of sleep. In the cool darkness of the adobe-walled hacienda, he slept deeply.

Or so he thought, until Henry Hooker greeted him at breakfast the next morning.

"That cough of yours could use a visit to the hot springs up Galiuro Canyon. Take one of my horses and tell Dr. King I sent you. You've heard of my stables? I raise some of the finest trotters in the Territory, carriage horses mostly. Last count, I had five-hundred brood mares and six pure-bred stallions."

"Sounds like nice odds for the stallions," John Henry commented.

"They're content, and make a good showing at the races in California. You can take your pick for the ride up the Canyon. Dr. King will get you from there to the railhead, and get the horse back to me."

"I thought you said there were still Indians in those mountains?"

"In the mountains, yes. But the Apache won't go near Galiuro Canyon, on account of the hot springs. They think it's evil spirits that makes the water boil up out of the rock, and I don't try to dissuade them. I'm looking at buying that property and developing it into a real resort."

"And let the Indians think you've made a deal with the Devil?"

But Hooker looked at him solemnly before answering.

"Seems to me we may have already done that."

It was a nine-mile ride from the Sierra Bonita to the hot springs, and John Henry was glad to have one of Hooker's best horses under him. On a lesser mount, the trail would have been just another arduous journey, following the foothills to the mouth of the narrow canyon, then pushing up through brush and cottonwoods growing thick between sheer rock walls. But on a spirited horse that knew the terrain, the ride felt more like an adventure. With the sky overhead a deep sapphire blue and a scent of wild witch hazel in the air, there was something intoxicating about the place. Then ahead of him, as the canyon walls opened up, he saw a column of smoke rising between the willows.

He might have thought it was smoke from a cabin chimney, if Hooker hadn't warned him otherwise. But the smoke was really steam coming up from the hot springs, and sign that he had arrived at Dr. King's Warm Springs Ranch, as the owner called it, though there were no cattle or even cows in that canyon. The title was just a grand name for what had been an Army hospital during the Civil War, then deserted for ten years until Glendy King came West, seeking his health. He heard of the springs, investigated them, and found the waters to be filled with healing minerals and heavy with Lithia, and proclaimed them a "fountain of life." He hoped they would also prove to be a fountain of riches as other health-seekers sought them out, and he went about building a home and bathhouses for his future guests. The fact that he had never actually graduated from Dickinson College, where he'd once studied medicine, didn't stop him from using the title of Doctor, especially if it brought customers to his resort. It was the water that mattered anyhow, not the doctor's credentials.

But King didn't need a degree to prove the efficacy of his hot springs. His own robust health was advertisement enough for John Henry. If the doctor had left Pennsylvania as a frail invalid as he'd claimed to be, he was now a hearty middle-aged man and happy to share his miracle cure with any paying customer, and John Henry reckoned it was worth paying the price. Though he didn't consider himself an invalid anymore, having had his own cure at the Montezuma Hot Springs, a little extra insurance couldn't hurt. And after a day of drinking in the mineral water and bathing in Dr. King's hot baths, his road cough would be gone and he'd be ready to travel again.

Dr. King's Warm Springs had nothing of the elegance of Montezuma, however, with its grand hotel on the hillside and its comfortable bathhouses, its attentive staff and soft Turkish towels. Here, the water boiled up out of a dark hole in the rocky pavement of the canyon floor, then overflowed into two rough wooden tubs set in a lean-to shelter. Yet primitive as the accommodations were, the steamy air and the slippery mineral water were soothing to a travel-wearied body, and John Henry let his usually tight-wound nerves relax. The Indians were wrong about this place, for no evil spirits could bring such calm and comfort. And Hooker was wrong as well in calling Gosper's plan a deal with the Devil, for it was the Devil they were fighting and justice that would win out. And what could go wrong with a plan like that?

In the mountains to the south along the border, near the Sonoran town of Fronteras, four cowboys were caught stealing cattle and were shot to death by Mexican soldiers. The cowboys had claimed to be filling a beef contract for Fort Bowie, and answered an order to surrender with gunfire. The Mexican government claimed the incident was proof that the United States was not willing to police the border and was asking for war.

That news, and an arrest warrant, were waiting for John Henry when he got back to Tombstone.

"I warned you," Wyatt said by way of welcome when the stage pulled into town. He'd been watching for John Henry's arrival and hoping to catch him before the law caught wind of his return. "Milt Joyce is a bad man to cross, especially now he's on the County Commission. And he doesn't forget a grudge. He's still suffering from that hand you shot up last fall, and means to make you pay for it."

"But I already settled that case!"

"Milt's claiming new evidence, and got the grand jury to send back an indictment. Like I said, he's got friends in high places. Sheriff Behan, to name one. It won't be so easy to get you off this time."

"I won't go to jail!" John Henry said vehemently. "Not for Milt Joyce, anyhow."

"You won't have to, if I can arrange bond money. But I'm hoping it won't come to that. Your attorney is going to ask the judge for a dismissal, on account of the grand jury being illegally impaneled, and that will be the end of it."

"My attorney?" he said with surprise, not having hired himself a lawyer yet.

"Albert George. His partner recommended him to me."

"And who might his partner be?"

"Fellow by the name of Fitch, just arrived from Prescott. Seems he's quite well known in the legal circles. Surprising that someone like him would take an interest in a case like this."

Wyatt wasn't the only one who was surprised.

John Henry never heard personally from Thomas Fitch, but felt better being in court with his partner, though even an able attorney couldn't sway the judge's decision. Milt Jones evidently had influence with the bench as well as the County Commission. So after two days of argument and a request for a change of venue, the best that Lawyer George could do was get the case off the docket for awhile and win a continuance until the fall. And by then, John Henry hoped, the law would have forgotten all about him.

But the law hadn't forgotten about the Benson stage robbery, though Sheriff Behan had given up the hunt for the robbers, and Wyatt was still working to find Luther King's accomplices. And as he told it to John Henry, an opportunity had presented itself in the person of Ike Clanton—one of the men Hooker had called a rustler and in league with the cowboys. Ike had come into town talking about Billy Leonard's New Mexico land, and how he had driven his cattle over there when Leonard went on the run. It seemed reasonable to Ike that since Billy wasn't around to use the ranch himself, he wouldn't mind a friend using it. But Billy minded very much, and let Ike know that he'd have to get his stock off the land, or buy it legally. So Ike was in Tombstone looking for money or some other solution to his land dilemma.

"Which got me to thinking," Wyatt said over drinks in the back corner of the Oriental, "and I proposed a plan to Ike. If he would deliver Leonard and the others so I could arrest them, I would let him have all the reward money and never let on who had arranged for the capture. The glory of bringing in the robbers would be enough for me, and make me look good in the next election for Sheriff."

"I reckon it's better for you to bring Billy in, than somebody else," John Henry said with a sigh, thinking that it would have been even better if Billy Leonard had stayed out of the robbery entirely. But now that it was over, he couldn't fault Wyatt for doing his duty to bring the robbers to justice. "So how did Ike take the idea?"

"He wanted to know how much reward money there would be. When I told him twelve-hundred dollars for each, he said that wasn't enough, so I offered another thousand out of my own pocket."

"Call it a campaign donation?" John Henry said, though he found it hard to be clever when it was the capture of a friend they were discussing.

"Then he wanted to know if the reward was good dead or alive. He said those boys would never come in without a fight, and he wanted to make sure he'd get paid either way. So I wired Wells Fargo in San Francisco, and they sent a telegram that I showed to Ike saying they would pay up, dead or alive. That seemed to satisfy him, and he brought Frank McLaury and Joe Hill in to help him bring the boys over from New Mexico to the Sulphur Springs Valley where I could arrest them."

"So if you promised Ike to keep things quiet, why are you telling me about it now?"

Wyatt, always spare with words, took a long time answering.

"Because we never got a chance to make the capture," he said slowly. "Joe Hill caught up with Leonard and his partners a day too late. By the time he found them they were already dead, shot down in a mining camp in the Hachita Mountains."

"Who did it?" John Henry said, eyes on his whiskey.

"Some ranchers by the name of Haslett, from over in the Animas Valley near Mike Gray's place. Mike wanted the Haslett's land, and put up a job for Head and Crane to drive them out. When the Hasletts got wind of it, they ran down Head in a saloon and commenced to shooting. Billy Leonard was along with him and got the worst of it. But the way I hear it, he'd already been wounded bad in the stage holdup, and was wishing somebody would shoot him and put him out of his pain."

John Henry took a fast drink of his whiskey, to cover his emotion. "Then I reckon I ought to find these Hasletts and thank them for doin' him the favor."

"If you're thinking about revenge, Doc, you're too late. When Jim Crane heard about his partners being killed, he came back with a gang of cowboys and shot the Hasletts to pieces, all three brothers."

"So how does it end, Wyatt?"

"What do you mean?"

"Billy's partners killed Bud Philpot. The Hasletts killed Billy's partners. The cowboys killed the Hasletts. So who's gonna kill the cowboys?"

"Nobody," Wyatt replied. "There's too many of them, up in those mountains, maybe three-hundred or more. And getting more organized all the time. Not even the law around here is up to handling that."

"Then where is justice?" John Henry asked, more a challenge than a question. For without knowing it, Wyatt had just led himself right to where John Henry wanted him to be.

"There isn't any justice, in Tombstone," Wyatt replied.

"But what if there were a posse commissioned with chasin' down these cowboys, goin' into the mountains to clean them out? Seems like that would be justice, and take care of the problem."

"There's no money for a posse like that. Hell, the bill we turned in to Behan for that chase after the stage holdup still isn't paid, and that was only a few hundred dollars. What you're talking about would take thousands."

"I know a man who has that, and more," John Henry said casually, as if the thought had just come to him.

Wyatt gave a half-hearted laugh. "Some lucky poker friend of yours?"

"No," John Henry replied. "I was actually thinkin' of Henry Hooker."

Wyatt didn't startle easily, but he was startled now. "How do you know Hooker?"

"Through mutual acquaintances in Prescott. I stopped at his ranch on the way back from there. He's concerned about the cowboy situation too, enough to offer money to help put a stop to it."

"He told you this?"

"He gave me a bank draft. All I need to do is find some men willin' to spend it, and get to work cleanin' out the cowboys."

"What you're talking about is against the law, Doc. What you're talking about is hiring mercenaries."

"I—we—are talkin' about vigilantes, bringin' justice where there is none. Would you rather see these killers go free and kill again? That's what'll happen, if you leave them to the law. You say it's three-hundred of them or more? Wait another year, and there'll be a thousand. I say it's better to stop them now, while the odds are more in our favor, than wait and lose the hand."

"Our favor?"

"Yours and your brothers, if they'll take the job. And mine, being the pipeline for Hooker and his money. Call it doing some work for the Cattlemen's Association, if you prefer. But somebody's got to do it, and sooner than later."

"And by somebody, you mean me."

"You're the only man who can do it, Wyatt," he said, and meant the words.

Wyatt sat quietly, the oil lamp overhead throwing unsteady shadows over his face. Then he pulled a cigar from his vest pocket, and considered it.

"I believe in justice," he said, "but I believe in the law, as well."

"But when the law is men like Johnny Behan and worse, when the law is a pack of outlaws . . ."

"I'll think on it," Wyatt said.

He should have known that Wyatt, who still fancied himself a lawman and was still hoping to win the Sheriff's badge in the next election, wouldn't forget the law completely and take Hooker's money without asking questions. Instead, Wyatt went to meet with Crawley Dake, the United States Marshal at Tucson, to clarify the government's stand on the situation. Yes, Dake told him, his deputies were trying to settle the trouble, and his office was authorized to pay expenses as needed. And yes, the Army was directed to assist in any way it could, as long as that didn't include police work. Dake's problem was there weren't enough deputies to go around or enough funds to pay for all the expenses they would encounter. So until the federal government hired more help or came up with more money, there was little more his office could do. As far as the Cattleman's Association offering funds in support of his efforts, he knew nothing of it.

Which left Wyatt with a decision to make: accept Hooker's money and act outside the law, or let the lawlessness go on because the law wouldn't act. John Henry, knowing him as well as any man did, thought he knew what that decision would be.

Though Wyatt's offer to Ike Clanton had come to nothing, Ike was still nervous about news of it leaking out. The cowboys could be killers, as the murder of the Haslett brothers had proven. They'd even killed Luther King who was one of their own, for giving away the names of his accomplices in the Benson stage holdup. So if they got wind that Ike Clanton had sold out Billy Leonard and his partners, they might just hang him, too.

Ike had a right to be wary, but John Henry had no sympathy for him. For it was his friend's ranch that Ike had tried to steal, and his friend's life that Ike had been willing to sell. So while he didn't fault Wyatt for doing his duty in trying to bring the robbers to justice, he couldn't forgive Ike Clanton for trying to profit from it.

But for a man who wanted to keep his business quiet, Ike was doing his best to draw attention to himself, getting into fights and wearing his gun on the streets against Tombstone town ordinance. He may have looked harmless, with his guileless face and unruly curls, like an over-grown boy in man's clothes, but Ike Clanton was dangerous when he was drunk—which was most every time he was in Tombstone. And when he was drunk, there was no telling what he would say. So if word of his failed plan to bring in the Benson stage robbers were to come out, it would probably come from Ike himself. And John Henry wouldn't mind seeing him shot down by his cowboy friends.

Wyatt, however, acted as though there had never been any failed plan at all. He still treated Ike as politely as ever, still played poker with him, still had drinks with him at the Oriental. To him, Ike Clanton was neither friend nor foe, only part of the tapestry of Tombstone.

And Wyatt had other things on his mind now, like looking for information that would help him trail the cowboys. It wasn't Wyatt's style to go riding into the mountains, guns blazing, shooting as many outlaws as he could. He was more interested in finding their hiding places and bringing them in under a Citizen's Arrest to face legal charges. Wyatt considered himself a detective, not a shootist—though John Henry was surprised at where his detective work led him.

"I want to sell our shares in the Last Decision," Wyatt told him, waiting with the news until John Henry took a break from his Faro game at the Alhambra. Though running a gambling table wasn't what Mattie would have called an honest profession, it was a profitable one in a town like Tombstone and John Henry took the work seriously. And Wyatt, who took everything seriously, respected that.

"You want to sell our mine?" John Henry asked in astonishment. "Has the silver played out in these mountains?"

"I doubt it. But I need something to entice some information out of Mark Smith, and I think a share in the mine might do it."

"And who is Mark Smith, that he should have the privilege of owning my silver mine?"

Wyatt paused a moment, waiting until the crowd sounds in the saloon covered his words.

"He's the McLaury's attorney."

He didn't have to say any more. Though the McLaurys put themselves out to be honest ranchers, they were easy, as Henry Hooker put it, in their association with the cowboys. There was even talk that they not only allowed stolen cattle to pass over their land, but that they made a profit off some of that beef as well. If anyone knew the cowboys' plans, they probably did. And though Mark Smith, as the ranchers' lawyer, would be duty bound to protect such information if he had it, in Tombstone almost everything had its price.

"So why don't you offer him money, in exchange for information? Hooker will pay whatever it takes."

"No," Wyatt said, shaking his head. "Smith will wonder where the money came from and know there's somebody behind me. And being a lawyer, he might just find out. But he'll never question taking shares in a mine."

"Even one that's not producin'?" John Henry asked.

For though they still believed the Last Decision might hold a fortune, they'd been a little too busy that spring, between stage holdups and arrest warrants, to act much like mining men.

"It's not the silver we're selling," Wyatt replied. "Just the hopes of it. I've run the idea past him, and he's interested. But I can't do it without your say so, along with Allen and the others. Being a lawyer, Smith's going to want everything done legal, with a deed drawn up."

John Henry gave a dramatic sigh. "And I was hopin' that silver mine would make my future!"

"If it puts us on the trail of these cowboys, it still may," Wyatt said.

Chapter Five

TOMBSTONE, 1881

AFTER A LONG AND TEMPERATE SPRING, SUMMER CAME WITH A vengeance, 108 degrees in the shade and downright deadly out in the sun. And along with the heat wave came Kate, who'd always had impeccable timing when it came to making an entrance, swirling into town in the middle of a desert dust storm. If she had forgiven John Henry for snubbing her when Warren Earp came to call, she didn't say, but she didn't seem to be holding it against him, either. She was as pleasant as ever, or as pleasant as Kate could ever be, and moved her things back into his room as though she didn't mean to ever leave again. But she'd only been back for two days when Tombstone caught fire.

The blaze started in front of the Arcade Saloon, where two barkeeps were measuring the liquor left in a whiskey barrel. One of them dropped his gauge rod into the whiskey, and the other tried to fish it back out again with a long wire, forgetting that he still had a lighted cigar in his mouth and that whiskey was flammable.

John Henry was dealing his Faro game at the Alhambra Saloon, just down Allen Street from the Arcade, when a sound like sudden thunder split the air. Around him, the board and batten walls started to shake and the oil lamps overhead started to swing. By the time he'd gathered his wits and got himself out into the street to see what hell had broken loose, the whiskey fire had ignited the Arcade Saloon and both buildings on either side.

"Wyatt!" he shouted, seeing the flames leaping toward the Oriental Saloon, two doors down from the Arcade, but his words were lost in the clamor of screams around him as all of Tombstone crowded out into the streets. The fire bell in the firehouse on Toughnut Street clanged, calling the volunteer fire department, but without a fire engine there wasn't much the volunteers could do. In the midst of the conflagration, no one appreciated the irony that Mayor Clum was at that very moment on a train from Benson, returning from a trip East to buy a fire engine for the town.

John Henry pushed through the crowds toward the Oriental, and found Milt Joyce frantically trying to salvage his own liquor stores while the fire took his roof and swept down into the saloon and the gamblers stumbled over each other toward safety. But Wyatt was nowhere in sight.

Behind the Oriental, the Safford, Hudson & Company bank stood in a shower of embers and smoke while the bank manager calmly locked up as if it were the end of any ordinary business day, ignoring the ceiling plaster falling all around him. And in a moment, the entire business block was in flames.

The fire should have stopped there, contained by the natural firebreak of the dirt streets, but the hot wind that had brought dust storms all week was still blowing, and the flames leaped across Fifth Street toward the Crystal Palace, then across Allen Street toward Vogan's Bowling Alley and the Grand Hotel. When the wind changed direction, the flames jumped back across Allen Street, and the Cosmopolitan Hotel caught fire. And in between the Cosmopolitan and the Crystal Palace, John Henry's Alhambra stood defiant for a few brave minutes, then surrendered to the blaze.

There wasn't enough water in all of Tombstone to put out such a firestorm. The only hope was to starve it to death, and the firemen set to work pulling down whatever would feed it—awnings, porches, balconies, lean-tos, sheds. But it was the adobe that finally put the fire out, after the flames had devoured everything else in sight. The adobe clay wouldn't burn, and by nightfall, only clay and brick were left where there had once been a raw wooden boomtown. With a waning crescent moon overhead and smoke blotting out the stars, Tombstone had never been darker than it was that night.

In all, sixty-six buildings were destroyed and four city blocks were left desolate. The lot owners, having invested all, couldn't chance losing whatever was left, and spent that night camped out amidst the rubble and the ash, sleeping on the still-smoldering ground where their businesses used to be.

John Henry's boarding house was on the far end of town where the fire hadn't reached, and when he finally got home long after midnight he found Kate there waiting up for him.

"Where have you been all this time?" she demanded. "When I heard the Alhambra was burning I went looking for you. But no one had seen you since the fire started. Where did you go?"

He was too tired to deal with her demands, too sick with smoke and shock to try to soothe her.

"I was lookin' for Wyatt," he said, as he pulled off his suit coat and unbuttoned his shirt collar. His clothes would smell of smoke for weeks, at least. "When I saw the Oriental take fire I was afraid he might be inside, but he wasn't there." Then he laughed to himself. "And do you know where he was?"

"Why should I care?"

"He was over at Brown's Hotel, helpin' a little old lady get down the stairs. Just like Wyatt, doin' the honorable thing even in the midst of hell. And Virgil's still goin' at it, standin' guard over the lots to keep off lot jumpers."

"And where was I?" Kate asked.

John Henry paused a moment, looking at her quizzically.

"I don't know, Kate. Where were you?"

"What do you care?" she said, her voice quivering with anger. "Tombstone burning down, and all you could think of was finding your precious friend! Did it ever occur to you to wonder if I were all right?"

"You're always all right, Kate. I've never known a woman who could take care of herself better than you."

He meant it as a compliment, but she clearly took it wrong.

"I could have burned up in that fire, too, and you wouldn't have even noticed!"

She was primed for a fight, but he had no fight left in him. All he wanted was sleep and a breath of air that didn't smell of smoke.

"Come, darlin'" he said, reaching his arms to her, "let's not quarrel. There's been too much drama in this town for one night already."

He was surprised when she came to him willingly, and even more so when he realized that she was crying.

Virgil's all-night watch after the fire won him the praise of a grateful town and election to the position of Chief of Police when his predecessor took a leave of absence and didn't return. And not surprisingly, his first commission from the City Council was to prevent the use of fireworks on the Fourth of July—not that anyone felt much like celebrating. With half the town burned to the ground, most folks were more interested in buying lumber and hiring builders than in having a patriotic holiday. But when word came from Washington, D.C. that President James Garfield had been shot, some kind of patriotic show seemed to be required.

The President had been on his way to visit his ailing wife in New Jersey when a madman in a Washington train station pulled a pistol and fired at him twice. The first bullet only grazed the President's arm, but the second went into his back and was lodged so deeply that his doctors couldn't find it, so had no way of knowing what damage had been done or if the President would live or die. And folks in Tombstone, remembering the shooting of Marshal White the previous fall, said that it seemed the streets of Washington were no safer than the streets of the Wild West.

So while the nation waited for daily news from the capital, Tombstone decided to show its sympathy by going ahead with the previously canceled Fourth of July celebrations, beginning with a fireman's parade through the still ashy streets and ending with a grand ball at the new Schieffelin Hall theater—advertised as the biggest adobe building in the country and completely fireproof—along with musical performances by the Tombstone Brass Band and the Men's Glee Club and an oration by a special guest, the honorable former senator Thomas Fitch.

Though it seemed more than coincidental that Fitch should show up in Tombstone so soon after their meeting in Prescott, the Senator had never yet made any move at communicating with John Henry. The closest their paths had come to crossing was Fitch's recommendation of the young attorney Albert George to handle John Henry's legal case. But now that Wyatt had started working on the cowboy problem, buying information and putting together a posse, it seemed they had something to talk about, and John Henry hoped that the Schieffelin Hall engagement would offer the right opportunity.

He had no difficulty convincing Kate that they needed to make an appearance at the Fourth of July ball. She lived for such entertainments, and immediately began trying on gowns, deciding which one would make her the biggest spectacle. She would have ordered a new dress from Addie Bourland, her favorite dressmaker, if there'd been time to have it sewn. But on such short notice she had to make do with something that she already had—for which John Henry was grateful, as his income had declined since the Alhambra was burned. Though the saloon's owners had already started to rebuild, it would be weeks before the Alhambra was doing its usual business again. For the time being, his only source of support was his own gambling wagers—always an unreliable living.

But Kate stopped complaining about wearing an old dress when the day of the ball brought a dark and threatening sky. It seemed a cruel irony that July should come in with a drenching rainstorm, after the heat and wind that had driven the firestorm of a week before. By the time the Tombstone Hook and Ladder Company had made their parade from the firehouse to Schieffelin Hall, the sky had opened up and let loose, and the dirt and ash of the streets had turned to mires of black mud.

So John Henry and Kate arrived at the ball wet and mud-splattered, but in good company at least. For the Schieffelin Hall ballroom, with its prettily stenciled board ceiling and globe-lamped chandeliers, was filled with the elite of Tombstone all equally sodden and muddy as themselves. And in spite of the weather, or maybe because of it, there was a feeling of friendly community in the gathering, as though by suffering together through fire and rain they had all shared in something important. It was, in fact, the first time that Tombstone had felt like a real town to John Henry, instead of just a collection of saloons and stores on top of a silver mine.

It was the kind of thought he would have to write in a letter to Mattie, as Kate would never understand. Kate would just laugh and ask if he'd been drinking again, and he, defending himself, would laugh along with her and tell her that he was always drinking. But the thought would remain with him until he put it into words on paper, and it became another part of the world he shared with Mattie and no one else.

Though he had hoped that the evening's gathering would give him an opportunity for some conversation with the Senator, all that passed between them was a greeting and Fitch recalling that when they had last met, Mark Twain was the topic of discussion. Anyone not knowing otherwise would think they were merely social acquaintances with a shared interest in literature, and nothing else. But when John Henry asked him if he meant to make Tombstone his permanent home, the Senator answered that he was interested in Tombstone for the time being, but would probably return to Prescott when the excitement of the place settled down. Which was as good as saying that he had come to keep an eye on things, and was watching out for John Henry, as well.

The Schieffelin Hall festivities ended at midnight without the fireworks that the City Council had banned but that Kate would have loved, and Morgan suggested a late-night poker game to make up for the lost excitement. And though John Henry invited Kate to come along if she wanted, he knew she would never choose to spend an evening with any of the Earp brothers. In fact, when Wyatt had given her a cordial greeting at the dance, she'd turned her head away as if she hadn't heard. And in ignoring Wyatt, she had also ignored Celia Blaylock, the woman Wyatt lived with as his wife and whom Kate was supposed to have been friendly with once, along with the rest of the Earp family, standing together as they always were. But though neither Virgil and Allie nor Morgan and his Louisa seemed to notice the slight, Celia most certainly did, and blushed deeply at the offense.

"Kate!" John Henry had scolded under his breath, "Mind your manners!"

"I always do," she had whispered back at him behind a stage smile, "when the company is mannerly." Then she flicked open her black lace fan, nearly slapping him in the face, a move too deft to be accidental, and said brightly: "Oh, look! There's that handsome Sheriff Behan! And who is that lovely creature he has on his arm?"

When Kate was acting she could outdo any Southern Belle at simpering, and she swept off in a rustle of silk and satin to entertain the Sheriff and his companion, a woman who looked familiar to John Henry—

"The girl behind the bar," he said to himself, remembering that Johnny Behan had once proudly pointed out the photograph of a fetching young

woman with dark hair and darker eyes. So there she was in the flesh—and most decidedly so, in a gown that Kate would have wanted to own, small through the waist and falling enchantingly off the shoulders—and Behan couldn't seem to keep his hands off of her.

John Henry had to hold back a laugh, seeing the Sheriff standing there grinning like a smitten teenager. And as he turned away in amusement, he saw that Wyatt had been looking in the same direction, and had noticed the girl as well.

"That's Josie Marcus," Morgan said, sharing their view, "Behan's fiancée. At least, that's how she introduces herself. More like his wife, since they're living together with no chaperone but his little boy. She's a looker, all right."

And when John Henry turned back to take another admiring glance at the lady, he noticed that Wyatt was admiring some, as well—for a moment. Then Wyatt turned away and put his hat back on his head, pulling it low over his eyes the way he did when he was hiding from the sun.

It was nearly dawn when his poker game with Morgan broke up and he returned to his boarding house room, expecting to find Kate fast asleep and the bed warm and welcoming. But Kate was awake already, or still awake, and still dressed in her mud-splattered gown from the dance the night before, her satin skirts spread out around her as she sat on the floor with a pile of papers in her lap. And she was weeping.

"What is it, Kate?" he asked. "What's happened?"

She looked up at him with tears running down her face, and didn't bother to wipe her eyes. "I was just looking for a drink," she said, "and I found these . . ."

And then John Henry realized what it was she was holding in her lap. She had Mattie's letters, the whole leather-tied stack of them that he'd been saving all these years.

"They're love letters . . ." Kate said in a daze, her breath smelling of liquor, "all love letters, from your cousin." Then she laughed, a hard bitter laugh. "And all this time, I thought you were just keeping in touch with the family, that your cousin was a man. But she's a woman. And she wasn't just your cousin, was she? She was your lover. And she still is."

John Henry stood silently, staring at Kate holding his precious letters, crying tears that were falling onto Mattie's dear words.

"Say something!" Kate cried. "Damn you, say something!"

He shrugged his shoulders. "What do you want me to say?"

"Say I'm wrong! Say you don't love her! Say it's me you love!"

"I do care about you, Kate," he said quietly.

She stood so quickly that the letters fell to the floor, and she threw her arms around his neck.

"Then prove it to me," she said with pleading eyes searching his face. "Marry me! Make me your real wife. Prove to me you don't love her like you love me!"

But as Kate clung to him, her face turned up to his and her lips eager for his kiss, John Henry took a ragged breath and slowly shook his head.

"I can't do that, Kate," he said. And for a moment longer she stood there clinging onto him. Then a tremor seemed to shudder through her body before she slid her arms from his neck and pounded her fists against him in a fury.

"Liar!" she cried. "Liar! You called me your wife, but it was her you loved all along, wasn't it? It was her you wanted, not me. It was her you were sleeping with in your heart, all this time, not me! Every time we made love, you were whoring with her!"

"How dare you!" he cried, the years of longing and guilt rising up inside of him and coming out in a fury, and he raised his hand and struck her across the face, the blow hitting so hard that she screamed and staggered backwards.

"You are forgettin' yourself, Kate. You're the whore, not her! I must have been deluding myself to think that I could ever make you into somethin' better than you are. You may be all dressed up in fancy clothes, but you're still nothin' but a damned, dirty whore!"

Kate looked up at him from where she had fallen on the floor, her bruised eye already starting to swell.

"And who do you think turned me into one, anyway?" she said, putting her hand to her injured face. "Do you want to know what I did before I met you again at Fort Griffin, and who I did it with?"

"What are you talkin' about?"

"I'm talking about your precious Wyatt Earp, your dear bosom friend!" she said, spitting out the words. "You two have shared so much, you might as well know you've shared the same woman. I didn't say it at first, not knowing that we'd ever run into him. And when we met up with him there in Fort Griffin, he had his wife along, and I pretended I didn't know him the way I did. But I knew him, all right! I knew him real good, ever since I started working at Bessie Earp's place in Wichita. Wyatt Earp was my first whoring job! And he was a damned good one!"

"You're lyin'!"

"Am I? Then ask him yourself. Ask him about how he found me in Wichita after my husband died and left me alone with our baby, about how I was desperate for work. Ask him how he sweet-talked me into going to Bessie's with him. How he made love to me and then paid me for it, like I was for sale. Ask Wyatt what your whore looks like without her fancy clothes on!"

"You've got a filthy mouth, Kate," he said, starting to turn away from her.

"But you're afraid I'm telling the truth, aren't you? You're afraid to find out that your hero is nothing but a whoremaster. You're afraid that I might think Wyatt's a better lover than you are. Well, maybe he is. At least he's not too sick to satisfy a woman when she wants it!"

Then he turned back to her, his blue eyes wild with anger and his hand raised to strike her again, and Kate laughed, triumphant.

"Then you do love me!" she exclaimed. "You wouldn't be so hell-fired about Wyatt if you didn't love me!" and she reached her arms around his neck, pulling him to her. "Make love to me, Doc," she urged him. "Prove to me that you're a better man than Wyatt Earp!"

John Henry resisted for a moment, staring down into her hot, hungry eyes, and seeing her mouth moist and waiting for his lips. Then the anger and the jealousy in him overflowed, and he bent his head and kissed her roughly, grabbing at her satin dress and tearing it from her shoulders. And as his hands slid down over her body, Kate laughed in that seductive voice of hers.

"Make love to me, Doc," she said again, arching her body up to his. "Love me, Doc. Love me!"

He awoke to the sound of a knocking at the door, and found Johnny Behan standing there.

"Afternoon, Doc," Behan said, looking uncomfortable.

"Is it?" he replied, running his hand through his sleep-tousled hair, his mind still groggy. "I don't know where Kate's gone to. She should have been polite and answered the door . . ."

"Kate's been with me this morning, at the Sheriff's office. She's sworn out a warrant for your arrest. You're going to have to come with me."

"Arrest? For what?" he asked, his mind struggling back through the haze of the past hours—the dance at Schieffelin Hall, the poker game with Morgan, the walk back home in the still hours before daybreak, Kate finding Mattie's letters . . .

Then he remembered the fight before their fierce lovemaking, and the bruise his hand had made on her face. "I didn't mean to hurt her," he said hurriedly. "We had a squabble, that's all, just a misunderstandin' . . ."

"It's not about that, Doc. Kate's sworn a warrant for your part in the Benson stage holdup. She says it was you who shot Bud Philpot that night. I'm here to arrest you for murder."

He had always been a careful dresser—something Mattie had liked to tease him about in their younger days. But he had never taken more care in dressing than he did on this day, making Behan cool his heels waiting for nearly an hour while he bathed and shaved and put on a fresh white shirt and his best suit. Though he knew that he was innocent of the charge against him, he also knew that innocence wasn't always enough when a man had enemies. If this were to be his final day of freedom, he wanted to make it last. And while he was taking his time carefully dressing, he sent a message to his landlady, asking her to send a message to Wyatt.

By the time they arrived at the county court offices, Wyatt was waiting there with John Meagher and Joe Melgren, the owners of the Alhambra Saloon, ready to post bond to keep him out of jail. It was a generous gesture for men who had themselves suffered terrible losses in the fire, as the Alhambra wasn't insured and they were having to raise the money to rebuild it. But they were willing, they said to Judge Wells Spicer, to put up all they did have to help a friend—then told John Henry that if he didn't show up for his court date, they'd hang him themselves for losing them the $5,000 bond money.

Judge Spicer accepted the bond and set the hearing date for the following Saturday morning, giving the District Attorney a few days to put his case together—and John Henry the same few days to worry that a case might be made. For innocent though he was, everyone knew he'd been friends with Billy Leonard and that he'd often gone to visit Billy at the Wells, and Old Man Fuller could testify that he'd been there the very day of the stage holdup, making him appear an accessory at the least and an accomplice at the worst. Some might suggest that he'd been the brains of the operation, since Billy's three partners weren't famous for their creativity. Some might even suggest that with his connection to the Earps and their connection to Wells Fargo & Co., he had used them to learn when the treasure stage was going out. And from that suggestion, it wasn't much of a stretch to imagine that the Earps were in on the deal, too, and get them all hanged.

And thinking of the Earps, he remembered what Kate had said about Wyatt: *"Ask him how he found me in Wichita, and how I was desperate for work. Ask him how he sweet-talked me into going to Bessie's with him . . ."*

He hadn't had to ask what she meant by Bessie's place. It had been the busiest brothel in Wichita, and a legal business in a town where good whorehouses were licensed and given police protection. The city fathers knew that cowboys coming in from long cattle drives were bound to find women one way or another, and felt it was better for them to do it legally than to risk the rapes of their own wives and daughters. So they took applications for houses of prostitution and approved the cleanest, issuing yearly licenses and offering the working girls a safer place to do their business than in the alleys behind the saloons. And the Earp brothers, always interested in a good business opportunity, backed Bessie's place and let Wyatt, who was already a Wichita policeman, do the policing himself.

He'd learned all that from Wyatt long before, while they were telling tales about their previous careers. "Funny how what's lawful in one town is against the law in another," Wyatt had said. "Makes you question the Ten Commandments, if they only apply sometimes."

"You're confusin' God with the local judiciary," John Henry had replied, "and mixin' up mercy with justice. God makes laws knowin' you're gonna break them, then gives you mercy when you say you're sorry. The legal system just gives you punishment, whether the law you broke was just or not."

Then they'd gotten into a discussion of whether breaking the law was a sin, or whether sin was always against the law, and Wyatt said that his brother James had taken such a liking to Bessie that he'd left his wife and married her instead. But he never mentioned that Kate had worked there too, and that he had been her first whoring job.

But what Kate had said about Wyatt wasn't his biggest concern just now, when what she'd said about himself could get him killed. He hadn't done the things she claimed he had, and he couldn't assume that Wyatt had done the things she said about him, either. They were both innocent, as far as he was concerned, and it was just Kate's drunken anger over finding Mattie's letters that had made her talk the way she did. But if he got out of his current dilemma alive, someday he would ask Wyatt more about Wichita.

While he was dealing with his legal troubles, Kate had drowned hers in more liquor, leaving Johnny Behan's office and heading straight for the Can Can Saloon, where she told everyone who would listen that her lover was a stage robber and a killer and she was looking forward to seeing him hang. And by the time John Henry had signed his bond papers and gone with Wyatt to the Oriental to do some drinking of his own, Kate was under arrest herself. Virgil, having heard from Wyatt what was happening in the courtroom, kept his eye on Kate and used his office of City Marshal to haul her in for being drunk and disorderly, then put her in a locked room at the Cosmopolitan Hotel while she slept off her spree. He could have thrown her in the city jail, an iron-barred shack just up the hill from the mines, but decided on the hotel in deference to Doc, so he said. As far as John Henry was concerned, he could have thrown her down a mineshaft and not looked back.

But Kate wasn't a happy drunk, and woke up even angrier than she had been the day before, especially when Virgil advised her to recant her story before it made any more trouble. Instead of recanting, she swore that Virgil would be her next target, and his damnable brothers along with him. They could all hang together for the Benson stage holdup, and go to hell with Doc Holliday.

Virgil was a temperate soul and wouldn't usually trouble a lady, but such unladylike behavior didn't sit well with him, and as soon as he had loosed her from her temporary jail cell at the Cosmopolitan, he went to the court recorder's office and swore out another warrant for her arrest, this time for Threats Against Life. She had, after all, threatened both him and his family, and knowing what she'd done to Doc didn't inspire any confidence that she was only teasing.

So while John Henry waited on the outcome of the District Attorney's investigation, Kate was in court herself facing Judge Felter, who found her guilty as charged and ordered her sent back to jail. And this time, she got herself under a little better control, and instead of cursing the judge and all the witnesses in the court, she asked for counsel and got Wells Spicer, who was off duty as a judge that day and back in his attorney's office across the hall from the courtroom. And by lunchtime, Spicer had filed a writ of habeas corpus to have her released while he appealed the guilty verdict.

Kate's good luck in obtaining the services of the experienced Wells Spicer was even better luck for John Henry. For once Attorney Spicer had heard Kate's story, he had a better idea about why she had sworn out a warrant against her lover. And as judge at John Henry's hearing two days later, Spicer was impartial but wary of believing the charges as presented.

"Make sure you have a solid case, Mr. Price," he cautioned the District Attorney, "and not just the rantings of a wronged woman. If you don't think you can prove the guilt of this prisoner beyond a shadow of a doubt—and I mean the smallest shadow on the darkest of winter days—then don't bother bringing this case before me. You will be wasting my time and yours, and I will remember the loss the next time you bring a case into this court."

Lyttleton Price, newly appointed District Attorney in a hotly contested race, was loath to earn the displeasure of the judge, and paid attention to Spicer's recommendations. When the hearing was called at ten o'clock on Saturday morning, he approached the bench and said in a steady voice:

"Your Honor, I have examined all of the witnesses summoned for the prosecution and from their statements I am satisfied that there is not the slightest evidence to show the guilt of the defendant. Indeed, the statements of the witnesses do not even amount to a suspicion of the guilt of the defendant. I am therefore asking that the complaint be withdrawn and the case dismissed."

And with a slap of a gavel on the bench, the hearing was over and John Henry was a free man.

It was the end of Tombstone for him. After the heat and the fire and the fear of being hanged for a crime he didn't commit, he'd had his fill of that boomtown and was ready to move on. And with Kate packed and gone again—back to Globe, he reckoned—it didn't take him long to pack his own things and pay off his landlady for the rest of the month's rent.

"And where are you going to?" she asked him, more by way of politeness than with any real care that she was losing a tenant. There were plenty of other boomers in Tombstone to fill up her boarding house.

"I don't know," he said with a shrug. For besides making his goodbyes to Wyatt and Morgan, his thoughts had only gone so far as getting out of town on the first stage to Benson, then buying a ticket on the Southern Pacific Railroad to somewhere, anywhere else.

"Well, then I suppose it's a good thing this wire arrived for you today," she said, "before you left with no forwarding address," and she handed him a telegram recently delivered to the house.

He didn't even need to open it to know who it was from.

Chapter Six

GOSPER HAD HEARD OF HIS ARREST AND WAS TROUBLED WITH THE NEWS, even though it had all come to nothing.

"You may be exonerated," he said, as they met in Gosper's rooms in the boarding house next door to the Buffums, "but that doesn't mean it's over, not when there's a woman involved."

"There is no woman involved anymore," John Henry said. "I reckon she's gone off for good this time. And even if she does come back, I won't take her. I can't give her what she wants, and she won't ever stop wantin' it. And I'd rather have her hate me from afar off than from close enough to cause me trouble. Hell would be a good distance."

But Gosper disagreed. "I think in your case, you're better off sleeping with the Devil."

"What do you mean?"

"I mean a woman scorned is a dangerous thing, as this one has proved. I don't know what caused the rift between you and I don't care, but I do care that one of our associates has a lady friend with a hot temper. As long as she's displeased with you, there's going to be more trouble ahead. And I can't afford to have you in jail, or worse, not when our plans are just getting underway."

"So what do you suggest I do about it?"

"I suggest you make amends with her, and the sooner the better. Whatever you have to do to make her happy, do it, at least for as long as we have bigger troubles to worry about. And after that, I don't care what you do with her."

"Always the gentleman, aren't you?"

"Only when I need to be, and what I need now is information. You wrote that your associate Wyatt Earp has made an arrangement with the cowboys' attorney?"

John Henry nodded. "That'd be Marcus Smith, the lawyer for the McLaury brothers. They own a ranch over in the Sulfur Springs Valley, close to the border with Mexico. The story is the cowboys steal cattle down in Sonora, then run it up to the McLaurys' place before the cows are sold on this side of the border. Their friends the Clantons do the same thing, with a ranch they own over the New Mexico line. But it's who they're working with that makes things interesting. Ike Clanton is friends with Curly Bill Brocious, and Frank McLaury's bought a ranch with Johnny Ringo. And Brocious and Ringo are two of the worst cattle thieves in the country."

"Which makes the ranchers hand-in-glove with the rustlers," Gosper said. "But which of them is heading it all up?"

"Wyatt says it looks like the Clanton's father is givin' the orders, making himself a little kingdom down there. He's the one you're gonna have to deal with to put an end to things. But Old Man Clanton stays close to his ranch most of the time and leaves the rustlin' to the cowboys."

Gosper considered the information. "And how many cowboys do you estimate this Clanton has working for him?"

"On his own ranch, maybe twenty. But Ringo and Curly Bill are said to have another two-hundred men at their call, and more drifting over from Texas every day, and all of them willing to do anything to make a dollar. It would take the whole Mexican army to stop them—if they could find them. They're headquartered at Charleston, but move from town to town. And rumor has it that they're plannin' some kind of retaliation for that raid near Fronteras."

"So the cowboys are becoming killers," Gosper said. "But without knowing when or where they will strike, we still can't stop them." Again, he paused to consider, then said quietly: "You tell Mr. Earp that once he knows where to find them, he should do whatever it takes to put an end to this. Whatever it takes."

John Henry was still thinking over Gosper's advice and still enjoying his respite in the cool pine-scented air of Prescott while he decided where he might go next, when word came of another raid in the mountains along the border.

The Mexicans called the place *El Cajon del Sarampion*, the Canyon of the Scorpion, a rugged pass through the Peloncillo Mountains that had long been a smugglers' route from Sonora to Tucson. The Americans called it Skeleton Canyon—a name that would seem even more appropriate after what happened there on a hot midsummer night, when a Mexican pack train was set upon by cowboys. The Mexicans, sixteen teamsters in all with thirty heavy laden mules, were attacked by a gang of fifty cowboys who had been lying in wait and came out with pistols blazing. The surprised Mexicans never had a chance to fight back, and were left with nine dead and thousands in goods and gold stolen. Even their mules were slaughtered, and the narrow canyon walls were covered with blood.

Gosper got the news from the Commandant of the Mexican Federales at Fronteras who wrote demanding action by the American government, while John Henry got the news from Wyatt who said he was satisfied that the attackers included not only Curly Bill and his gang, but Ike Clanton and the McLaury brothers as well. The cowboys had made their move and made themselves known, and John Henry replied as Gosper had directed him: "Do whatever it takes, Wyatt. But be careful."

He knew, of course, that he would have to go back to Tombstone himself.

Having given up his boarding house rooms when he'd left Tombstone behind him in a cloud of stage coach dust, he had to find a new place to stay—not an easy task in a boomtown where every empty space was quickly filled and hotel rooms were often fought over. So he couldn't be too particular when the only place available turned out to be a single room in a small house next door to a horse yard. But at least the nights would be quiet at Camillus Fly's boarding house near the back entrance to the OK Corral, and when he was restless and couldn't sleep, there was the interesting gallery of Mr. Fly's photographic work hanging in the hallway to entertain him.

He was looking over those photographs one afternoon, admiring how well the photographer had captured the sights of a silver camp, when Wyatt came bearing news.

"Looks like our mine has finally brought in a mother lode," he said, after making sure no one was around to overhear. "Mark Smith just sent word that Frank McLaury is expecting Old Man Clanton to head up a rustling party down into Sonora."

"The old man himself?" John Henry said in surprise. So far as he knew, Old Man Clanton always directed his rustling operations from the safety of his ranch, leaving the dangerous work to his sons and their associates.

Wyatt nodded. "He doesn't trust his cowboys to make a clean work of it, after all that mess at Skeleton Canyon. He wasn't interested in killing those Mexicans, he said, just stealing their treasure. It was Curly Bill and Ringo who wanted to teach the greasers a lesson. So he's handling this trip personally. If I can catch him in the middle of things I can bring him in on a citizen's arrest and put an end to this business." Then he paused. "There's only one problem."

"And what's that?"

"The Old Man's already down in Sonora, and starting back tonight with the stolen beeves. With Morg in Benson playing cards and Virg in Tucson on U.S. Marshal business, I'm in this alone."

John Henry didn't have to think twice before answering.

"You're not alone, Wyatt. Not as long as I'm still breathing."

Guadalupe Canyon crossed from Mexico through the southeastern corner of Arizona and into New Mexico—a long shallow valley with stony cliffs above and a grassy floor below, and wide enough to handle a whole herd of cows. It was a perfect highway for driving cattle, especially cattle collected in Mexico and headed for the Animas Valley in New Mexico where the Clantons had one of their ranches.

Wyatt's plan was to hide in the cliffs near the Mexican side of the canyon and wait until Old Man Clanton himself came into sight down below with his stolen herd, then fire warning shots and announce his arrest, trusting in the surprise to effect an easy surrender. But though

John Henry was willing to go along and do whatever Wyatt wanted, he doubted that Clanton would come in so easily. A man who could command the likes of Ringo and Brocious, as well as holding the McLaurys in thrall, wasn't likely to give up without a fight.

But the rustlers weren't their only problem, as they discovered after a day's ride from Tombstone and a hard hike up through the scrub oak to the canyon rim above. With nightfall coming on, they used the last of the light to find a lookout spot with a screen of hackberry and a clear view of the canyon floor below, then settled themselves in for the wait.

Like all wild places, the canyon seemed silent at first, until their own talking quieted and the animal sounds took over: bobcat in the distance, wolves howling closer by, an owl hooting somewhere overhead. And then came a sound that John Henry didn't know, a chirping and a clicking coming from the edge of the rocky rim below them, like a cloud of angry katydids about to take flight. And suddenly, their lookout was overrun by a pack of long-snouted creatures with ringed tails, clambering up from the rocks and clawing past them toward a stand of piñon pine, where they leapt like cats into the trees.

"What the hell?" John Henry said, reaching for his pistol.

"Coati," Wyatt answered, unconcerned, "Canyon raccoons. They're thick in these mountains. But don't worry. They eat plants, mostly."

"Mostly?"

"Well, that and small animals. They wouldn't try a man unless he was alone."

John Henry was about to say that in that case he was grateful to have friends, when another sound interrupted him—a sound they both recognized too late as the click of a cocked gun.

"*Alto! Quién va?*" a voice commanded, and they looked past the trees to see two dismounted Mexican Federales taking aim at them through the piñons.

"*Qué negocio tiene usted en suelo mexicano? Si eres ladrones?*" the same voice said, clearly expecting a response.

It had been years since John Henry had spoken Spanish, since he'd played cards and pulled teeth at the Mexican Presidio across the Rio Grande, but enough of it came back to answer, "*Sólo los viajeros, que hemos perdido nuestro camino.*"

"What do they want?" Wyatt asked, reaching for his own pistol.

"Seems we didn't measure our steps well enough. We're on the Mexican side of the border. They think we're rustlers."

"Can you talk us out of this?"

"I'll try," he replied, then threw out another stretch of Spanish, which made the second Federale raise a shotgun and take aim.

"I guess the answer was no," Wyatt said, "or your Spanish isn't as good as you think."

"So I reckon there's only one thing to do," John Henry said, and glanced at Wyatt long enough to see him nod a reply.

"Back me up, Doc," Wyatt said.

"I always do."

It was the second time he had followed Wyatt into the heat of a gunfight, but the first when he'd had to shoot to kill, and it left him shaking and winded. But there was nothing much else they could have done, with the Federales so eager to make a battle.

"Blame it on the cowboys," Wyatt said, as they dragged the bodies back to the stand of Piñon pines where the Coatis chirped and waited with long snouts quivering. "They've left these greasers so spooked, they'll shoot at anybody."

"So we just leave them here?"

"There won't be enough of them to identify, once the Coatis and the buzzards are done."

"But the uniforms . . ." And he paused a moment, considering the whole strange situation. Then he thought of something he'd been too busy to consider before. "Wyatt, why were there only two Federales, and not on horseback?"

Wyatt looked up quickly, sharing his thought. But before he could answer there came a volley of gunfire from somewhere nearby and an echo of shots from the floor of the canyon, and they both dropped to the ground, edging close to the rim and keeping their heads low.

In the thin moonlight, they could just make out a newly laid camp where a party of cowboys was scrambling for rifles and firing in all directions as if they couldn't tell where their attackers were hiding. Behind the camp, a herd of cows crowded the canyon and made escape impossible.

"Like target practice," John Henry said, as he watched one after another of the cowboys go down. "I reckon the Federales beat us to it."

But as the sound of screams and gunfire echoed off the canyon walls, Wyatt's only comment was, "I would like to have arrested them."

There was no time for conversation as they beat a quick retreat to the mouth of the canyon where their horses were tied, then rode hell-bent to Tombstone before the story of the ambush could make it there. And riding clear through the night and into the early hours of dawn, they were safe in their beds by the time the news arrived, brought by the two lone survivors of what a special edition of the papers was calling the *Guadalupe Canyon Massacre*. The newspapers laid the blame on Mexican Federales and reported that the dead men were Old Man Clanton and rancher Billy Lang, along with a cowboy named Charley Snow and young cowhand Dick Gray whose father Mike owned the Tombstone Townsite Company. But in spite of the party's questionable enterprise, the only real outlaw among them was Jim Crane, who was still wanted for his part in holding up the Benson stage.

A vengeance party was quickly raised by Mike Gray and the father of Billy Lang, and Ike Clanton was said to be gathering two-hundred cowboys to go after his father's killers, and the newspapers warned that blood would flow like water. But it was Milt Joyce's response to the shootout that made John Henry nervous. Milt was telling anyone who would listen that it was Jim Crane's murder that accounted for the whole business, and that no one had wanted Crane dead more than Doc Holliday, who had been with him in the Benson stage holdup. Chances were it wasn't Mexicans who had done the murders at all, but Holliday and his friends who had arranged for the whole thing. And hadn't someone seen Holliday and Wyatt Earp riding out of Tombstone in that direction just awhile before?

It was just Milt's saloon talk, but enough to rouse suspicions again, and this time it brought John Henry a new enemy—Ike Clanton, whose grief over his father's death made him willing to blame anyone. Someone was going to pay for the Old Man's murder, and whether it was Mexicans or the Earps and Doc Holliday, it didn't matter so much to him, as long as somebody died.

But before Ike Clanton could trail his father's killers, an act of God washed away whatever evidence may have been left in Guadalupe Canyon when the rains came and stayed for a week. Toughnut Gulch was a foaming torrent ten feet wide, while the San Pedro River washed over its banks and took the dam away with it. The railroad came to a standstill, the mines and the mills closed down, and parts of Tombstone collapsed as the water swept away new-laid foundations. The roads and trails across Cochise County were underwater or washed out, and food supplies were dwindling fast. And worst of all for an isolated town, there was no mail for ten long days and no word from the world outside the deluge. It might as well have been Noah's flood, separating the sinners of Tombstone from the rest of creation and leaving them to their own miserable selves—especially John Henry, who was hungry to hear from Mattie. There had been too much trouble in his life of late and not enough of the peace her words always brought to him.

But when the rains stopped and the roads dried out, it was John Gosper he heard from instead, reminding him that with the renewed rumors of his supposed part in the Benson stage holdup, he needed to do whatever he could to keep his troublesome lady friend happy. And it was only because Gosper asked him to do it that John Henry wrote to Kate and invited her to meet him at the San Augustin Festival in Tucson. Truth was, he could use a little time away himself, with Ike Clanton still fuming and looking for someone to blame for his father's death.

He was only a little surprised when Kate wrote back that she would be happy to attend the fiesta with him. Kate loved a good show, and the fiesta was the biggest tourist attraction in Tucson, a town that before the arrival of the railroad had been little more than a collection of adobe houses along the Santa Cruz River. *The Old Pueblo* the locals called it, with its hundred year-old walled Presidio and bell-towered church of San Augustin, its flat-roofed barrios and chicken fights in the streets. But with the coming of the Southern Pacific the year before, the sleepy pueblo had suddenly awakened. Now with a population of eight-thousand, San Augustin del Tucson was the biggest city between San Antonio and San Diego, with as many Anglos as Mexicans, and all the amenities of a railroad boomtown—including the Pleasure Park of Alexander Levin where the fiesta welcomed revelers from the end of August to the middle of September.

Levin's was three-acres of ground located close outside the city limits and encompassing a brewery, a beer garden, a bowling alley and a shooting range, all encircling a thatch-roofed ramada that was part open-air dancing pavilion and part gaming room. And once the religious ceremonies honoring the city's patron saint were over, Levin's would be the most popular place in Tucson.

But first came the church services, with a procession of children in brightly colored Mexican dress carrying a figure of San Augustin, a vespers service and a ringing of bells, a High Mass and an evening rosary, a benediction and another processional—and Kate, arriving on the stage from Globe with her usual impeccable timing just as the ceremonies ended, and making it seem like the parade was really in honor of her.

She reached for John Henry's arm as she stepped down from the coach onto the crowded plaza, gathering her skirts in her other hand to make a graceful entrance, but not asking for her usual kiss in greeting, nor did she offer one in return. And John Henry could tell by that small oversight that things were not all forgiven between them. But why should they be? Neither one of them had apologized for what had happened in Tombstone, and without an apology there wasn't likely to be any forgiveness, only tolerance. But he wasn't going to pretend that he was sorry for his actions, when he didn't think that he had done anything wrong. Her finding his letters from Mattie was nothing compared to her infidelity in having him arrested, so if there were any apologies to be made, they would have to come from her.

But Kate made no mention at all of that summer's troubles, and acted as though their most recent separation had been just like all the others—she was, after all, an actress and good at pretending. So he followed her lead and acted as though they had never been apart, or that he had spent four days imagining himself hanging because of her.

"You look ravishing, my dear," he said, as he guided her to the Cosmopolitan Hotel where he had already registered them together, then added as if they were on better terms, "I hope you won't mind bein' ravished."

And since Kate didn't object, he considered that as good as an invitation. Anger had never yet gotten in the way of their lovemaking, and sometimes made it even more interesting.

There was something comforting about waking up with a woman one was accustomed to, even when she was as challenging as Kate. There was no need to put on airs with her or try to make conversation when he was still too groggy to talk. She knew, after all these years together, that he liked to start his day slowly, clearing his head with a shot of whiskey and then soaking in a warm bath until the congestion of the night settled from his lungs. She knew that he preferred his shirts freshly laundered and that he only liked a certain scent of cologne after his shave. She knew how to order his breakfast and when to open the drapes so he could read the paper while he ate. And though he had no intention of making it a permanent reconciliation, he still wondered, as he found himself settling into the return of their comfortable routine together, if he could ever have found such comfort with Mattie. But it was a thought that didn't sit well with him, as though he were somehow being unfaithful to his truer love, as though being comfortable with Kate was worse even than sleeping with her.

As for Kate, she seemed comfortable to be spending his money again, visiting the concessions at Levin's Pleasure Park and sampling the delicacies of the fiesta—brown sugar Panoche, green quince, red pomegranates, black Mission figs—while John Henry made more money at the gaming tables. Under the open-air ramada, the roulette wheels were crowded with fifty revelers at a time and the braver sports laid down $10,000 on a single hand of poker. There were Faro layouts and keno chances, Monte cards and rondo, and Mexican games that John Henry had never even seen before: Mallia, Chusa, Lotería.

It was the Lotería that most intrigued him, like bingo with picture cards instead of numbers, and the barker would make a guessing game out of it. Instead of calling out "*gallo*" meaning rooster, he would say, "*El que le canto a San Pedro*," meaning "that which sang for Saint Peter," and the players would have to figure out the riddle before they could guess the card. For John Henry to whom Spanish was mostly just a memory, the game was doubly difficult. Yet he made money even on such puzzles as "*El que la pica por atras,*" when he correctly covered the picture of a scorpion.

"And do you know what the riddle means?" Kate asked, implying that he had only managed an accurate guess.

"The one who stings from behind," he answered back, "like you, my dear."

"And where did you learn all this useful Spanish?" she asked, refusing to sound impressed.

"From a man I knew as a child. And from the Commandant of the Presidio at Nuevo Laredo, as well."

"Where?"

"It's a Mexican town across the border from Eagle Pass, in Texas. I practiced dentistry there for awhile, after leavin' Dallas. You might say it was the beginnin' of my second career. I was there long enough to start thinkin' in Spanish instead of English, and that's when I knew that long enough was too long."

"So say something to me in Spanish," Kate said. "Tell me that you love me."

It would have been easy enough to appease her, as Gosper had told him to do. But his sense of honor wouldn't let him say in Spanish what he couldn't say in English, so instead he said: "*Mi señora es la mejor puta en el territorio!*"

The other players at the table, mostly Mexicans who had understood every word of it, gave approving nods, and Kate seemed satisfied and kissed him heartily, which won a round of appreciative applause. And as she replied with a low stage bow, showing off her décolletage before flouncing away toward the concessionaires, John Henry gave a smile to his Loterio partners.

Kate didn't know that he had called her the best whore in the Territory.

She had other friends who thought better of her, however, like Josie Marcus, who was also in Tucson to visit the fiesta and with whom Kate had spent a day doing whatever it was that women did.

"You remember her, don't you? Sheriff Behan's fiancé?" she asked John Henry later, as they were dressing for another profitable evening at Levin's Pleasure Park.

"I seem to recall the name," he said, not adding that he certainly recalled the face and the figure, more alluring in person than in the photo Behan had kept proudly behind the bar when he worked at the Grand Hotel. But that kind of comment would only make Kate jealous, or worse, so he kept it to himself.

"Well, she's broken their engagement, and I can't say as I blame her. You know she came back after being away a year in San Francisco and found him sharing their house with another woman."

"Only a year? You'd think he could have waited a little longer than that."

"So she's thrown him out, and I think she's right, don't you?"

It sounded like a loaded question, so he sidestepped it. "Poor Behan. But I reckon there's plenty of bachelor accommodations available in Tombstone."

"Who cares about his accommodations?" Kate said with irritation, letting him know that he'd said something wrong. "It's Josie who has the problem, after the fool way the Town Lot Company arranged things."

If it wouldn't have made her even more irritated, he would have told her that she was making as little sense with her story as Morgan always made with his tales. But mentioning Morg was almost as dangerous as mentioning Wyatt, so instead he said: "And what's the Town Lot Company got to do with Josie Marcus?"

"They sold the land to Behan after Josie's family paid for her to build the house. So now that she's broken off their engagement, he says she has to move her house off of his lot. And since he's the Sheriff, there's no one to tell him he can't do it."

"Virgil would tell him," he said. "He's Marshal of Tombstone, and ought to have some say with the Town Lot Company."

"Always the Earp brothers!" Kate cried, her irritation now turning to anger. "You think they walk on water, all three of them!"

"There's actually five of them in Tombstone, Kate, if you add in Jim and Warren. You remember Warren, don't you? The nice boy you were so rude to a few months back?"

"I don't know why I even try to talk to you! All I wanted was some help for poor Josie, and you offer me the Earps! Where's your money purse?" And she started to rummage through the drawers of his dressing table.

"What are you doing?" he said, grabbing her hand away from his things.

"I'm taking some money for Josie," she said, pulling away from him, "so she can buy her lot back and not have to move her house."

"And why should I fund this lover's quarrel? Aren't you spending enough of my money all by yourself?"

"Because you've got more money just now than anyone else I know. I see how much you make off these gaming tables."

"And you think my hard work should go to buy something neither one of us can use? Why Kate, how very altruistic of you!"

"Curse me all you like!" she said, glaring at him, and reached again for his money purse.

"I wasn't cursing you, Kate, I was giving you a compliment! I've never seen you be so generous before—though your generosity is a bit less impressive when it's bought with my labors."

"Are you going to give me the money or not?" she demanded, but this time held her hand out to him expectantly.

"And if I don't pay for your friend's romantic folly?" he asked

"Then I will leave you once and for all."

It was almost too tempting an offer to resist, but he remembered Gosper's warning, and decided otherwise. *Whatever you have to do to make her happy, do it*, the Governor had cautioned. But he hadn't imagined that keeping her happy would clean out his own purse.

"And how am I supposed to pay our livin' expenses, once I have saved Miss Josie's house for her?"

"The same way you always do—cheat at cards. You seem to have a way of sweet-talking these Mexicans out of their money."

It was true that he'd done well in Tucson, almost making up for what he'd lost when his Faro game at the Alhambra was closed by the fire. The fiesta had been lucky for him, and the games were still going on.

"All right," he said with a sigh. "I'll buy your friend's lot back for her. Call it charity, or a last attempt at chivalry. I always did fancy myself as a Knight in Shining Armor, riding in to save the day."

"You can save the romance for me," Kate said, bristling. "Josie's got her eye on someone else already."

"And who might the lucky man be? Or should I say unlucky, having Sheriff Behan for a rival?"

"She hasn't told me yet, which I think means he's still a married man."

"*Still* married?" he asked, catching her meaning.

"The Sheriff was married too, when she met him. It didn't take her long to end it, once she set her sights."

"Sounds like a lovely girl," John Henry remarked, "a pillar of womanly virtue."

"Who needs virtue in a town like Tombstone?" Kate replied. "All anyone needs is money, and a little luck."

There were plenty of other Tombstoners visiting Tucson during the fiesta, though some, like Virgil Earp, came for work instead of pleasure. As Deputy U.S. Marshal, it had fallen to him to bring Cochise County's newest stage coach bandits to federal court in Tucson.

The robbery had happened near midnight on the road from Tombstone to Bisbee, fifty miles south into the Mule Mountains. The stage was loaded with passengers and a Wells Fargo box worth $2500, and had just passed the small mining town of Hereford when two men stepped into the road.

"Hold on!" said one of them, covering the stage with his pistol while the other robber reached up into the coach for the mail sack and the treasure box. Then the man with the pistol called for the passengers to come down from the coach and line up neatly while he collected their valuables—$600 in cash money and a gold pocket watch. The second robber, brandishing a shotgun, climbed up to the box and said to the driver, "Maybe you have got some sugar," and proceeded to go through his pockets. When he found nothing, he jumped down and told the passengers to get on their way.

There were no shots fired, no murders on the road this time, and with the darkness of the hour and the way the robbers had their faces hidden behind bandanas, it seemed there might be no identifying the robbers, either. Except that the highwaymen had been a little too loose in their conversation, especially the man with the shotgun who had asked for "some sugar"—a phrase everyone back in Tombstone knew was a favorite of Sheriff Behan's assistant deputy, Frank Stillwell.

It was an odd posse that went out after the robbers, with Stillwell's partner, Deputy Sheriff Billy Breakenridge, following after him, and Wyatt and Morgan Earp along for the ride to make sure Breakenridge didn't do Stillwell any favors. As for the other robber, there was speculation it was Pete Spence, who owned a mine together with Stillwell and had a hard reputation and a murder charge or two behind him. And because of the possibility that a desperate character like Spence might be involved, a second posse joined the first, with two Wells Fargo agents on the hunt and another of Sheriff Behan's deputies keeping an eye on them. Back in Tombstone, word went around that the hunters were hunting themselves.

The two posses met up at the scene of the robbery and then reorganized, with the Sheriff's deputies heading on toward Bisbee, and the Earps and the Wells Fargo agents tracking the robbers' trail. It was near the summit of the Mule Mountains where they made the find that would crack the case—a cowboy's boot heel that matched the footprints left at the robbery site—and matched the high heels that Frank Stillwell was known to favor.

They took the boot heel down into Bisbee where Wyatt found a shoemaker who had recently mended a pair of cowboy boots with just such a missing heel. His customer, as the shoemaker recalled, was a man named Stillwell. Then it was only a matter of finding where the robbers were hiding in that town and bringing them in. It was no surprise to anyone that Stillwell's partner in the poorly planned crime was Pete Spence. What was a surprise was that Frank Stillwell, as deputy sheriff, should be so bold as to pull off a stagecoach robbery right there in his own county and that his $7,000 bail was put up by none other than Ike Clanton, son of the late rustler boss.

"Which looks a lot like the Sheriff's office is in league with the cowboys," Virgil said, when he and John Henry ran into each other at Levin's one night.

"Meaning that Old Man Clanton's murder hasn't put an end to anything," John Henry observed.

"And worse than Stillwell making bail," Virgil went on, "his case was dismissed for a lack of evidence. Lack of evidence! I never saw so much evidence in a stage holdup! So Wyatt had me get a federal warrant to go out and arrest Stillwell and Spence on a charge of robbing the mails instead. Which is why I'm in Tucson, bringing them in. But it's not making us any friends in law enforcement, arresting other officers."

"I reckon not," John Henry said.

"And now there's a rumor that we mean to do more than make arrests."

"Says who?"

"Says Frank McLaury. He stopped me on the street in Tombstone last week to accuse us of raising a vigilance committee. I told him I didn't understand his meaning, and he told me that he'd heard that Wyatt and I meant to hang all the cowboys, including himself and Ike Clanton, and Ringo and Curly Bill, as well."

"Well, they deserve hangin'," John Henry remarked.

"But I told him to remember who had guarded Curly Bill after Marshal White was killed, and who run him up to Tucson the next morning to keep the vigilance committee from hanging him. 'Who was it who did that?' I asked him, and Frank says, 'You boys.' And I asked him why he believed we would be going after him now. 'Well, I can't help but believe the man who told me about it,' Frank says, and I asked him who that might be."

The whole dialogue was making John Henry decidedly uncomfortable, as Virgil was not a party to Gosper's plan as far as he knew, and so had no reason to arouse suspicion from Frank McLaury. But Wyatt certainly was planning to hang the cowboys, one way or another, and now someone was getting a little too close to the truth.

"So who told Frank this ridiculous story?" John Henry said lightly, trying to sound more amused than anything.

"Johnny Behan," Virgil said under his breath. "And I don't doubt that Frank McLaury believes him. For the last thing Frank told me was that it will make no difference what we do, he will never surrender his arms to us. 'I'd rather die fighting than be strangled,' he says. And by strangled, he means hanging by vigilantes."

But John Henry let out a laugh to mask his wariness, and said: "Sounds like Sheriff Behan is tryin' to shift the attention away from his own highly questionable dealings, make the Earp boys look bad so he looks better by comparison. Sounds like he's worried that Wyatt might steal his office away from him, come next election day."

Virgil pondered the thought. "Maybe so. But there was something about the way Frank looked at me when he said it, like he had cause to be afraid. And a cause like that can be trouble."

With all the difficulties in Tombstone, John Henry was beginning to think that Tucson might be a better place to take up residence. It was certainly a more charming town, with its old city walls surrounding the Presidio and its rows of brightly colored adobe houses backed by brilliant flowering gardens. And with the lucky streak he'd been having at the gaming tables, he'd stayed on awhile past the end of the fiesta and might have stayed even longer if he hadn't been interrupted in the middle of a Faro game at the Congress Hall Saloon by a tap on the back and a familiar voice.

"Doc, we need you back in Tombstone," Morgan Earp said. "Better come up this evening."

He didn't need to ask what Morg was doing there. The solemn sound in his usually jolly voice meant that something important was going on. And the way he'd said "we" meant that the message had come from Wyatt.

"All right," John Henry said, and cashed in his chips, much to the surprise of Kate, who had been sitting bored beside him while he gave his attention to bucking the tiger.

"You're leaving in the middle of a game? But you're winning!"

"Better to leave winnin' than losin', isn't it, my dear?" Then he turned to the banker and his fellow players, "Gentlemen," he said, and pushed his chair away from the table.

But when Kate pushed her own chair back and stood quickly in a rustle of new silk and taffeta, Morgan shook his head.

"Not you, Kate, just the Doc. It's business."

"You can't tell me what to do!" she said, glaring at him.

"Now, Kate," John Henry soothed, "maybe it's better for you to stay here and let me take care of this. You go on over to the hotel, and I'll be back to get you in a few days."

"I'm not staying here alone! If you're going back to Tombstone tonight, then I'm going, too!"

"You might want to wait 'till tomorrow, Ma'am," Morgan said with more politeness than she ever showed him. "There's no more passenger cars 'till morning, so we'll be on a freight."

But she ignored him and turned her answer to John Henry. "If you can ride a freight, so can I."

"We're only on the freight as far as Benson, Ma'am," Morgan said. "Then we're on a buckboard, since there's no stages so late and all."

"You left a buckboard at the station?" John Henry asked, and Morgan nodded.

"Wyatt wanted me to hurry."

"If you can ride a buckboard, so can I," Kate said to John Henry, thinking only of comfort and not hearing the urgency in Morgan's voice. If Morgan had driven a buckboard all the way from Tombstone to Benson to catch the train, that meant he had news that couldn't wait on the stage schedule, and there wasn't time for either of them to listen to Kate's arguments.

"All right," John Henry said again, this time to Kate, "you can come. But whatever you don't have packed and ready in an hour isn't comin' with us."

While Kate ran to the hotel to gather her things, John Henry listened to Morgan's news.

"You know Ike Clanton's been having his suspicions ever since that Guadalupe Canyon shootout? Well, now somebody's talked and he's putting two and two together, coming too close to the truth. He knows you and Wyatt went after the Old Man, and he thinks you might have killed him, too. Rumor has it he plans to murder you and Wyatt some dark night as payback."

"If he's makin' threats, Virgil can bring him in on charges."

"Like I said, it's rumors mostly: somebody says Ike says. Until he says it out loud himself, there's nothing much the law can do."

"But it was Mexicans that killed his father," John Henry said defensively. "Wyatt told you how we ran into those Federales before we could find Clanton's outfit . . ."

"I know. But Ike's been drinking hard since he got the news about his father, and he'll believe anything. Especially after what Marsh Williams said. Never trust a secret to a telegram, Doc."

At any other time, he would have found Morgan's convoluted story-telling amusing, but not now when there were desperate matters involved.

"What the hell does Marsh Williams have to do with anything?"

"He's the one who got that telegram for Wyatt over at the Wells Fargo office, saying the company would pay dead or alive for the capture of Billy Leonard and his partners. And he's the one who told Ike that he hoped he'd got his money all right."

"The damn fool!" John Henry said, knowing what trouble such an unguarded comment could make. Ike had been nervous enough about his failed deal with Wyatt, without hearing that anyone else knew of it. If his outlaw companions heard that he'd been ready to sell them out for a piece of ranch land, they'd be glad to bury him on it.

"But that's not all," Morgan said, going on with the bad news. "Seems someone's been talking to the Sheriff about Wyatt's deal with Mark Smith. And Behan's guessing that Wyatt has more than just information in mind."

"And who is it that's talkin'?"

Morgan shrugged. "Don't know. Maybe Smith himself, or maybe one of his law partners. Doesn't make much difference who leaks, once the story's out. And now with what Marietta Spence told Josie Marcus . . ."

Once again, Morgan's story was taking its usual confusing turns.

"You mean Behan's former fiancée? What's she got to do with anything?"

"She told Wyatt what Marietta heard from Pete Spence, that the cowboys are making plans to get us before we get them. And that's why Wyatt wants you back right away. He's worried there's going to be an ambush, and we're better off all together."

"But Stillwell and Spence are here in Tucson on trial. They won't be dangerous for awhile yet."

"Maybe not, but Ike Clanton's still in Tombstone, drunk and mad and looking for a fight. And Frank McLaury's getting nervous too. And to tell you the truth, Doc, so am I."

But there was something missing in the story still, for it wasn't like Wyatt to act on news that came from women's gossip.

"And why would Josie Marcus be doin' us the favor of passin' information?"

"No favor for us, Doc," Morgan said with a grin. "More like a favor for Wyatt. Seems like she's sweet on him, and he doesn't seem to mind too much. Lucky for us she was Behan's woman, and knows some things."

Luck and money were all that counted in Tombstone, Kate had said. He hoped they had enough.

Chapter Seven

IT WAS A HARD RIDE BACK TO TOMBSTONE, JUMPING A FREIGHT AT
the railyard in Tucson then being jostled on the bench of a buckboard
the last thirty miles from Benson. By the time he and Kate arrived at
Fly's boarding house in the small hours of the dawn, he was cold and
sore and more concerned with sleep than with the cowboys' plans. Let
them come and kill him—there were worse ways to die than asleep in
a soft feather bed.

He was awake again by suppertime and back at work banking Faro at
the newly reopened Alhambra Saloon, and other than a little trouble over
a contested card, it looked to be a quiet evening. There'd been no more
word of threats from the rustlers, and until Wyatt learned something
more definite, they were all just waiting and staying close together. But
waiting was worse than action, keeping his nerves on edge and making
him look up sharply whenever the saloon doors swung open. So he was
the first to notice when Ike Clanton stepped into the saloon sometime
after midnight, his round face reddened from liquor.

"Why, look who's here!" John Henry said out loud, meaning to attract
the attention of Wyatt who'd been having a discussion with the bartender,
and Morgan who'd been having a sandwich at the lunch counter. "If it
isn't the Outlaw Heir Apparent! Evenin' Ike. What are you doin' here in
enemy territory?"

Ike's bleary eyes narrowed as he focused on the voice that had called
his name, then he said with a look of surprise and almost sinister pleasure: "I didn't know you were back in town, Doc."

"I'll take that to mean you're glad to see me. So were you lookin' to lose some money at cards? 'Cause I'd be happy to oblige. Or were you just stoppin' in for a bite to eat?"

"I was looking for someone," Ike replied, "and I wouldn't eat shit with you."

"Well, I wouldn't eat shit with you, either, Ike. And I think it highly impolite of you to suggest that this fine establishment serves anything less than real food. That isn't shit there in your sandwich is it, Morg?" he said, and in spite of the tense situation, he almost laughed when Morgan stopped eating and took a long suspicious gaze at his bread and meat.

Ike's sinister smile faded at the sight of two Earps within fighting distance, and he said darkly, "You know what I'm talking about, Doc. Somebody's been saying I made a deal with Wyatt Earp, and it's a damned lie."

"And who exactly are you accusin', Ike?"

"You know who. You know more than you ought to know. You know enough to get a man killed."

"Is that a threat or a confession?" John Henry said, his blood rising. "'Cause if you're threatenin' me, you might as well put your pistol behind it."

"I ain't heeled, or I would go to shooting! And then I'd start on your friend Earp there, and his brothers next. You may think you know everything, but I know who's going to pay for my father's murder, and when they're going to pay up!"

"You son of a bitch of a cowboy!" John Henry cursed, pushing away from the Faro table so fast that the coppers went flying. "If you're not heeled, go heel yourself! I won't be threatened by you for somethin' I haven't done, and I won't wait for you to shoot me in the back. If you want to fight, you can have all the fight you want right now."

It was bold talk, considering the fact that his own pistol was still behind the bar where he'd checked it before his Faro session. But with Wyatt and Morgan to back him up, he didn't much fear a drunken Ike Clanton, even if the cowboy somehow managed to find himself a weapon. Wyatt, however, seemed less willing to make a fight, turning from the bar and saying coolly:

"Why don't you move this outside, Morg? You're the officer on duty here. We don't want any damage indoors," and Morgan quickly obeyed, climbing over the lunch counter.

"Let's go, boys," Morgan said. "Doc, you can finish him off in the street."

But Ike Clanton was more talk than fight, and he stood breathing hard before spitting onto the saloon floor and turning on his bootheel, pushing angrily through the batwing doors.

"He'll be back," Morgan said. "Ike don't like being bullied."

"And I don't like being threatened."

"Then one of you is going to have to do some shooting," Morgan replied with a grin.

"We'll let Virg handle it for now," Wyatt commented. "He'll find some excuse to arrest Ike and get him off the streets until he calms down. But keep your eyes open, both of you. This isn't over yet. And Doc?"

"Yes, Wyatt?"

"Remember what your father told you about keeping that temper of yours reined in. We don't want anymore trouble than we've already got."

Other than the run-in with Ike, the rest of the night was uneventful, and when Kate woke John Henry the next day he was having a pleasant dream that faded before he could remember it.

"Get up, Doc," she said, sitting next to him on the bed. "Somebody's looking for you."

"Who?" he asked groggily. "What time is it?"

"Past noon. Ike Clanton's been here with a rifle. Mrs. Fly told him you weren't in. He said he wants to see you about something."

"What time did you say?"

"Twelve-thirty."

"Twelve-thirty," he repeated, then cleared his throat. "Hand me that whiskey glass, will you, darlin'?"

"What's this all about?" Kate demanded. "Why would Ike Clanton be here looking for you, and with a rifle in his hand? What does he want to see you for?"

"I have no idea," he lied. "But if God will let me live long enough to get dressed, he'll see me. Now draw me a bath. And Kate, you'd best go on to breakfast without me."

It was a disagreeable day, gray and overly chill for late October, and John Henry bundled into his heavy wool overcoat, steel gray as the sky. In his hand, he carried the gold-headed cane Barney Ford had given him in Denver. In his overcoat pocket, he had the nickel-plated Colt's revolver Bat Masterson had given him in Dodge City, loaded up and ready. If Ike Clanton wanted to talk with a rifle in his hand, John Henry would be happy to oblige him. And if Ike's conversation were on the same subject as the evening before, full of anger and threats, it was better to be safe than sorry.

Ike hadn't said where he was going when he left the boarding house unsatisfied, so John Henry started by inquiring after him at the Grand Hotel where the Clantons and the McLaurys always stayed while they were in town. But Ike wasn't there, though the barman said his firearms were.

"Yessir, Dr. Holliday. Marshal Virgil Earp came in here this morning and gave me Ike's rifle and six for safekeeping. Him and Ike had a set-to in the street, and Ike got hisself buffaloed. Marshal Earp told him he couldn't go around with his rifle in his hand, especially drunk as he was, and Ike said he was looking to kill somebody and needed his guns."

"Seems like a bold thing to say to a lawman," John Henry commented, though he was glad to hear that Virgil was taking care of things.

"Yessir. So that's when Marshal Earp knocked him down and arrested him. Took him over to pay a fine to Judge Wallace."

"So where's Ike now?"

"Off nursing his sore head someplace, after getting buffaloed. But his guns are here," he said, nodding behind him, "so he's not dangerous anymore. Just drunk, like half of Tombstone."

So John Henry left the Grand Hotel feeling a little more relaxed, knowing that Ike was disarmed at least if not in jail, and when he ran into young Billy Clanton out in the street, he tipped his hat and offered the teenager a good-day. As far as he knew, Billy wasn't a party to his brother Ike's rantings. Then he strolled over to the Alhambra to see how the crowd was shaping up there, and was happy to run into Morgan who had stopped by looking for him. Since it was nearly two o'clock in the afternoon and he'd missed his breakfast with Kate, he invited Morg to join him for some lunch.

"You heard about what happened to Ike Clanton this morning?'" Morgan said.

"I did, and glad to hear it. Too bad Virgil only buffaloed him, instead of shooting him down. Ike came by my place this morning lookin' for me with a rifle in his hand, and probably would have used it if he'd a chance."

"The McLaurys are in town too, and riled about what happened to Ike. And now Tom McLaury's the one with a bloody head."

John Henry sighed, knowing that when Morgan was telling a story, there was always a lot of unraveling to do.

"So what happened to Tom?"

"He ran into Wyatt on the street, and they had words and got to fighting. Or Wyatt got to fighting, since he was the one with a pistol."

"Meaning that Tom was unarmed?"

"So he said, but Wyatt said it looked like he had a pistol in his pocket. Easy to mistake a wad of money for a pistol, sometimes. But Wyatt wasn't taking any chances, since Ike had been out on the streets with a rifle."

"Better safe than sorry."

"So he slapped Tom across the face, then hit him with his pistol too, in case Tom was heeled and wanted to make a fight right there."

"And did they get to shooting?"

Morgan shook his head, looking disappointed. "Nope. Tom didn't pull, so Wyatt let him go, but he's beat up pretty bad. I hate to think what's going to happen when his brother finds out about it. Frank won't go so easy as Tom did."

"As long as we keep them in clear sight," John Henry said, "things will be all right. It's an ambush that Wyatt's nervous about. He's probably tryin' to bring on a fight out in the open, where no one gets surprised."

"Well, there's a fight coming, I think," Morgan said, "after what Wyatt did to that horse."

"You mean after what he did to Tom?"

"No, the horse!" Morgan said with exasperation, as though John Henry were simple-minded for not following the story. "After Wyatt hit Tom he went off to Hafford's looking for a cigar, and seen Ike and Billy Clanton and the McLaurys in Spangenberg's gun shop next door, looking at pistols. Their horse was looking too, I guess, 'cause it was standing on the sidewalk with its nose in the door of the shop, and Wyatt went up and tried to move it back into the street. But that horse wasn't going to move, so Wyatt told Frank and Tom they'd have to move their horse off the sidewalk or pay a fine."

"And what did they say to that?"

"Something that wouldn't sound very good in church. But they were done in the shop by then, and moved the horse anyway, and Wyatt just kept his eye on 'em. He says they went into that gun shop without any weapons that he could see, and come out with pistols stuck down in their belts. And Billy Clanton was busy pushing cartridges into his gun belt."

"So now they're heeled," John Henry said, "and the ball opens."

They found Virgil on the corner of Fourth and Allen Street, in front of Hafford's Saloon, and Wyatt was with him. And for the first time that John Henry could remember, they were arguing.

"I say we bring it to a fight right here and now," Wyatt was saying, "and not wait for them to make an ambush."

"You know I can't allow that," Virgil said, trying to keep his voice quiet. "I'm marshal of this town. It's my job to keep things peaceful."

"And I tell you there won't be any peace until those damned cow thieves are run out."

"Then let's run 'em," Virgil said, "give 'em a police escort right out of town and tell 'em not to come back. But I can't condone violence."

"Then you're signing our death warrants, Virg. 'Cause Ike Clanton won't stop until he makes somebody pay for his father's murder, and he don't much care who."

"And if you hadn't gone up that canyon looking for the Old Man, Ike wouldn't have any cause to think you had part in it."

Their heated words were drawing a crowd, and brought Sheriff Behan to see what was causing the commotion. The sheriff, having slept late and then gone for a shave, hadn't yet heard about the trouble with Ike Clanton and the McLaurys that morning, and was surprised when Virgil told him that they were armed and on the streets looking for a fight.

"They're down at the OK Corral right now," Virgil said to him, "and I want you to go down there with me and help disarm them."

"Hell, Virgil," Johnny Behan said, "if you go down there they'll make a fight for sure. You know they've sworn to never turn their arms over to you. Better let me go alone and see to it. They won't hurt me."

"I suppose they won't," said Wyatt darkly, and Behan gave him a glare.

"Well, that is all I want you to do, Johnny," Virgil said, "I want you to make them lay off their guns while they are in town."

But as Sheriff Behan headed down Allen Street toward the corral, a man pushed his way through the crowd.

"Marshal Earp," he said to Virgil, "I heard those cowboys making threats against you, and I want you to know that we will stand with you if there is a fight."

But Virgil declined the offer. "I won't bother them if they stay in the corral or start out of town. But if they go out onto the street, then I will have to take away their guns."

"Why, Marshal Earp," the man said, "they are out of the corral now and all down on Fremont Street."

"So much for Sheriff Behan's able assistance," Wyatt said. "So now what do you propose to do?"

Virgil answered by handing his shotgun to John Henry.

"Put this under your coat, Doc," he said, "and hand me your cane. I don't want to draw any attention carrying my shotgun on the street."

And as they stepped off the sidewalk and moved into Fourth Street, Morgan commented, "They have horses. Shouldn't we get some horses ourselves, in case they make a running fight?"

"No," Wyatt answered. "If they try to make a running fight, we can kill their horses and then capture them."

John Henry, holding his coat closed against the wind to hide the shotgun, whistled softly as they walked four abreast toward Fremont Street.

At the corner, Wyatt slipped his pistol into his hand and cocked it. A half a block ahead, in front of Bauer's Meat Market, Johnny Behan stood facing them with hands outstretched. "Hold up, boys! Don't go down there or there will be trouble!"

But Virgil kept on his deliberate pace, and answered, "I am going down there to disarm them, Johnny. Step aside."

"But I have already been down there to disarm them!"

"Then there won't be any trouble," Virgil replied.

But Wyatt was less trusting than his brother, and said, "If they pull anything, let them have it."

"All right," John Henry answered.

A few yards ahead of them, the Clantons and the McLaurys stood close together in the empty lot that opened onto Fremont Street, behind the OK Corral. It could be no coincidence that the lot was also next door to Fly's Boarding House, where John Henry had his room, and where Ike had come hunting for him earlier that day. But they weren't out on the street, as Virgil had been told, sign that Sheriff Behan had contained them, at least.

But he hadn't managed to disarm them, and Frank McLaury and Billy Clanton were both brandishing pistols, while Tom McLaury had one hand on a horse with a rifle in its scabbard. They didn't look much like men heading peacefully out of town, and Virgil held up the cane and called out, "Boys, throw up your hands!" Beside him, Wyatt and Morgan stood close together between the lot and the street, and John Henry waited out on Fremont with the shotgun in his hand.

But instead of surrendering as ordered, Billy Clanton and Frank McLaury moved their hands toward their six-shooters, and Virgil cried, "Hold on! I don't mean that!"

For a moment there was the tense silence of a showdown, both sides waiting for what would happen next. Then Billy Clanton, young and nervous, jerked his pistol and cocked it in one deadly move, and Wyatt seeing it said, "You sons of bitches! You have been looking for a fight and you can have it!"

The two shots rang out in a single report, then all hell broke loose.

John Henry, standing out on the street, couldn't tell who had started it, but saw Tom McLaury moving out of the lot behind his horse and reaching over the saddle for his rifle. Then the horse wheeled and left Tom in the open, and John Henry pulled up the shotgun and squeezed both triggers. Tom staggered from a double load of pellet pounding into his side, and crumpled to the ground near a telegraph pole.

The shotgun spent, John Henry threw it aside and pulled the Colt's from his coat pocket, circling for a target. Through the haze of gunsmoke he saw Virgil take a hit and fall, then drag himself up again. He saw Ike leap at Wyatt and wrestle with him before Wyatt pushed him off, shouting, "Commence to fighting or get away!" He saw Morgan take a hit and go down, screaming, "I've got it, Wyatt!" Then he saw Frank McLaury, wounded and bloodied, stumble out into the street with Tom's horse as a shield. When the horse broke and ran, Frank squatted in the street, catching his breath.

"'Afternoon, Frank," John Henry said, taking aim, and the wounded man looked up at him in a daze and raised an unsteady shooting arm.

"I've got you now, Doc," he whispered.

"You're a good one if you have!" John Henry answered with a laugh. "Blaze away!" Then taunting, he spread his arms to make himself an easy target.

But Frank had some life in him yet, just enough strength to squeeze the trigger of his pistol, and John Henry seeing it spun himself sideways and felt the bullet slam against his pistol pocket and skim across his hips.

"You son of a bitch!" he shouted as he aimed again at Frank's chest, ready to finish the work. But before he could get off the shot, another blast roared from behind him and crashed through the side of the cowboy's head.

"I got him for you, Doc!" Morgan Earp cried, and John Henry turned to see him sitting in the street, shot up but still game.

But the fight was over, finished as fast as it had begun. And as the gray haze of the gunsmoke slowly lifted, the snow began to fall.

He stumbled back to his room at Fly's Boarding House, his whole body shaking. His nerves that had been taut as a stretched wire during the gun battle had frayed apart in the sudden silence when it was over. "This is awful!" he kept saying to himself, "awful . . ."

Frank McLaury was dead, his brains blown out by Morgan's final shot. Tom McLaury lasted a little longer, dying wordlessly from a dozen buckshot wounds. Young Billy Clanton held on the longest, shot in the gut and bellowing in agony before a dose of morphine let him go quietly down to his death. Ike Clanton was the only cowboy to survive unscathed, after running like a coward from the fight that he had started.

While the doctor attended to Tom and Billy's last moments, Virgil and Morgan were carried away in a wagon—Virgil shot through the leg and Morg shot through both shoulders, with Wyatt alongside to keep away the crowd. Three men dead and three men wounded, all in the space of not more than two minutes.

"This is awful!" John Henry said again, and heard a voice behind him asking:

"Are you hurt?"

It was Kate, though he hadn't even noticed her being in the room. Had she been there when he arrived, or had she come in after? Had she seen what happened out in the empty lot next door?

"Are you hurt, Doc?" she asked again, and he had to pull his mind away from the scene in the street and make himself focus on her words.

"Am I hurt?" he asked, repeating her question and trying to find an answer. Was he hurt? His back burned where Frank's bullet had skimmed past him, but he didn't think it was serious. He shrugged off his coat and pulled his shirt from his trousers, uncovering his chest. He ran his hand over the pain, and felt the wet blood at the back of his hip—a flesh wound, nothing more. But the bullet had left a black hole in his white shirt, and a stain of blood surrounding it. He touched the stain and looked up at Kate with tear-filled eyes. "No, I am not hurt."

"Can I do anything?"

"No, nothing. Just leave me alone, please. I just want to be alone."

"Doc . . ."

"For hell's sake, Kate! Just leave me alone!"

And for once, Kate said nothing, and did as he asked.

He stayed in his room until dusk, trying to settle his mind and sort out all that had transpired, and then he went looking for Wyatt. The afternoon's snow had brought an even colder wind with it, and on the streets people huddled in their coats and spread whispers about what had happened and what was to come. The marshal and his brothers had done right to kill the men who had threatened them and the town, but killing three cowboys would only bring retribution from the rest, and a raid was feared at any moment. And as the darkness fell together with the snow, the wind moaned through the town like an omen.

He found Wyatt at the Oriental, and walked with him from there down to Virgil's house on First Street, where Virgil and Morgan were laid out in bed and being tended by the doctor. Virgil's leg wound, a bullet through the fleshy part of his thigh, would heal on its own, but Morgan's injuries would take more care. The bullet had entered his right shoulder and chipped a vertebra before passing out through his left shoulder, and even the small movement of breathing left him groaning in pain.

"Now I know how you feel every morning, Doc," Morgan whispered, while his pretty wife Louisa, her face tear-stained with worry, straightened the quilt that lay over him.

"Then you need some of my mornin' remedy," John Henry replied, and pulled the whiskey flask out of his vest pocket, holding it to Morgan's lips. "I reckon you saved my life with that last shot, Morg."

"Wyatt always did say I was the best shot in the family!"

"I said you'd need to be the best shot," Wyatt corrected him, "seeing as how you were the worst poker player in the family," and Morgan replied with a strained smile.

"Ol' Wyatt, always has to be right!" he said, and closed his eyes to rest.

Beside him on the one large bed in the room, Virgil turned slightly, shifting the weight off his bandaged leg. "Behan came down to see us," he said, "saying he's our friend and will do all he can to help us. But I wasn't buying it. He let us think those boys were disarmed, knowing they'd make a fight before they'd surrender their weapons to us. He might as well have taken a shot at us himself."

"He still may," Wyatt said, "one way or another. He's already tried to arrest me, when I went up to town. I told him that I will answer for what I have done, but I will not be arrested by the likes of him. Any decent officer may do it, but not Behan."

"But he arrested Ike Clanton," Virgil said, and Wyatt nodded.

"More likely for safe keeping than on charges. Ike's brother Phin rode into Tombstone an hour ago. He's with him at the jail, keeping guard. I don't know if Behan still means to arrest us, but I don't want you opening the door to him if he comes back here again."

"How'd we get into this fix, Wyatt?" Morgan asked, taking a painful breath.

Wyatt looked down at both of his brothers, then turned his gaze toward John Henry. "I thought we were doing the right thing," he said. "I believed we were bringing justice to this town . . ."

Virgil nodded. "We did right, Wyatt. They were breaking the law and threatening our lives. We did right to defend ourselves. And it don't matter to me who fired the first shot, if their intent was to kill us. You remember that, Wyatt. It don't matter who started it, only who finishes it."

"I'm only afraid it's not finished yet," Wyatt said, looking toward the long windows that fronted the porch and into the dark night outside. Then he stood up and put on his hat, pulling it low, and turned to Virgil's wife: "Allie, better drag some more bedding in here and get it up against that glass, just in case the cowboys come calling. And don't answer the door unless you know it's me."

And as he and John Henry left and Allie Earp bolted the door after them, they heard Morgan say to her, "Take my six and keep it handy, Al. If the cowboys come around tonight, you'll know they got Wyatt and are coming for us. You kill us before they get to us, all right?"

The wind blew all that night, while Allie Earp sat up with Morgan's heavy pistol in her lap, waiting, and Wyatt and John Henry walked the streets, watching for trouble. Then morning came with a change in the wind and a threat from a different direction. For while they had kept their moonlight vigil looking for cowboys, the town undertaker had spent his night making up Billy Clanton and the McLaury brothers for their debut as corpses, their open coffins displayed in the funeral parlor window under a sign that declared *Murdered In The Streets of Tombstone*.

The funeral procession commenced at three o'clock in the afternoon with three-thousand spectators lining the streets of the town while the Tombstone Brass Band played a solemn cadenced march of the dead. Two silver-festooned, glass-windowed hearses carried the coffins of the McLaury Brothers and Billy Clanton, while Ike and Phineas Clanton rode atop a wagon so that all could see their mourning, their hats banded in black and black baldrics slung across their chests. Following the Clantons came a cadre of three-hundred mourners on foot and a line of twenty-two black-draped carriages and buggies, and by the time the parade reached the cemetery at Boot Hill, the mood of the town had changed from one of apprehension to anger. Three men had been murdered on the streets of Tombstone and someone would have to pay.

It was all, the viewing and the procession and the elaborate funeral show, part of Ike Clanton's plan to hang the Earps and Doc Holliday. And when the Coroner's Jury, hastily called to examine the bodies and determine the cause of death before the undertaker went to work, deliberated and returned their verdict, it seemed his plan would succeed. The report read that *William Clanton, Frank and Thomas McLaury, came to their deaths in the town of Tombstone on October 26, 1881, from the effects of pistol and gunshot wounds inflicted by Virgil Earp, Morgan Earp, Wyatt Earp, and one Holliday, commonly called 'Doc Holliday,'* with no mention that the shootings were done in the line of duty. So when the Town Council met later that day to discuss the trouble, there seemed no other option but to suspend Marshal Virgil Earp pending a full investigation. And then Ike Clanton filed an official complaint, and Sheriff Behan came with arrest warrants.

"Well, Kate, this is a turn around," John Henry said. "Last time I was arrested for murder, it was all your doin'. This time, you're sittin' there cryin' like you might actually regret my demise."

"My only regret is that I can't do the hanging myself!" she said, her bitter words belying her tears. "And I'd start with your precious Wyatt Earp! I told you no good would come of this. I told you he'd bring you nothing but heartache. And now look what's become of us!"

"It's what may become of me that's more to the point," he replied, as he packed a traveling case. Considering the state of affairs in town, he didn't know when, or if, he'd be coming back to his room. Which meant that Kate had no idea who would pay the rent the next time it came due—likely cause enough for her tears.

"But how can they make a murder charge stick against you?" she asked. "You were only defending yourself after Ike came hunting for you. Wyatt's the killer, since he fired the first shot. And it wasn't even his fight in the first place."

"Then you could say that he was defending me, which means that you owe him a thank you, at least. If he and his brothers hadn't stood with me, Ike would have had an easier time shootin' me down. It was Virgil who took away his rifle that mornin', remember?"

"And it was Virgil who decided to disarm them all, instead of running them out of town. So he's as much to blame as Wyatt and Morgan."

"And how is Morg to blame for anything?" John Henry asked, growing weary of her twisted logic. "If he hadn't fired that last shot, I might be dead instead of Frank."

"And if Frank McLaury weren't dead, or Tom, or Billy Clanton, there'd be no murder charge at all. It's Wyatt and his brothers who brought this on us," she said again, including them both in the trouble as though she were off to jail too. "And it's Wyatt and his brothers who deserve to hang, not you."

"Well, I'm sure the courts will appreciate your savin' them the trouble of renderin' judgment. But I'd feel a little easier if you weren't campaignin' for the execution of my friends. Whatever Wyatt and his brothers get will be my fate, as well."

"Wyatt again, always Wyatt! You'd rather hang with him than run away with me!"

"I'd rather not hang at all, if I had my choice. But I don't see as how runnin' anywhere right now is an option. Sheriff Behan is waitin' outside the door with a warrant and a pistol in his hand, remember?"

"I remember," Kate said. Then she looked up at him with something almost like real feeling in her eyes. "And I remember when a lawman at the door didn't scare you into surrendering. I remember when you dared a fire to run away with me, back in Fort Griffin. We were happy then, do you remember that? Weren't we happy?"

And there was such a sudden wistfulness in her voice that he couldn't disagree. No matter that he had escaped from Fort Griffin with no plan of taking her along, and only took her because she'd told him she was carrying his child. No matter that he'd wished he could leave her in Sweetwater and then Dodge, or that she had left him too many times to count. None of that mattered now when he might be at the sudden end of his life, so they might as well remember their time together wistfully, as though it had been something worth keeping. And as he thought back over it, some things about it had been.

"Did I ever thank you for savin' my life?" he asked. "I would have died if you hadn't taken me over those mountains and down into Las Vegas."

"No," she said, "but you called me your wife when we signed at the hotel. And I figured that was better than a thank you. I thought it meant that you loved me, even when you were cruel."

"I did love you, Kate, in my fashion."

"And do you still?"

She looked up at him, waiting and wanting what he had never been able to give her—his whole heart, his whole life. And when he didn't answer, she shook her head and sniffed back the tears, always the actress.

"Well then," she said, "I suppose this is as good a night as any for goodbye. Especially if they really do hang you this time."

"Kate," he said with a heavy sigh, "believe me, there is nothin' I would rather do right now than have a roaring good fight about this, but I don't have time. There is a man outside my door with a gun in his hand, and he will shoot me down if I even think about runnin'. So pour me a drink while I finish packin', and refill my flask. 'Cause I plan on gettin' very drunk and stayin' that way until this is all over."

There were worse ways to be jailed than being locked up in Judge Spicer's private office. There were no barred windows, no rope-slung cots, no slop jars stinking in the corner. Spicer's couch made a comfortable bed and the Judge had ordered a pallet laid out, as well, and even allowed the prisoners to use the outhouse behind the building when the need arose. But there was no doubt that they were under arrest, with a heavily armed guard posted at the door keeping them from walking out onto Fremont Street toward home and freedom—a home that for John Henry was close enough to see, since the office building was across the street from Mrs. Fly's boarding house. And seeing it from his incarceration only made the improvised prison seem even more prison-like.

It was the continued threat of retribution from the cowboys that made Judge Spicer elect to hold Wyatt and John Henry in his office instead of the city jail. Safe as the jail might be, the four-block walk from there to the courtroom would make the prisoners a perfect target for an assassination attempt as they passed by all the saloons and hotels in town, and Tombstone was still too skittish to tempt any more shootings. So until bond was posted—assuming anyone could raise the exorbitant $10,000 each the Judge had ordered—the prisoners were safer where Spicer could keep an eye on them.

There would have been four prisoners, not two, if the warrants had all been served. But Virgil and Morgan were still in bed recovering from their gunshot wounds and couldn't be moved, and Spicer was content not to have them. The case was only a preliminary hearing, after all, to see if there were cause to call a grand jury, and not a real trial, and the fewer participants there were the quicker things would go.

It seemed a lucky draw that had brought Wells Spicer as judge for the hearing, as he had also heard Kate's murder charge against John Henry the summer before and had thought so little of it that he'd instructed her attorney to rescind it before a trial. And the fact that Kate's former attorney, Lyttleton Price, was now lead attorney for Ike Clanton, seemed even more fortuitous. As Judge Spicer had warned Attorney Price then, he'd better come with sufficient evidence to make a case, or the judge would not look kindly on him. Considering their past association, Wells Spicer would probably be the judge least likely to rule in favor of Lyttleton Price's prosecution now. But it would take a good defense attorney to get the case dismissed.

It took three days for bond to be posted, coming from an encouraging cross-section of the townspeople: mining investors, sporting men, the local Wells Fargo agent, the owner of the Bird Cage Theater, the manager of the Cosmopolitan Hotel. Even a local attorney threw in $1,000 after James Earp offered $5,000 of his own money. But the biggest donation of all, and the biggest surprise, as well, was the $10,000 posted by the man who then signed on as lead attorney for the defense—the honorable Senator Thomas Fitch.

Chapter Eight

TOMBSTONE, 1881

JOHN HENRY WANTED NOTHING MORE THAN A GOOD NIGHT'S REST IN his own bed, but the Senator had other ideas for the newly freed defendants, proposing that they spend the evening in his legal office, reviewing all of the testimony offered at the Coroner's Inquest and discussing every possible scenario that might be imagined up by the prosecution. It was good legal practice to prepare a defense, he explained—and precious little time to do it with the preliminary hearing scheduled to begin at eight o'clock the next morning.

He also explained that while he would represent the Earp brothers, he had asked Attorney T.J. Drum to represent John Henry, saying only that his former acquaintance with the defendant might be deemed a conflict of interest.

"Your former acquaintance?" Wyatt asked.

Fitch paused a moment to flick a piece of lint off the sleeve of his suit coat, as though the question weren't worth his full attention. "The doctor and I knew each other socially in Prescott," he said. "But why give the prosecution even that tenuous of a connection as cause to have me dismissed?"

It was a little bit of theatrics, John Henry knew, but the answer seemed to satisfy Wyatt, and Fitch didn't elaborate on it. Nor did he explain why he would be willing to volunteer such a large amount of money and his time as defense counsel for a man he barely knew, and Wyatt, more concerned with the health of his wounded brothers than which attorneys chose to battle out the case, never bothered to ask. And once Fitch went to work reviewing the testimony of witnesses from the Coroner's Inquest, there wasn't time to think of anything else.

"The prosecution can make a good case for manslaughter," the Senator said, noting that not a single witness claimed that the Cowboys had fired first. "According to Behan, Coleman, and Claiborne, it was your party that started the shooting, almost immediately with Marshal Earp's order to throw up hands. And Mr. Claiborne claims it was you, Dr. Holliday, who fired the first shot. Sheriff Behan doesn't go that far, but does insist that it was a nickel-plated revolver that started the shooting. And you are known to own just such a weapon."

"I do, but I was carrying Virgil's shotgun at the time. I'd have to be a daisy of a shootist to hold a shotgun in one hand and pull off a pistol shot with the other. You can't believe such a fantasy."

"It doesn't matter what I believe, but what Judge Spicer will believe. And no matter which of your party started the shooting, it seems a clear case of homicide one way or another. You shot; they died. The legal question is: what kind of homicide was it? Did you act in the sudden heat of passion, without due caution or circumspection? Was there a spirit of revenge involved? Or was there malice aforethought that would lead to a supposition of premeditation? Which, gentlemen, is what the prosecution will need to prove to win a judgment of First-Degree Murder, the charge Mr. Clanton has preferred against you. Which makes it not so much a matter of *what* happened, but *why* it happened."

"You know why," John Henry said, irritated that their own attorney should be challenging them. "Ike Clanton was threatenin' my life, and the Earps' lives as well. We were only defendin' ourselves."

"It'll be hard to claim self-defense against an unarmed man," Fitch replied, "regardless of what threats Mr. Clanton had previously made. And as far as anyone knows, the McLaurys hadn't made the same sort of threats."

"Frank told Virgil he'd rather die fighting than be strangled," Wyatt said. "And Tom challenged me on the street that morning."

"And you dispatched him handily even though he wasn't armed either. Do you always brutalize defenseless men?"

"I hit a man when he needs hitting," Wyatt replied coolly.

"And you kill him when he needs killing?" Fitch said, his tone turning badgering.

"Wyatt didn't kill Tom," John Henry said, jumping to his friend's defense, "I did."

"Yes indeed, as a double load of buckshot proves," Fitch said. "You didn't even wait to find out if he were armed before letting loose with that shotgun."

John Henry's irritation was turning to ire. "When a man makes threats against your life, you have a right to take action!"

"I thought you said it was Ike Clanton who threatened you?"

"He did, the night before."

"Then why did you shoot Tom McLaury?"

"Because he was in on it with Ike. Because they were all in it together."

"In on what?"

"Planning to assassinate us!" John Henry said, his blood rising. "That's why Ike came to my room that morning with a rifle! That's why they were next to my boarding house that afternoon, waitin'. Maybe Ike and Tom weren't armed, but Frank and Billy were, and they would have killed us all if we hadn't stopped them!"

"But why would they want to kill you, Dr. Holliday? Why would the McLaurys have any cause to join in on Ike Clanton's little vendetta? Why on earth would you think the Cowboys were gunning for you and the Earps? Are you delusional? Are you insane?"

"You know why!" John Henry said, his voice hot with anger at the affront. "You know what we were doing! You know how Wyatt was goin' after the rustlers, and how the McLaurys got wind of it. You know how they planned to kill us before we got to them!"

He was breathless with anger and emotion, and had to stop to let his racing heart slow down, and in the silence Senator Fitch said:

"And that, Dr. Holliday, "is why you will not be testifying."

And that was when John Henry knew that he'd been caught in a lawyer's trap. Fitch had purposefully goaded him into saying too much as a sort of test, and even Wyatt, who still didn't know the whole of the plan, sent him a questioning look.

"There is too much at stake here, for all of us," Fitch said, "to chance any wrong words. So Dr. Holliday will not be called to testify, and Mr. Earp will give his testimony in the form of a written statement, taking advantage of an antique clause in the Arizona legal code. And neither of you will be examined or cross-examined on the stand."

"I'm not much of a writer," Wyatt said. "Wouldn't it be better for me to just tell the truth as I know it?"

"It's not truth that will win this case, Mr. Earp, but good strategy. The statement you will read will have been carefully crafted by myself. And if all goes according to plan, this trouble will end with the preliminary hearing and never go to the grand jury. Indeed, gentlemen, it must never go to the grand jury. Now, tell me everything you know about the Clantons and the McLaurys, and let's build a defense."

It was past midnight when John Henry finally returned to his room at Mrs. Fly's Boarding House, letting himself in quietly and finding the bed empty and cold. Kate hadn't been there yet and John Henry was relieved not to find her. He didn't need another argument just now, when come morning he'd have to be sitting in court at his own murder trial—though as the Senator had told them several times over, it wasn't really a trial but only a hearing looking for cause to become a trial. But whatever the legal name, he needed sleep before facing it.

But his sleep was interrupted in the dim light before dawn by the sound of laughter in the hallway outside his door—a man's voice, his words slurred with liquor; a woman's voice, sweet and insistent:

"He's not here, he'll never know! What do I care if he knows? He doesn't care about me anymore. To hell with him. But you," she said, her words rich with seduction, "you want me, don't you? You want this, don't you?"

There was a long pause, then a laugh and a moan, and the door swung open.

And Kate stood there in Johnny Ringo's arms.

To hell with him, she'd said. And to hell with her, John Henry thought, over and over again when he should have been paying attention to the first day's court proceedings. To hell with her, ungrateful, unfaithful whore. He'd thrown her out as soon as he saw them standing there together in the doorway—standing? No, clinging, cloying, coupling almost, as if they couldn't wait for the privacy of a bed—his bed, where she'd probably brought other men before. And she called him faithless, because of his letters to Mattie? She railed against words, when her own sins were scarlet as blood on the snow? If he'd used up all the words in the world pouring out his heart to Mattie, it wouldn't have equaled one drop of the infidelity poured into Kate. Whore, he thought, *whore!* And glad that she was gone.

But not gone enough, with her things still there in his room, waiting to be packed and taken away: the gowns he'd paid for, the jewelry he'd bought her, the traveling trunks and bonnets and books of fashion plates, the perfume bottles left open to scent the air, the face powder that spilled out of jars across the top of his dressing table. His room was filled with her things, and he wanted it cleared of them all—cleaned out, washed clean.

And by the end of the day, it would be, if Mrs. Fly followed the instructions he'd left for her. "Take away every female thing," he'd told her as he left for court that morning. And when she asked what she was to do with all of those things once they were out of his room, he shrugged. "Whatever you want, Mrs. Fly. Send them to Miss Elder, if you can find her. Or keep them for yourself, and take it off my rent. I paid for most of them, anyhow."

But when Mrs. Fly blushed and looked embarrassed—Kate's gaudy things were hardly suited to a proper married lady, after all—he reconsidered.

"Donate them, Mrs. Fly. Send them all down to the Bird Cage Theater for the costume collection. I reckon the acting company would welcome such a magnanimous benefaction."

And knowing that other actresses would be wearing what used to belong to Kate who had never stopped longing to be an actress again herself, somehow satisfied him, as well as giving him something pleasant to ponder on while the preliminary hearing got underway.

It was a macabre irony that the start of the hearing came a year to the day after the Halloween funeral of Marshal Fred White, murdered on the streets of Tombstone. If John Henry were a more superstitious man, he'd think that Tombstone had a curse and he was caught up in it.

The prosecution, led by attorney Lyttleton Price, showed its cards from the start, bringing in a parade of witnesses who all claimed that the Earps and Doc Holliday had shot down unarmed men, and making a case for manslaughter at least, and maybe murder.

"I ain't got no arms!" the first witnesses remembered Tom McLaury saying, as he opened his coat while young Billy Clanton was yelling, "I do not want to fight!" And then the Earps began to fire, the first shot coming from a nickel plated revolver and the second from a shotgun.

But Sheriff Behan's testimony which followed confused the issue of which gun fired first, though he clearly meant to lay the blame on the Earp party.

"I ordered the Earps not to go down there to the OK Corral," he said after being sworn in, "but they refused my order, looking like they wanted to make a fight. It was the Earps who fired the first shots—eight or ten altogether, I believe, before the McLaurys and the Clantons could begin to defend themselves."

But Senator Fitch was equal to the challenge, and he asked on cross-examination: "I understand you to say you had your eye on a nickel-plated pistol. Was it pointed the first time you saw it?"

"Yes, it was pointed at Billy Clanton."

"Was it the commencement of the expressions, 'You sons-of-bitches,' that diverted your attention from the Clanton crowd and concentrated it upon the Earp crowd?"

"My attention was already on the Earp crowd."

"How long had your attention been especially on the Earp crowd?"

"From the time I turned to go with them," said Behan.

"Did you see the shotgun in the hands of the Earp party, and if so, which one of them?"

"The last time I saw the shotgun, it was in the hands of Holliday," Behan said, looking toward where John Henry sat at the Defense table between Wyatt and Attorney Drum.

"And did you see the shotgun employed in the difficulty?" Senator Fitch asked.

Behan paused a moment before replying, as if considering the politically correct answer. "I did not," he said.

"Sheriff Behan," Senator Fitch chided, "with Dr. Holliday having a shotgun just preceding the difficulty, and on the way to the difficulty, and your attention being especially directed to the Earp party, how does it happen that you do not know what became of the shotgun?"

"It might have been used and I not know of it," Behan replied, seeming confused.

"And do you still insist that the first shot was fired from the nickel-plated pistol?"

"Yes."

"This nickel-plated revolver being the same pistol supposedly owned by Dr. Holliday?"

"That's right."

"Oh, come now, Sheriff!" Fitch said with a laugh. "Do you mean to tell us that, in your opinion, Dr. Holliday carried a shotgun into the battle, then put it aside in order to pull his revolver to make the first shot, then discarded the pistol in favor of the shotgun, firing it in time to kill Tom McLaury, and all of this within the space of two minutes' time?" And being the performer that he was, Fitch then acted out the whole ridiculous scenario, which sent a ripple of laughter through the crowded courtroom.

"Order in the court!" Judge Spicer said. "We'll have no theatrics, Mr. Fitch."

"My apologies, Your Honor," the Senator said graciously, but his point had already been made and he went on with his questioning.

"Is it not a fact that the first shot fired by Holliday was from a shotgun; that he then threw the shotgun down and drew the nickel-plated pistol from his person and then discharged the nickel-plated pistol?"

"I—I don't know," Behan said, and Fitch turned to his clients with a satisfied nod. Though he hadn't been able to keep John Henry's name out of the trouble, he had succeeded in making Johnny Behan's testimony look confused and unreliable. Then to counter Behan's claim that he'd tried to disarm the cowboys and that the Earps had been in the wrong, Fitch asked:

"And did you not say to Virgil Earp the evening of the fight: 'I am your friend and you did perfectly right,' or language of such substance and like import?"

But Behan's rambling reply never got to the point of a real answer, and Fitch finished his questioning. And so it went through two days of questions, with Senator Fitch deftly deflecting the prosecution testimony, and for the first time in a full week, John Henry started to breathe easily.

But then a stranger from Texas showed up in Tombstone.

William Rowland McLaury had been busy in his Fort Worth law practice when a wire came telling him of the murder of his brothers, Frank and Tom. Will was the oldest of the three McLaury brothers, darkly handsome and well-respected, and aiming toward a Texas judgeship while helping to support an elderly father and two unmarried sisters. He was also recently widowed, being left with two young children of his own to raise, and he was about to leave work for his son's birthday party when the telegram from Arizona arrived. A week later, he was stepping off the stage in front of the Grand Hotel, armed with rage and a sharp legal mind, and intent on seeing justice done one way or another.

He arrived in Tombstone in time to hear the end of Johnny Behan's two days of ambivalent testimony, and was furious to find the defendants free on bail and still walking the streets while his murdered brothers were moldering in Boot Hill Cemetery. So he quickly had himself sworn in as Associate Counsel for the Prosecution, and began the legal paperwork to have bail revoked and Wyatt and John Henry jailed once again. And while he waited for Judge Spicer to consider the motion, he spent his evenings in the saloons, spreading lies about the Earps and drumming up support for a murder charge. But though John Henry was incensed, Wyatt seemed more accepting. If it had been his brothers shot down in the streets, he said, he'd have gone after the killers too.

Judge Spicer took his time contemplating Attorney McLaury's request, as revoking bail would mean rescinding his own judgment that the defendants were of no danger to the citizens of the community and would not try to flee if allowed their freedom. Indeed, there were only two legal reasons for rescinding bail: an error in the first judgment, or a likelihood that the evidence as already presented would result in a murder charge by the grand jury. And while he pondered the issues, the prosecution continued to bring witnesses to the stand, including housewife Martha King who had watched the Earps and Doc Holliday walk down to the OK Corral and heard one of them say the damning words, "Let 'em have it," with Holliday replying, "All right." Words that sounded painfully like malice aforethought and premeditation. And when butcher James Kehoe took the stand next and told how the Earps had fired shots before Frank McLaury even drew his pistol, Mrs. King's words seemed even more ominous.

So it was not surprising when Judge Spicer finally rendered his judgment on Will McLaury's motion and announced that the defendants would return to jail after the day's proceedings ended. But if McLaury had expected fireworks from the defendants over the decision, he was disappointed, for Senator Fitch had spent the last two evenings coaching his clients on the best response should such a decision be made.

"You will not in any way seem to be surprised or frightened. Rather, you will take whatever decision comes with perfect calm and composure, as though you have no apprehension at all that the final verdict will work against you in any way. And I will, of course, immediately file a writ of Habeas Corpus to have you released again. This, gentlemen, is nothing but a scare tactic on behalf of Attorney McLaury, trying to shake your resolve and bring you to confession of guilt in the murders of his brothers. Which you, of course, will never make."

So John Henry put on his best poker face, and joined Wyatt in an unemotional response when Monday afternoon's ruling sent them back to jail again—this time to the cold confines of Sheriff Behan's county lockup behind the saloons. Bad enough to be incarcerated and condemned to a bad sleep on a dirty cot—worse to be under the supervision of Johnny Behan, who had already testified against them and would probably welcome a quick lynching to put an end to things. So it was some small comfort when Fitch assigned an armed guard to the jail, surrounding it with Earp partisans, though John Henry still didn't sleep well.

The prosecution didn't need to bring Ike Clanton to the stand, who was himself a party to the shooting. Indeed, it might have seemed cruel to make him relive in front of a crowded hearing the horrific last moments of his younger brother's life. But Ike seemed intent on having his day, or days, in court, and telling the story his own way—which was an imaginative fantasy about how the Earps and Doc Holliday had badgered and bullied him for no reason the night before the shootout. As Ike told the tale, he was only trying to defend himself from their unprovoked brutality.

"I never threatened the Earps or Doc Holliday," he lied, and John Henry had to hold back a curse. Ike had done nothing but threaten him for the whole evening before the shootout, and had come looking for him with a rifle the next morning, intent on making good on his words. According to Ike, he was as innocent as a choir boy, as were the rest of the Cowboys.

But when Senator Fitch took over the questioning, he challenged Ike's claims.

"Did you not tell the saloonkeeper at the Oriental that as soon as the Earps came on the street, they had to fight?"

Ike said he couldn't remember whether he was in the Oriental on the night in question.

"Do you remember being in Kelly's saloon on the morning of the fight, with a Winchester rifle in your hand?"

Ike said that he did remember being in Kelly's and the barkeeper there asking him what was the matter, as his head was bandaged.

"Did you not reply that the Earp crowd had insulted you the night before when you were unarmed, and that as you were now heeled, they would have a fight on sight?"

Ike squirmed uncomfortably, but said that those were very near the words he'd spoken at Kelly's that morning. Then Senator Fitch threw out the most challenging question of all, trying to make a reason for Ike's unreasonable threats and confuse the real causes behind the fight:

"Did not Wyatt Earp approach you, along with Frank McLaury and Joe Hill, for the purpose of getting you three parties to give away Leonard, Head, and Crane, the robbers of the Benson stage, so that he could capture them?"

Ike's face went pale and his gaze darted about the courtroom, no doubt looking to see which of his cowboy comrades might be there listening. If they hadn't yet heard of his failed plan to profit off the arrest of some of their own, they had heard enough now to get him strung up.

But instead of answering, Ike put a shaky hand to his temple, and stammered: "I've . . . got a terrible neuralgia of the head. Been bad ever since Wyatt Earp buffaloed me, the morning of the gunfight. He's a killer and deserves to hang, along with the rest of them!" Then, moaning, he asked to be excused from the stand, a request Judge Spicer answered with a two days' recess.

Will McLaury, seated at the Prosecutor's table and smiling darkly, seemed strangely pleased with the turn of events.

Behan had arranged for separate cells for the two defendants, more out of a desire to keep them in isolation, John Henry thought, than to afford them some small privacy. Not that privacy was possible in such close quarters, anyhow. His cell was at the back of the jail, with three board walls and bars across the front allowing anyone to see him at any time. His cot was the same as the kind the miners used, canvas and wood slung together and warmed by one rough blanket. His toilette was a water bowl and pitcher and a slop jar emptied every day or so. There was no mirror for shaving, so Senator Fitch had obtained permission for his clients to visit the barbershop each morning on the way to court—under heavy guard, of course. As though John Henry would be inclined to escape down the middle of Main Street with the whole town watching him go. And exposed as he was, he didn't even feel comfortable writing to Mattie—though what he would say to her in these circumstances, he didn't know. *I am incarcerated, awaiting the court's judgment on a murder charge . . .* It was impossible to tell her what had become of him, though he wanted more than ever the comfort of her company, if only in the words he sent to her.

And lonely as he was for some comfort, he was almost glad when the guard announced that there was a woman come to see him.

"Hello, Doc," Kate said, when the guard brought him into the office of the jail—the only place where a prisoner could entertain company. "You're looking well, all things considered."

"You're lookin' well, yourself," he replied, and noted that she had somehow found replacements for the face paints and jewels she'd left behind and that he'd discarded. She was, as she ever was, impeccably overdressed. "Purple satin might seem ostentatious for a prisoner visit, but it suits you," he commented.

But Kate had no teasing, taunting reply for him, as she usually did, only a look of something like remorse, or maybe pity.

"I wanted to say goodbye, before I leave. I'm done with Tombstone," she said with not unexpected finality. "I'm going back to Globe. There's a man selling a hotel there for a good price, and I've decided to take him up on the offer."

"And where will you get the money?" he asked. "As you can see, I'm fresh out of pocket these days. Maybe you could put those earrings in soak for a little cash?"

But she ignored his caustic tone, and answered back coolly: "I don't need your money anymore. I'm with Ringo now."

Of course he knew that already, having seen them tangled up together at his door, but that was when Kate was drunk and not thinking clearly. Now, she seemed sober as a schoolmarm.

"So what do you want from me, Kate? Don't tell me you're havin' second thoughts and want to rekindle our past association."

"Oh, I've had plenty of second thoughts, right from the start. If I'd paid mind to them, I wouldn't be where I am now. And maybe you wouldn't be here either," she said, glancing around the jailor's office and giving a shiver. "It's too cold in here for you. You should have them stoke the fire."

"A prisoner doesn't get many privileges. I'm lucky to be out of my cell and talkin' with you now."

"Are you?" she asked, and for a moment there was a trace of wist-fulness in her voice. The she shook it away, as though shrugging off a costume after a performance. Always the actress, his Kate.

Except that she wasn't his anymore, she was Johnny Ringo's, at least for the time being. He couldn't imagine her staying for long with the melancholy cowboy. Kate needed more liveliness than Ringo could offer, more of a challenge. That was what she had seemed to thrive on with John Henry, anyhow. The more trouble he gave her, the more fire she gave him back. And thinking back on their tempestuous time together, he was almost a little wistful himself. Some of Kate's fire would do well to warm up his jail cell now.

"So why are you here, Kate?" he asked.

"I wanted to ask you something. I wanted to know, once and for all . . ."

"Know what?"

She hesitated a moment, as if she'd forgotten her lines. Then she said in measured tones, "I always thought it was Wyatt who was coming between us. Always Wyatt. Until I found those letters. It was her, wasn't it? Right from the start? And I never even had a chance."

He could have lied to her, said something soothing for her to remember him by. But what was the point now? She was leaving for good and he would likely never see her again. And if Will McLaury had his way and got a hanging, John Henry would be facing his Maker soon enough, confessing all his sins. He might as well start telling the truth now.

"It was always her," he said quietly, and though he couldn't bring himself to say her name out loud, in his heart he said it—*Mattie*. He had loved her for as long as he could remember, even before he knew what love was. It was always Mattie to whom his thoughts turned and to whom his heart fled for solace. It was Mattie who knew him, through and through, and who somehow made sense of his senseless world. It was Mattie he still dreamed of at night. And though time or distance or God himself conspired against them, it was Mattie he would someday have again.

"It was always her," he said again. "But I loved you the best I could, Kate."

"But that's not enough."

And before he could say that he was sorry, truly sorry, she gathered herself together and swept from the room, making a last final exit. Always the actress.

Attorney Will McLaury had made good use of the recess, for when Ike Clanton came back to the stand he suddenly had a new story to tell, one that played on the previous line of questioning and turned it back around on the Earps and Doc Holliday.

"Tell us more about this so-called deal with Wyatt Earp," McLaury said when Ike was resworn for the day's testimony. And Ike, evidently not having heard the part about telling the truth, the whole truth, and nothing but the truth so help him God, launched into a tale so melodramatic it would have impressed dime-novel author Ned Buntline.

"Wyatt Earp told me that he wanted me to help him put up a job to kill Crane, Leonard, and Head," Ike said, aiming for a look of innocence in his round childish face, and looking stupid instead, "and he would pay me six-thousand dollars to do it."

A noisy wave of disbelief washed over the courtroom, followed by astonished silence as Ike went on with his story.

"Earp told me there was between four and five-thousand dollars reward for the robbers and he would make up the balance out of his own pocket. He said that his business was such that he could not afford to capture them, but would have to kill them or else leave the country, for they were stopping around the country so damned long that he was afraid some of them would be caught and would squeal on him."

"And did he tell you what it was that he was afraid they might 'squeal' about?"

"Yes," said Ike. "He told me that his brother Morgan had piped off to Doc Holliday the money that was to be going out on that stage, and he could not afford to capture the robbers and have them talk. He then made me promise on my honor as a gentleman not to repeat the conversation if I did not like the proposition."

John Henry didn't know whether to laugh or get to fighting. Ike Clanton, a gentleman? Wyatt stealing money from Wells Fargo and piping it off to him and Morgan? And how had Wyatt piped off money that was still in the strongbox after the holdup? But Wyatt, sitting stonily beside him, wasn't laughing, having just heard himself accused of robbery, embezzlement, and several murders. And things only got worse when Will McLaury continued the questioning.

"And what made you believe Mr. Earp's story?" McLaury asked.

"I believed it because he wasn't the only one who talked about the robbery. His brothers told me of it too, Marshal Virgil Earp and Morgan Earp, as well."

"So all three of the Earp brothers confessed to you their part in the holdup of the Benson stage?"

"That's right."

"And did anyone else add to this confession?"

"Doc Holliday," Ike said, nodding toward the defense table. "He told me that he shot Bud Philpot through the heart, on the night of the holdup. Then Morgan Earp told me that he'd piped off fourteen-hundred dollars to Doc, and Virgil Earp admitted to me that he had helped the robbers escape by leading Sheriff Behan's posse in the wrong direction. Which is why they wanted to kill me and Frank McLaury, on the after-noon of the gunfight. We knew about their business and could get them into trouble over it."

And there was the reason for Ike's fanciful new story, no doubt made up by Will McLaury during the two days' recess: premeditation. According to Ike's perjured testimony, the shootings at the OK Corral were part of a plan to cover up the Earp party's other crimes, with malice aforethought enough to bring a judgment of murder in the first-degree and get them all hung.

"Thank you, Mr. Clanton," Attorney McLaury said, and sat down smiling like a cat with a bird in its claws.

Ike came back to the stand after a lunch recess, and Judge Spicer turned the questioning over to the defense for cross-examination.

"It seems, Mr. Clanton," said Senator Fitch, "that you are the lucky recipient of most of the confessions in Tombstone."

"Some," said Ike.

"But isn't it also true that Marsh Williams, the Wells Fargo agent, stated to you that he was personally involved in the attempted stage rob-bery and the murder of Philpot? Isn't it true that James Earp, a brother of Virgil, Morgan, and Wyatt, also confessed to you that he was a murderer and a stage robber?"

The courtroom rippled with laughter at the absurdity of the proposi-tion, and Lyttleton Price shot to his feet as if excited to have something to say at last.

"Objection, your Honor! The defense is badgering the witness!"

"Sustained," said Judge Spicer. "I hope, Mr. Fitch, that this line of questioning is going someplace."

"It is indeed, your Honor," replied Fitch, then he turned back to Ike on the witness stand. "Mr. Clanton, didn't you actually have four or five conversations with Wyatt Earp about Leonard, Head, and Crane?"

"Might have done," Ike said with wary eyes, less confident now that his coached story was done being told. "I don't recall exactly."

"And didn't Mr. Earp explain that he was planning to run for sheriff, and that he was therefore interested in the glory of a capture rather than the reward money?"

"He said I could have the reward," Ike responded. "I don't remember if he said anything about running for sheriff."

"Didn't you then insist on a reassurance that the reward would be paid dead or alive, because you worried that the outlaws might make a fight rather than be arrested?"

"All I know is he wanted them dead," Ike said. "I don't recall anything else."

"So you didn't ask him for proof in the form of a wire from Wells Fargo that they would pay for the capture, whether the robbers were taken dead or alive?"

"No," said Ike, and it looked like Fitch had gone up a blind alley in his questioning, until he turned to the Defense table, where Attorney Drum was holding a piece of blue-inked paper.

"Your Honor," said Fitch, "I have here the Wells Fargo telegram in question, if I may read it to the court."

"Go on," said Spicer.

Then Fitch smiled and said in his best stage voice: *"Regards your inquiry, yes we will pay rewards for them dead or alive."*

The courtroom erupted and Senator Fitch smiled as he said, "I have nothing more for this witness, your Honor," having made the point, at least, that Ike Clanton's testimony could not be trusted—and without it, there was no evidence of premeditation.

Fitch had planned all along to start the defense testimonies with Wyatt reading a prepared statement, and now that the prosecution had played all its cards he knew just what to write—though Wyatt still had some doubts.

"I don't feel right doing this," Wyatt complained as he sat in Senator Fitch's office and rehearsed his part, the defendants being allowed one evening out of jail to consult with their attorney. But Wyatt was no more easy reading than he was talking, and he stumbled and faltered through the first two recitals, trying to find his own rhythm in Fitch's well-crafted words.

"You'll feel worse hangin'," John Henry said encouragingly. "Anyhow, a bit of uneasiness will add some humility to your performance, makin' it seem more natural."

"And how'd you learn so much about the theater?" Wyatt asked.

"Kate," John Henry replied. "Everything was a show to her."

It was the first time he had thought of her in the past tense, after all the years of having her be part of his daily life. But there would always be part of her with him, somehow.

"I heard Kate left town with Ringo the other day," Wyatt said, not glancing at John Henry for a reaction. "I guess she's done with this silver camp."

It was Wyatt's way of acknowledging the end of his friend's longtime relationship, and John Henry responded with equally little emotion.

"So I hear. May God save Globe from Kate and the other terrors of Tombstone."

"Gentlemen," Senator Fitch said, "we have work to do. Mr. Earp, if you'd please read that last passage again."

Except for the shadow of a noose hanging over their heads, the recitation reminded John Henry of Professor Varnadoe's classes, back in Valdosta.

"*More than kisses,*" he quoted, "*letters mingle souls, for thus friends absent speak . . .*"

When both Wyatt and the Senator turned to give him a questioning gaze, he shrugged and replied:

"Somethin' I memorized back in grammar school. I don't know why I thought of it just now. Forgive the interruption, Senator. Go on, Wyatt. I'm breathless with anticipation to hear what you have to say this time around."

It was no surprise when the defense's first day in court started with an objection from the prosecution.

"Your Honor!" exclaimed Lyttleton Price, "this man means to use a manuscript for his statement!"

"And what is your objection to the use of a manuscript, Mr. Price?" Judge Spicer asked. "Does the statute disallow a written statement?"

"No, Sir, your Honor, but it doesn't allow for one either."

"Which leaves the interpretation of the statute to the will of the court," replied the Judge. "And as I interpret it, the defendant can make a statement in any form he pleases."

"But this is highly unusual!" protested Price.

"Agreed. But as there is nothing usual about this case, I see nothing wrong with an unusual statement being offered. Sit down, Mr. Price. Objection overruled. Mr. Earp, you may continue."

John Henry heard a whispered curse come from the Prosecution table, where Will McLaury sat brooding as Wyatt started over again with his statement, reading it word for word and with as little emotion as he had mustered in his all-night rehearsal:

"The difficulty which resulted in the death of William Clanton and Frank McLaury originated last spring when I followed Tom and Frank McLaury and two other parties who had stolen six government mules from Camp Rucker. Myself, Virgil Earp, and Morgan Earp, Captain Hurst and four soldiers; we traced those mules to McLaury's ranch."

"Objection, your Honor!" Lyttleton Price said again. "This tale is irrelevant to the matter being heard! It's the Earps themselves who are on trial here, not the murdered McLaury brothers! I move this testimony be stricken from the record!"

"May I remind you, Mr. Price," replied Judge Spicer, "that this is not a trial, but only a preliminary hearing? There is no one on trial here, only the circumstances which may or may not warrant further legal action. I have allowed Mr. Earp to make a statement in this proceeding, and I will allow him to state whatever he may consider important to his own defense. As to the relevance of Mr. Earp's testimony, that remains to be seen. Objection overruled—again."

Judge Spicer was clearly growing impatient with the interruptions, and the prosecutors sat in frustrated silence through the rest of Wyatt's statement, unable to either comment or cross-examine—which meant that whatever Wyatt said, true or not, would become part of the court record. But it was true for the most part, outlining the animosities between the cowboys and the law without mentioning Wyatt's more clandestine efforts to end the outlawry.

"It was generally understood among officers and those who have information about criminals," Wyatt went on, "that Ike Clanton was sort of chief among the cowboys; that the Clantons and McLaurys were cattle thieves and generally in the secret of stage robberies, and that the Clanton and McLaury ranches were meeting places and places of shelter for the gang. I knew all these men were desperate and dangerous men, that they were connected with the outlaws, cattle thieves, robbers, and murderers, and I was satisfied that Frank and Tom McLaury killed and robbed Mexicans in Skeleton Canyon two or three months ago, and I naturally kept my eyes open, as I did not intend that any of the gang should get the drop on me if I could help it."

Then he went on to detail the failed deal with Ike Clanton to turn over his fellow cowboys who had robbed the Benson stage, and how Ike had become skittish about it and suspected Doc Holliday of giving him away, although it was actually Marsh Williams' carelessness with the Wells Fargo telegram that had caused the trouble.

"The night before the gunfight I walked in the Eagle Brewery, where I had a Faro game which I had not closed. I stayed in there for a few minutes and walked out to the street and there met Ike Clanton. He asked me if I would take a walk with him, that he wanted to talk to me. He told me when he ran into Holliday that night that he wasn't fixed just right. He said that in the morning he would have man-for-man, that this fighting talk had been going on for a long time, and he guessed it was about time to fetch it to a close. I told him I would fight no one if I could get away from it, because there was no money in it. He walked off and left me saying, 'I will be ready for you in the morning.' I got up the next morning about noon, and was told that Ike Clanton was armed and saying, 'as soon as those damned Earps make their appearance on the street today the ball will open, we are here to make a fight. We are looking for the sons-of-bitches!'

"I was tired of being threatened by Ike Clanton and his gang, so when I found Ike I said, 'You damned dirty cowthief, you have been threatening our lives and I know it. I think I would be justified in shooting you down any place I should meet you, but if you are anxious to make a fight, I will go anywhere on earth to make a fight with you, even over to the San Simon among your crowd.' He replied, 'I only want four feet of ground to fight on!' Pretty soon after I saw Tom McLaury, Frank McLaury, and William Clanton down to the gunsmith shop. I followed them to see what they were going to do. I saw them in the gunshop changing cartridges into their belts. About ten minutes afterwards, and while Virgil, Morgan, Doc Holliday and myself were standing on the corner of Fourth and Allen Streets, several people said, 'There is going to be trouble with those fellows,' and one man said to Virgil Earp, 'They mean trouble. They have just gone down into the OK Corral, all armed, and I think you had better go and disarm them.' Virgil turned around to Doc Holliday, Morgan Earp and myself and told us to come and assist him in disarming them.

"I believed then, and believe now, from the acts I have stated and the threats I have related and the other threats communicated to me by other persons as having been made by Tom McLaury, Frank McLaury, and Ike Clanton, that these men last named had formed a conspiracy to murder my brothers, Morgan and Virgil, Doc Holliday and myself. I believe I would have been legally and morally justified in shooting any of them on sight, but I did not do so, nor attempt to do so. I sought no advantage when I went as deputy marshal to help disarm them and arrest them. I went as part of my duty and under the direction of my brother, the marshal. I did not intend to fight unless it became necessary in self-defense and in the performance of official duty. When Billy Clanton and Frank McLaury drew their pistols, I knew it was a fight for life, and I drew in defense of my own life and the lives of my brothers and Doc Holliday."

Wyatt's closing words weren't just a defense of his honor—they were a legally perfect defense against a charge of manslaughter, and Attorney Will McLaury glowered as the day's proceedings ended. If the gunfight had been a deadly battle between lawmen and outlaws, the hearing had become a war of words between lawyers.

But Senator Fitch had written parts for other characters in his legal drama. as well, or so it appeared to John Henry, when the hearing adjourned from the courtroom to be reconvened in Virgil Earp's sickroom at the Cosmopolitan Hotel—though without the formality of the courtroom the whole procedure seemed more farce than drama, with men who all knew each other too well expecting justice to make a blind decision between them.

Virgil's testimony not surprisingly supported Wyatt's version of things, adding that Wyatt and Morgan were both deputies to the city marshal and that he had personally asked Doc Holliday to go along and help. What was surprising was his mention of a stranger who'd just happened along in the last moments before the gunfight.

"There was a man met me on the corner of Fourth and Allen Streets about two o'clock in the afternoon of the day of the shooting," Virgil related. "He says to me: 'I just passed the OK Corral, and saw four or five men all armed and heard one of them say, *Be sure to get Earp, the marshal.* Another replied and said, *We will kill them all!* When he met me on the corner he says, 'Is your name Earp?' and I told him it was. He says, 'Are you the marshal?' and I told him I was. I did not know the man. I have ascertained who he was since. His name is Sills, I believe."

The fact that the man named Sills was a stranger to Tombstone with no ties to any of the parties involved and therefore no reason to lie, seemed to make him the perfect impartial witness. And his testimony that the Clantons and the McLaurys had made death threats against the town marshal seemed to sew up the case and show that the defendants were not cold-blooded killers—if his testimony could be believed. For even John Henry had his doubts that Sills wasn't just another of Senator Fitch's theatrical inventions, with his too perfect testimony coming at a too perfect time. But would Virgil have memorized a script, as Wyatt had, for the sake of a good defense case? Virgil was not one to bear false witness—unless he too were protecting someone. And thinking that, John Henry remembered the look on Allie Earp's face as she waited out in the hallway while her husband gave his testimony—a mix of fury and fear and womanly tears. Would Virgil lie to put an early end to the trial and save his wife anymore grief?

And what of the man named Sills? He claimed to be a furloughed locomotive engineer on the Santa Fe Railroad, just passing through Tombstone on the day of the gunfight and who just happened to have witnessed the shooting from beginning to end. One thing was certain: he knew his lines, as he proved when the hearing was reconvened in the county courtroom and he was called to the stand.

Sills was nothing remarkable to look at, as he sat round-shouldered in his faded brown suit and thinning brownish hair. One might have seen him in a crowd and never even noticed he was there. But his testimony was riveting.

"I saw four or five men standing in front of the OK Corral, who were talking of some trouble they had had with Virgil Earp, and they made threats at the time, that on meeting him they would kill him on sight. Someone of the party spoke up at the time and said that they would kill the whole party of the Earps when they met them. I then walked up the street and made inquiries to know who Virgil Earp and the Earps were. A man on the street pointed out Virgil Earp to me and told me that he was the city marshal. I went over and called him to one side and told him the remarks I had overheard this party make. One of the men had a bandage around his head at the time, and the day of the funeral he was pointed out to me as Isaac Clanton. I recognized him as one of the party."

"And what do you know of the shooting in question?" Senator Fitch asked.

"A few moments after I had spoken to the marshal, I saw a party start down Fourth Street. I followed them down as far as the Post Office. Then I got sight of the party I had heard making those threats. I thought there would be trouble and I crossed the street. I saw the marshal and party go up and speak to the other party. I wasn't close enough to hear their conversation, but saw them pull out their revolvers immediately. The marshal had a cane in his right hand at the time. He threw up his hand and spoke. I didn't hear the words, though. By that time, Billy Clanton and Wyatt Earp had fired their guns off and the marshal changed the cane from one hand to the other and pulled his revolver out. He seemed to be hit at that time and fell down. He got up immediately and went to shooting. The shooting became general at that time and I stepped back into the alleyway along the side of the courthouse."

"And how did you know it was Billy Clanton who started the fighting?"

"I saw him after he was dead, and recognized him as the same who fired at Wyatt Earp."

The prosecution could hardly wait for their chance to cross-examine the witness and prove him a fraud, asking him question after question designed to trip him up: "When did you come to Tombstone? How did you come? Where have you been since?" And for every question, Sills had a plausible, if unprovable, reply. In the end, Attorney Price descended to asking Sills where he was born, which railroads he'd worked for, and the names of all the conductors on those lines—fishing, it was clear, for some break in the man's identity that would belie his testimony. Price even asked for a description of the horses that pulled the stage that brought Sills to Tombstone just before the fateful gunfight.

"I think there was a white horse and one bob-tailed horse in the team," Sills replied without hesitation.

It would have taken a better prosecutor than Lyttleton Price, or one more knowledgeable about the people involved than Will McLaury, to notice and pursue a point that caught John Henry's notice: the almost familiar way Sills twice mentioned a man he had never met.

"I saw the marshal pick up a shotgun when they started alongside of the building and hand it to Doc Holliday. Doc put it under his coat and the marshal took his cane."

Then, when asked about his usual place of residence, Sills replied: "I lay off at Las Vegas, and stop at my own house."

Had John Henry known the man there in New Mexico, or had the man known him? John Henry wasn't sure on either point, but was somehow certain that the senator was behind the man's well-timed testimony.

Sills' first-hand recollections seemed enough to win the case for the defense, but Senator Fitch had one more witness to call before the end of the day, who reaffirmed Ike Clanton's threats before the fight.

"I was tending bar on the morning of the 26th of October," related bartender Julius Kelley, "when Ike Clanton and Joe Stump came in and called for drinks. At the time I was waiting upon other customers when I heard Ike Clanton telling Joe Stump of some trouble he had the night previous. I asked Clanton what trouble he had been having. He stated that the Earp crowd and Doc Holliday had insulted him the night before when he was not heeled; that he had now heeled himself, and that they had to fight on sight."

When Senator Fitch moved that the preponderance of the testimony to that point would lead to the conclusion that his clients were not guilty and should be released from jail for the duration of the hearing, Judge Spicer agreed and set them free.

It would be the best Thanksgiving vacation John Henry had ever had.

It was ironic that he had Abraham Lincoln to thank for his four days of freedom, but there had been no official Thanksgiving holiday until Lincoln had made one. Before then, there were just the traditional celebrations of turkey and pumpkin pie in honor of the Pilgrims. But Lincoln, claiming a spiritual awakening after his visit to the bloody battlefield of Gettysburg, decided that the whole country should have a day of religious devotion, and turned the traditional celebration into a national holiday. Which meant that in Tombstone, the legal system shut down for a long weekend and the saloons opened wide.

John Henry had planned to spend the time drinking and playing cards, forgetting for a few days at least that his life was hanging on the outcome of a legal hearing. But things seemed to have changed some in the Tombstone sporting community, and he found himself greeted by an uncomfortable silence wherever he went—as though people suspected he might have another shotgun hidden under his overcoat, ready to be used again at any moment. It seemed as if he'd gone from being a sporting man to a shootist in two minutes' time, and men he used to rub shoulders with in the saloons and gambling houses now gave him a wide and fearful berth. And the way they whispered behind his back didn't make him feel any easier—who knew what they were saying, or what they might be planning?

Still, he was safer in a crowd than he was alone in his room, where the cowboys might yet finish their unfinished business and furnish another corpse for the Coroner's Jury. So he stayed close to the saloons and kept his back against the wall, and was almost relieved when the holiday weekend was over.

The hearing reconvened on Monday morning, with the first testimony coming from a U.S. Army surgeon who'd observed the supposedly unarmed Tom McLaury obtaining a pistol in the hour before the gun-fight, and the next testimony coming from Albert Billicke who repeated the same observation.

"When Tom went into the butcher shop," Billicke testified, "his right-hand pocket was flat and appeared as if nothing was in it. When he came out, his pants pocket protruded, as if there was a revolver therein."

This accusation against his brother was too much for Attorney Will McLaury to accept, and he launched into a pointed questioning:

"How did it happen that you watched Tom so closely the different places that he went, and the exact position of his right-hand pocket when he went into the butcher shop, and the exact form of a revolver in the same right-hand pocket when he came out?"

Billicke seemed unruffled by the question, and replied easily:

"Every good citizen in this city was watching all those cowboys very closely on the day the affray occurred, and as he was walking down the street my attention was called to this McLaury by a friend and so it happened that I watched him very closely."

"And do you mean to say that you know every good citizen of Tombstone?" Attorney McLaury asked, his voice ripe with ridicule.

"I know not all of them, but a great many," replied Billicke, to the laughter of the courtroom. For what Will McLaury didn't realize was that Albert Billicke was the owner of the Cosmopolitan Hotel, and knew more folks in Tombstone than most anyone else in town. And though Senator Fitch didn't join in the laughter, he must have been happy to hear his defense theory so well expounded—that the cowboys were a menace to the city and the Earps and Holliday were only defending themselves and the good citizens of Tombstone. The play, it seemed, was playing very well.

The next witness was Winfield Scott Williams, a newly appointed assistant district attorney, whose testimony must have been hard for his boss, District Attorney Lyttleton Price, to hear. For Williams not only added to the defense case, but contradicted Sheriff Behan's supposedly irreproachable testimony. Though Behan had claimed to have never assured the Earps that they had acted rightly in shooting down the cowboys, Williams quoted him as saying just that.

"As I remember it, Sheriff Behan's comments to Virgil Earp were, 'I heard you say, *boys, throw up your hands. I have come to disarm you,* when one of the McLaury boys said, *We will!* and drew his gun.' The shooting then commenced. In another conversation that I heard, Behan said to Virgil Earp, 'I am your friend. You did perfectly right.' This is as I remember it."

This time there was no laughter from the courtroom, only the uncomfortable affirmation that the county sheriff had lied on the stand and that justice in Tombstone depended on whose side had the fastest guns. And according to seamstress Addie Bourland, who'd made all of Kate's expensive frocks, there were fast draws on both sides of the law.

Addie had been in her dressmaker's shop on the day of the shooting, sitting close to the window as she always did for the best sewing light—which on that gray October day was slim. So when her window was shadowed by a party of dark-coated men passing by, she looked up to see what was happening.

"I did not know there was going to be a difficulty," she said, "but I observed four men coming down the street toward where a group of cowboys were standing near Mr. Fly's Photo Gallery."

"Go on, Mrs. Bourland," Senator Fitch said. "And what did you see next?"

"I saw Dr. Holliday—I knew it was him by his long coat and because we have spoken in the past—I saw Dr. Holliday walk up to a man holding a horse and put a pistol to his stomach and then he stepped back two or three feet, and then the firing seemed to be general."

"And did you notice the character of weapon Doc Holliday had in his hand?"

"It was a very large pistol."

"Did you notice the color of the pistol?"

"It was dark bronze," Addie Bourland replied.

"Was it or was it not, a nickel-plated pistol?"

"It was not a nickel-plated pistol."

"Did you see at the time of the approach of the Earps any of the party you thought were cowboys throw up their hands?"

"I did not."

Senator Fitch turned from the witness stand in triumph, for as everyone in the courtroom—and especially Judge Spicer—knew, if Doc Holliday did not start off the shooting with his nickel-plated revolver, as the prosecution claimed, then the Earp party had not started the fight. And if they hadn't begun the shooting, then they had to have been shooting in self-defense. And though the cross-examination should have left Addie Bourland's testimony there, Will McLaury couldn't let it rest—and only added power to the defense case.

"About how many shots were fired before you left the window, Mrs. Bourland?"

"I could not tell; all was confusion, and I could not tell."

"Were all of the parties shooting at each other at the time you were looking at them?"

"It looked to me like it."

"Had any of the parties fallen at the time you left the window?"

"I saw no parties fall."

And as the whole courtroom would have to agree, if no one had yet fallen when the shooting became general, then the Earps could not have opened the ball by shooting down any of the cowboys. It was another triumph for the defense—so much so that Judge Spicer took the unusual step of personally interviewing the witness during the long lunch recess. He explained that he believed she knew more about the case than she had testified. So when the hearing resumed that afternoon, he recalled her to the stand and asked one question himself:

"Please state the position in which the party called the cowboys held their hands at the time the firing commenced; that is, were they holding up their hands in surrender, or were they firing back at the other party?"

"I didn't see anyone holding up their hands; they all seemed to be firing in general, on both sides. They were firing on both sides, at each other; I mean by this at the time the firing commenced."

If Kate had been around, John Henry would have given her a thousand dollars to buy a new dress from Addie Bourland, by way of thanks.

Judge Spicer read his written decision to a packed courtroom, with heavily armed guards keeping watch over the audience. Whichever way the decision went, one side or the other would be fighting mad and there had already been enough bloodshed in Tombstone.

"This case has now been on hearing for the past thirty days," Judge Spicer said, the measured cadence of his words a cool contrast to the heated atmosphere of the courtroom. "During this a volume of testimony has been taken and eminent legal talent employed on both sides. The great import of this case, as well as the great interest taken in it by the entire community, demand that I should be full and explicit in my findings and conclusions and should give ample reasons for what I do. From the mass of evidence before me, I have found it necessary for the purposes of this decision to consider only those facts which are conceded by both sides or are established by a large preponderance of testimony."

He paused a moment, seeming to review the notes before him. Wells Spicer may have had more difficult legal questions to answer in his long and storied career, but there was likely none as publicized as this one would be. The gunfight had already been reported in papers from San Francisco to New York, and the hearing was likely to follow suit. He cleared his throat and went on.

"In view of these controversies between Wyatt Earp and Isaac Clanton and Thomas McLaury, and in further view of this quarrel the night before between Isaac Clanton and J. H. Holliday, I am of the opinion that the defendant, Virgil Earp, as chief of police, subsequently calling upon Wyatt Earp and J. H. Holliday to assist him in arresting and disarming the Clantons and McLaurys, committed an injudicious and censurable act, and although in this he acted incautiously and without due circumspection, yet when we consider the conditions of affairs incident to a frontier country, the lawlessness and disregard for human life;

the existence of a law-defying element in our midst; the fear and feeling of insecurity that has existed; the supposed prevalence of bad, desperate, and reckless men who had been a terror to the country and kept away capital and enterprise; and consider the many threats that have been made against the Earps, I can attach no criminality to his unwise act. In fact, as the result plainly proves, he needed the assistance and support of staunch and true friends, upon whose courage, coolness and fidelity he could depend, in case of an emergency.

"When, therefore, the defendants marched down Fremont Street to the scene of the subsequent homicide, they were going where it was their right and duty to go; and they were doing what it was their right and duty to do; and they were armed, as it was their right and duty to be armed, when approaching men they believed to be armed and contemplating resistance. The defendants were officers charged with the duty of arresting and disarming armed and determined men who were expert in the use of firearms, as quick as thought and as certain as death and who had previously declared their intention not to be arrested nor disarmed. Under the statutes as well as the common law, they have a right to repel force with force.

"In view, then, of all the facts and circumstances of the case, considering the threats made, the character and positions of the parties, and the tragic results accomplished in manner and form as they were, I cannot resist the conclusion that the defendants were fully justified in committing these homicides—that it was a necessary act, done in the discharge of official duty.

"There being no sufficient cause to believe the within named Wyatt S. Earp and John H. Holliday guilty of the offense mentioned within, I order them to be released."

John Henry gasped as he felt relief flood through him, as though he'd been holding his breath the whole while. Then he turned to Wyatt and grabbed ahold of his hand, half for congratulations, half for support. Beside him, Senator Fitch was already answering the questions of eager reporters. But on the other side of the courtroom, Ike Clanton's prosecution team gathered their disbelieving dignity and Will McLaury shook with anger and turned a black look to the back of the crowd—where Johnny Ringo and Curly Bill Brocious nodded back at him and smiled.

Chapter Nine

TOMBSTONE, **1881**

THE DEATH LIST WAS RUMORED TO INCLUDE EVERYONE FROM JUDGE
Spicer and the Earps and Doc Holliday to both defense attorneys and
the mayor who'd been their vocal supporter, and was said to have been
signed in blood in a midnight ceremony in one of the cowboys' canyon
hideaways. But rumor or not, the truth was that Tombstone had turned
into an even more dangerous place than it had been before the gunbattle,
with fighting in the streets and the saloons and the crack of pistol shots
echoing through the dark December nights.

For safety sake, the Earps had moved out of their neighboring cottages on the outskirts of town and into adjoining rooms on the second
floor of the Cosmopolitan Hotel where Wyatt could keep them all better guarded. John Henry spent a few nights at the hotel, as well, before
moving into a rented room in a boarding house nearby, Fly's place next to
the OK Corral having lost some of its charm for him. But no sooner had
they got themselves settled than the cowboys took a suite of rooms across
the street from the Cosmopolitan at the Grand Hotel, with the shutters
closed and one slat missing as though to allow the barrel of a pistol to
peek through, and things didn't seem any safer than they'd been before.
And with Will McLaury still in town, spreading the word that he was
going to hang the Earps and Doc Holliday one way or another, there was
little doubt who was putting the cowboys up in their elegant new digs.

Mayor Clum's response to the situation was to send a wire to Governor Gosper, asking for the protection of additional arms, and Gosper

wired back that he'd asked President Chester A. Arthur to rescind the Posse Comitatus act, allowing for martial law in Tombstone. But while Washington discussed and deliberated, as slow as ever to answer the needs of the Arizona Territory, the rumors and the tensions mounted and Wyatt and John Henry went about their business heavily armed and wary.

But it was Mayor Clum who took the first fire, when he left town on a long-delayed trip to the Indian Bureau in Washington, D.C., and ran into road agents halfway to the railhead in Benson. He was one of five passengers on a coach with no treasure box and no shotgun guard, and knew at once what the shooters wanted as they fired a volley that killed a horse and wounded the driver. And not wanting to put the other travelers into more danger, Clum grabbed for his six-guns and jumped from the stage, running across the lots and into the darkness. It took him all night to walk back to Tombstone, where he learned that after he'd left the stage the robbers had disappeared without taking so much as a pocket watch from the other passengers. And what kind of stage robbers held up a stage without robbing it? Their intent, he told Wyatt and Virgil when he came to visit, was nothing less than his own murder.

The local papers, one backing the cowboys and the other siding with the Earps, battled out the holdup in fiery editorials, the *Nugget* calling Clum a paranoid coward who saw cowboys at every turn, the *Epitaph* calling for better policing of the roads in this time of local trouble. But other than that one attack the roads were safe enough, and the rumored Death List seemed to have been just a rumor after all.

Then, three days after Christmas, Tombstone erupted again.

There had been a chilly rain all morning, clearing in the afternoon and followed by a brilliant starry night—good light to see by for anyone out late, as were John Henry and Wyatt, playing poker with Virgil and Morgan Earp at the Oriental Saloon. The game was something of a cel-ebration of the departure of Attorney Will McLaury from Tombstone, who had seemingly given up on his scheme for revenge and gone back to Texas where he belonged. And though Virgil still limped from his leg wound and Morgan still winced when he coughed, they were both healed enough to hold their own in the game for most of the evening.

Their conversation was purposefully spare, mostly about the game and nothing to draw attention to themselves. Even Morg was uncharacteristically quiet, his only comments being about how Doc was robbing him blind and surely cheating because no honest player would be able to take so many hands. John Henry had to laugh at that, as he had played nothing but honest cards all night, and had never had to cheat to beat Morgan, anyhow. Then, sometime close to midnight, Virgil decided he'd had enough celebrating and a little too much losing at cards.

"Well, gents," he said, "I suppose Allie's wondering if I'm ever coming home tonight. Better get there before tomorrow starts. You'll have to steal from each other from here on out."

"I'll walk you home," Wyatt said, putting down his cards and reaching for his hat, but Virgil shook his head.

"No need for a bodyguard, Wyatt. I've got my six and a bright moon outside. No one will get the slip on me tonight. Besides, if Allie sees me limping home on your arm, she'll think I'm not man enough for a night out. And that would be a sorry end to my social life."

Morgan laughed at that, but Wyatt hesitated a moment before picking up his cards again.

"Take care, Virg," he said.

Virgil took his hat, lit up a last cigar, and limped toward the door. It was a short walk home, less than a block, and the sky was very bright, as he had said.

He couldn't have made it more than across the street when a volley of gunfire filled the night like fireworks. Then silence, and Wyatt went lunging for the door.

In the street outside, gunsmoke was thick as fog. And coming back through it, limping more slowly than before, was Virgil.

"Wyatt," he said, "I think I'm hit . . ." Then he collapsed into his brother's arms.

They carried him back to the Cosmopolitan Hotel and summoned the doctor, who found him torn up by buckshot, his left elbow blown away.

"There's wounds to the kidney and the liver, as well," the doctor said, "and I fear there's a bullet lying near to the spinal column. I'll have to do surgery immediately, here in the hotel. Too dangerous to move him again."

Virgil moaned in pain, while Allie wept at his side.

"It's hell, isn't it!" he said, then "never mind, girl. I've still got one good arm to hug you with!"

And that was the last he said before the doctor covered his nose with a chloroform-soaked rag, putting him out of his misery before cutting into him.

"You know they were gunning for all of us," Wyatt said to John Henry, as they waited out in the dark hallway. "Hell, they probably thought Virg was me, coming out of the saloon."

"Then we've got to end this before they do," John Henry said. "We've got plenty of men who'll back us up. You just say the word." Already the hotel was surrounded by an armed guard, and more would come if Wyatt wanted them.

But Wyatt wavered. "We can't give the law anymore cause against us, Doc. Judge Spicer let us off this time, but another street fight and the grand jury will take it up. No, for now we're better off cleaning them out of the mountains, like we planned."

"But they're not in the mountains anymore, Wyatt! They're right here in town, shooting us down like target practice. First it was Mayor Clum, now Virg. Tomorrow night, maybe it'll be you."

"All I want is a fair fight, Doc, if it comes to that. But I won't go skulking around this town, shooting through saloon doors like a hired assassin."

"Maybe you won't," John Henry said, "but the cowboys will."

Virgil's wounds were feared fatal and the doctor considered removing his shattered arm to save his life. Instead, he took out five inches of bone and sewed the arm back together and gave him a one-in-five chance to live. To Virgil, that seemed like pretty good odds. And the odds were good, too, that it was Ike Clanton who had done the shooting, as his hat was found in the vacant building from where the crippling shots were fired.

"Will McLaury's behind this, I'm sure of it," Wyatt told John Henry, "or at least his money is. And if Clanton and McLaury are in on this, then you know Ringo and Curly Bill can't be far away. And Behan sure as hell won't try to stop them."

But with Virgil wounded and unable to go after the assailants, there was nothing much Wyatt could do about bringing them in. It was one thing to chase cowboys in the mountains in a clandestine operation, and another thing to hunt them down openly, and for that he needed proper authority. So he sent a message to U.S. Marshal Crawley Dake at Tucson, asking to be appointed deputy in his brother's stead. *"Local authorities are doing nothing,"* he wrote, *"and the lives of other citizens are threatened."*

But before he received Dake's answer officially deputizing him, the cowboys were back to robbing stages again—this time the Bisbee stage, loaded down with $6500 payroll for the mines. The attack came as the coach passed near the Clanton ranch, with three highwaymen shooting from a distance. The shots downed a horse and brought the coach to a halt, and the robbers sent a note demanding the treasure box be thrown down. But even from a distance the guard could name the assailants, and when the Benson stage was robbed the next day, word went around that both jobs were headed up by the same man: Pony Diehl, one of Johnny Ringo's old gang. The cowboys were getting bolder, and even more dangerous.

Wyatt's deputization as a U.S. Marshal arrived with a pledge of $3,000 operating expenses, allowing him to outfit his own small official posse with each man promised $5 a day pay for his services, along with horse and bridle, saddle, carbine, six-shooter, and rations. The men he picked weren't the usual civic-minded citizens out to do some good, but a mix of gamblers, ranchers, and sometime outlaws—all familiar with the territory and unafraid of a show-down. But on the night before they were to ride out in search of Virgil's would-be assassins, one of the cowboys rode into Tombstone and ran right into them, instead.

Snow was falling that third week of January, dusting the dirt streets and frosting the town like a fairyland. But the pretty façade couldn't cover the murderous mood of the place, so when Johnny Ringo stepped out of the Occidental Saloon into the middle of the Earp posse, a crowd quickly gathered. He'd been drinking, that was clear by both the smell of him and the bravado with which he came into town and challenged a whole street-full of men.

"Evenin' Deputy Earp," Ringo said, tipping his hat, "Evenin' Doc. Hear you boys are planning to make a raid on Charleston. You know Charleston is cowboy territory?"

"Then I guess that would be a good place for a raid," Wyatt replied, without answering the question.

"You won't find any cowboys there," Ringo said. "We're not stupid enough to sit around town, waiting to be shot down like dogs. Not like you Earp dogs, anyhow."

"You're drunk, Ringo. Go home."

"And let you sneak in and shoot me while I'm sleeping? I'd rather fight you here and now. So what do you say? Are you game? Or are you scared?"

Wyatt was never scared, but he wouldn't bring on another street fight, putting the whole town in danger. "I'm not going to fight you, Ringo. There's no money in it."

"Well, there's money in fighting you. Plenty of money. Plenty of people want you dead, you and your brothers. And Doc Holliday. In fact, there's more that wants Holliday dead."

"What are you talkin' about, Ringo?" John Henry asked, and the cowboy answered with a laugh.

"I'm talking about Kate. You remember her, don't you, Doc? Well, she sure remembers you. And she told me to give you a message when I next saw you," and he smiled as his hand moved toward his pistol.

John Henry saw the motion and reached for the Colt's he kept ready in his pocket. "You want to fight, Ringo? We'll fightin's just my game! All I want is ten paces out in the street."

It might have been another street shooting, but John Henry was only playing for time by asking for ten feet between them. He could have easily shot Johnny Ringo down right where he stood, and been happy to do it. But from where he was standing, he could see what Ringo couldn't: the Chief of Police moving in behind the cowboy, ready to make an arrest. And with Wyatt armed and ready at his own side, he was betting on the odds.

"Count to ten," he told Ringo, and started backing away. Ringo smiled and did the same—and backed right into the arms of the waiting police.

John Henry was fined for carrying a deadly weapon in town limits, but it was worth the money to see Ringo in jail at last—for the judge, noting that Ringo had an outstanding warrant for a stage robbery from the previous fall, kept him locked up for that charge, as well.

"That's one cowboy down," Wyatt said, "and a gang of them to go. Are you still game, Doc?"

"I'm always game," John Henry replied.

Though Ringo was a disturbance in Tombstone, the real troublemaker was Ike Clanton, who Wyatt was sure had fired on his brother. So it was Ike whom Wyatt's posse was hunting when they rode into the cowboy hideout of Charleston the next day, arriving just as dusk was settling on the town and finding nothing but silence to greet them. It seemed that someone had spread the word that a posse was on its way, and the inhabitants had left their adobe-walled houses empty and their fires still smoking.

"Ringo," said John Henry, as he sat his horse and considered the apparently deserted town. "So that's what he was doin' in Tombstone: keeping watch. So what'll we do now, Wyatt? Seems disheartening for the boys to ride down here for nothin'."

The rest of the posse was gathered at the far side of the narrow bridge that crossed the San Pedro, waiting for orders.

"We don't know there's nothing," Wyatt replied. "Take your men and circle back around, search every house. But be pleasant about it. We don't want the folks to confuse us with cowboys, and shoot us down."

But there was no trace of the cowboys, and the posse spent the rest of their time riding through the back country of Cochise County, carrying unserved warrants for Ike Clanton and Pony Diehl, while Ike had gone back to Tombstone and turned himself in. By the time Ike made his appearance in court, he had seven witnesses to his whereabouts the night of the shooting, all of them swearing he had been in Charleston the whole time, happily drunk, while all the prosecution could muster was the presence of Ike's hat at the scene of the crime.

The Judge had no choice but to dismiss the case for lack of evidence, then he took Wyatt aside and said, "You'll never clean up this crowd this way; next time you'd better leave your prisoners out in the brush where alibis don't count."

John Henry's thoughts had already been going in that direction.

His lying alibis behind him, Ike Clanton wasted no time in riding down to Contention City to swear out a complaint of his own, charging Wyatt and Morgan Earp and John Henry Holliday with murder in the death of his brother Billy. It was the same charge they'd just spent a month fighting in Tombstone, but since that court proceeding was only a hearing and not a jury trial, double jeopardy didn't apply—which meant that they could be rearrested as often as anyone liked on the same charge until the case was finally tried.

"I reckon Will McLaury's behind this, as well," John Henry said as he rode beside the Earp brothers on their way to Contention, accompanied by Wyatt's hand-picked posse for protection. "Ike doesn't know the law except to run from it."

"So what do you think our odds are, Doc?" Morgan asked.

"Better than last time, I reckon, if we get there safe. I trust the courts more than I trust this road." They suspected that Ike had brought the charge in Contention just to get them all together in an open place—though even with Wyatt's posse on guard, a fight on the road could still be a duck shoot.

They reached Contention City at noon and walked into the courtroom fully armed and pistols drawn, and Wyatt announced:

"Your honor, we come here for the law, but we will fight if we have to."

But the judge, not wanting any of their fight, ordered the prisoners back to Tombstone instead where the court dismissed the case on the grounds that another magistrate had already dismissed it and the grand jury had already failed to indict, and a new examination on the same matter would be unwise during such turbulent times.

So it seemed the game had come to a draw, with the Earp posse unable to hold the cowboys and the cowboys unable to hold the Earps, and everyone waiting for the next card to turn.

It was dangerous times for men; too dangerous for women, and most of the Earp wives had gone to the family home in California until things calmed down in Tombstone. Only Virgil's wife Allie remained behind, continuing to nurse her crippled husband back to health, and leaving the men with no female presence to entertain them. So it fell to Morgan and John Henry to make a party for Wyatt the night before his thirty-fourth birthday, and they decided to invite him to the Bird Cage Theater to take in the show. Of course they knew that Wyatt wouldn't be interested in such frivolities as *Stolen Kisses: Twenty-Two Hours of Incessant Laughter*, nor would he think it safe to be in a darkened theater where the cowboys were known to congregate, and they weren't surprised when he declined the invitation. But Morgan was hungry for some amusement and convinced John Henry to accompany him in spite of Wyatt's absence. Though John Henry agreed with Wyatt about the safety of the situation, somehow Morgan always brought out the daring in him.

The show was as frivolous as Wyatt would have expected, though it wasn't anywhere near twenty-two hours of laughter. But there were enough laughs to make for a good evening, and enough long-legged show girls to make up for the absurdities of the script. From the rows of wooden benches on the floor to the box seats that hung above, men were drinking and smoking and cat-calling, and all in all having a fine evening. And for the first time in weeks and maybe even months, John Henry almost forgot about the cowboy menace.

Morgan seemed to have forgotten altogether, as the show ended and he walked from the theater singing boisterously the bits he could remember from the unmemorable score, and John Henry laughed at the sight of him, though he didn't join in the singing. One tipsy troubadour was enough for Tombstone.

"You fellows will catch it tonight if you don't look out," one of the other men leaving the theater told them, a lawyer by the name of Briggs Goodrich who was known to have ties to the cowboys.

"That's a harsh critique," John Henry said. "My friend here isn't all that bad of a singer."

"I wasn't making mention of his singing," Goodrich said, then he looked around him a moment. "I'm just suggesting that you might want to be a little less enthusiastic this evening."

"But theater demands enthusiasm!" Morgan replied. "Isn't that right, Doc?"

"Theater demands an audience," John Henry commented, "which you seem to have acquired."

"More audience than you know," Goodrich said, "and maybe more than you can handle." Then, taking another quick glance around, he tipped his hat, and said, "Good evening, gentlemen."

"And what do you suppose he meant by that?" Morgan asked.

"I reckon he's tellin' us it's time to call it a night," John Henry replied. "Advice worth takin', maybe."

"Well, I'm not ready to go home. And there's not much home to go to, now Louisa's gone. Damn Wyatt."

"You shouldn't damn a man the night before his birthday," John Henry replied. "And what's Wyatt got to do with Louisa, anyhow?"

"Nothing, as far as I know. But he was the one who told me to send her home, just to be safe. But now that I think of it, I wonder if he wasn't just being jealous."

"Wyatt jealous of you?" John Henry said with a laugh. Wyatt was a man other men envied, not the other way around. "And what would he be jealous of, anyhow? Seems to me like Louisa's as smitten with you as you are with her—sodden, almost. You're not imaginin' infidelity, are you?"

"Hell no, or there'd be hell to pay. I'm just saying that maybe Wyatt wanted my Louisa to go off because his Josie had to go off. Which is probably all your fault, come to think of it."

"And why is any of this my fault?" John Henry said, knowing that once Morgan started a story, it would be a while before it made any sense.

"Well, you're the one who bought Josie that house. And if you hadn't bought her a house, then Johnny Behan wouldn't have been drunk and mad."

"Morg, you are the sorriest story teller I ever knew! What does Behan gettin' drunk have to do with Josie's house? Which I didn't buy, anyhow. I only gave her the money to hold onto her land when Behan wanted to throw her off of it. Or so Kate said. I reckon that might have been just another story, as well."

"This ain't a story, Doc, it's the Gospel truth. You know how Wyatt started staying at Josie's after the hearing?"

"I heard of it."

"Well, Celia was crying about Wyatt's leaving her for another woman, so he went back home for a night to talk things out, and he asked me to stay at Josie's to keep an eye on her."

"Sounds like the gentlemanly thing to do," John Henry remarked, though a real gentleman wouldn't have found himself in such a duplicitous situation in the first place.

"Well, I was a gentleman, all right, but Johnny wasn't. He came by while I was there, mad as hell, half drunk and pawing at Josie when I came out of the bedroom. Naturally he figured I'd been with her, and that only made him madder. He grabbed her hard and called her a whore, said if she had enough room in her bed for all the Earp boys, she ought to have enough room for him there too, especially since it was his land she was doing her whoring on."

"His land?"

"That's what he said. I guess Josie forgot to tell him about you buying the land for her. So then she gets the deed out of the drawer, shows him his name isn't on there anymore, says it's her land and her house too, and he'd better get his worthless self out of it, or she'll have me beat the hell out of him."

"Which, of course, you were glad to do."

Morgan grinned. "I can't have my brother's woman being called a whore, can I? Besides, I'd had a hankerin' for a long time to knock some humility into Johnny Behan. First hit, I think I must have broke his nose, 'cause the blood was pourin' out, but he was too mad to care. He came after me like a little bull, head down and aimin' at my middle, so I kicked him hard in the belly. Doc, you should have seen him go flyin' clean out of the house and into the street! I don't think Johnny Behan's ever been beat so fast before. Josie went runnin' to him to see if he was all right, but he just pushed her aside and picked himself up off the ground, mutterin' and wipin' that blood off his face as he went. Funniest damn thing I ever saw, Johnny Behan groveling in the dirt like an old sow."

"You never told me this entertaining tale before," John Henry said.

"We've been kind of busy lately," Morgan replied with a shrug, "chasing cowboys and all. I guess it slipped my mind."

"So what does this have to do with Louisa leavin' Tombstone?"

"'Cause that was when Wyatt decided Josie had to get out of Tombstone, since her being here with him was making more trouble with Behan. And Celia wasn't too happy about the situation, either."

"I reckon not."

"So Wyatt sent them both packing: Celia down to Colton to our folks' house, Josie back to San Francisco."

"A girl in every port, so to speak."

"And as long as Celia was going, he decided my Louisa should go along to keep her company. Which leaves me mighty little company here. So like I said, if you hadn't bought that land for Josie then Behan wouldn't have had cause to fight with me, and Wyatt wouldn't have sent the women away. So it's all your fault, the way I see it."

John Henry had to smile at the absurdity of Morgan's logic, especially when a solution was so easily had.

"Well, there's plenty of women left in Tombstone, if it's female company you want. Maybe even one those leggy show-girls you were whistlin' at back at the theater."

"I don't want a show-girl, Doc. I want my Louisa. She's twice the looker of those dancers. And she loves me, like you said."

"And what's love got to do with company?" John Henry said with a laugh. He'd found it easy enough, in his life, to separate the two things, living with Kate while he longed for Mattie. And Kate had been good company, when she was so disposed. But he also understood, better than he could explain to Morgan, what it was like to hunger for something he couldn't have—to wait, and wait, and wait.

"Tell you what, Doc, I'm about to be fed up with Tombstone. If it weren't for Wyatt wanting to track down these cowboys, I'd be on the next train to California myself."

"Next train doesn't leave until tomorrow, Morg," John Henry pointed out, "so you might as well enjoy what's left of the night. As for me, I am headed to bed."

"But we haven't said a proper Happy Birthday to Wyatt yet!"

"Wyatt's birthday isn't until tomorrow either. You can wait until then."

"And miss these fine fireworks?" Morgan said, his face brightening as the desert sky lit up with lightning. "Looks like a storm moving in. I wonder if there's a game of pool open somewhere?"

John Henry laughed again. Even lovesick, Morgan couldn't stay sad for long—or on the topic at hand.

"You be careful, Morg," he cautioned. "Remember what Goodrich said. You just keep your eyes open, all right?"

Morgan was right about the storm, and by the time John Henry reached his boarding house room, the wind was blowing into dust devils in the streets and the rain was coming down hard. It was fine weather to be indoors, and even better for letter-writing, as Mattie loved the rain and would like to hear his description of it as it sheeted down on the tin roof overhead. And in between the sound of the wind and the rain, the thunder echoed after every lightning flash, thunder that rolled like canon and cracked like gunfire. A nice simile, he thought, and pulled out his writing paper.

He was partway through the third page and contemplating the next phrase when there was a knock at his door, and he opened it to find Warren Earp standing in the hallway.

"Doc," Warren said, "Wyatt says come now . . ."

He didn't need to say more, for when Wyatt called, John Henry always answered. Especially now, with Warren standing ashen-faced and speechless.

"What is it, Warren? What's happened?"

"It's Morg. He's dying."

Warren told the story in short breathless sentences as they ran through the windy rain toward Hatch's Billiard Hall, where Morgan Earp was laid out with a bullet hole in his back.

"Wyatt heard there might be trouble tonight, so he went to the theater looking to warn you and Morg. But you were already gone, and Morg was on his way to Hatch's for a game of billiards. Wyatt told him not to go, but you know Morg and how he don't take no for an answer. So Wyatt says that's all right, I'll stay with you while you play one game. So Morg was playing a game with Bob Hatch, standing by the table while Bob lined up his ball, when somebody breaks in the glass at the back door. Bob thinks it's the wind and he ducks so's the glass don't hit him, but Morg just stands there watching the table. Then there's a shot comes through the broken window, and it hits Morg in the back and goes right through . . ."

Warren stopped for a moment, bending over to catch his breath, and John Henry could see that he was crying.

"It's all right, " he said, not knowing what else to say and touching a hand to the young man's shoulder, and Warren sniffed back tears and went on.

"Morg falls down where he's standing, and Wyatt runs to pick him up again, and Morg says, "No, I can't stand it!" so they lay him down on the billiard table instead and take a look at him, and he's bleeding all over the table and moaning. Then Wyatt tells me to fetch the doctor and go get Doc."

They were at the front door of Hatch's Billiard Hall, and John Henry stopped a moment to take it all in: the crowd of men pushing to get a view, the town doctor bending over the billiard table, and Morgan lying in a pool of blood while the wind whistled in through the broken glass of the back door.

He stared at the scene, knowing it would never leave him. Then something like a sickness came up from inside of him, swelling like vomit into his chest and tearing at his throat.

"No!" he screamed, pushing past the others, nearly knocking the doctor over as he ran headlong to the billiard table and Morgan's side. "No!" as Wyatt stepped forward and held him by the shoulder, keeping him back.

Then the doctor spoke. "The bullet entered left of his spinal column, looks like it passed through the kidney and came out here at the loin. There's nothing I can do to repair this. It's too much," he said as if talking to himself, "too much . . ."

Morgan was still breathing, every breath coming with a gasp, but his eyes were closed and his body was still. Then his eyelids flickered and opened, and he looked up at his brother.

"Wyatt . . ." he whispered.

"I'm here, Morg, I'm here," and he took hold of his brother's hand.

"Wyatt," Morgan said again. "Be careful . . ."

And with Wyatt's face pressed close to his, Morgan whispered something more. "What did he say?" John Henry asked.

Wyatt sniffed back tears, the first time that John Henry had ever seen him cry.

"He said, '*Watch your back.*' He was making a joke . . ."

And that was when John Henry felt the tears running down his own face. Always making a joke, Morgan was. Right to the end.

By midnight he was gone, while the wind continued to mourn across the desert and blow like a banshee through the town, and Wyatt arranged to have his brother's body moved back to the hotel where he'd be safer dead than he'd been alive. And while Wyatt and Virgil and Allie attended to their brother, John Henry went on a rampage. He wasn't going to wait for another cowboy to get away with murder.

He went back to his room and gathered his gunbelt and cartridges, his Colt's and his Winchester. Then he slipped the Hell-Bitch into its scabbard and strapped it around his waist, and headed out into the howling night.

"Murderers!" he cried into the darkness, his voice flying out into the wind. "Murderers!"

He had no idea where to find Morgan's killers, but that didn't stop him. He ran from one street to another, screaming like a wild man and shooting at shadows. He slammed into every saloon in town, swinging his Winchester before him like a sword, leaving the denizens speechless and terrorized. He ran through the liveries, startling the horses and setting them to whinnying. He searched every alleyway, every dark yard, every corner of Tombstone.

When Wyatt found him at dawn, he was sitting in the middle of Allen Street, too spent to cry, too sad to sleep.

"Come on, Doc," Wyatt said, reaching a hand to help him to his feet. "It's time to go home."

But John Henry ignored Wyatt's outstretched hand, and said stonily, "He told me once how you held onto him when he fell out of an apple tree. How you fell down with him because you wouldn't let go."

"And I'd have died tonight with him, if I could have," Wyatt said. "I should have made him go home. I shouldn't have let him play that game . . ."

"What'll we do, Wyatt?" John Henry asked, his voice breaking like his heart. "What'll we do?"

And for the first time, Wyatt had no answers.

Morgan went home the next day, his body laid out in a wooden coffin loaded onto a freight at Contention City. Then Wyatt went back to Tombstone to get the rest of the family out of town. With one brother wounded and one brother dead, he wasn't going to risk any more lives. But although Virgil pleaded with him to get himself out of the Territory too, Wyatt wouldn't listen. He'd gotten them into this, he said, seeking justice. Now justice would have to come at his own hand.

But sending a living Earp brother home was more dangerous than sending a dead one. So Wyatt and John Henry went along as far as Tucson, and Virgil, with his mangled shooting arm still in a sling, was grateful for the escort.

"Keep your eyes open," Wyatt told his posse as they boarded the car—brother Warren, hired guns Jack Johnson and Sherman McMaster, and John Henry. "There's an hour stopover between trains, once we get to the station. Hard to hide Virg and Allie while we wait."

"Tucson is Marshal Dake's town," John Henry noted. "You reckon he'd allow us these shotguns, under the circumstances?"

Wyatt considered a moment, then said, "Better keep the guns out of sight, best you can. But keep your pistols handy in case there's trouble."

It was a warning he didn't need to bother giving. They all knew that trouble was coming, just didn't know when or how. But while Sherm and Jack and Warren roamed through the cars, watching over Virgil and Allie and keeping their eyes open for anything untoward, Wyatt took a seat near a window and sat staring into the gathering darkness, his long-barreled pistol in his lap. Across the aisle from him, John Henry sat quiet, as well, respecting his silence. And what was there to say, anyhow? They'd lost Morgan, and that was a loss beyond words.

Then at last Wyatt looked away from the window and said, "I don't understand it."

"What is there to understand?" John Henry replied bitterly. "They're huntin' us down, one a time. Ike wants revenge, and Will McLaury's willin' to pay for it."

"But that's the thing. It wasn't Ike Clanton this time."

"How do you know? Did you hear something?"

"I saw something. I saw a face through that broken glass on the door, right after Morgan was shot." He paused a moment, looking perplexed. "It was Frank Stillwell. I'm sure it was him. But why him? Stillwell's a road agent, not a cowboy. He wasn't in on the Guadalupe Canyon raid; he wasn't in on the street fight. What's he got against Morgan—against us? It doesn't make sense."

"You arrested him after the Bisbee robbery," John Henry said. "I reckon that's a sore point with him."

"But it's not worth killing over. It's not worth this . . ."

It didn't make sense to John Henry either—until he remembered the last nonsensical story Morgan had told him, about protecting Josie and besting Johnny Behan.

"It wasn't Stillwell behind it," John Henry said, suddenly understanding too well. "It was Behan. Stillwell's just his henchman, like always. It was Johnny Behan who wanted Morgan dead."

Wyatt looked up sharply. "Behan? But why?"

John Henry was slow in answering, knowing how Wyatt would take the answer—Wyatt who was always protecting Morgan. For though Morgan may have been the target, it was Wyatt who was the cause.

"Did Morg tell you what happened the night you left him guardin' Josie?"

Then he recounted the story the way Morgan had told it to him, but without the laughter that Morgan brought to every tale. For there was nothing funny now about the altercation with Behan that left the sheriff blustering and bloodied and eager for revenge. And John Henry didn't have to point out that if Wyatt had stayed faithful to his own woman, instead of keeping company with the sheriff's fiancée, Behan wouldn't have had cause for bluster in the first place. But if Wyatt were guilty of infidelity to Celia, he had never been unfaithful to his brothers.

"So if Behan is behind this," said Wyatt, "then we have the law against us now, as well as the outlaws."

"So what do we do?" John Henry asked.

Wyatt turned his face back toward the window as the dusk descended into darkness.

"Kill them," he said. "Kill them all."

The train yard at Tucson seemed quiet enough, but Wyatt sent out a scouting party before allowing Virgil and Allie to be escorted off the car, and the report brought back by Sherman McMaster and Jack Johnson was worrying: Ike Clanton had been seen in town, supposedly attending a trial at the Pima County Courthouse. Whatever his excuse was for being there, Wyatt wasn't trusting him. And worse, Clanton had a companion along with him, a narrow and pale-eyed man who might be Frank Stillwell—"possum-like" folks back in Georgia would have called him, sneaky and mean.

But there was no sighting of Stillwell or Clanton anywhere near the train, so Wyatt cautiously let Virgil and Allie cross the train yard and go to supper at the Porter House Restaurant nearby—closely guarded, of course. What the other diners must have thought about the mourning-dressed couple hovered over by three heavily armed men, they didn't say, but a hush fell over the place and everyone ate in respectful, wary silence. Outside the restaurant, Wyatt and John Henry watched the shadows.

And so an hour passed and the train yard grew busy again. The railroad fireman filled the tender car with coal and water, the locomotive hissed and sighed sending out clouds of steam into the night, the conductor announced the Southern Pacific to California and called "All a'board!" for the westbound passengers. And still there was no sign of the assassins.

"Maybe they won't show," John Henry said. "Maybe they got wind we're here with Virg, and took off for home. Ike always was a coward."

"Ike maybe," Wyatt replied, "but not Stillwell. And if he's here, I'll find him."

He didn't have to say what he'd do to Frank Stillwell once he did find him. He'd already passed sentence on the man who had murdered his brother, and anyone else who'd helped him. After having spent his whole adult life defending justice, now Wyatt was ready to be judge and jury and executioner all by himself.

The crowd of passengers pressing toward the train may have been hiding Ike and Stillwell, but it also gave cover to Virgil and Allie as they made their way back from the restaurant.

"Pull your window shades down," Wyatt advised them as soon as they were settled on the railcar. "We don't want any more broken glass."

He didn't need to explain that with the darkness of night outside the railcar and the glow of gaslights inside, they'd be an easy target for a shooting. Then the porter passed through the car, taking tickets and signaling that it was time for those not traveling on to say their goodbyes. But Wyatt lingered.

"We'll be all right," Virgil said to him.

"I ought to send Warren on home with you."

"He won't stay there, if you do. He's got a venture streak in him, like the rest of us. It's a bad trait, I suspect."

"I suspect so."

Then Virgil reached toward his brother with his one good arm and gave him an embrace.

"You end this, Wyatt," he said, "and you live to tell the tale."

McMaster and Johnson were the first off the railcar, followed close by Warren, and they fanned out into the train yard, pistols drawn.

"They'll be lucky not to lose each other," John Henry commented as he and Wyatt followed them off the train and into a cloud of steam from the engine, "let alone find Stillwell in this. It's like lookin' into a fog, only darker."

But Wyatt wasn't listening—wasn't even standing by him anymore, taking off at a run along the tracks.

"Wyatt!" John Henry called, then broke into a run following after him.

He heard the scream before he could see what was happening, then the cloud cleared and he saw too well, even by moonlight. Ahead of him, Wyatt was standing face to face with Frank Stillwell, holding his shotgun against the man's belly.

"Drop the pistol!" Wyatt ordered, and Frank Stillwell did as he was told, his pale eyes wide with terror. "You killed my brother!" Wyatt said, and Stillwell mumbled something in reply.

"Are you confessing to me?" Wyatt said, "Are you making a confession? Say it then! Say you murdered Morgan Earp!"

"It wasn't me," Frank Stillwell said, "it wasn't me! It was somebody else, I swear! You ain't gonna shoot an innocent man, are you?"

"No, Frank," Wyatt said, "I ain't gonna shoot an innocent man," and for a moment something like relief spread over Stillwell's narrow face and he put his hands on the barrel of Wyatt's shotgun as if to push it away.

"But you're not innocent," Wyatt said. "You're guilty as hell." Then he let loose with both barrels, blowing Frank Stillwell wide open.

A heartbeat later Warren was there, running up behind John Henry and breathing hard. "You killed him, Wyatt!" he said in astonishment as Frank Stillwell wavered a moment before teetering to the ground, his guts spilling onto the dust. "You killed him!"

But before Wyatt could reply, John Henry's shotgun opened up and emptied into Frank as well. "No, Warren," he said evenly, "*we* killed him." Then he threw the shotgun to the ground and pulled out his pistol, firing a load into Frank's chest.

In a moment McMaster and Johnson were alongside, and John Henry said "Shoot him, boys. Let's give him a firin' squad."

For whatever else Wyatt Earp was, he was not a murderer, and he didn't deserve to bear the burden of Stillwell's killing alone.

Chapter Ten

Tombstone, 1882

They expected that the shooting would have brought some notice, the noise of it calling whatever law was around, but as things turned out no one paid any attention at all. For Tucson was having another kind of fireworks that evening, celebrating the lighting of the first gas lamps in town, and anyone hearing the gunfire would have imagined it was just part of the party. So it was morning before Frank Stillwell's bloody corpse was found alongside the Southern Pacific Railroad tracks, and by then Wyatt Earp and his posse were halfway back to Tombstone, having walked most of the night before flagging down a freight train headed to Benson.

But telegraph messages traveled faster than freights, and by the time the travelers reached Tombstone there was a wire from Pima County to Sheriff Behan, notifying him of the murder of his former deputy. And it was only because the telegraph operator was a friend of the Earps that the wire hadn't yet been delivered. The operator had been holding the telegram for half a day, waiting for some word from Wyatt, when John Henry arrived at the Western Union office with a telegram of his own to send. For though John Gosper was no longer directing the affairs of the Territory since the swearing-in of newly appointed Governor Edward Trittle, he would still want to know first-hand what was happening in Tombstone. John Henry just hoped his wire would reach Gosper before the press stories did—and that Gosper still had some influence with the government. But it was the wire for Sheriff Behan that was the more pressing matter.

"It says here you and Wyatt are wanted for the murder of Frank Stillwell," the Western Union operator said, as he handed the wire to John Henry. "I shouldn't even be showing you that, but I think a heap of Marshal Earp and not a hell of a lot of Deputy Stillwell."

"I don't suppose you can just lose this somewhere?" John Henry asked, knowing what the answer would be. A Western Union operator who didn't deliver the wires wouldn't be long in his job.

"Sorry, Doc," the operator said. "I got to give it to the sheriff soon. But I thought you and Marshal Earp ought to know about it first. For what it's worth Doc, I don't believe Wyatt would do such a thing."

"I didn't believe it, either," he said as he tipped his hat and turned to leave. It was heartening to know that Wyatt had such a staunch supporter, and disheartening to know that the man hadn't thought him equally incapable of murder.

Wyatt's plan was for the posse to stay together at the Cosmopolitan Hotel, for safety sake, while they decided on what to do next—though it was Johnny Behan who made the decision for them as soon as the wire from Pima County reached his hands.

"I'm here to arrest you, Wyatt," he said, as he met them returning to the hotel from supper, "you and the rest."

"On what charge, Johnny? I don't see a warrant in your hand."

"Warrant's on its way from Tucson. I got a wire here from Pima County that says you and your men killed Frank Stillwell."

"Is that so?"

"I got a wire, and I have come to see you about it."

"I'll see Sheriff Bob Paul about it, but not you. I have seen you once too many times already. Next time I see you, you'll be on the other end of the shotgun."

Johnny Behan reddened with anger. "Are you threatening me, Wyatt Earp?"

"No need to do that, Johnny. You're as good as dead already."

Then Wyatt turned on his boot heel and motioned his men to follow him, heading down Allen Street toward Smith's Corral and their horses.

Justice may have been served on Frank Stillwell, but he surely hadn't acted alone and his accomplices still needed to pay for their crime, and it was clear that Sheriff Behan wouldn't be the one to make them settle up. So Wyatt and his men left town but stayed near enough to catch wind of the inquest into the death of Morgan Earp, where the conspirators were being publicly named. The list was incomplete but not surprising: Frank Stillwell, his friends Pete Spence and Hank Swilling, a German by the name of Fritz Bode, and a Mexican called Florentino Cruz. It was the source of the accusation that was unexpected, the information coming from Marietta Spence, Pete's wife, who had overheard the men talking before and after the shooting of Morgan Earp. Pete had beaten her, she said, when he learned about her eavesdropping, and threatened to kill her and her mother both, and she was only telling the story so the law would protect her from her husband. And somehow it pleased John Henry's gentlemanly Southern soul to think that killing Pete Spence would save a lady from harm.

Wyatt knew all the men named in the inquest and where to find them, and he meant to track them down before they had time to disappear into the desert. So his posse camped that night near Watervale, then rode east the next morning toward Pete Spence's wood-cutting operation in the South Pass of the Dragoon Mountains. But they were disappointed to learn that Pete wasn't there, having ridden back into town ahead of them to turn himself in to the sheriff, taking his chances with Johnny Behan's easy law instead of Wyatt's revenge.

But Florentino Cruz wasn't as clever as Pete Spence and didn't comprehend that the fate that had taken Frank Stillwell was coming to take him, too. So while Pete made his cowardly run back to Tombstone, Cruz stayed on at the wood camp, cutting trees as though he had a whole life's work yet ahead of him.

They found him near the Chiricahua Road, working in a sunlit stand of poplars, and Wyatt called out a greeting in the few Spanish words he knew:

"*Buenos Diaz, Señor*," he said, and the man looked up pleasantly—until he saw who was talking him.

"*Qué quieres?*" he said, looking wary, and Wyatt turned to John Henry.

"Talk to him, Doc. Ask him what he knows about the murder of Morgan Earp."

"Why not just shoot him, and save yourself the time?"

"Could be he has some information we could use."

"That's Wyatt, always the law man," John Henry said, "even when you're an outlaw." Then he turned toward the Mexican and said in Spanish, "*You heard that Morgan Earp was murdered?*"

"*I heard of it,*" Cruz replied.

"*Did you hear what happened to the man who shot him?*"

"*I heard Frank Stillwell is dead.*"

"*And we're the men who did it,*" John Henry said. Then he drew his pistol and pointed it at Cruz. "*So one killer to another, what do you know about the murder of Morgan Earp?*"

The Mexican wavered a moment, his fingers flexing on the hatchet in his hand, as if he might use it as a weapon. But one hatchet wasn't much protection against five men with rifles and handguns, and he seemed to reconsider.

"*I didn't have nothing to do with it. I didn't have nothing against Morgan Earp. I was just the lookout. They paid me to keep my eyes open, that's all. So I keep my eyes open, in case anyone comes into the alley. But I didn't shoot nobody. I didn't kill nobody.*"

"What's he saying?" Wyatt asked John Henry.

"He says he was just the lookout. He says they paid him for his time."

"Who paid him?" Wyatt said, and John Henry turned to the Mexican again.

"*Who gave you the money?*"

The Mexican's answer came as a surprise. "*Johnny Ringo paid me,*" Cruz said. "*He came to the camp one night with Brocious. They said they had a job for me to do, that all I had to do was keep my eyes open and they would pay me. They said somebody important had a job that needed doing. They paid me just to keep my eyes open.*"

"Ringo and Brocious," Wyatt said, understanding that much at least, and John Henry nodded.

"He says they told him somebody important had a job for him to do."

"How much did they pay him?" Wyatt asked, and John Henry put the question to the Mexican.

"Twenty-five dollars," the man answered in English, then lapsed back into Spanish. "*They paid me to keep my eyes open. But I didn't kill nobody.*"

"So that's what a man's life is worth?" Wyatt said bitterly. "Twenty-five dollars?"

"He's a regular Judas," John Henry commented, "going to hell for a handful of silver."

"I give you the money back," the man said, struggling for the English words. "I get it for you! Let me go and I get it for you! Twenty-five dollars. I give it to you!"

"I don't want the money!" Wyatt said fiercely. "I want my brother! Can you buy me another brother for twenty-five dollars? Is that what a man's life is worth, twenty-five dollars?"

Then he reached into his saddle bag, and the man shrank and cowered as if another gun would be coming out against him. But instead of a gun, Wyatt pulled out his money purse and counted out twenty-five dollars in coins and tossed them to the Mexican. "How about twenty-five dollars for your life?" Wyatt said.

And as the Mexican, not comprehending, scrambled for the coins, Wyatt Earp lifted his rifle and blasted a bullet through the man's heart.

Hank Swilling and Fritz Bode were luckier than Florentino Cruz, being arrested for the murder of Morgan Earp instead of being hunted down by his brother. With the law in Tombstone being as corrupt as the cowboys, they'd likely get off without doing anything more than a week or two in jail. But if what the Mexican had said was true, there were other conspirators still roaming the mountains, and Wyatt wasn't leaving it to Sheriff Behan to bring them in. The fact that Behan had appointed Johnny Ringo to his own posse to chase down the Earps only made the hunt more interesting.

They learned about Behan's posse on their way back through Watervale, where they stopped just long enough for provisions and news before heading west toward the Whetstone Mountains. Now that they'd done a killing in Cochise County, they couldn't linger anywhere for long, and the Whetstones were known for hiding men who were hiding from the law. With luck, they could lose themselves there for awhile—and maybe find some outlaws, as well. As for Behan's posse, they'd be thrown off by some misinformation Wyatt left with the shopkeeper in Watervale, saying that he was taking his men northwest toward Kinnear, when they were really headed to Iron Springs on the south end of the range.

They added Texas Jack Vermillion as another hired gun at Watervale but left one man behind, as Wyatt charged Warren with carrying messages back to Tombstone. They were running low on funds and needed some quick cash, and Wyatt said he knew a few businessmen who might be willing to send it along by way of his brother. So against protests that the fight was just getting good and he was man enough to take it on, Warren stayed behind, and Wyatt's only comment, as they rode away, was, "I've lost one too many brothers already."

The Whetstones rose like a dark wall west of Tombstone, their jagged peaks as sharp as the cutting stone for which they were named. The foothills were covered with mesquite and scrub plants; the narrow canyons filled with hackberry and walnut trees; the few watering holes shaded by cottonwoods and sycamores and wild grape vines. There were herds of mule deer and antelope, packs of coyote and javelina, and enough cotton-tails to make rabbit stew every night. There were also enough caves and caverns to shelter most of the outlawry of the Arizona Territory. But while the Whetstones were a good place to go hiding, they were a bad place to go seeking, the narrow canyons too narrow, the watering holes too scarce. And without knowing every cave and cavern, a posse could get turned around or trapped and never make it out again.

Going into the Whetstones with a posse on their trail, especially one with Johnny Ringo who'd spent his share of time in those same mountains, might have seemed like a bad gamble—except for a bit of news Wyatt had gleaned in Watervale. For Curly Bill Brocious was in those mountains too, laying low while Wyatt's vengeance swept across the desert like a dust storm, and tracking him down was worth all the gamble. The only question was, where in that hundred-mile range of wilderness might he be? So they rode warily, shotguns loaded and ready.

The day was hot for March, the temperature already soaring to somewhere near ninety degrees, and by noon the men were taking off their suit coats and rolling their shirtsleeves. All but Wyatt, who kept his frock coat on, tails spread over his horse's flanks, saying he preferred the heat to the scratch of the wild grape vines. And soon, he said, they'd be at Iron

Springs where they could water the horses and rest awhile in the shade of the cottonwood trees.

It was a rest that John Henry hungered for, having spent too many days in the saddle and too many nights sleeping on the hard ground. Even with warm spring weather, the desert nights were cold and chilled him to the bone—leaving him coughing and choking again every morning, undoing the miracle of his cure at the Montezuma Hot Springs. But though Wyatt asked after his health, he didn't suggest slowing the hunt any—and how could he, with Behan now carrying arrest warrants and eager to serve them? And this time, there'd be no easy acquittal coming down from the court, only a verdict of guilty for the murders of Stillwell and Cruz. And that was the thing that most disturbed John Henry's rest—the nightmare he kept having of standing in the dark train yard in Tucson, pumping lead into Frank Stillwell. He'd done it to back up Wyatt, to make amends to Morgan, to right the wrongs of the wicked world around him, even. But noble as his reasons had seemed, he was beginning to feel a growing sense of unease at what he'd done, like Stillwell was haunting him somehow. And it was that, more than the morning chill that made him wake up sick every day. But Wyatt had no such nightmares, only a heroic resolve to finish a job, and John Henry was honor-bound to follow him.

They came to the springs in mid-afternoon, with Texas Jack as scout leading the way and Wyatt riding close behind him, followed by John Henry and the rest stretched out single-file along the narrow wooded trail. Ahead of them, Iron Springs glinted in the sun, a smallish pool of water surrounded by a muddy bank and a stand of cottonwood trees. Then something moved in the trees on the far bank, and John Henry shouted out, "Wyatt! Watch out!" For the movement in the trees glinted like sun on water, or like the steel of a gun, taking aim. And all at once the muddy bank was a commotion as a band of cowboys rose up, rifles and pistols flourished.

John Henry yanked back on the reins, turning his horse and nearly colliding with the horse and rider behind him as they all made for a retreat, with Texas Jack and Wyatt following fast while the shooting began. But when he finally slowed his mount and swung around in the saddle to look behind him, Wyatt wasn't there and neither was Texas Jack.

"Wyatt!" he hollered, to no reply, as he spurred his horse to a run and plunged back toward the springs, nearly stumbling over Texas Jack who lay pinned beneath his downed horse. He would have stopped to help him, but for what he saw at the water's edge: Wyatt standing beside his mount, the reins tossed over one arm and his shotgun in the other, taking aim across the springs at Curly Bill Brocious while a barrage of gunshots exploded all around him. Then Wyatt's shotgun jumped and a double load of buckshot slammed into Curly Bill, tearing him wide open.

The cowboy leader screamed in agony and fell forward into the water, turning it to blood, and his partners ceased firing for a stunned moment. Then the fusillade began again, and Wyatt reached for the rifle in his scabbard while John Henry pulled Texas Jack up onto his own horse.

"Wyatt! Get out of there!" he screamed as he turned his horse to retreat again.

But Wyatt stood his ground, pulling his pistol and emptying it into the woods across the river, while his horse spooked and reared in a fury of gunfire.

He should have been dead, shot to pieces by the cowboys. But somehow Wyatt managed to get astride his horse and ride to safety while the cowboys blazed away, with the only wound he had to show for it being a boot heel shot off and the tails of his frock coat torn to shreds by the gunfire. And John Henry knew then, if he had never known before, that Wyatt Earp was a hero worth following to hell and back.

There would be no more hiding in the Whetstone Mountains for them now, with another man dead and cowboys and lawmen both after them. So they rode back the way they'd come, stopping at Watervale just long enough to collect Warren and the cash he'd managed to obtain, before heading north toward the Dragoon Mountains. At Summit Station in the north pass of the Dragoons they crossed the tracks of the Southern Pacific Railroad, where Wyatt wanted them to board the train and head west to Benson and on to Tucson. His friend Bob Paul was sheriff there and would fight for their freedom, so he said. But John Henry didn't trust the law any more than he did the outlaws, and he had another plan in mind. North of the Dragoons, past the Galiuro Mountains and into the Sulfur Springs Valley was the ranch house of Henry Clay Hooker, a stone fortress in the middle of three hundred-thousand acres of private land, and a sanctuary even the Apaches hadn't been able to defile. And Hooker, he told Wyatt, had connections even higher than Sheriff Paul could claim.

But it was a hard ride to the Sulfur Springs Valley, two days and nights in the saddle with only a brief layover along the way, and by the time they arrived at the Sierra Bonita, John Henry was almost too tired to talk.

"Back for another respite are you, Dr. Holliday?" Henry Hooker said as he met them in the courtyard of his home, his Yankee accent now sounding comforting instead of irritatingly foreign as it had the first time they'd met. "I heard you boys have been busy down there in Tombstone. I presume this is the esteemed Marshal Earp?" he said, offering his hand up to Wyatt. "Rumor has it you've killed Curly Bill."

"Rumor gets around fast," Wyatt replied.

"Well, that's good work. I hope you'll keep it up and kill the rest of them as well."

"I plan to, once I get Sheriff Behan off our trail."

"We're hopin' you can offer us safe haven, for awhile," John Henry said, and Hooker smiled as though receiving guests for a holiday.

"You're more than welcome, gentlemen. I'm sure your horses would enjoy a rest, as well. I can loan you fresh mounts, if you'd like. I keep some of the finest saddle horses in the Territory, as you may have heard."

Hooker was just as John Henry remembered him: a calm of civility in an uncivilized world, seeming to be merely entertained by the arrival of eight trail-weary outlaws on his doorstep. But then, Henry Hooker was always happy for whatever amusement entered into his remote kingdom.

"Well then," he said genially, "let's get you all settled. I can offer beds in the house for Dr. Holliday and Marshal Earp, and cots in the bunkhouse for the rest of you. But there's always enough room at the supper table for everyone. I hope you all like beef and brandy."

While the men tended the horses and washed themselves for supper, John Henry and Wyatt met privately with Henry Hooker in his book-lined office, where his former bright demeanor became more businesslike.

"You're right about Sheriff Behan's posse following you," Hooker said. "My men spotted them this morning, past the south fence. They'll be here by breakfast tomorrow, I expect."

It was, as before, hard to fathom the immensity of Hooker's holdings—a ranch so large it would take a man four days to ride clear around it.

"I'll keep him off the best I can," Hooker went on, "but he may have a warrant to search the house. Until we're rid of him, you'll be safer away from here. There's a stone cottage on a ridge three miles west of here, toward the Galiuro. It's on a piece of the property I don't use for ranching so the hands don't know about it. I lived there when I first arrived in the Territory. I've kept it up since, as sort of a memorial to my younger days. Only the Apache know it exists."

"And the Apache won't go near the Galiuro on account of the hot springs," John Henry said, recollecting, and met a smile from Henry Hooker.

"That's right."

"We're obliged," Wyatt said, "but I don't want anyone to think that we're afraid of the law. I'd speak to any honest lawman, but not Behan."

"You'd be hard-pressed to find an honest lawman in these parts," replied Hooker. "The rustlers are in pocket with most of the authorities, as you surely know. Your best defense, under the circumstances, is to get out of the Territory as fast as you can."

"I'll leave when I'm done with my work, and not before," Wyatt said resolutely. "My brother was murdered, and I aim to bring the men who did it to justice."

"A noble aim, if justice were possible in this situation."

"I don't follow."

"Marshal Earp, I have been in the world a good deal in my days, and have seen much of both justice and injustice. And it seems to me that justice is either for all, or is not at all. If you can't take your vengeance without injuring innocent men, then there is no justice."

"What innocent men? You just said yourself there's no honest law in this country."

"I mean the men behind your vigilante efforts on the border. If you continue this fight now, with the newspaper-reading public paying avid attention, you may well shine a light on things that were meant to be done in the dark, in secret if you will. And that could, indeed, destroy the very cause of justice for which you have been paid to fight."

"I thought you were the man behind the vigilantes," Wyatt said slowly, his eyes narrowing. "I thought it was your money Doc was depositing to pay our way, yours and the Cattleman's Association."

"Our money, yes," Hooker said, "but not our fight alone. Suffice it to say that there are many parties interested in cleaning up the border, many good men whose only aim is to keep peace for the rest of us. Many good men with nothing to gain and everything to lose, should your work on our behalf become public. So while I applaud your desire to seek justice for your brother, I must warn you that continuing this fight now will only bring injustice for the rest of us. And what justice can you or your brothers have then?"

It was an eloquent speech, especially if one knew the men to whom Hooker referred. But without that knowledge—which Wyatt would never have—it likely made a weak defense.

"I appreciate the philosophy, Mr. Hooker, but it doesn't change my aim. I made a promise to my brother Morgan, and I intend to keep it. And to hell with anyone else."

"Colonel Hooker," John Henry said, beginning a defense of his friend, "Wyatt is just speakin' out of his grief . . ."

"And you wrote of this sad situation to your friend, Mr. Gosper?" Henry Hooker said, taking John Henry by surprise.

"I sent him a wire just before we left Tombstone," he admitted.

"That's what I surmised," Hooker said, then he opened the drawer of his roll-top desk, withdrawing a long envelope, and turned back to Wyatt.

"Marshal Earp, I have here a letter from Governor Trittle which arrived just today. He says he will be seeking remedy from the Federal Government and pardons for any man who has helped to quell the border difficulties. But pardons, he points out, take time to obtain. Which is why I suggest that once you are rested and refreshed and we've sent the Sheriff away, you make haste to leave this Territory. While the Governor can't issue a pardon, he can decline an extradition order if the local law desires to bring you back. But you've got to get out of Arizona first."

"And why would the Governor send this letter to you?" Wyatt asked, rightly confused, then he turned to John Henry with an angry rise in his usually tempered voice. "Was this your plan all along, in bringing us here? Did you send a wire here, as well, announcing our arrival?"

"He didn't have to," Henry Hooker replied. "And yes, this was the plan all along, and longer than you know. Believe me when I say that you aren't the only one seeking justice, Marshal Earp, and that your sacrifices have not gone unappreciated. We offer our deepest condolences on the loss of your brother."

And though Wyatt may have wanted to ask more, Henry Hooker stood up abruptly, ending the conference.

"And now, gentlemen, it's time to dine."

Hooker was done talking, but Wyatt wasn't done wondering, and he spent the supper meal watching John Henry the way one poker player watched another, measuring him. John Henry had been observed that way all too often, and had done plenty of the same himself, and he knew what was going on in Wyatt's mind. Why had John Henry sent a wire to John Gosper? And why would that wire elicit a reply from the newly made governor of the Territory? And what did Henry Clay Hooker know that he wasn't telling? But with Hooker at the head of the table and the rest of the chairs filled with Wyatt's posse, he couldn't ask those questions.

But after supper, when the rest of the men had gone to the bunk house to sleep and Wyatt lingered in the courtyard with a cigar, the questions came. John Henry did the best he could to answer without answering, knowing that by keeping his counsel he was protecting the men who could best protect them all. But Wyatt deserved some explanation, at least.

"You remember when I stayed behind in Prescott, when you and Virg went on to Tombstone?" he said, starting into the story at what was a sort of beginning.

"I remember," Wyatt said, taking a slow draw on his cigar while he waited to hear more.

"Kate was there with me. After she left, I took a room in the same house where John Gosper boarded, so he and I grew acquainted. He was Secretary to Governor Frémont then, and Acting Governor every time Frémont left the country, so he had an interest in the affairs of the Territory. Especially the situation down on the border. When I moved on to Tombstone, he asked me to stay in touch, keep him informed of doings there. So I started up a correspondence with him. I thought it might prove advantageous to have some connections with the Territorial government, that's all."

Wyatt took another slow draw, then spat onto the paving stones at his feet. "That's all?" he said. "What about Senator Fitch coming along all of the sudden as your legal counsel, best damned attorney in the whole Territory? Was that on account of your government connections too?"

"I don't know how he came to be there," he replied honestly. "I didn't ask for him. But I reckoned Gosper might have sent him, and I was grateful for his help. We'd have all hung by now, without him."

"I don't like operating without knowing what I'm in for," Wyatt said, "or who I'm in with. You should have told me about your correspondence with Gosper. I might have used his influence myself in chasing down these cowboys."

John Henry nodded, aiming at a look of chagrin. "You're right, Wyatt. I don't know why I didn't think to tell you. Things were busy, I reckon."

"Things are still busy," Wyatt said, and for a moment John Henry thought he had side-stepped having to say anything more. Then Wyatt flicked the ash from his cigar and gave him another long, appraising look. "So you wired Gosper from Tombstone," he said, "to tell him what?"

Now he had no need to give half-truths or leave anything out. "I told him the sheriff was a murderer and we killed his hired gun. I reckon he figured out the rest by himself."

Wyatt was quiet, considering. Then he took a last draw on his cigar and said: "Well, I suppose there's no going to Bob Paul now, or finishing what we started. Not when you've brought the whole government of the Territory down on our heads. And I would like to have finished off Ringo before I left Arizona."

"No reason you can't come back, once things quiet down."

"Once things quiet down," Wyatt said, repeating the thought. "You know they're saying I carry the head of Curly Bill in a flour sack, just to prove he's dead?"

"That's absurd," John Henry replied. "You don't need a whole flour sack to hold a man's head, even with a head full of hair like Curly Bill. Though I reckon you'd have enough space to add Ringo's head, once you get it."

Morgan, he thought, would have found that funny.

They stayed three days at Hooker's stone hideaway in the Galiuro, seeing neither cowboys nor Indians, with Wyatt chafing at the bit to fight Behan and his posse. But though he didn't fully understand the reasons behind Henry Hooker's counsel, he was wise enough to follow the cattleman's advice. So they cooled their tempers and their heels, and waited until Hooker sent word that Behan had been turned off their trail before they returned to the Sierra Bonita.

The lawman evidently hadn't gone easily, accusing Hooker of misinformation and downright lies when he wouldn't divulge the whereabouts of Wyatt and his men.

"You are upholding murderers and outlaws," Behan had told Hooker, and the Colonel didn't take the insult kindly.

"Damn such law and damn you and your posse!" Hooker said hotly. "They are a pretty set of fellows you have got with you, a set of horse thieves and cut-throats," then he spat at the ground beneath Ringo's horse.

Having gained no advantage at Hooker's ranch, Behan next rode north to Fort Grant where he went looking for Indian scouts to help track the Earps. But the Indians at Fort Grant would have nothing to do with a man Hooker had insulted, and the sheriff came back to the ranch just long enough to refresh his horses before heading back to Tombstone. He was empty-handed and over-spent, having tallied up a thirteen-thousand dollar expense bill with no prisoners to show for it, and would return to town a laughing stock. And John Henry couldn't resist adding to his injury by writing the tale in a letter to the Tombstone *Epitaph*, and closing with:

"Our stay was long enough to notice the movements of Sheriff Behan and his posse of honest ranchers, with whom, had they possessed the trailing abilities of the average Arizona ranchman, we might have had trouble."

Surely, Behan reading the letter would know that his quarry had been there at Hooker's ranch all along, watching him and laughing. And for John Henry and Wyatt, the ridicule was some small recompense for not being able to send Behan to hell with Curly Bill where he belonged.

Leaving Henry Hooker's refuge at the Sierra Bonita, they followed Behan's route north to Fort Grant where they received a much warmer welcome than had the sheriff and his outlaw posse. Colonel James Biddle, commanding officer of the camp, warned Wyatt that he had been shown warrants for the Earp party and would have to hold them, but insisted that they all come in for a bite of something to eat first. Then he instructed his orderly to leave fresh mounts at the gate and excused himself from the dinner table, leaving Wyatt's posse to ride out of camp with full stomachs and rested horses and not a single soldier following after them.

They were four days on the road from there, crossing through the mountains between Arizona and New Mexico and then across open desert and hardly resting for keeping watch all the time, before making it to Silver City. John Henry could have used a layover there to regain some of the strength that seemed to be failing him all at once, but there was no time as long as they were still within riding distance of the border and the cowboys. So they spent one uneasy night in the only hotel in town before leaving their horses at the local stable and buying stage tickets to Fort Cummings and train tickets from there north to Albuquerque. And it was only then that Wyatt finally ordered them to rest for a few days, while he reconsidered his plans and re-outfitted his posse.

Wyatt got the best of the respite, putting up at the home of a local merchant with whom he had some past acquaintance, while John Henry and the others camped just outside of town and out of sight of the townsfolk. But while they slept on the hard ground and Wyatt slept in a comfortable feather bed, John Henry didn't fault him for it. Wyatt was a hero, after all, and a better man than any of the rest of them, and probably deserved a better night's accommodations. But when he said as much to the others, recounting the way Wyatt had stood up to Curly Bill, untouched by a hail of gunfire like some ancient immortal, the men outright laughed at him.

"Damn, that warn't no God you saw standin' there, Doc!" said Texas Jack. "That was jest Wyatt in his steel vest, takin' aim. I'd have braved old Curly Bill too, if I'd been bullet proof. But who'd want to wear somethin' like that on a hot day in those Arizona mountains? Like to have sweat to death before the bullets came flyin'. And then Wyatt had on that frock coat in addition. I reckon he knew what he was gettin' into, and counted it as a precaution. You know Wyatt's careful like that."

And as John Henry thought back on that bloody afternoon when they were all in mortal danger, he remembered how they went in their shirt-sleeves for the heat while Wyatt kept his frock coat on, saying it would save him from being scratched by the brambles.

"Wyatt's careful, all right," added Sherman McMaster, "but mostly about hisself. I didn't notice him warning the rest of us to suit up."

"You got warned in cash," Warren Earp said. "Wyatt paid you for your trouble, and he'll pay you again, soon as he gets done dealing with this merchant."

"True, true," replied Jack Johnson. "Though seein' Curly Bill blown up was worth payin' for myself. But I don't mind takin' the money for goin' along."

But John Henry hadn't gone along for money, only as friend to Morgan and Wyatt both, and willing to put his own life on the line for their sakes. He'd have died defending Wyatt, if it had come to that—but would Wyatt have done the same for him?

He scarcely slept that night, pondering on the thought, and was the first one up the next morning, heading into town where he found Wyatt still at breakfast in the merchant's comfortable home.

"You're early, Doc," Wyatt said, wiping at his long mustache with a linen napkin. "Are you having breakfast instead of whiskey this morning?"

Wyatt may have meant the comment as a friendly jest and John Henry might have taken it as such in times past, but this morning he took it as an insult, adding to the injury he already felt.

"Hard to sleep late on the ground," he replied, "not that you care much about the comfort of your men."

"You're welcome to find a room in town, if you prefer," Wyatt said. "Nothing's stopping you but money."

"Which is what it's all about, is that so? You won't fight a man unless there's money in it, but you'll pay a man to do your fightin' for you. Except for me. Me, you didn't even bother payin', just took my fight like it was your due, like I owed you my life somehow."

"What the hell are you talking about?"

"I'm talkin' about the hell you put me through back there at the Iron Springs! Makin' me ride along with you unprotected while you went in there armed."

"We was all armed, as I recall. Wasn't a man there without a pistol and rifle at least, and you had a shotgun alongside as well. How much more armed did you need to be?"

"I'm not talkin' about arms, I'm talkin' about armor! Like you had on under your coat that day, accounting for why you wouldn't take that coat off. You said it was brambles you were avoiding, when it was a steel shirt you were hidin' underneath. No wonder you stood up to Curly Bill like you did, knowin' you were armored, while the rest of us were open targets. While I was followin' you like a dog, ready to be shot down for your sake! And you coverin' yourself in steel and not botherin' to tell me anything about it. You're no hero, Wyatt Earp! You're not even much of a man!"

John Henry stood there shaking as he finished his tirade, expecting something similar from Wyatt in return, a fight maybe, or apologies. But Wyatt did the unexpected, and answered him with a laugh—Wyatt who never laughed and rarely even smiled, said with amusement:

"Whoever said I was a hero? And why would I tell you about something you couldn't handle? You're not strong enough to wear steel, Doc. You can barely sit your horse some days."

John Henry felt the sting of Wyatt's words like a slap across the face, and his hand reached instinctively for his pistol. "Are you callin' me a coward, Wyatt?"

"I'm calling you what you are: a sick man. There's no offense in that, so you can forget challenging me to a duel."

But John Henry was offended, all the same. For as his Father had drilled the truth of it into him years ago, so he still believed: illness was weakness. And the one thing he feared the most was being thought weak.

Then Wyatt made matters worse by reaching into his pocket and pulling out his money purse, counting out coins and handing them to John Henry.

"Here Doc, get yourself a room in town, someplace quiet if you can find one. Get some sleep and you'll feel better about this. We'll be heading out of here in a few days, going north to Colorado, soon as I get us organized. I hear there's some good resorts there for consumptives."

Wyatt might as well as have called him *lunger* or put a bullet through John Henry's heart, finishing him off right there and then. And that was all it took to make up his mind.

"I don't need your money, Wyatt. I don't need anything from you. I can find my own way to Colorado. I used to live there, as you may recall. I reckon I still have some friends in Denver. I sure as hell don't have any here."

And Wyatt, who had never been fast with a reply, was too slow in answering now.

Chapter Eleven

COLORADO, 1882

"DAMN RAILROAD TRAVEL!"

John Henry wheezed out the words and put a handkerchief to his mouth, catching a bright foam of blood. Although he'd taken offense at Wyatt's words, he couldn't deny that the outlaw trail had taken a toll on him, and the long train ride north from Albuquerque had only added to his discomforts. And as the Santa Fe steamed across the Raton Pass between New Mexico and Colorado and down into Trinidad, he cursed the black smoke that seemed to be sucking the life out of him. What was the name of the doctor who'd treated him in this town before? Who was it that Kate had called when he was overcome with the altitude and the air? And where was Kate when he needed her now?

But Kate was gone, as Mattie was gone, far away and leaving him alone to care for himself. And thinking of Mattie, he thought of one place that he might go for help, a place that never turned anyone away and actually welcomed those seeking refuge. For in the Sangre de Cristo Mountains, on the Purgatory River, in the city named for the Holy Trinity, there would of course be a Catholic church somewhere.

There was a church, along with a school and a convent for the nuns who did the teaching, and when the Mother Superior saw the fevered face of the man the priest had sent over from the sanctuary, she took him in without questions, lodging him in the guest room kept up for visiting dignitaries. And John Henry, grateful for some rest at last, didn't trouble her with any answers.

But rest was slow in coming, as he coughed until his chest felt like fire, and he bloodied through all of his handkerchiefs and the toweling the nuns brought after that. Then, too worn out to even cough, he finally slept.

And dreamt, strange dreams brought on by that strange accommodation. He dreamt he was with Kate, who smelled of flowers and quinine, then of Morgan, playing billiards on a tabletop soaked with blood. Then Morgan turned into Wyatt, and the billiard cue in his hand turned into a pistol and he took aim at John Henry.

"Why, Wyatt?" John Henry asked him in his dream. *"What did I do wrong?"*

"My brother is dead," Wyatt said back to him.

"I thought we were brothers," John Henry said, but Wyatt turned cold blue eyes on him.

"My brother is dead," he said again, *"and you're the one that killed him."*

"No!" John Henry cried, the words tearing out of him. *"Not me! It wasn't me!"* But there was blood all over him, smeared on his face and filling his open hands, and he was standing in the train yard in Tucson and knew that he was a murderer. Then, panic and terror as a noose ringed around his neck, cutting off his breath.

He woke, gasping for air, and saw shadows in the room, ghosts in white who whispered and hovered over him. Then he slept again and dreamt of Mattie, wearing white like the ghosts. Wearing a wedding gown and veil? But where was he, if not standing beside her at the altar? Who was the groom who slid a ring onto her finger and called her his bride?

"I love you, Mattie," he said, *"I always have . . ."*

"Always . . ." she answered, then she joined with the ghosts and was gone.

He woke with a throat dry as the desert, and reached for a glass of water that stood waiting on a bedside table.

"The fever is broken," said the Sister who tended him. "And now, we must call for the sheriff."

He choked on the water. So this was sanctuary? The nuns took him in, then turned him over to the law as soon as he was healed?

"You tell Sheriff Behan he can go to hell, but I'm not goin' with him!"

"That's rough language for these good ladies," said a man's voice, "and the wrong sheriff, as well. They mean me, and I have no intention of sending you back to Behan."

The voice belonged to Bat Masterson, who stood smiling in the doorway, derby hat in his hand and a shiny new badge pinned to his stylish topcoat.

"You're sheriff here?" John Henry asked. Had he even known Bat was back in Trinidad?

"City marshal, actually, by a landslide in the last election, and recently appointed under-sheriff for the county, as well. Seems the citizens of Trinidad heard about my record of service in Dodge City and wanted some of the same for themselves. Which I am hard at work to supply. I keep an eye on who comes and goes, and keep the town safe. When the Sisters told me they had a stranger in their midst, I stopped by to see who that might be. And lo and behold, look who it was. Long time no see, Doc. I'd ask how you've been, but that's obvious."

"You know what's been goin' on down in Tombstone?"

"I heard of it. Bad news about Morgan, but not unexpected, with tempers what they are down there. Hard to lose a brother though," he added, remembering no doubt his own brother Ed who'd been shot down while serving as city marshal of Dodge. "And how's Wyatt?"

John Henry took another drink of water, throwing it back like a shot of liquor.

"He's plannin' his revenge, once things quiet down. He won't rest 'till Johnny Ringo's stretched out alongside Curly Bill. He'd take Behan along for good measure, if he could."

"That doesn't sound like Wyatt," Bat said. "At least not like the Wyatt I knew."

And though John Henry could have taken the opportunity to say how Wyatt had changed and become someone none of them knew, instead he found himself defending him. "He's just tryin' to make sense of it all," he said, which seemed to be enough for Bat.

"So what are your plans now? The nuns are happy to help a sick man, but they can't keep a healthy one in the convent."

"I reckon I'll find a poker game in town, and try my hand. Although I'm a little out of pocket these days, as you can imagine. My trunk and most of my things got left behind in Tombstone when we decided to go for a ride."

"I thought as much, when I found out you'd thrown yourself on the mercy of the nuns. Good hotels are more your usual style than the Sisters of Charity."

"Is that who they are?" he said, then more to himself than to Bat he added: "*Faith, hope, charity, these three: but the greatest of these is charity.*"

"What?"

"First Corinthians, the Epistles of Paul. My mother made me recite for her every night before I went to sleep. It still comes back, sometimes."

Bat shook his head. "I always did need a translator to understand you. Which is probably what makes you so good at gambling. You're inscrutable. But sadly, I won't be able to allow you into any of the games in this town."

"What are you talkin' about?"

"I'm sorry, Doc, but you seem to have a way of bringing trouble wherever you are, whether you mean to or not. And I can't have trouble coming to my town. I can't take a chance on the cowboys following you here and hurting innocent people in the crossfire. Besides, gambling is against city ordinance in Trinidad now."

John Henry laughed at that. "So what are you gonna do? Arrest me?"

"If I have to. But I'd rather you just left town."

"You're runnin' me out of Trinidad?" he said, disbelieving.

"Consider it a shove in a better direction. Pueblo, for instance, has plenty of games. And the law there is lenient enough, for a price. I'm going there myself next week to wager on a big prize fight. You should come along. I'll even loan you a stake until you win something on your own, just to prove my good intentions."

"Isn't prize fightin' illegal too? Won't that bother your conscience, kickin' me out of town for doin' the same as you're doin' someplace else?"

"I'm City Marshal of Trinidad. It's none of my business what goes on in Pueblo, unless I want to be in on some of it. So what do you say?"

"I never did fancy prize fightin'. It's too chancey. But I don't reckon I have much choice, do I?"

Bat smiled and put on his derby hat. "I knew you'd come to the proper decision, with a little persuasion. Now pack your things and move out of here before I charge you with loitering."

"You have a funny way of playin' with the law, Marshal Masterson."

"Let's say I'm practical about things."

Pueblo, Colorado was badly situated between high bluffs and the Arkansas River. Problem was, the Arkansas liked to flood every few years, overflowing its banks and exploring into the city. But though there was talk early on of moving the city in deference to the river, when the Denver & Rio Grande built a depot there for its narrow gauge railroad, Pueblo became permanent. So the Union Depot, with its Romanesque red sandstone walls and its mosaic tile floors and stained glass windows, seemed to represent the city's answer to the Arkansas: if the river really wanted to move the city, it would have a lot of work to do. And soon Union Avenue was filled with the usual business of a railroad town—hotels, restaurants, saloons, bordellos, all daring the river to rise again.

It was that defiant Pueblo attitude that brought prize fighting to town when the local law forbade it, and filled the newspapers with veiled stories of the coming fight. Since the match wasn't supposed to be happening at all, the location of the fight was kept secret—except that everyone in the sporting class, as well as law enforcement officers from all over southern Colorado, knew just where to find it.

The fighting ring—four stakes joined with rope around a twenty-four foot square of ground—was located far enough from town to require a short train ride, but near enough for the entire sporting community to attend. And with a $500 purse to the winning contender and hundreds more on the wagers, it was a fight every gambling man in Pueblo wanted to witness. There was something elemental about a sport wherein grown men pummeled each other senseless, the rules of frontier boxing being somewhat less than civilized, that drew blood-lust from the most genteel of an audience. So the crowd grew along with the anticipation, while the fight promoters had their own fight over who would referee the match.

Being referee for such an event meant being willing to take the abuse of the losing side, and with both sides armed and ready to continue the fight should the judgment go against them, the job was declined by everyone to whom it was offered. Which, of course, only raised the excitement level of the evening, with the audience taking bets on who would referee and too many men losing their stake before the real fight even began. Clearly, someone needed to fight or the attendees would be fighting amongst themselves, and that could end up being deadly.

John Henry watched it all with amusement and one hand on the pistol in his pocket. He'd put his own small wager on the match, betting on a silver miner from Leadville. Though as it turned out, even his small wager ended up being too much. For when no referee could be found and the audience howled for blood, one of the reporters covering the story suggested throwing a couple of dogs into the ring instead and letting them fight it out, to give his readers some kind of story at least. And blood being blood, the audience agreed to the trade and put their money on the dogs instead, and cheered as the curs tore into each other. Then, when the first two dogs were dead, the audience found another pair and threw them into the ring to add to the carnage.

It was a disgusting sight and not worth the money John Henry had invested in the fight, and he went back to town and a good bed at the Fariss Hotel to sleep off the memory of it. And come next morning, he was glad he'd gone to bed instead of following the rest of the sporting crowd from the fight ring to the continued merriment on Union Avenue. For as he sat at a late breakfast, drinking coffee and reading the *Pueblo Chieftain*, he was greeted with headlines of the "Prize Dog Fight" and a smaller police item about a midnight raid on the gambling houses and bordellos in South Pueblo. There'd been more than fifty arrests, so the paper reported, and if John Henry had gone along with the other sports, he'd have spent the morning hours in police court instead of reading the paper in the comfortable dining room of the finest hotel in town.

He was only able to afford such luxury because of the loan he'd taken from Bat Masterson before he left Trinidad, and which he needed to repay as soon as possible. So his first occupation, once evening came, would be to invest in a high-stakes poker game and make a quick profit. But until then he had time on his hands, and he considered how best to spend it. Should he take in a show at the new Tivoli Theater? Or should he visit the mineral baths and the barbershop in the hotel's basement? Or maybe he would travel out to the new "magnetic" springs the young desk clerk had boasted of.

"Clark's Magnetic Mineral Springs, yessir, they're famous around here. They say if you throw a knife into the water, it'll come out magnetized."

"And what use would there be for a magnetized knife?" John Henry questioned, trying not to sound too doubtful. Some mineral springs, like the Montezuma Hot Springs at Las Vegas, really did seem to have miraculous powers, but a knife-magnetizing spring seemed a little beyond belief.

"The springs cure illnesses too, lots of 'em," the lad said, seeming eager to show his town in a good light and himself as a worldly gentleman. "They have a pamphlet all about it down there at the bath house: *All diseases of the sexual or urinal organs yield readily to treatment by the use of the water alone,*" he quoted, then reddened at having said so, and John Henry gave a laugh.

"I'll remember that, next time I need help in the romance department."

"You can take the electric streetcar out to the springs. It runs right past the hotel every ten minutes. It's only a nickel for the fare. It's a popular ride."

"I reckon it would be," John Henry said. "And what do you know about the show at the Tivoli?"

The young man shrugged. "It's all right, if you like dramas. It's mostly serious. If you want to see a show, go over to the Comique. That's all music and such. And dancing girls, if you like those." And when his face reddened again, it was clear that the young man who had been able to quote the sexual benefits of the mineral springs liked dancing girls, too. Well, what was not to like?

So it was the Comique that John Henry chose for his afternoon's amusement, and found Miss Amelia Dean's performance to be worth the price of admission, even without the addition of the banjo music and a comic in blackface. The girls were always the best part of the entertainment.

It was late afternoon when he came out of the theater, and stood on the street to have a smoke before heading off to supper and a night of wagering.

"Excuse me," a man said, coming out of the theater behind him and brushing past, then stopping as if he'd suddenly recognized an old acquaintance. "Aren't you Doc Holliday?"

John Henry turned to look at a stout little man with bluish eyes and a bristle of red for a beard. And all he could think, trying not to laugh at the thought, was that he'd just found a leprechaun. "Have I had the pleasure of your acquaintance?"

"Hell, yes!" the man said, "don't you recall? Why, you saved my life one time in Santa Fe, got the testimony right here to prove it." And with embarrassing swiftness, the little man pulled down his trousers to show a scar across the top of one naked hip. "That's where the bullet went, which would have gone worse if you hadn't been there. That was one clean shot you got, Doc, killing that Mexican before he got better aim. I owe you my life, and I have sworn to repay the debt. And now, here we are running into each other in Colorado, and me knowing something that could turn around and save your life. So what are the odds of that?"

"Mighty slim," said John Henry, "as I have never been in Santa Fe, other than passin' through on the train a couple of weeks back. And I don't recall bein' in any kind of gunfight while I was there, not to mention which that scar is too old for such a fresh wound. So I thank you for the honor, but believe you must have me confused with someone else."

"Well, a train is just what I'm here to tell you about," the man said, not letting go of the conversation but pulling his trousers back on, at least. "I met a man on the train who is looking for you, and swears he will shoot you down when he finds you."

"Is that so?"

"That's so. I suppose you know a man named Frank Stillwell?"

Odd as the man was and probably deranged, he had John Henry's full attention.

"I knew a man named Stillwell," he said carefully. "He was a stage robber and a murderer. But he's dead now, so I hear."

"Well, the man I met is none other than Frank Stillwell's brother Josh on his way to find you, for he says that you killed his brother, and here I have found you first. What are the odds of that?" he said again, and John Henry decided that the man must, indeed, be deranged. But what if Stillwell really did have a brother and that brother were looking for him? Or what if this odd little man were the very same Josh Stillwell himself, a misshapen fruit fallen from the family tree?

"I don't know why this Stillwell would be lookin' for me," he said, confessing nothing. "I know that Frank Stillwell is dead, but I do not know that I had anything to do with his death."

The little man snorted, "I'm not accusing, I'm just giving information by way of repaying a debt. But if you don't care to have your life saved like you saved mine in Santa Fe . . ."

"I told you, I have never been in Santa Fe, other than passin' through. And I do not remember savin' your life there, or even meetin' you for that matter. And I assure you, I would have remembered that. But I did know Frank Stillwell, and it might be of interest to me to know if he had a brother anywhere hereabouts."

It was the perfect opportunity for the man to introduce himself as the very same Josh Stillwell, ready to take revenge for the murder of his brother. And in case he did, John Henry let the roll of tobacco slip through his fingers, ready to reach for his pistol. But the man passed the chance at revenge, and said as if greatly offended:

"He has a brother all right, just like I said. And I met him on a train, just like I said, and he was looking for you, just like I said. But where he is now, I couldn't say. Not knowing I was going to run into you, I couldn't very well tell him the same."

"So what good is this information to me?" John Henry asked, growing frustrated. What good was a warning that didn't warn? Was he supposed to watch for this supposed Josh Stillwell behind every rock? Then the man made an offer that may have been his intention all along.

"Tell you what, how 'bout I keep an eye out for Stillwell in exchange for a little something to pay me for my efforts? Five-hundred dollars, let's say. Tit for tat, so to speak, for me saving your life after you saved mine. That would make us about even, don't you think?"

But John Henry just laughed, having finally found the cause of the confrontation. "I think you are a poor extortioner! First you make up a story to get my attention, then you make up a threat to go along with it. And all I have to do is pay your exorbitant price to be done with you? I wouldn't buy you a drink!"

"Are you telling me no?" the man asked, his face growing as red as his scraggly beard.

"I am telling you to leave me alone. I won't pay your protection money, even if there were something you could protect me from. Which I highly doubt. Good-day, Sir."

But as he turned his back, ending the absurd conversation, the man hollered after him: "You'll be thinking about that again, Doc Holliday. You'll be wishing you'd dealt better with me. You'll be ruing the day you turned down an offer from Perry Mallen."

Chapter Twelve

THE PRIZE FIGHT IN PUEBLO NOT HAVING AMOUNTED TO MUCH, Bat Masterson determined to travel on to Denver for the bigger purses on the horse races there, and invited John Henry to go along. And though he was just settling into the sporting life in South Pueblo, John Henry readily agreed to the invitation. He hadn't believed most of what Perry Mallen had told him, but he still found the encounter unnerving. Bad enough that Frank Stillwell might have left a brother behind to avenge him, without crazies coming out of the woodwork to collect on the deal. And with such men roaming around Colorado, John Henry felt safer in the company of old friends—and especially old friends who were lawmen.

He'd had friends in Denver once too, but that was when he was calling himself Tom McKey and working as a Blake Street Faro dealer. He'd lived a whole lifetime since then and it probably wouldn't do him any good to resurrect Tom McKey now, after he'd left town on a skipped court date and never looked back. But the place felt familiar, and just knowing he knew people there made him feel more comfortable, some-how.

And since it wasn't Tom McKey who was returning to Denver, on the run after shooting a Buffalo Soldier and soon to be running again, he felt no need to hide himself the way he'd done before. Besides, he had nothing to hide himself from in Colorado, with the troubles of Tombstone far behind him and the best men in the Territorial government working on his behalf. Other than the odd run-in with the mad Mallen in Pueblo, he felt comfortable enough in his new surroundings—even though the Denver he found himself in was remarkably changed since his last visit there. In the six years since he'd left town, the city had polished itself to a shine with the profits from the silver mines in the mountains to the west. In towns like Silverton and Silver Cliff and Leadville, the money was coming up out of the ground almost too fast to spend, though the new Colorado millionaires were doing their best to spend it—like Horace Tabor who'd almost lost his shirt before happening on the Matchless Mine and now had more than enough to spoil his beautiful young mistress, Baby Doe, and Denver too. Baby Doe got a pretty mansion with a fine carriage lined in blue satin to match her eyes and a team of black horses to pull her wherever she wanted to go, and Denver got a new Opera House and a whole block of city buildings to go along with it. Then Horace Tabor, having still more money to spend, built a grand exposition hall for his first annual National Mining and Industrial Exposition, promised to best the World's Fair and bring the whole world to Denver's door.

John Henry arrived in town on a warm May afternoon and checked into the new Windsor Hotel, another of Horace Tabor's investment projects. Tabor had bought the building for a half-million dollars, then put another quarter-million into making it the most lavish hostelry in the west, with French diamond dust mirrors, Havilland china, English furniture, and a full mile of fine Brussels carpeting. Then, as a memorial to the source of his wealth, Horace had three-thousand silver dollars embedded in the floor of the basement saloon. Like all fine hotels, the Windsor catered to gentlemen, giving them a separate entrance from the women and children so they could easily access the bar and billiard room, and a Gentlemen's Reading Parlor with the latest newspapers and a boy to fetch smokes from the basement humidor. There were three dining rooms, a floating ballroom with a walnut floor suspended over steel piano coils, an Otis Steam elevator that rose all the way to the Mansard-roofed fifth floor, and elegantly appointed sleeping rooms with marble fireplaces, private baths, hot and cold running water, and shiny brass gaslights. There were even telephones in a few rooms, thanks to the forest of telephone wires that stretched across the street from the Colorado Telephone Company housed, of course, in the Tabor Block office building.

The Windsor was pricey accommodations, but settling himself into a fine hotel meant he'd brush shoulders with the finer men in Denver society—men who had plenty of money to spend on a friendly game of cards, along with information on other investment opportunities. For though he'd lost his stake in the Last Decision Mine in Tombstone, he hadn't lost his interest in silver mining and the money it could make. So as soon as he unpacked his valise and treated himself to a hot bath and a fresh suit of clothes, he sent a message to Mr. John Vimont, a Leadville mining speculator who happened to be checking into the Windsor at the same time he signed the register, and asked if they could meet for a drink later in the evening. Then, feeling flush and ready for a prosperous few hours, he hailed a horse-drawn cab and took a ride out to the exposition fairgrounds to look things over.

The National Mining and Industrial Exposition wasn't set to open until the beginning of August and the grand exposition hall was still under construction, but it was already impressive: a great stone, brick, iron, and glass gallery modeled after the National Museum in Washington and surrounded by forty acres of park land. Inside, the gallery would host displays of mineral wealth and mining machinery from all thirty-eight states and eight western territories, showing the world what treasures America had to offer and hopefully inviting foreign investments. But the more immediate treasure was the harness racing facility inside that forty acre park, where visitors to the exposition could bet some of their silver and gold fortune on the horses. The racing track was already open to the public and drawing sporting men from all over Colorado, and John Henry wanted to see where he'd be placing his bets on the upcoming races.

He also wanted to see just what this harness racing was all about, before betting on it. For much as he'd been raised on horseback and had seen plenty of men race their horses for wagers, he'd never seen the kind of citified racing that had taken over Denver. He hadn't admitted his lack of education on the matter to Bat, when he was invited to attend the harness races—he'd just nodded and said he'd be happy to go along and take some money from the sporting men in the Queen City. But he was smart enough to know that just because all race horses wore harness didn't make all horse races harness races, and he wasn't going to admit his ignorance about the particulars when race day arrived. Every sport had its peculiarities and a smart sporting man made sure he knew them before wagering.

There'd been horse races in Tombstone, of course, where men showed off their saddle horses in a one-on-one straightaway contest. Wyatt had won a few races there, as had his brother Virgil before the cowboys' bullets crippled his arm and ended his riding career. But these harness races were something else entirely—instead of a man mounted on his animal, the rider rode behind in a two-wheeled cart while the horse did a dainty two-step trot called a pace. It wasn't just speed that won a harness race, but form as well. The pacer lifted right front and right hind leg, then left front and left hind leg, the legs hobbled together to keep the horse from breaking stride.

"But how do y'all pick a winner, before he races?" John Henry asked the manager of the race course, as he stood at the newly planted fence and watched a workout session. It was a glorious day for being outside, the sun bright overhead and a trifling breeze, and he was enjoying the weather as much as he was enjoying watching the horses run.

"Pedigree, mostly," the manager said, his eyes on the track, "and watching the exercise, like you're doing now. The best pacers come from a long line of the same, like Hambletonian, come down from Henry Astor's Messenger. That was the first of the lot on this side of the Atlantic. We've got a grandson of Hambletonian coming to the track next week. You'll want to put your money on him, no matter who else is racing."

"So where's the strategy?" John Henry asked. "Has to be something left to the jockey."

"Ah!" said the manager with a smile, "that's where the fun of the sport comes in! Watch for when the race nears three-quarter mile, and you'll see how the drivers go for position—they'll fight to take the lead early, then circle the field, then move up on the rail to keep the others riders out. Then they go for broke to the end. Harness racing is fastest in the last quarter, not like thoroughbred racing. Makes the finish hard to decide sometimes, which makes it all the more exciting."

And all the more risky for wagering, John Henry decided, though he'd be willing to put some money on that horse with the good bloodline. Leave the rest of the racing to Bat Masterson, for himself he still preferred a good game of cards—which he found as soon as he returned to the city and the familiar saloon district west of 16th Street. This was the Denver of Tom McKey's memory, where he'd spent his nights dealing Faro at Babb's Variety House and his days sleeping in a dingy room over Long John's saloon, with only occasional forays into the card rooms of fine hotels like Barney Ford's Inter-Ocean. Now the Inter-Ocean Hotel had been eclipsed by the more luxurious Windsor, and the new palace of gambling was Elitch's Arcade, and John Henry was glad to be moving in that better society. Even in the sporting community there were class distinctions, and Doc Holliday was considerably above the world where Tom McKey had lived. Tom would never have had lawmen for friends, for instance, or spent an evening sitting at poker with the likes of Bat Masterson, who had also found his way to the Arcade.

Bat's conversation was mostly about the coming races, which meant that his attention wasn't on the cards the way it should have been, and that turned out well for John Henry. And by suppertime, he was feeling flush enough to pay back the loan Bat had made him in Trinidad, and offer to treat him to a meal, as well—an irony not lost on the sheriff, who said that as long as he was actually paying for the food himself he might as well make it filling. So two beef steaks, half a roast spring chicken, and an apple and rhubarb pie later, Bat was a little heavier in the belly and John Henry was a little lighter in the pocket but still showing a profit for the evening, and he headed back to the Windsor Hotel for his meeting with the mining speculator from Leadville.

It was a short two blocks walk to the Windsor, up Larimer Street from the corner of 16th to the corner of 18th, but he'd only gone a few steps when his way was blocked by three men who appeared out of a darkened doorway.

"I have you now, Doc Holliday!" one of the men said. "Throw up your hands!"

In the new-fallen darkness John Henry couldn't see the men's faces, but there was no mistaking the glint of gunmetal on two revolvers. But as he went for his own pistol he remembered that it was back in his hotel room, abiding the Denver gun ordinance, and he had no defense when the other two assailants yanked his arms behind him and clasped handcuffs around his wrists.

Perry Mallen was a madman, all right, having followed John Henry from Pueblo to Denver, and there swearing out a warrant for his arrest—which the Arapahoe County Sheriff's office honored by sending two armed policemen along with him to do the arresting. And even when he had John Henry in hand, hustled off to the Sheriff's office before being remanded to the County Jail, Mallen kept his pistol aimed on his prisoner.

"You can drop that," John Henry said angrily, "I'm not heeled."

"You killed my partner, you blood-thirsty coward," Mallen said, "and I would have taken you at Pueblo if the men I'd had with me had stood with me. But you won't get away from me again!"

"Nobody is tryin' to get away from you," John Henry said. Then, disgusted, he turned to one of the officers who had taken him in. "I don't know what this man is talkin' about, and I doubt very much even he knows."

"You can tell that to the judge," the officer said. "This ain't no court of law."

"And how long do you intend to keep these cuffs on me?"

"Long enough," Perry Mallen said, pushing his pistol at John Henry.

"Why is this man armed?" John Henry said, again appealing to the officers, "I don't see a badge on him."

"That's official police business and none of yours," the officer replied, "so you can keep your complaining to yourself."

"Is it customary in this country to deny a citizen the right of speech?" he fumed. "Is it right? Is it just?"

But his words made no headway with the officers, and Perry Mallen smiled over his pistol sights.

"I can expose this man as a fraud!" John Henry said in desperation, "I can show you he has no reason for bringin' me here, I can show—"

"You can show the judge," Sheriff Spangler said, joining the group and handing over a document to his officers. "Take him to the County Jail, boys, and watch out for reporters. Seems we've got a famous prisoner here."

Although he'd had plenty of trouble with the law in his life, he'd never before been arrested for something he hadn't done. And he'd never been in handcuffs.

Bat Masterson arrived at the jail at three in the morning, along with an attorney and a writ of habeas corpus ordering Sheriff Spangler to have his prisoner in court within the day.

"Like I said, trouble seems to just naturally follow you," Bat remarked, using his position with the Las Animas County Sheriff to secure a private interview with the prisoner. "Though this time, it seems the trouble was waiting for you. What do you know of this Mallen character?"

"Nothin' more than what he's told me, which is all a delusion, I've no doubt. I only met him last week, down in Pueblo. He accosted me outside the theater and insisted I'd saved his life in Santa Fe, and he was determined to return the favor."

"Seems an odd bit of life-saving, having you arrested for murder."

"I reckon I disappointed him, not acceptin' his offer. He wanted five-hundred dollars to protect me from a man he claimed was trailin' me. I thought it was pricey."

"Five-hundred dollars? That's an interesting coincidence."

"How so?"

"That's the same purse Behan is offering for your apprehension, along with five-thousand more for all of you taken together."

"So you think Mallen is a bounty hunter?"

Bat nodded. "He probably thought he'd make the money easier by guarding you. Did he make mention of being a sheriff in California?"

"I don't recollect that."

"Well, that what he's calling himself. Says he was sheriff of Los Angeles County when you murdered his partner over a card game in St. George, Utah. Or so the arrest warrant says."

"I've never even been in Utah!"

"That's just the start of it. Mallen says he failed to catch you there, and he's trailed you for seven years since, from the Indian Territory to Tombstone. He claims you were the leader of the cowboys and killed six men single-handedly in Tucson, and he means to make you pay."

"I reckon I should have given him the five-hundred dollars."

"It's a ridiculous story, of course, but it won't go away until the judge hears it. And I'm more concerned with what happens after that."

"What do you mean?"

"I mean this bounty hunter's story is just a ploy to bring you in. It doesn't matter if it's a pile of buffalo shit. Now that he's got you, he'll let Behan know—and Behan can bring charges that will stick. It's too bad you didn't stay with Wyatt. You'd have been safer up in the Black Canyon country, laying low."

"Where?"

"Up in the Gunnison," Bat said, "west of Pueblo." And when John Henry looked quizzical, he added, "I thought you knew where Wyatt was . . ."

John Henry hesitated, not wanting to explain the situation. But this wasn't the time for pride, not when he needed all the friends he could get, and he said with a sigh: "I haven't heard from Wyatt since I left Albuquerque. We had somethin' of a fallin' out there."

"Well, this would be a good time to mend fences, in case you need a place to go when I get you out of here. Seems Pueblo has a claim on you for stealing four-hundred dollars from Charley White, and I intend to bring you there to answer the charge. That will spring you from here, at least."

"What are you talkin' about? I don't even know a Charley White."

Bat smiled as he carefully placed his derby hat back on his neatly macassar-oiled hair, "You do now. And in the meantime, start talking to the press."

Bat's hastily concocted plan, the best he could do under the circumstances, was to bring another charge against John Henry accusing him of petty larceny in Pueblo, and insisting that the court consider the Colorado claim before another coming from Arizona Territory. But such legal maneuvering would take a few days, assuming it even worked, and all John Henry could do was try to stay calm in the confines of the Arapahoe County Jail and tell his story to every reporter who came to call. For as Bat pointed out, though the reading public had no influence in a court case, the voting public did—especially in an election year like 1882.

The papers were more than happy to take an interview with such a notable prisoner as Doc Holliday, late of the Arizona Territory and the already famous gunfight at the OK Corral. For the story that had gone by wire from Tombstone to San Francisco had been reprinted around the rest of the country, as well, and there likely wasn't a paper in America that hadn't headlined the street fight and its bloody denouement. Now the capture of Doc Holliday became an even bigger story—especially when Perry Mallen's fantastical charge was followed up by another naming John Henry Holliday in the murder of Frank Stillwell in Tucson.

The second warrant was personally carried to Colorado by Bob Paul, the sheriff from Tucson where the killing had taken place, though John Henry would have thought Paul more friend than foe and not likely to bring such bad tidings. But Paul had his reasons for playing messenger.

"Behan wanted to come himself," Sheriff Paul said, when he stopped in to see the prisoner. "But you know without my saying how that would have turned out. Word is, the cowboys have all deserted Tombstone and are taking to the road, getting ready for a welcoming party. Not that you'd like the welcome they'd give you."

"But how could Behan bring a warrant from Pima County? That's out of his jurisdiction."

"That's right, but he made a play for it anyhow, claiming Stillwell was his deputy and it was his duty to see justice done. The courts thought otherwise, so here I am."

"You couldn't have just gotten lost along the way or misplaced the paperwork?" John Henry said, with only faint sarcasm. It seemed harsh to him that having escaped from Arizona with the Earps, their old associate would be willing to bring him back again.

"Somebody was going to do the job, and I reasoned it might as well be me, so folks don't say justice isn't honored in Tucson. But the warrant's only a technicality. Until the governor sends an extradition order, you're safe here in Colorado."

"So you're just here for show?"

"I'm here to do my job, nothing more, nothing less. But I'm happy to leave it as such, and leave you be. If the governor wants you, he can come calling for you himself. But my guess is he won't want you back. The Earp gang has caused him enough grief already."

John Henry couldn't dispute that point, for there'd been far too much grief all around. Gosper's plan to protect the border had been effective, but costly. But there was a new governor in the Arizona Territory now who might not have much sympathy for the former administration's hired guns.

"So supposin' Governor Trittle does sign an extradition?" he said, posing the question he didn't really want answered.

Bob Paul shrugged. "Then I'll have to take you back. That's the law. But I'll do my best to protect you from the cowboys and get you back to Tucson to stand trial, if it comes to that. You'll remember how I saved that stage coach when Billy Leonard's gang tried to hold it up? Got the treasure and the stage both safe to Benson in spite of the fight."

John Henry did remember, but remembered as well that two men had died that night and his friend Billy had died not long after. And that kind of assurance didn't make a man feel too secure.

The court hearing that should have happened within a day of his arrest was postponed a full week while the judge recovered from a sudden illness and John Henry languished in the Arapahoe County Jail. He slept fitfully, he ate poorly, and even the weather seemed to have a malaise, with a steady rain that obscured what little sunlight might have snuck into the jail cell. The whole world looked gray and dismal, like his chances would if the Governor of Arizona signed an extradition order for his return. So he took what chance he did have and followed Bat's advice in speaking to every reporter who came to call, like the young writer from the *Denver Republican* who sat quietly taking notes and only occasionally interrupted with questions.

"The men known as cowboys are not really cowboys," John Henry told him, starting at something like the beginning of the story. "In the early days the real cowboys, who were wild and reckless, gained a great deal of notoriety. After they passed out their places were taken by a gang of murderers, stage robbers, and thieves who were refugees from justice from the Eastern States. The proper name for them is rustlers. They ran the country down there and so terrorized the country that no man dared say anything against them and will not until some respectable citizen is shot down, when the people will rise and clean them out, as they did at Fort Griffin, where twenty-four men were hung on one tree when I was there. The Tombstone rustlers are part of this Fort Griffin gang. Trouble in Tombstone first arose with them by the killing of Marshal White by Curly Bill. Marshal White fell into my arms when he was shot. The trouble since then is familiar to all."

"What did Perry Mallen have to do with the Tombstone troubles?"

"Nothin' that I know of, other than bounty huntin'. From what I know of him, he is a crank. But one thing which Mallen tells gives him away badly. He said in your paper that he was standin' alongside Curly Bill when the latter was killed. If that is true, then he was with one of the worst gangs of murderers and robbers in the country. As for Mallen's claim that I killed his partner in Utah, at the time I was supposed to be doin' that killin' I was here in Denver, dealin' for Charley Foster in Babb's house, where Ed Chase is located now."

"What do you know of the killing of Frank Stillwell, for which you are also charged?"

He paused, carefully choosing his words.

"I know that Frank Stillwell was a stage robber and one of Morgan Earp's assassins, but I do not know that I am in any way responsible for his death."

His answer, though meant to be obscure, was also true. Although he had emptied his pistol and his rifle both into Stillwell's body, so had the rest of Wyatt's posse, and there was no telling which of them had actually done the killing. It had been a firing squad that night, backing up Wyatt, and none of them could claim the death—which was how it was meant to be.

"Do you apprehend trouble when you are taken back?" asked the reporter.

"I do, as soon as I cross over into that Territory. We hunted the rustlers, and they all hate us. John Behan, Sheriff of Cochise County, is one of the gang and a deadly enemy of mine, who would give money to have me killed. It is almost certain that he instigated the assassination of Morgan Earp. Should he get me in his power, my life would not be worth much."

"But Sheriff Paul of Tucson will take you to that place, will he not?"

"Yes, and there lies my only chance for safety. I would never go to Tombstone alone. I'd make an attempt to escape right outside this jail and get killed by a decent man. I would rather do that than be hung by those robbers there."

"Cannot Paul protect you?"

"Paul is a good man, but I am afraid he cannot protect me. The jail there is a little tumble down affair which a few men can push over, and a few cans of oil thrown upon it would cause it to burn up in a flash, and either burn a prisoner to death or drive him out to be shot down. That will be my fate." And staring out into the rain, he said: "If I am taken back to Arizona, that is the last of Holliday."

While John Henry was talking to the papers, the papers were checking up on Perry Mallen, who was turning out to be nothing that he said he was. He claimed to be a sheriff from Los Angeles, California; he was in reality a shyster from Akron, Ohio. He claimed to be single; he was actually married to three women in three different states all at the same time. He claimed to be avenging his murdered partner; he was really hoping to collect a rich reward for the capture of Doc Holliday. And as far as anyone knew he had never been in a gunfight in Santa Fe, New Mexico. So no one was surprised when the judge, returning to court after a week's illness, quickly dismissed Mallen's equally questionable claims against Doc Holliday and warned him to get out of town before he found himself in the County Jail.

But the second warrant for John Henry's arrest, the one carried by Sheriff Bob Paul of Tucson, couldn't be so easily set aside. So Judge Elliot had no choice but to remand the prisoner back to the County Jail to await the arrival of the extradition order from Arizona.

John Henry's lawyer, hired for him by Bat Masterson the night he was arrested, was Colonel John T. DeWeese of the firm of DeWeese and Naylor, assisted by attorneys from Decker and Yonley, so no one could say that he wasn't well represented. The two firms were the finest Denver had to offer, and John Henry was as confident as the circumstances would allow in following their advice. But when DeWeese came to his jail cell the day after the Judge's hearing with a legal proposal, he wasn't sure how to respond.

DeWeese was a former military man, brevetted Major General by President Andrew Johnson at the end of the War before turning to a career in the law, and he still carried himself with that authoritative air. When Colonel DeWeese spoke, men listened and followed orders, and even the jail guard scurried away when DeWeese said he needed to speak to the prisoner privately.

He didn't waste any time getting to the point.

"Judge Elliot called me to his home last evening," DeWeese said, "on a matter too confidential for the courtroom. A matter which has to do with you and Mr. Perry Mallen."

"I thought we were through with him. What fantasy is he chargin' me with now?"

"Nothing new, but Judge Elliot did some inquiring about the five-hundred dollar bounty Mallen was aiming to receive for turning you in. Seems that was just part of the reward: five-hundred for you, with another five-thousand for the entire Earp posse."

"What of it?"

"As I said, Judge Elliott made some inquiries and found that the bounty was indeed offered by Sheriff Behan and his associates as he believes the entire posse is guilty of the same crime for which you have been charged. But though he'd rather have all of you back together, he'll take you piecemeal if he has to. Hence the five-hundred dollar reward for you alone."

"And I thought he just favored me personally," John Henry remarked. "How disappointin' to find out otherwise."

"Which is just the point," DeWeese said, "and to your great advantage."

"I don't follow."

"It's simple. If Arizona wants all of you but will settle for one, they might be persuaded to take the rest and let you alone."

"You mean make a deal? Trade me for the Earps?"

"That's just what I mean, and what the Arizona authorities will likely be willing to accept."

"And why is Judge Elliot so eager to deal with the Arizona authorities? Seems like it's no loss to him either way, whoever gets sent back. It's all just paperwork and jail food, as far as I can see."

"That would be true in any other year, but this is election year in Colorado, along with the rest of the country. The judge would like to keep his courtroom past this coming November, and ending this case well would look good for him. And for the rest of us, of course. You may have noticed how much publicity your arrest has generated. Why, you're a national celebrity now, Dr. Holliday. There will be thousands of newspaper readers cheering at your release."

"And thousands of voters ready to thank the courts that saved me?"

"Precisely," DeWeese said with a nod.

"So what do I have to do to secure this prize? I'm a little constrained these days, being behind bars and all."

DeWeese gazed at him steadily. "All you have to do is tell us where your friends the Earps are hiding out."

"You want me to turn them in?" he said, incredulous.

"Not quite. There's no warrant for their arrest, as there is for yours. But it might be a bargaining point for your release if we knew where to find them. As your attorney, it's my obligation to make you aware of all the possibilities of your case. And I should remind you that if an extradition order does arrive, your case will move from the County Court to the Governor's office, and we'll have no control of the matter at all. As your attorney," DeWeese said again, "it's my obligation to keep you informed—and alive, if possible."

"I would like to speak to Marshal Masterson," John Henry said, knowing Bat would understand the legalities of the situation. Though the judge had not yet honored his invented charge from Pueblo, Bat was still working on that angle as well.

"I'm afraid Marshal Masterson has left the country," DeWeese replied.

"Left? To where?"

"He's gone south to arrange for a guard, in case you are taken back to Arizona."

John Henry's confidence faltered at the news. For Bat Masterson was an odds player, and if he were putting together a guard for John Henry's return to Arizona, it was a good bet he'd be returning there.

"Think it over," DeWeese said. "But don't take too long."

He thought he knew what hell was like, waking up too many mornings with the memory of Stillwell's murder bright in his mind. For much as he had prevaricated his answer to the *Republican* reporter, the truth was that he was as guilty as anyone for the death of Frank Stillwell, and the law could rightfully make him pay for it. In the street fight in Tombstone he was only defending himself from being murdered. In the train yard in Tucson he'd become a murderer himself, and that, he had thought, was hell. But he'd been wrong. Hell was being alone in a jail cell, waiting to be sent off to die with life dangling unreachable before him. Unreachable, because he could never turn his friends over to the law even if it meant sending himself to the gallows.

Blame Mattie for his lingering sense of gallantry, blame his mother for raising him with a moral conscience that refused to be drunk to death, blame his father even for cursing him with too much pride to be disloyal. Though he spent the whole night wide-awake and wishing he could do it, he couldn't bring himself to betray his friends even for the sake of his own life. And Wyatt, safely hidden in the Black Canyon country of the Gunnison, would never know the sacrifice John Henry was making on his behalf.

Colonel DeWeese was disappointed in his client's response, though it was probably more professional regret than anything personal. He didn't know John Henry well enough to care much about his longevity, but he certainly cared about his own legal reputation, and it didn't look well for a noted lawyer to lose such an important case.

And then the extradition papers arrived.

He'd been a fool to trust in the assurances of the Prescott plotters, to believe that John Gosper and the others could protect him if things went wrong. How could they protect him when they were no longer the power behind the Territorial throne? Governor Trittle didn't know him and didn't owe him any favors, for all he'd risked his life to serve the good of the Territory, and it was Governor Trittle who was running things in Arizona now. But surely Gosper could have done something on his behalf, said something to forestall the extradition or even prevent it. But Gosper had failed him, as Wyatt had failed him, and John Henry was alone to face the injustice of the law.

But it took two governors to execute an extradition order: one to send the request to have a prisoner returned and another to honor the request. And blessedly, Governor Pitkin of Colorado was out of town when the Arizona extradition request arrived, and when he did return home he elected to take the request under consideration, and think about it for a day or two. And once again, John Henry found himself alone in a dismal jail cell, waiting.

He wrote to Mattie, telling her once again to not believe everything she might read of him, as the story of his arrest had certainly made its way back to Atlanta by now. "*Have faith,*" he wrote to her, "*listen to your heart to know the truth. And know that I love you always.*" But then he couldn't bring himself to send the letter, for fear that it might fall into the wrong hands and somehow bring dishonor to her. He would hold onto it just until he got out of jail, he told himself.

And since he was writing letters he couldn't send, he wrote one to Wyatt, as well, something for Bat to deliver someday if he didn't get out of jail again. "*I reckon Damon did no more for Pythias than I have done for you,*" he said, hoping the lawman would know enough about Greek literature to understand the allusion and appreciate his sacrifice. Then, because Wyatt probably wouldn't understand without an explanation, he added, "*When Pythias was arrested on false charges and threatened with death, Damon gave himself as a ransom so Pythias could go free to prove his innocence, and would have been killed in his friend's place if Pythias hadn't returned in the nick of time.*"

But Wyatt was no Pythias and hadn't come to save him, and his only hope was that the Governor of Colorado would have pity on him, and refuse the extradition request. As he had told the reporter from the

Republican, if he were sent back to Arizona that would surely be the end of him. But Governor Pitkin didn't know him any better than Governor Trittle did, and without friends in high places, the odds of his being released were slim to none.

It was near midnight when the jailor came, waking him from an uncomfortable sleep.

"Sorry to bother you, Doc,"

"No more sorry than I. Seems bad news could wait until mornin' at least." Why wake him to send him back to Arizona to his death? Was Colorado so eager to see him strangled or shot to pieces?

"Sometimes darkness brings good news," the jailor said.

But it wasn't the jailor's voice, but another that spoke—a voice that John Henry remembered from somewhere long ago. It was a carefully modulated baritone, smooth as warmed honey, fluid as poetry and music put together. It was a voice that should have belonged to a cultured white man, but came from a black man's mouth instead.

"Good evening, Dr. Holliday," Barney Ford said, as the jailor unlocked John Henry's cell and let him in. "Or is it Mr. McKey? I must say, I was surprised to find that both are one in the same."

"But how did you know . . ."

"I make it my business to know," Barney Ford said, as he took off his hat and sat in the chair the jailor had placed for him, the man's deference showing that he knew this was no ordinary Negro, but one of the wealthiest men in Denver. Then Barney Ford nodded and waved the man away, leaving him alone with John Henry. "You mentioned in a newspaper interview having been in this city before. You said you worked at Babb's Variety House where Ed Chase is located now. That interested me, as Babb and I are old friends and Ed Chase and I have long been competitors, so I made some inquiries. As I said, I make it my business to know."

John Henry replied warily. "So you've come to make me pay for what Tom McKey did?" Didn't he have trouble enough already, without having an old court case brought to mind? Would the city court even care about a gambler who had once skipped bail over a saloon fight? He'd had worse charges brought against him since then, and worse consequences hanging over him—or hanging him. The last thing he needed was Barney Ford bringing up the painful past.

His poker face must have been out of practice, for Barney Ford seemed to read his thoughts and replied with something like a laugh, saying, "No, Dr. Holliday! I haven't come to make Mr. McKey pay for anything. I've come to pay him back."

"I don't follow."

"You saved my life once, as you may recall, standing up between me and a drunkard's pistol. There's not a lot of white men who would put themselves in such a situation, ready to take a bullet for a black man. But whatever your reasons for doing it, you did it, and I owe you my life."

John Henry's thoughts went back to his last stay in Denver, when he had first met Barney Ford and Bud Ryan both, and joined in an altercation at the Inter-Ocean Hotel. And though his own troubles with Bud Ryan had overshadowed that first meeting, he did remember shielding Barney Ford from Ryan's wildly waving pistol. What had made him do that, he still didn't know.

"You paid me back, Mr. Ford. You gave me a gold-headed cane. I used it some, in Texas," he said, though he didn't add that the cane had almost cost him his own life in another saloon fight. It was a sad statement on the course of things that so much of his life had been lived in saloons and jail cells . . .

"The gift of the cane was all I could do at the time, but hardly a proper price for a man's life. So tonight, I am settling my debt."

And again, Barney Ford had him stumped. "How so?"

"By being the one to tell you that you will not be going back to Arizona, not now nor ever again. I have just come from a late night meeting with my good friend, Frederick Pitkin, looking over some papers he has received concerning you."

"You know Governor Pitkin?" John Henry asked in surprise.

"I make it my business to know most everyone who has influence in this city, and making sure that I am on the good side of that influence. When one rises from nothing, every step of the staircase is the most important. Though you may not understand that, having started out at the uppermost landing."

And come down a ways, John Henry thought. But he wasn't interested in a discussion of class distinctions, only in finding a way out of the low place in which he currently found himself. "So you met with Governor Pitkin? What did he say?"

"He said he was facing a difficult decision, whether to honor an extradition order and lose the good opinion of the voting public, or deny the extradition and lose the good opinion of his fellow governors. Assuming the extradition request was properly rendered, that would make for a most difficult decision." Then he paused before adding, "If, as I told him, the document was properly rendered."

"What do you mean, 'properly rendered?'"

"Say, for instance, that he found some flaw in the wording, some jot or tittle left undone. Then the whole of the document would be compromised—like a fence with a missing board that would allow one imprisoned to escape from bondage. A wise man, feeling himself to be so unrighteously bound, would make use of that hole and run through it."

"And was there a hole?" John Henry asked, his heart skipping a beat. "Was the document flawed?"

Barney Ford shrugged. "I can't say, having never seen the papers. It was, of course, a confidential matter and I would never presume to advise the Governor of the fine state of Colorado on such things. I only stopped by to make a social call and mentioned the story of the hole in the fence in recollecting my own early experience, by way of conversation. Though I did note that as I was leaving, Governor Pitkin was calling in his Secretary to consult on some matter about a signature not being appended where it should have been. I dare say that document is likely to be lost in the Secretary's files and will have to be redone by the sender. Assuming, of course, that the Secretary remembers to ask for a better copy to be sent. You know how busy the work of government is, how many things can be lost or forgotten."

"Then I am free?"

"My dear Dr. Holliday, you have always been free. You have merely suffered the consequences of your own agency. The only real prison is having no agency at all."

"So how do I thank you, Mr. Ford?" John Henry said, offering his hand.

"There is no need," Barney Ford replied, as he rose from his chair and took John Henry's hand in his. "My debt is repaid. Which makes us equal now."

But one of them was more than equal, John Henry, thought, amazed to be thinking such a thing.

He walked out of the Denver City Jail the next morning, squinting into the glaring light of the last day of May, and was immediately taken into custody by Bat Masterson, come to escort him to Pueblo to stand charges there.

"But it's a bogus case!" John Henry protested, as Bat made all the pretense of his office, including handcuffing the prisoner to keep him from escaping on the train ride south.

"It was the best I could come up with, under the circumstances. And if Pitkin hadn't found the extradition order to be flawed, the Pueblo charge would have been our only hope of keeping you here in Colorado."

"But did you have to come up with somethin' so plebian? Swindlin' a man out of a few hundred dollars? If I'd cheated a man, I'd have taken him for a helluva lot more than that!"

"Yes, but the point was to make up a charge that we could get you out of. I wasn't trying to make you look good at the crime. But don't worry, as long as you can come up with bail money, you won't be in Pueblo long. The town is full of swindlers and so is the county court. They'll probably delay your case for weeks or months—or forever, if you're lucky. Then Arizona won't ever get you back."

John Henry sighed. "I reckon I can play a swindler if it saves me from the cowboys. And I'll have some bail money, as soon as you take these handcuffs off me."

"How's that?"

"I can't very well beat you at poker without two hands to play the cards."

He made his appearance in court, paid his $300 bail, and smiled when his case was postponed until mid-July. He'd rather have cleared his name of such a petty charge, but he knew that Bat was right and that the longer the charge remained on the books the safer his life would be. And though he could have left Pueblo then, he decided to stay on for the better part of two weeks. His month in the Denver City Jail had left him worn out and wheezing again, and he was content to rest awhile before heading to the thinner air of the mountains—while his meeting with the Leadville mining investor had been unexpectedly cancelled, he was still interested in the opportunities that city had to offer. And as long as he was headed in that general direction, he thought he might take a week or so and stop into Gunnison, as well.

He had no apology to offer, nor did he expect one from Wyatt. After all he'd been through in Denver, he only had a hunger to see his old friend again and know that they might still be friends. And he wasn't surprised when Wyatt welcomed him back with nothing more sentimental than a "Hello, Doc," and an offer of a bedroll at his posse's camp alongside the Gunnison River.

It was just like Wyatt to eschew the more comfortable lodgings of the town itself in favor of seclusion out under the stars. Wyatt had never been one for much socializing in the first place, and he'd only grown more reclusive after Morgan's murder. Maybe he felt safer away from the crowds; maybe he was tired of answering too many questions. Whatever his reasons, being Wyatt he would never explain, and John Henry knew him well enough not to ask.

Wyatt's camp beside the river looked more like a fishing expedition than a hideout. Though the Gunnison wasn't much more than a stream at that point, it was well-stocked with trout, and the men took turns casting to catch their supper. The campfire smoldered during the day and stoked to a blaze at night, and the gang sat around it and swapped stories over tin cups full of hot coffee. It might have been an idyll, except for the fact that they were all still wanted by the law in Arizona.

"Feels like Eden before the serpent arrived," John Henry commented on his first night there, "like paradise before all hell broke loose."

"It's quiet all right," Wyatt replied. And for a while they both sat and listened to the silence and the river. Overhead, the sky was velvet black and studded with points of silver.

"I'm thinkin' of goin' into the mining business again, up in Leadville," John Henry said. "I know of a man who's got some interests there."

Wyatt nodded. "Mining's a profitable venture in these parts. I might look at that myself, after the pardon comes through."

"What pardon?"

"The pardon Hooker said he'd get us, if we left the Territory. We left, like he told us to. So I figure the pardon should be coming soon."

"Then I reckon you'll be livin' by this river for a long time," John Henry said. "Arizona's done helpin' us, Wyatt. You know they sent an extradition order for me?"

"I heard about it. Bat's come to call a few times."

So Wyatt had known the trouble he was in, and hadn't come to his aid. The knowledge settled on him painfully, and he had to be careful to choose his words.

"Turned out the order was flawed," he said, "or I'd have been in Arizona now instead of here with you." Then he took a gamble, and added: "I thought you might have come to help me out."

Wyatt shrugged. "What could I have done? I'm not the law anymore. Hell, I don't even know if I believe in the law anymore. I don't know if I believe in anything anymore. Morgan's dead. Virg's a cripple. My family's all gone, all except for Warren here. You heard Celia left me?"

"I hadn't heard. But I'm not surprised, with things what they were in Tombstone."

The ladies had all left, one way or another: Louisa going away to the Earp home in California before Morgan's murder; Allie taking Morgan's body and Virgil to California, as well; Kate leaving John Henry for her old lover, Johnny Ringo. Tombstone had been the end of too many things.

Wyatt nodded. Then, looking into the fire, he said: "I'm sorry if I disappointed you, Doc. I'm sorry I didn't turn out to be what I thought I was."

And then John Henry finally understood why Wyatt hadn't come to rescue him in Denver: Wyatt was still trying to be rescued himself. This camp alongside the river wasn't an Eden; it was Purgatory, and Wyatt couldn't find his way out.

It only took two nights sleeping out of doors to remind John Henry why hotels had been invented, and he gladly gave up the rugged life for a room at the St. James Hotel in town, where the bed had a real mattress and the early morning sun was shaded by heavy drapes at the window. But hotel living cost money and that meant finding a fast income, so he took a place at the poker tables on Main Street and gambled his way to room and board.

The downside of staying in town was that Gunnison had two newspapers, one in the morning and one in the evening, and two reporters to gather the news—which meant that he was hounded for a story both day and night. As a newly-minted celebrity after his month of publicity in Denver, everything he said and did suddenly made the papers.

"He is usually dressed in a dark close fitting suit of black," wrote the reporter for the *Gunnison Daily News-Democrat, "and wears the latest style of round top Derby hat. His hair is seen to be quite gray, his mustache sandy, and his eyes a piercing blue."* The *Gunnison Evening Review* added that *"his handshake is a strong free and friendly grip of a hand, which says very plainly, 'here is a man who, once a friend, is always a friend; once an enemy, is always an enemy.'"* And when the same reporter accosted him again the next day, he quoted John Henry as saying, *"I'm not traveling about the country in search of notoriety, and I think you newspaper fellows have had a fair hack at me."*

But there was no getting them to leave him alone, so when the *News-Democrat* writer begged for an interview, he acquiesced, recounting yet again the tale of the gunfight in Tombstone, the maiming of Virgil Earp and the murder of Morgan, and the end of Curly Bill Brocious and the cowboy menace—and hoping that someday soon the reading public would tire of the story of Doc Holliday and he could return to his anonymous life.

The news that didn't make the papers in Gunnison was that Johnny Ringo was dead, killed by a bullet through his troubled brain. Bat came bringing the story to the campsite by the river, knowing that both Wyatt and Doc would want to know that the last of the cowboy leaders was gone.

"But who killed him?" John Henry asked. "All his old enemies are dead."

"And so are all his old friends," Bat replied. "Curly Bill, Frank Stillwell, the McLaurys, Old Man Clanton, even Jim Crane and Harry Head. All the masterminds, such as they were, are gone. Word is he went to

California to try to make amends with his sisters there, the black sheep of the family, but they threw him out. He even bought some fancy new boots for the reunion that he owed money on back in Tombstone. The boots were too small, the shoemaker said, but he wanted them anyway. Wanted to look dapper for his sisters, maybe. I figure he was despondent over the whole situation, and killed himself."

"And where did they find him?" Wyatt wanted to know.

"Up Galiuro Canyon, sitting in the crook of a tree. His boots were off and his gunbelt was buckled on upside down. His pistol was on the ground, alongside of a whiskey bottle. He blew his brains out, I guess. That's all anyone can figure."

"And made his dreams come true," John Henry said, and Bat and Wyatt both looked at him quizzically. "That was how his father died, when Ringo was a boy. They were in a wagon train, and his father went out in the night to check on something troubling the stock. His shotgun misfired and put a load of buckshot through his head. Ringo had night-mares about it, and used to say he wondered what it would feel like to have your head blown off."

"And how do you know about Ringo's nightmares?" Wyatt asked.

"Kate told me. I guess she must have left him, too." And in some small way, he was sorry for Ringo's bitter end. If the Galiuro Canyon hadn't been haunted before, it likely would be now.

But Wyatt wasn't sorry, only disappointed in a missed opportunity. "I should like to have killed him myself," he said, "for Morgan and for Virg."

But having lost his chance for the last revenge, Wyatt seemed to lose some of his melancholy too, as if Tombstone were finally letting go of its hold on him. There was no reason to go back there now, with only Behan left behind and not much chance of justice for him. Nor was there any reason to keep hiding out in the mountains, if things in Arizona were coming to a close. And though one might have expected that to leave Wyatt with no reason to live at all, it seemed to have given him a new lease on life, and he began to think about plans again. But when John Henry asked if he'd like to travel along with him up to the silver country and Leadville, Wyatt declined.

"I believe I'll try my hand in California for awhile. I hear Virg is headed to San Francisco to see some fancy doctor there, maybe do something to save that arm of his. I believe I'll go along and see what I can do for him."

What Wyatt didn't say, but John Henry already knew, was that Josie Marcus was in San Francisco too.

Chapter Thirteen

LEADVILLE, 1883

THEY CALLED IT THE CLOUD CITY, TEN-THOUSAND FEET HIGH WITH
air so rarified it left a man dizzy and out of breath for days after arriving. The nights were no better, the altitude making for restless sleep and
morning nausea and a tiredness that was almost painful. If it hadn't been
for the silver-lining in that city in the clouds, Leadville wouldn't be worth
much more than a stop on a mountain stagecoach road. But ever since
shopkeeper Horace Tabor grubstaked a couple of German immigrants
out prospecting the nearby hills, Leadville had become a boom-town.
The prospectors hit pay dirt in carbonate ore that assayed at two-hundred
ounces of silver to the ton, and Tabor, with a one-third interest in the
claim as repayment for his $100 stake, became a rich man almost over-
night. The Germans' good fortune, and Tabor's lucky grubstake, inspired
other fortune-hunters, and soon the Leadville mining district was war-
rened with mine shafts, cluttered with stamp mills, and overhung with
the haze of the smelters that never stopped burning. The Germans' claim,
named the *Little Pittsburg*, was just a start, and was quickly joined by the
Little Chief, the *Chrysolite*, the *Matchless Mine*, and a hundred others, all
making fortunes for their owners.

By the time John Henry arrived, Horace Tabor was a millionaire
many times over and Leadville had become a city of nearly 40,000 people
with talk of taking over Denver's place as the state capital. Its two-mile
long main street was crowded day and night with coaches and carriages,
ore wagons and delivery drays, foot-traffic and fine horses and trains of
burros bound for the mines, and over it all the shouting of newsboys

announcing the morning paper and bootblacks singing "twenty-five cents a shine!" There were brick and stone sidewalks fronting tall business buildings, stores filled with every description of merchandise, and enough law offices to handle all the legal entanglements of claims and claim jumpers, mine deeds and multiple-owner partnerships. There were, in fact, nearly as many lawyers in Leadville as there were saloons—and there were nearly a hundred of those, making saloonkeeping the biggest business in town. And where there were saloons, there were the lesser establishments that went along with them: gambling houses, dance halls, bordellos, opium dens. Anything a man could want was available in Leadville—for a price, of course. But there were also the more priceless pastimes, like Sunday services at the five Protestant churches in town, or daily mass at the Catholic Church of the Annunciation, its spire towering righteously over the populace. Godlessness may have reigned in Leadville, but God wasn't giving up on the town just yet.

While John Henry admired the churches and appreciated the numbers of saloons, it was the mining that had drawn him to Leadville. For having caught the silver fever in Tombstone and then having lost his silver mine soon after, he was hoping to be luckier in Leadville and maybe even make a fortune, as Horace Tabor had. And how could one walk around Leadville and not think of Horace, when the Tabor name was everywhere? There was the Tabor business block, the Tabor hotel, the Tabor Bank of Leadville, and most impressive of all the Tabor Grand Opera House, billed as the finest theater between St. Louis and San Francisco. And seeing Tabor's theater, how could John Henry not think of Kate?

Kate would have loved the Tabor Opera, with its eight-hundred red-velvet upholstered seats, its eight hand-painted canvas backdrops, its fifty-foot stage lit by seventy-two gaslights—the gas, of course, supplied by Tabor's Leadville Illuminating Gas Company. John Henry saw that bank of gaslights fronting the velvet curtain and remembered how he'd first met Kate. "*You watch out for the Valkyrie!*" Jameson's Tante had warned him before he left for the theater and a cyclone blew into town. And Kate had been a cyclone, a regular storm in his life. But what else could one expect from an actress? She was, if nothing else, entertaining.

And she had been so much else, besides. Yes, Kate, wherever she was now, would have wanted to be on that Opera House stage.

His first order of business on arriving in Leadville, even before finding a permanent place to live, was paying a visit on Mr. John Vimont of the Big Pittsburg Consolidated Silver Mining Company, the investor he'd missed meeting in Denver—though as it turned out, that meeting would have been the second time their paths had almost crossed. Before coming to Colorado, Vimont had done some work in the Tombstone mining district as well, and he greeted John Henry like an old acquaintance.

"Doc Holliday!" he said with a smile, rising from his desk and reaching out a hand as John Henry was ushered into his office, a suite of rooms on the second floor of a Harrison Avenue business building. "I've been looking forward to meeting you! Never got the chance, in Tombstone, as I left there shortly before the shooting that's made all the news. Of course, you've been in the news quite a bit yourself here in Colorado. Impressive piece of legal wrangling, with the extradition order and all. I was pulling for your release, having known your friend Wyatt Earp. He and I sat a jury together, a year or so back. A fine man, and a good family. Such a shame about his brother Morgan."

Vimont seemed a pleasant enough man, his eyes kindly behind wire-rimmed glasses, but his mention of Morgan took some of the brightness out of the day, and John Henry had to wonder if there would ever be a place where the tragedies of Tombstone weren't waiting to haunt him. But Vimont didn't leave the conversation to languish there. "So what can I do for you today? I assume you're interested in mining opportunities?"

"I am," John Henry said, taking note of the collection of framed mining certificates on the walls around him, the comfortable furnishings, the soft carpeting covering the wooden floors. The company was doing well, by the look of things. And since Vimont had mentioned an acquaintance with Wyatt, John Henry played on his lead: "Wyatt Earp and I had shares in a mine claim down in Tombstone, and I thought I might get into the same sort of arrangement here. I was hopin' a man of your associations might have some suggestions for me, bein' new to the Leadville mining district myself."

"Well, you've come to the right place," Vimont said cheerily, "though I'm sorry to say there's not a lot of claims left for the sharing, unless you happen to win one in a lucky game of chance. There was such a rush of prospectors in the first years of the Leadville strikes that most of the locating work's already been done. Now the business is more about development, with big companies buying up the smaller ones and big money coming in to finance operations. Like the Consolidated." He nodded toward the framed certificates on the wall, and said, "We own ten of the best lodes on Fryer Hill and fourteen smelters for processing the silver, with some of the deepest pockets backing us. Like Cyrus McCormick from Chicago, one of our trustees. No doubt you've heard of him."

Who hadn't heard of Cyrus McCormick? His harvesting machine had helped to revolutionize the American farm industry and made its patent owner a rich man. But John Henry wasn't a millionaire looking for someplace to stow his money.

"So I reckon that leaves me out of the game," he said with disappointment, "not havin' made my fortune yet."

But Vimont still smiled encouragingly. "Which is why I said you've come to the right place. We've just made a public offering of 200,000 shares in the company, and at only one-hundred dollars each, it's an excellent investment."

"So for a hundred dollars I own a one in 200,000th share in your mines?" John Henry said, doing the calculation. "Seems like a mighty small piece of the pie."

"That's not quite how it works. What you get for your money is a share in the company, whatever its holdings, whether mines or smelters or even railroads. Your investment goes to help us build the business, and when we make a profit, you make a profit. It's that simple."

"And when you take a loss, I take a loss too?" John Henry said warily.

"You would," Vimont agreed, "if there were any losses. But the way the silver industry keeps booming, there's never going to be a loss. We're a well-managed company, I can guarantee you. Solid as any other listing on the New York Stock Exchange; you can read about us in the stock reports."

John Henry was interested, but it was big profits he was looking for, not percentages on a hundred dollar investment, and he said as much.

"But that's where the stock market gets interesting," Vimont replied. "Once all the shares are sold they start being traded, and once the trading starts the value of your shares can go up indefinitely. It's all based on the performance of the company and how many investors want to get in. Like a big stakes poker game, you might say, where everyone wants in and the ante keeps going up. And your one-hundred dollars can become a fortune with no effort at all on your part. It's the best game in town."

It was the mention of poker that caught John Henry's imagination, and made Vimont's offer seem worthy of more consideration. He was still a sporting man, after all, and there was nothing he liked so well as the thrill of winning a wager. So though he'd come to Leadville hoping to put his name on a mine claim, he put it instead on a certificate of shares in the Consolidated Silver Mining Company, and started his new career as a player in the stock market. And Leadville, he felt sure, was going to be lucky for him.

He took up lodgings in a little shotgun house, ten-feet by twenty-feet, on West Third Street between a restaurant and a Chinese laundry. One block to the west was the Episcopal Church; one block to the east was the red light district of Cat Alley; and three blocks to the north, where West Third crossed Harrison Avenue, was the City Marshal's office keeping a watch over everything. And feeling himself settled again at last, he sent for his trunk that had been left behind in Tombstone. Then he went to work banking a Faro game at the Monarch Saloon for living expenses, and started reading the papers to keep a watch on his investments.

The papers, of course, were full of news of the mines: the daily haul of carbonate ore by the ton and the going price of silver by the ounce; details of railroad construction as the tracks made their way from Denver to Leadville, promising a shorter, cheaper passage across the mountains and faster delivery of silver bullion to the banks in the east; descriptions of the state and national political races and results of the fall elections and their impact on the silver-mining economy; and now and then a weather report. Besides that, there were the usual notices of engagements and marriages, babies born and old folks dying, school board meetings and spelling bees and Saturday night church socials. And occasionally there was something novel, like the earthquake that shook Denver on

Election Day, seeming a heavenly approbation or a curse, depending on one's political views, as Chester A. Arthur was voted into the Presidency.

John Henry's own political views were ambivalent. From what he could see, both parties had their strong points and both parties were wrong about a lot of things, and neither party had done all that much for him personally. So when a petition went around the saloons asking for signatures in support of the new Leadville Independent Party, he signed up and even joined the other sports at the organizational meeting held at one of the local watering holes. And though the party didn't have a candidate of their own, their block of votes did keep a Leadville Republican from becoming Governor, which called for something of a celebration and a round of drinks, at least.

But with or without an election going on, there was always plenty of drinking in Leadville. The papers estimated that something like 30,000 drinks were poured every day, from sunup until nearly sunup again. The miners on the night shift came into the saloons first thing in the morning before heading to bed, the miners on the day shift came in right after work and before having supper, and in the early afternoon hours between the sporting men arrived and started on their daily dose of beer and hard liquor. At night, of course, everyone was drinking. It was only in the two or three hours before daylight that the saloons and the beer halls were quiet, and the barkeeps would catch their own sleep before starting to pour drinks all over again.

It was during one of those quiet spells that a Harrison Street business building called the Texas House caught fire. The blaze started innocently enough when an oil lamp ran too low on fuel and exploded, catching the canvas-covered ceiling in flames.

John Henry was on the second floor when the fire began down below, playing a late poker game in Con Featherly's gaming room, and was only a little distracted by the sound of the initial explosion.

"Sounds like someone's settin' off fireworks," he commented, keeping his eyes on the cards and letting the other players lose their concentration. In his experience, whenever a player lost his train of thought, he pretty much lost the game, as well, and he was close to winning this one.

"Damn if it ain't!" the man across the table from him said, "or else they're settin' off the fireworks downstairs. There's smoke comin' up through the floorboards!"

He was right about the smoke, and before they could fold the game there were flames coming up as well.

"Gentlemen," John Henry said, realizing that things had come to a halt, "shall we split the pot now, or watch it burn?" Then, as his polite question went unanswered in the sudden commotion, he gathered up the coins and greenbacks himself and pocketed them for safe-keeping, then grabbed for his coat and headed to the door.

The stairs were clear, but the air was so thick with smoke that finding them was the dangerous part. He reached out a hand and found the rail, scalding hot to his touch, and followed it down into the back of the saloon below. The stairs exited near the alley door, and the men stumbled through just as the flames fanned toward them and blew upwards into the stairwell. Outside, the sudden cold of the December air burned his lungs like fire.

By the time the Leadville Hose Company arrived the entire first floor saloon was ablaze and the second floor was about to join it, and the fire brigade hurried to get things under control.

"Hey you there!" one of the firemen hollered down to John Henry from a precarious position atop a pile of crates. "Grab ahold of the bottom of the hose and help me keep it steady!"

"But the fire's down here!" John Henry hollered back. "Why are you aiming up there?"

"Saloon's too far gone to save! But the water may keep the flames from spreading out and taking the rest of the block. Hold the hose with your arms, not your hands!"

So John Henry did as he was told, and held on while his arms ached and his lungs burned from the heat of the blaze before him. Even the frigid winter air didn't chill him, as he sweated in spite of the cold.

It took more than an hour to put out the flames, leaving the Texas House Saloon gutted and charred and the second story rooms ruined by water. But the building still stood, its walls smoking as the sun came up and the town gathered to see the spectacle. And as John Henry stood in the crowd, shivering in his sweat-soaked clothing and his face blackened by ash and soot, a reporter from the *Leadville Daily Chronicle* asked: "Did you help with the fire, Sir?"

He couldn't very well deny his involvement, wet and blackened as he was, and by the next morning his name was in the papers alongside the mining reports, with thanks from the Leadville Hose Company for his valiant services.

There was a spectacular sunset the evening after the fire, so fiery red that the fire department was called out again, and John Henry thought he might be mustered back into service as a volunteer. But when no flames appeared to go along with the scarlet sky, the fire bells stopped ringing and the town relaxed some—until the same phenomenon occurred the next night and every night for a week after that. Something was burning somewhere, to make such a show, and folks began to wonder if the smoke of the smelters was having an effect on the atmosphere. But no one was worried enough to shut down silver production in the richest silver city in the country.

January came with heavy snow and packs of wolves prowling the darker streets of the city. Though Harrison Avenue glittered with gaslights, only a few of the side streets were lighted, and folks had to carry lanterns against the darkness and pistols against the wolves. Problem was, the city had recently announced stricter enforcement of the concealed weapons law after a flurry of Christmas Day frolics and gunfights, and the wolves seemed to be getting the better deal of the arrangement. One pack chased a miner while he made his way on horseback toward Twin Lakes, and another pack killed a woman and her baby out alone on the roads.

The cold brought sickness with it, as well, with pneumonia taking fourteen lives and Smallpox causing the city to open a pesthouse in a vacant building at the lower end of Fourth Street. But that was too close for comfort, and when the disease refused to be contained, the city ordered the pesthouse removed to outside of town and a general vaccination begun. Smallpox vaccine had been in use since the 1780's, when an observant doctor noted that his milkmaid, once exposed to Cow Pox, did not contract the closely-related Smallpox. But one-hundred years later, few people had been subjected to the puncture-induced inoculation, and the people of Leadville mostly ignored the city's advice. The railroads took it, however, making a mandatory vaccination day for all railroad workers, and offering free drinks for everyone who complied. The free drinks clinched the deal, the workers rolled up their sleeves, and the spread of the Smallpox slowed. In the end, only sixty-nine lives were lost, and Leadville breathed a collective sigh of relief and looked forward to the end of the hard winter.

It was amazing to John Henry that the city didn't just shut down during the long cold months, when the mountain passes became impassible and the street cars had to be changed out for horse-drawn sleighs. The air, already thin and hard to breathe, was so dry it seemed to catch in the throat and hang there and the constant cold permeated every fiber of his being. Life would be easier, he thought, as he slipped on the snow-packed sidewalks and shivered in his heavy wool coat, if the whole town could winter elsewhere and come back again when spring returned—if indeed there were a spring in Leadville. Old timers said there were only three seasons in those mountain valleys, not four, counting Early Winter, Full Winter, and Late Winter and not much else. But the snow and the cold couldn't cool the silver fever of Leadville, and it somehow seemed fitting that Leadville's great love story—the romance of Horace Tabor and his beloved Baby Doe, came to a blissful climax while the winter winds blew.

It was blissful for Horace and Baby Doe, anyhow. Horace's newly divorced first wife, Augusta, was understandably bitter when Horace took his mistress to Washington, D.C., and married her in a lavish ceremony with a guest list that included President Chester A. Arthur and most of the Congress and Senate. Augusta deserved better than that kind of public humiliation, especially since it was her dogged determination that had helped Horace amass his millions. Who was it who had married him when he was a penniless man from Maine, then followed him to the gold fields of Colorado so he could sell groceries to the starving miners? Who was it who had kept the store and balanced the books, then tended to Horace when his own gold panning days ended empty-handed? And when Horace finally made his fortune, what thanks did Augusta get? She got divorced against her wishes so her husband could take up with a tart half her age and then flaunt his infidelity by marrying Elizabeth Bonduel McCourt Doe in the most public marriage ceremony of the century. It was no wonder that Augusta Tabor was bitter, and that the rest of the nice ladies of Leadville sided with her.

But neither Augusta's bitterness nor the loss of his own place in Leadville society bothered Horace Tabor. What was Leadville without his money, anyhow? He didn't need the city's goodwill to know that it needed him. Besides, now that he had his fortune and his beautiful young bride, he was aiming at bigger things than a silver camp in the sky. Horace aimed at becoming a senator himself, even if he had to buy himself the seat, and then perhaps he'd run for President . . .

The ladies of Leadville, they who supported the five Protestant Churches and the Catholic Church of the Annunciation, knew that God would reward such great pride with an equally great fall someday. They just hoped it wouldn't happen until all the silver was sucked out of the ground underneath Leadville and they were all as rich as Augusta, whose divorce settlement lost her a husband but left her with half of his properties and a fine mansion in the middle of town. She might have been bitter, but Augusta Tabor was rich, as well.

Whatever Horace Tabor's faults were, being frugal wasn't one of them, and while the gossip over his divorce and remarriage raged, he continued to pay top dollar to book shows for his Opera House in Leadville as if to prove that however much he'd had to give to Augusta, he still had plenty more left over for himself and Baby Doe. And that was how *Mazeppa*, the famous and expensive equestrian spectacle, came to town. John Henry, of course, had to see the show.

It was as gaudy and overblown as he remembered it, with a pretty girl in skintights playing a Tartar prince and a stableful of trained horses parading around the stage. But though the production was beautifully mounted and the acting more than adequate, somehow the play seemed tired and worn out, its melodrama more fitting to a past decade than to the modern 1880s. Or maybe it only seemed that way because the last time he had seen it Kate had been the star, and no new staging could be the same without her. Last time he had seen *Mazeppa* there was a real storm to go along with the storm on the stage, a gaslight fire in the curtains, and a girl with blue fire in her eyes taunting him to follow. And for too long, he had.

He left the theater feeling lonelier than he had in months, and found himself wondering where Kate might be, now that all her lovers had left her. Not that he wished he could be one of them again. It was Mattie that he loved and always would, and wished that he could have with him in Leadville or any other place. But having seen Kate's show again after so long, he couldn't help but think of her, and the thinking made him remember things he'd long since forgotten—like the seductive sound of her actress voice, the warmth of her honey-colored skin against his, the way her anger turned to passion in a mercurial moment. And though he tried to deny it, he knew that there was still some part of him that belonged to Kate, that belonged with Kate.

"Shows over for the night, if that's what you're waiting for," a voice said, startling him out of his thoughts as he stood on the stone sidewalk in front of the Opera House, and he turned to find Wyatt Earp looking down at him, bemused.

"I thought you were in San Francisco with Virgil," John Henry said, somehow not surprised to see his old friend sharing the sidewalk with him. With his thoughts going back through the years like that, he wasn't even sure he was in Leadville anymore.

"I was in San Francisco, 'till Virg started doing better. Now I'm back. Lucky I found you the first night. I figured you might be at the theater, when I heard about the show."

"You came all this way to visit me? How very flatterin'."

"Yes and no. Mostly I come looking for you, hoping you'll be willing to help us out."

"Help who out?"

"The old Dodge City gang. Seems Luke Short has got himself into something of a bind, back in Dodge, and needs support."

John Henry remembered Luke Short as a bandy-legged little gambler who drifted from town to town along with the rest of them, but no one he'd had much to do with personally.

"So why would Luke Short ask for my help?"

"It's not Luke who's doing the asking. It's Bat Masterson. They're friends from way back, and Luke asked for Bat, so Bat's asking for us. I figure we all owe Bat a favor, one way or another."

He couldn't argue the point, but he still didn't see how Luke Short's problems—whatever they were—were any problem of his. But if Wyatt were willing to come all this way to talk to him, he was willing to listen.

"Story is, Luke bought up the Long Branch Saloon, which put him into competition with the Alamo next door."

"The Long Branch has always been in competition with the Alamo. But I reckon there's plenty of Texans to go around."

"Used to be. The big cattle drives are pretty much over for Kansas, which means there's not so many drovers as there used to be. So the competition is tougher than before."

Wyatt stopped his story to pull out a cigar and bite off the end before lighting it, taking his time as he always did, as if he could only say so many words at once without taking a break. But John Henry knew his style, and waited for him to go on.

"So now the Alamo's new owner decides to back Larry Deger for Mayor and Deger returns the favor by enforcing the vice laws against the Long Branch, the Alamo's only real competition."

John Henry nodded, following the thought, "Which means that only the Long Branch has to pay a fine for the dance halls girls and the gamblin'. That would make for bad business."

"It's even worse than that. They're not just collecting fines, the way we used to do. They're arresting the whores and the dealers, and threatening to drive them out of town."

"While leaving them be in the Alamo?"

"That's right. So Luke straps on his guns and heads to the jail to bail out his employees and fix things. And runs into the Deputy Marshal on the way."

"Who doesn't take kindly to seeing Luke armed on the streets of Dodge, I wager," John Henry said.

"So the deputy fires at Luke, and Luke fires back and misses—Luke's not all that much of a shootist—but he thinks he hit the deputy, so he runs back to the Long Branch to hide out. Takes the marshal all night to convince him the deputy isn't dead, and if Luke'll come out and turn himself in, there's only a Disturbing the Peace against him. Which was a ploy, as when Luke shows up at the jail, they arrest him for Assault with a Deadly Weapon instead."

"Well, he did take a shot at the deputy."

"Which is two-thousand dollars bail and maybe jail, if he's convicted, which under the circumstances it looks like he will be, until Mayor Deger sends an armed guard to run Luke and all his employees out of town. Says he's doing it to preserve the peace."

"Which leaves the Long Branch empty and not so much competition anymore, I reckon."

"And ignores due process, which is breaking the law. But when Luke complains to the governor and the governor wires Mayor Deger to find out what's going on, the mayor says everything is quiet in Dodge. Which makes the governor look like a fool, if he believes it."

"Which is where Bat comes in?" It seemed like Bat was making a habit of helping out when a governor was involved.

"And the rest of us, if you'll come along."

"To do what?"

"To be there, mostly. Make a show of force on Luke's side of things until Mayor Deger changes his mind about denying due process. We used to be the law in Dodge, me and my brothers and Bat. I hate to see the law dishonored now."

"I thought you didn't believe in the law anymore, Wyatt."

But Wyatt was out of words on the matter and didn't reply. And John Henry had to wonder just what had happened to Wyatt between Gunnison and San Francisco that had changed his mind about things—or maybe what had happened in San Francisco.

"And how's Josie Marcus?" he asked, taking a chance.

Wyatt took another draw on his cigar before answering.

"She's over in the Gunnison, waiting until we're done with this business."

And he didn't need to say any more.

Wyatt laid over the night in Leadville, sharing supper and an evening of cards and doing his best to persuade John Henry to go along with him back to Dodge. But though John Henry entertained the idea for an hour or two, he knew he couldn't go. He wasn't free, like Wyatt was, to move around the countryside and take a stand whenever he wanted to. He was only free by the good graces of the Governor of Colorado, who'd ignored the extradition order from Arizona but could decide at any moment to honor it. If the show of force in Dodge City ended badly, as another show of force had ended badly in Tombstone, John Henry might find himself behind bars again and answering to Johnny Behan's crooked justice.

So they drank and wagered and talked of old times, and John Henry said he would have to decline Wyatt's invitation and miss the chance to relive the glory days in Dodge. And though it was good to have the company of his old friend again for a few hours, their friendship wasn't what it once had been. Maybe it was losing Morgan, whose easy laugh had balanced Wyatt's laconic nature. Maybe it was the steel vest that Wyatt had worn into battle while John Henry had gone in brave but unprotected. More likely, it was the two weeks he'd spent in a Denver City jail awaiting the extradition order while Wyatt, knowing of his precarious strait, hid out in the mountains and left him to his fate. Like a dry river bank bearing down under a desert rain, there was only so much strain a friendship could take before beginning to give way.

As for their common crime in the shooting of Frank Stillwell, neither one of them mentioned it at all, and by the next afternoon Wyatt was gone.

There was something else Wyatt had told him, by way of warning. There'd been another Tombstoner on the train with him who'd also gotten off at the Leadville depot: Johnny Tyler, their old adversary from Arizona.

John Henry remembered Tyler as the cocky leader of the Sloper gang that had tried to take over the gaming tables in Tombstone. But though he'd had a little set-to with Tyler in his early days in that silver boomtown, getting them both thrown out of Milt Joyce's saloon, it was Joyce who'd caused him real trouble by confiscating John Henry's prized Colt's Navy pistol. When he'd gone back to get it, he got himself buffaloed and nearly killed for his efforts, and made Milt Joyce into a mortal enemy. But with all that had happened in Tombstone since then, he'd pretty much forgotten about Milt Joyce and Johnny Tyler both.

Now here was Tyler again, ready to make the rounds of the Harrison Street gambling halls, and it seemed the best strategy was to follow Wyatt's advice and simply avoid him, though surely in a city of 40,000 the odds were slim of them ever running into each other face to face. But just to be cautious, John Henry stayed close to his own Faro game at the Monarch, sweeping up the wagers on every losing bet and investing most of his share in Consolidated Silver Mining stocks, and hoping Tyler didn't happen in while he was dealing.

But he had more to worry about than staying shy of an old adversary, when the silver market stumbled on the heels of the failure of Horace Tabor's Bank of Leadville. The failure wasn't entirely Horace's fault, for by the time of the collapse he had sold off his controlling interest in the business, and Mr. E. L. Campbell, the recently defeated Republican candidate for governor, was acting bank president. But Horace was still connected with the establishment, and news that his Wall Street investments had taken a sudden decline caused a minor run on the bank he had founded. Then Campbell was accused of using the bank's money to fund his own political campaign, causing more investors to take their money elsewhere, and in a matter of months, the Bank of Leadville went from deposits of nearly two million dollars to only a few hundred-thousand, and the remaining customers emptied their accounts as well. The failure of the Bank of Leadville caused its subsidiary Bank of Kokomo to fail, and set off a summer of declining confidence in banking in general which caused even more failures, and by September the First National Bank of Leadville and the City Bank of Leadville and the Merchants and Mechanics Bank were all teetering.

John Henry didn't care much about the banks, as most of his money was in stock certificates now instead of cash deposits, but the mention of Tabor's losses on Wall Street made him nervous. If Tabor's businesses were suffering, would his own be far behind? And would the recently reported death of Cyrus McCormick, the Consolidated's biggest backer, have a detrimental effect on the company? But when John Henry went to the offices of the Consolidated Silver Mining Company to address his concerns, he found that Mr. John Vimont was no longer with the company, having sold out his shares early and left town.

He hadn't written to Mattie much during the troubled days in Tombstone and after, but once he'd gotten settled in Leadville he'd become a regular correspondent again. And though he didn't tell her everything about what he'd been through, not wanting to have her worry over him or think badly of him, he told her as much as he could, writing long letters about the silver-rich city and the too-thin air, the fire he'd helped to put out and the politician he'd helped to defeat, the white-spired Catholic Church of the Annunciation and the snow-covered peaks that towered nearby. And he'd written to her proudly about his silver interests in the Leadville mines and how much money his investments might bring in, and she wrote regularly in return, praising his efforts and wishing him success.

But now he wrote instead about his fear that he may have lost a great deal of money in the declining market. For though he should have been more cautious, spreading his investments over several companies instead of trusting everything to just one, the Consolidated had seemed so solid, its holdings so secure. And worse than the sudden losses—twenty percent of par was all the market was paying now—the twenty dollars in shares he'd make on every one-hundred dollar investment wasn't even cash money. So all he had to show for his year in Leadville was a pile of share certificates and the daily take off his Faro game, and he was no further ahead than when he'd first stepped off the train from Arizona.

It had been hard writing to her of his failures when he so wanted her to be proud of him, but he knew that Mattie of all people would understand and offer kind words to comfort him. But for the first time in as long as he could remember, she didn't write him quickly back. And after two weeks had gone by, and then a month and more, he feared that there was something amiss in her life as well. Was there an illness in the family that occupied her attention? Was she herself ill, and couldn't write to tell him of it? Or was she simply so disappointed in his failures that she had finally lost her affections for him?

It was a beautiful fall day when her long-overdue letter finally arrived, the kind of day that made one forget that winter was coming again soon. On the western horizon the peaks of Mount Elbert and Mount Massive, soaring past 14,000 feet into the deep-blue Rocky Mountain sky, were already crested with snow, but on the lower elevations the blue spruce forests were bright with the gold of aspen groves. And though there was enough wind to make a chill, it was blessedly blowing the haze of the smelters away to the east, leaving the air clean and almost glistening.

John Henry noted it all as he walked home from the Post Office, memorizing every detail so he could describe it to Mattie in his soon-to-be-written reply to the letter he had safely tucked into the pocket of his overcoat. He might have opened her letter as soon as the Postmaster had handed it to him, but for the size of it. It was a long letter, he could tell, and he wanted time and privacy to read it. Then, home in his narrow shotgun house, he slit open the envelope and pulled out the pages filled with her delicate handwriting, as familiar and dear as the sound of her voice. It was funny how written words could almost have a sound to them, how the shape and slant of the letters could hold the heart and soul of someone so far away. *More than kisses, letters mingle souls,* he thought, remembering the poem learned in his youth, *for thus friends absent speak.* She had always been there for him; would always be.

My dearest John Henry,

Please forgive my long delay in writing to you, but you will understand, I hope, as you read this. Most of all I hope that you will be happy for me at the announcement of some wonderful news. I am happy, happier than I ever thought to be . . .

A sudden chill swept through the room as if the wind outside had taken a change of direction, making the light of the oil lamp waver and the pages of the letter shiver in his hand. What wonderful news? What happiness? Then the chill in the room seemed to run right through his heart. Had another man come along to steal Mattie away from him? He'd never contemplated such a calamity, not since the days of his rivalry with their cousin Robert, but his mind was suddenly full of imaginings. And hands trembling, he forced himself to keep reading.

It was only then that he took notice of the heading at the top of the first page, where instead of *Atlanta* was written *Saint Vincent's Convent, Savannah.*

It was the place she had been sent for refuge as a child during the War, when her father had come home on furlough and packed his daughters off to the nuns for safe keeping. Now she'd gone there again, seeking refuge from the battle that raged around her, for the national coverage of the OK Corral gunfight was nothing compared to the sensational stories about the capture of the notorious Doc Holliday in Denver. And because of the stories which made it all the way back to Atlanta, his cousins were sudden celebrities, a fame that was unwanted and unwelcome. The Hollidays were a fine Southern family, but the Black Sheep in their midst made them all seem somehow improper.

Mattie didn't mind so much what other folks said, as she knew John Henry better than anyone and still thought the best of him, but she couldn't ignore the comments of her mother and sisters, of her Aunt Permelia and her Uncle John, of her cousin Robert who loved her like a sister. It had been John Henry's duty they said, as oldest son of the oldest son, to uphold the family honor. Instead, he'd brought dishonor on them all, and every family conversation seemed to center on all he'd done to disappoint them, until Mattie couldn't bear to listen anymore.

So she'd sought refuge again, as she had as a child, taking sanctuary with the nuns in Savannah, where life had no impossible problems to solve. With the Sisters, there were no lost loves or romances denied, only the love of God who was husband to them all. And as she hid for a few weeks from John Henry's fame and the family's railings, she realized what she should have known all along. She wasn't meant to marry, not John Henry nor anyone else, and her impossible love for her cousin was really a blessing, freeing her for something more worthy. If she couldn't marry the man she loved, the man she would always love, she could give her life to God instead.

Her letter had been so long delayed, she said, because she had taken vows at Saint Vincent's Convent, after going there at first only seeking sanctuary. And she hoped it would be some solace to him, as it was to her, to know that her service as a Sister of Mercy would be pleasing to the Lord. Then she signed her letter, not with her given name as she always had, but with the new name she had taken as a nun, a name she had chosen to honor a Roman saint who was married to a first cousin before giving up her marriage to serve her God. Saint Melania, she hoped, would approve and understand her sacrifice.

"*Her* sacrifice!" John Henry cried aloud to the darkness that crowded him, to the emptiness that threatened to engulf him.

Her sacrifice? What about *his* sacrifice? What about his life, his longings? Did her greedy God demand his life, as well, laying himself down like Isaac on some bloody altar, a willing offering? Well, he wasn't willing! He wanted Mattie, had always wanted her. He needed her, more now than ever. And his first thought, when he could think clearly at all, was that if she couldn't come to him, he would go to her. He would scale those convent walls, lay siege if he had to, and take back what God had stolen away from him. And once he had her with him again, he would never let her go.

But how to get there? Atlanta was a week away by rail and the trip would cost him more cash money than he had on hand. Though he didn't know much about nunneries, he was sure that the longer he waited the higher those walls would be. And as he drank himself insensitive, downing a bottle of whiskey while the wind outside keened and cried, he imagined those walls as a prison and Mattie as a prisoner waiting for him to come to her rescue. She would want him to come, would cry tears of joy to see him again. All he had to do was get himself there.

He'd done his best to avoid Johnny Tyler but now he sought him out, knowing that the riskiest games were usually the richest, as well, and wherever Tyler chose to place his bets there was sure to be some real money on the table. All he had to do was beat the Sloper at his own game, as he'd beaten him in Tombstone, putting up with his sass and outsmarting him. He only had to steady his hands and calm his shattered nerves, the result of reading Mattie's awful letter. He only had to stop his heart from racing at the thought of losing her forever. So he steeled himself with another dose of liquor, and went looking for Johnny Tyler.

He found him fortuitously enough playing poker in a game at the Monarch Saloon, as if luck had sent him there on purpose. Luck or God, one or the other, and it didn't seem like heaven was on his side just now. So he thanked Lady Luck and anted into the game, taking a seat across from Tyler, as if sharing a poker table with him were the most natural thing in the world.

"Well, if it isn't Doc Holliday," Johnny Tyler sneered. "I suppose I should say it's nice to see you again, but that would be a lie. You look like hell."

"I'm dealin' with the Devil," John Henry said darkly. "But then, you probably sold your soul long ago."

"Still the same old Doc, full of smart talk," Tyler replied. "Seems like the last time we played, you got thrown out of the saloon."

"Seems like you did the same, Johnny. But at least I was man enough to go back and do somethin' about it."

"And got yourself beat up, doing it!" Johnny Tyler said. "Doesn't look like you have much to brag about anymore. Hell, I'm surprised to see you still walking the streets. Thought you'd have coughed up your lungs long ago—or got shot down like your friend Morgan Earp. Shame that took so long to happen. I was wagering on the Earps losing Tombstone from the start. You in this game or just sitting down to catch your breath? I haven't got all night to beat you."

The mention of Morgan got John Henry's blood boiling, but there was enough cash on the table to get his attention, and as good a pot as he was likely to find anywhere that night.

"Deal me in," he said, "'cause this won't take all night."

Johnny Tyler was an uninspired poker player, relying on threats to cow his competition and scare men into folding when they might have taken a hand, and without the big wagers he made, he couldn't have gotten a game at all. But a rich pot was appealing no matter what the company, and he used it to draw in opponents before insulting them back out of the game. It was the same old Sloper business that had made him so many enemies in Tombstone while making him so much money at the same time: offer big payouts and the other players will put up with anything, for a time.

On any other night, John Henry would have found besting Johnny Tyler no challenge at all. He'd have turned deaf ears to the insults and kept his mind on the cards, playing a better game than Tyler knew how to play. But on this night, with his nerves already rattled and his mind running circles around a convent in Savannah, he found himself losing time and again on plays that should have easily gone his way. He took two pair and threw away a card that would have brought him three of a kind. He had the start of a straight and got confused, thinking he was working on a flush. He raised when he should have folded; bowed out when he should have called.

And then, miraculously, he found himself looking at his favorite hand—three of a kind sevens and a pair of Jacks, the hand Kate used to deal him when he needed to cheat. But Kate wasn't sitting beside him now and this wasn't cheating, just a miracle when he needed it. A full house could beat most other hands, with a little bluffing to beat the rest.

But even a full house wouldn't be enough, if he couldn't afford to stay in the game. And as the wagers went around, then went around again, he found himself in a difficult position: fold on his best hand of the night, having lost his stake with not even a dime to show for it, or ask for credit from Johnny Tyler.

"Looks like you're out of pocket, Doc," Johnny Tyler said as he hesitated over his cards. "Raise me or get out of this game."

He couldn't get out, not until he'd won back what he'd brought; not until he'd won enough to get himself back to Georgia again. And thinking of Georgia and Mattie, he fingered her little Irish ring, an unthinking habit that had brought him both comfort and luck through the years— and suddenly he knew what he had to do to stay in the game. The ring was so loose on his thin fingers now that it slipped off easily, and he closed his hand around it for a moment, thinking a prayer and making a wish. Then he tossed it into the pot, saying, "I raise and call. That's pure gold, worth as much as you've got in that pot, I reckon."

The ring caught the light as it settled down onto the pile of chips and coins and greenbacks filling the table: two hands for friendship, a crown for loyalty, a heart for love. There was enough money in that pot to fund his way to Georgia twice over. Soon, soon he'd be back with her again, rescuing her from her convent, rescuing both of them.

"Gold is it?" Johnny Tyler said. "Well, it'll be melted down quick, 'cause it's mine now unless you can beat this."

Then he fanned his cards out on the table: four of a kind hearts, beating a full house.

"No!" John Henry cried, pushing himself to his feet and cursing. "You palmed those cards! I know I had you! I know I had you!" But the room swayed around him, and he could feel the words come sliding out of his mouth.

"What was that, Doc?" Johnny Tyler said, taunting him. "I didn't understand you. Did you say I was cheating?"

"Give me back my ring!" he said in a slur and Tyler laughed in his face and swept up the winnings for himself.

He was too distraught; he was too drunk. He jumped at Johnny Tyler, grabbing after Mattie's ring, and came up against a fist in his jaw.

The fist belonged to Bill Allen, the bouncer and former policeman whom John Henry knew by sight and nothing more. "No fighting in this saloon," the big man said.

"But he stole my property! He stole my gold ring . . ."

"He wagered it and lost," Johnny Tyler said. "But I don't want to make a scene. If it means so much to him, he can have it back. Here," he said, and tossed Mattie's little ring onto the table like it meant nothing at all. "Just do us all a favor and get him out of this establishment. Riff raff gives a good place such a bad name."

"You can't throw me out!" John Henry protested as Bill Allen wrapped muscular arms around him, pinning him. "I have a Faro table in this saloon! I work here!"

"He has a Faro table here?" Johnny Tyler said, smiling. "Why, that's even better. Now he's out of pocket and out of a job. I'd say that's a winning night for me." Then he tossed a gold coin to Bill Allen. "Here's a tip for your efforts, Mr. Allen. You've rid me of a nuisance."

"I work here!" John Henry said again, protesting as Bill Allen hustled him out onto the street.

"You can see Cy about it tomorrow," Bill Allen said. "But I'm in charge of things tonight and I don't want any trouble. And you are trouble, Doc." Then, as if taking pity on him, he dropped the tip money at John Henry's feet—a five dollar gold piece that clattered onto the stone sidewalk.

"I don't want your charity," John Henry said bitterly.

"And I ain't giving any. Call it a loan until you find another Faro game. Severance pay, but with interest due. Listen, Doc, I don't like Johnny Tyler much either, but he just bought a quarter share in the place, so I got no choice. You ran up against the wrong man tonight, that's all. Better luck next time."

He had Mattie's ring and the five-dollar gold coin, and that was all. If he put them into another game and lost, he'd have nothing at all.

But without Mattie, he'd already lost everything.

The snow came early that year, bringing a hard winter, and the haze of the smelters hung like a pall over the valley. The price of silver was down, the lead markets unsteady, and the mines started laying off workers. Then the last of the troubled Leadville banks failed and no one had much money left to throw around. Even the saloons and the gambling houses slowed down some without the steady stream of thirsty miners with fresh pay in their pockets. Only the brothels seemed unaffected by the slump, the cold of winter making the painted whores of Cat Alley look almost inviting.

And then the blizzards began, one fierce storm after another, with days of heavy snowfall and hurricane winds blowing drifts twenty feet deep. The snow buried the tracks of the Denver & Rio Grande and filled up the mountain passes, and Leadville closed itself off from the world. And as John Henry walked the snow-drifted streets looking for a lucky break and coughing in the endless cold, his spittle hit the icy sidewalks and froze like red-tinted glass.

He pawned his jewelry to make ends meet, putting his cufflinks and tiepins in soak until he made a little cash in small-stakes games and could buy his things back again. He didn't care so much about the jewelry, anyhow. Most of it had come from Kate, gifts she'd bought for him with his own money when she was feeling well-disposed towards him. If he lost it forever, he wouldn't weep over the loss. But he never again wagered with Mattie's ring, even when he knew he had a winning hand. He kept it close to him, tucked into his vest pocket lest anyone see it on his finger and try to steal it away.

He was turning careful about many things, counting the coins in his money purse every night and denying himself the little luxuries that he once took for granted. Even the newspaper seemed an extravagance, and he took to reading the discards he found lying around the saloons. Day-old news was better than no news, especially when it came for free, and he needed to stay up on the mining business in Leadville. The Consolidated was foundering but not yet drowned, and he kept hoping that his shares might yet bring him something in return.

It was still snowing in February, with months of the same to come, when the *Leadville Democrat* reported a tragedy on the Ypsilanti mine ground, with a story that put fear into miners and townspeople alike. According to the paper a surveyor for the Magnolia Mining Company, out measuring for leases, had stumbled into a snow drift and disappeared. His partner saw him go down and ran to help him, discovering that the snow had hidden the yawning mouth of an abandoned mine shaft and the surveyor had unwittingly stepped into the opening, falling down two-hundred feet to the black depths below. It took a crowd of miners and a windless with an iron hook rigged to it to find his body and fish him up out of the twenty feet of icy water at the bottom of the shaft. And there were hundreds of other open pits and abandoned mine shafts in the hills surrounding Leadville, all of them covered over with snow and waiting to swallow up another victim.

It was the wrong sort of reading for bedtime, especially for a man who was already feeling chilled and achy, as John Henry was, and no wonder that he had a hard time going to sleep. And when he did sleep, it was fitful and filled with nightmares—a monster that opened its mouth to swallow him up, an icy blackness, an emptiness that waited to engulf him. But when he tried to fight against the thing, beating at it with his fists, the blows went right through it like rocks thrown into water, and when he tried to scream, the water filled his mouth and drowned him in the darkness.

It was the pneumonia, the doctor said, the illness sweeping through the city as Smallpox had done the year before, but this time there was no pest house or quarantine for the afflicted. Pneumonia victims coughed and got better, or coughed and died, depending on their own constitutions, and the doctor was too busy to stay long in one house waiting to see who would recover and who wouldn't.

John Henry's was a particularly bad case, the illness complicated by the consumption that had already weakened his lungs. The coughing, when he had the breath to cough, tore at his lungs and left him crying out in pain, and the undulant fever left him sweating and shivering and aching all over. When he couldn't breathe, he was near delirious, dreaming that he was back in Philadelphia where Jameson had given him rat poison and saved his life. But there was no Jameson in Leadville, and he was left to the kindness of the tenants in the house next door, when they remembered to check on him.

He was two weeks in bed altogether and another sitting in a chair close to the fire, trying to gather his strength before he was well enough to walk the two blocks up to Harrison Avenue—hard exercise for a man who'd just beaten the pneumonia. Third Street was a long rise that left his heart racing and his breathing labored, but he had no choice but to make the walk. With no work for nearly a month and no way to pay his rent, he was in danger of losing his house and had to find something else soon.

He was lucky to have some friends left in town, like Joseph Daniels who'd been his roommate when he first moved to Leadville and was glad to see him up and around again. Joe worked as a bartender at Hyman's Club Rooms next to the Opera House, and suggested that Mannie Hyman might give him a room in lieu of pay.

"Pay for what?" John Henry asked him.

"Bartending, if you're interested, the shift after mine. It's all he's got open right now, and only because the last man drank himself out of a job. But I'll put in a word for you, if you want. You sure you're feeling well enough to be out in this cold?"

He was sure he didn't feel well enough, but if Mannie Hyman had a room and a job both, he was willing to take them. But it was only temporary, he told himself, just until his fortunes turned and he was on his feet again. He wasn't a bartender, after all, and couldn't pour drinks for a living for long. But for now, he was grateful for the help.

Harrison Avenue had always been brightly lit, lined with gas lamps supplied by Horace Tabor's gasworks. But that March, the gas lamps suddenly seemed to dim when the first electric lights arrived, a string of forty-five of them that dazzled like daylight in the lingering darkness of late winter. The papers announced their coming with editorials about the economics of electricity and debates raged about the efficacy of such a fragile marvel, but the citizens of Leadville celebrated with a street party the night the lights first came on, cheering and toasting a brighter future to come. But it was the children who made the most of the new illumination, staying out until after midnight and playing as though the daylight would never end.

Chapter Fourteen

LEADVILLE, 1884

HE HADN'T WRITTEN BACK TO MATTIE AFTER SHE TOOK HER VOWS, too devastated at first to find the words and then too sick to hold pen to paper. And after that—well, what did one say to a sweetheart who'd become a nun? Their correspondence was over the way their life together was over, gone and better forgotten.

But Mattie, it seemed, had not forgotten, and once she was settled into her new life she started writing to him again almost as if nothing had changed between them. Almost. For she was careful now to sign her letters with the Saint's name she had taken, as a proper Sister should do—or as if to remind him that she was God's now and not his. But that was the only change in her writing. She had always been discreet, and continued to be so. She had always sent her love and still did the same. And if it hadn't been for that Saint's name and the address of a Savannah convent on the envelope, he might have imagined that things were as they had always been between them. And maybe somehow, they were. For what had their love ever really been but words, anyhow? Just words and wishes that almost, but not quite, came true.

And so he took up the correspondence where it had left off, as though they might still have a future together one day, in God's due time. Were nuns cloistered forever? he wondered. Were there angel convents in heaven? Then he laughed at his own folly. Where he was going, angels dared not tread. But as long as Mattie still loved him, maybe there was hope for him yet.

He told Mattie about the pneumonia that had nearly killed him that winter, and how the doctor said he was a miracle to be still walking the streets. What he didn't tell her was how the illness had left its mark upon him after it passed. He was thinner than he had been in all his adult life, his suitcoats hanging loose around him and his trousers bagging about his legs. He spoke in a hoarse whisper, his throat ravaged by weeks of constant coughing, his lungs ruined. And worse, he had become a laughing stock in Leadville.

In spite of his fearsome reputation in Tombstone, men who had avoided him before now took advantage of his delicate condition to taunt him. Wasn't he the notorious Doc Holliday? Hadn't he helped to gun down a hundred cowboys in his day? Well, show your stuff, Doc! Skin that smoke wagon and let's have at it! And when he declined the invitations, too weak to pull a pistol even if he had one on him, he got more abuse. Hell, you're not all that dangerous! Why, I could whip you twice before you saw me coming! Leave him alone, boys, he ain't worth fighting! And then, the laughter.

He didn't tell Mattie about the taunts, nor about the threats that followed when Johnny Tyler, seeing an opportunity and taking it, tried to revive the old trouble between them. Word in the saloons was that Tyler was ready to settle old scores, and meant to finish in Leadville, once and for all, what had started in Tombstone. And John Henry, thinking himself unable to make a defense, turned to the only help he could find.

It was a strange play for him to seek attention from the law, after so many years of running from it. But what other choice did he have? Johnny Tyler had become a prominent man in Leadville, at least among the saloon society, with plenty of friends to stand by him. John Henry had friends, as well, but not the kind with money and influence. So with appreciation for the irony of the situation, he asked for help from the local police, filing a complaint against Johnny Tyler for Threats Against Life.

Except that it wasn't Tyler himself who had made the threats, but various members of his gang, passing the word along over a game of cards or a drink across the bar. So though all the sports in town knew that Johnny Tyler had plans for Doc Holliday, the police were powerless to do anything about it.

"You let us know if he pulls on you, and we'll take care of him," Officer Robinson told him in the waiting room of the marshal's office at the corner of West Third Street and Harrison. "Be glad to do it, in fact. I hear Tyler killed a cop in Frisco, and got away with it. More than glad to pay him back for that one. But we can't act on hearsay, Doc. And it don't look like you got more than that, as yet."

"If he pulls a pistol on me, it'll be too late for help," he said. "I'm not armed these days, being deferential to the gun ordinance, but I doubt Tyler is as law-abiding as myself."

But it wasn't so much his respect for the law that made him leave off his pistol while he was on the streets as his fear of being arrested again, and giving any cause for a return to Arizona. While Barney Ford had engineered his release from jail in Denver and Bat Masterson had arranged for an endlessly continued court case in Pueblo, he still sensed the Damocletian blade of Johnny Behan hanging over him.

So when the police declined to protect him, he took his cause to the local papers, as he had done in Denver, giving an interview to a reporter from the *Leadville Democrat*.

"Why don't you arm yourself, if you're fearful of an attack?" the reporter wanted to know.

"It's my history that stops me," he explained. "If the battle ended badly—if I should kill someone here, no matter if I were acquitted the governor would be sure to turn me over to the Arizona authorities, and I would stand no show for life there at all. I am afraid to defend myself, for legal reasons, and those cowards kick me because they know I am down. I haven't a cent, have few friends to stand beside me, and Tyler's gang will murder me yet before they are done."

When the interview was printed in the next day's paper, the reporter had added his own assessment of the situation:

It looks very much as though a gang of would-be bad men have put up a job to wipe Doc Holliday off the face of the earth. There is much to be said in favor of Holliday, who has never since his arrival here made any bad breaks or conducted himself in any other way than a quiet and peaceable manner. The other faction does not bear this sort of reputation.

And still, the police did nothing.

He had told the *Democrat* reporter that he hadn't a cent, and that was nearly true. He had no money of his own to speak of, and certainly not enough to pay for an armed guard, which was probably what he needed. But he did have a little something he kept in reserve—the five dollar gold piece the bouncer Bill Allen had thrown him when Johnny Tyler had him ousted from his saloon. He'd kept it close, along with Mattie's gold ring, as a kind of security. As long as he had her ring and that five dollar gold piece, he'd never be flat broke. But other than that, he hardly had enough for a low-stakes poker game—and when he did scrape together an ante and came up with a winning hand, his partners often weren't solvent enough themselves to pay up. His days of high stakes play and profitable pots were over for the time being.

So when Bill Allen came calling to collect on his five-dollar loan, John Henry didn't have the wherewithal to repay him—at least not in cash money. He wasn't going to let loose of that gold piece like he'd let loose of Mattie's ring. And what difference would it make to Allen if he got his money in gold or greenbacks, anyhow? "But I'll make good on it in five or six days, or a week," he said, mentioning a young man who owed him that much and more who was off at a mine works but soon to return.

"I'll give you that," Allen said, "as long as it don't take no longer. I said it wasn't charity and I stand by that. But if you don't make good, Mr. Tyler himself will be doing the collecting for me. It was his money at the start, as you may recall."

He recalled, all right, and cursed himself for having taken the money in the first place. But now that he had it, he wasn't eager to part with it. And surely a week or so wouldn't make all that much difference, one way or another. But when one week became two and two became three, he knew he was headed for trouble.

He should have been more circumspect, when he walked into the Monarch Saloon looking for Bill Allen to beg a little more time. The young gambler who owed him money hadn't yet paid up, so he had nothing to pay up with himself, an inequity over which he had no control—and having to come begging now was a downright injustice. For the way he saw it, Johnny Tyler was really the one to blame for Bill Allen's unpaid loan—which wasn't Allen's money to start with, but Johnny Tyler's anyhow. And the last thing he was inclined to do was pay money to Johnny Tyler. So instead of being circumspect, as a debtor ought to be, he was vexed and showing it.

He swung though the batwing doors like a lawyer striding into a courtroom, ready to make his case, then had a coughing fit that knocked a little of the bravado out of him. Past the smoke and the crowds and standing behind the bar pouring drinks, was Bill Allen.

John Henry had never paid Allen much mind before, but took a moment to appraise him now, the way he appraised his opponents in a card game.

Allen was a big man, hard-muscled as if he worked at staying that way, but quick on his feet like a prize fighter. He'd been a policeman in the past, a fitness trainer for the fire department, a bouncer at more than one Leadville saloon. And in between, he tended bar and kept an eye on the customers. Which meant, no doubt, that he kept a gun handy underneath the bar, in case things got rowdy. Strong and armed, he would be a formidable opponent, if one opposed him.

"Well, it's about time," Allen said, looking up to find himself being scrutinized. "You said a week, Holliday, and it's been three. I was about to run out of patience."

"You're gonna have to be patient a little longer," John Henry replied, his tone only sounding polite through long years of mannerly training, "for I haven't the money to pay you back just yet."

"Is that so?"

"That's so. An inconvenience for both of us, I am afraid."

"More than an inconvenience for you. Do I look like a damned banker?"

John Henry had to stifle a laugh at the question. Bill Allen looked nothing at all like a banker, especially with his street clothes covered in a liquor-stained apron.

"Something funny, Holliday?" Allen asked, his muscular forearm flexing as he lifted a heavy whiskey bottle, holding it aloft as though he might make a weapon of it.

"Nothin' funny at all," John Henry said, chiding himself for the inopportune laughter. It wasn't wise to taunt a man like Allen who had a wall full of glass bottles behind him to go along with the hidden pistol.

"Good," Allen said, and finished pouring whiskey into a waiting glass. "I was afraid I was going to have to teach you a lesson. So what did you have in mind to offer me, if you ain't got the money?"

"What do you mean?"

"You didn't come in here just to tell me you ain't gonna pay up? That wouldn't be very smart. And I hear you think you're mighty smart—or so says Mr. Tyler. So what did you have in mind?"

If Allen were trying to goad him, it was working. But he couldn't let it show.

"I'm afraid I don't have anything much to offer. I'm not drawin' pay just yet, and all my jewelry is in soak."

"I'm not interested in baubles. But I'll be happy to take that pearl-handled Colt's revolver I've seen you carry. That should bring me more than enough at the pawn shop."

"You will not take my gun!"

"I think you're wrong about that, Holliday. I think I'll take whatever I please, if you don't make good on our deal. I'd rather have the money, but . . ." Then, making his point, he slid a hand under the bar and slipped a pistol beneath his apron.

"No need for violence, Allen," John Henry said, keeping his voice to a level calm. "I'll have your money. Just give me the weekend to work things out. 'Til Tuesday, say."

Bill Allen scowled a reply. "All right. I'll give you until Tuesday to pay up, one way or another, or I'll kick your damned brains out. Understood?"

"Perfectly," he said, though the truth was, being threatened made him even less interested in paying up on the debt. And he sure as hell wasn't going to let Bill Allen steal his prized pistol. It was the principle of the thing now, along with his stubborn pride.

As for the five-dollar gold piece, the thought of simply returning it never even crossed his mind.

Bill Allen meant what he said, according to every sport who happened to run into John Henry that weekend. They were even taking bets on the outcome of things, should an altercation arise, with most of the bets going in favor of the bouncer, and only a couple of sports taking a risk and putting money on John Henry. But willing as the sporting community was to make money on his misfortune, no one was offering to make him another loan to settle the debt. That would spoil all the fun.

And so the weekend passed and Monday along with it, and John Henry knew when he went to bed in his room above Mannie Hyman's Saloon in the wee hours of Tuesday morning that his time was up, and he had no one but himself to count on.

"Why don't you just give him his gold piece back?" Mannie said, when John Henry came downstairs to work the next afternoon. Sleeping until three in the afternoon sounded like a luxury, except that his work day had ended at six in the morning, so he still wasn't all that rested. "Allen's already been by here, looking for you, I guess. I sent him back to the Monarch, but he'll be coming along again and I don't want any trouble when he shows up."

"I don't see as how givin' him the gold will solve anything," John Henry replied, as he reached for his apron—clean and white, unlike Allen's dirty one. Even while doing such menial work as bartending, John Henry had his standards. "This business about the money is just a front for Johnny Tyler's gang. They've been lookin' for an excuse to do me in, and this is it. I reckon Allen's just one of his henchmen. If I settle up now, they'll find some other cause and be comin' after me again soon enough. I'd rather pick my ground than have them ambush me."

"This saloon is my ground, Doc," Mannie corrected him, "and I don't want anybody fighting here. So why don't you forget bartending for the day? Go back to bed until this thing blows over, and I'll have one of my dealers keep an eye out for Allen. Then you can take your fight outside and beat each other senseless, if you like."

Mannie Hyman sounded mean-hearted, but he'd been generous enough in offering John Henry a room in exchange for pouring drinks these past months. And now Mannie was considering setting him up at a Faro table in the game room, as well—although that was less likely if he raised a ruckus in the saloon.

"All right," John Henry said, shrugging and untying his apron. "But just for safety sake, I want you to keep an eye on my pistol for me. Allen threatened to take it away, and I'd hate to have him lift it from me while I was sleepin'."

So Mannie Hyman took John Henry's revolver and tucked it away beneath the bar for safe keeping—and where John Henry could find it easily, should Bill Allen come to call.

His second-floor room above the saloon faced onto Harrison Avenue, giving the narrow window an unobstructed view across the rooftops of Leadville and west toward Mount Elbert, still crested with snow this late into the summer. But there was no easy line of sight down to the street below, unless he stood at the window and risked being seen. So he had no way of knowing if Bill Allen were making his way from the Monarch Saloon to Hyman's Club Rooms two doors down the street, or if he were already downstairs, ready and waiting.

And not knowing, he jumped at a rapping on the door.

"Who's there?"

"Pat Sweeney," the visitor answered, and John Henry relaxed only a little. Pat was one of the regulars at Mannie's place, a fellow gambler who had never done him wrong before.

"Are you alone?"

"I am," said Sweeney, and John Henry unchained the door, letting the gambler in. "Bill Allen's been back, looking for you," he said. "Mannie sent him away again, but he's getting impatient."

"So what does Mannie suggest I do?" John Henry asked. "I can't hide up here forever."

Sweeney shrugged. "If I were you, I'd call for the police. Looked to me like Allen had a pistol in his pocket. I think he means to murder you, or scare you at least. And I wouldn't wait around to find out which."

"Could you guard the stair, if he tried to come up?"

"Allen's a big man, Doc. It'd take more than me to bar the way. And he's got more friends than you do, sorry to say."

John Henry considered the situation, then sighed heavily.

"Well, there's nothin' else to be done, I reckon. Go find Deputy Bradbury, tell him I'm in need of police protection. He should be out on the street somewhere. Tell him Bill Allen is armed and I don't think it right for one man to be able to carry a gun and not another. Tell him if Bill Allen comes at me, I will shoot him on sight. I don't want it bein' said, after the fact, that I didn't give the police a chance to do their job."

"And where will you be, Doc?"

"Downstairs at the bar, waitin'."

Mannie Hyman's saloon was the largest in Leadville, as he'd pushed it into the two adjoining stores and added a separate gaming room at the back of the building. Under its fancy pressed-tin ceiling and newly-hung electric lights, Hyman's could accommodate hundreds of customers an hour. So it was always crowded and always noisy—and no one paid much attention as a solitary sport made his way down the back stairs and into the drinking parlor, taking a stand near the front end of the bar.

"What'll it be, Doc?" said Henry Kellerman, the bartender on duty. "You drinkin' tonight?"

"Not yet," John Henry replied, and Kellerman turned back to his other customers. Not yet, he thought, but soon enough, though a drink might have steadied his shaking hands.

At the front of the saloon, two plate-glass windows faced onto the street, giving him a clear view of the street and sidewalk outside, so he saw Bill Allen coming even before he reached the door. There was a cadre of gamblers trailing behind him, and no doubt Johnny Tyler somewhere nearby as well. And though there was a policeman on the opposite sidewalk observing the parade, he didn't seem to be making any effort to stop it.

"*Time's up,*" John Henry said to himself, as he reached around beneath the bar for his pistol and steadied himself against the cigar case. All he needed was one clean shot before Allen commenced to shooting, just one chance. He didn't dare wait around to have a conversation about it.

Behind him at the bar, Kellerman was still busy pouring drinks, while somewhere in the card room at the back of the saloon, Mannie Hyman was occupied with his game tables. So nobody else was paying attention as Bill Allen paused at the threshold, turned to say something to his cronies, nodded to the officer across the street, then stepped into the saloon.

"Times up," John Henry said again as he took aim and fired, the bullet slamming into the doorframe just above Allen's head. His second shot tore through Allen's right arm, taking flesh and bone and blood with it as the big man hollered and slid to the floor.

He still had his finger on the trigger when someone jumped him, knocking the Colt's out of his hand to go skidding across the saloon floor. It was Kellerman, pinning him against the cigar case as Deputy Bradbury sauntered into the saloon.

"Doc, I want your gun," the officer said, finally taking action.

"I want you to protect me! These men mean to kill me!"

"Looks more like they need protecting from you."

"Is there a problem here?" Mannie Hyman asked, pushing through the crowd at the sound of the gunfire.

"Not anymore," the deputy replied. "But you just lost yourself a bartender. Let's go, Doc."

"But I was only defendin' myself!" he protested.

"You can save your apologies for the judge."

And John Henry was headed to jail again.

If he'd been in a better humor he might have appreciated the irony of his $5,000 bond being a thousand times the dollar amount of the loan that had got him into trouble in the first place. Where did the Judge think he'd come up with that kind of money, considering his inability to find an extra five dollars to save his life?

But his bond was posted the next day, arranged by Mannie Hyman and guaranteed by a couple of other saloon owners. They knew he wouldn't be running from town before he had a chance to speak his mind, which was to say that he had fired in self-defense, and which he repeated to everyone who would listen.

As for Bill Allen, his wound was grisly but not fatal, a disappointment that was actually good luck, according to the defense attorney assigned by the court.

"Easier to get you acquitted of Assault with Intent to Kill than First-Degree Murder, as there's no question who did the shooting. Fortunate for you, you're not as good a shot as folks say you are."

"I wasn't tryin' to kill him, just wing him. If I'd wanted to kill him, I'd have done it. But he's not worth hangin' for."

"Well, you winged him all right. Doctor had to sew up an artery to keep him from bleeding to death. They're worried about the gangrene now. Bill's bound to remember you for the rest of his life."

He reckoned that made them about even.

Leadville loved a good show, and counted two theaters on Harrison Avenue: Tabor's Grand Opera House and the even grander Lake County Courthouse, two-stories of red brick with a soaring clock tower and a life-sized statue of Blind Justice teetering above. The courthouse wasn't really intended for entertainment, but in Leadville legal cases often turned into a sideshow. And judging by the size of the crowd that turned out for John Henry's hearing, a show was what the citizens expected. The courtroom was as packed as the one in Tombstone had been for the month-long deliberations over the street fight there. But this time there was no Wyatt sitting beside him to share the scrutiny, and no eloquent Senator Fitch to maneuver through the legal loopholes. This time, it was only John Henry and a parade of prosecution witnesses no doubt paid off by Johnny Tyler.

The crux of the case, as the prosecution presented it, was that Bill Allen wasn't armed when Doc Holliday shot him, giving the defendant no defense. No matter that Allen had been making death threats for weeks, or that he'd come into Hyman's saloon clearly armed earlier that very day; when he came to visit Holliday that afternoon he had nothing but good wishes in his heart. Or so his spokesmen said. Allen himself was still in bed, recovering from his gunshot wounds, and couldn't testify on his own behalf—which only made things look worse for John Henry.

So when the defense took over and called John Henry to the stand, he laid his hand on the Bible and swore to tell the whole truth—or the truth as he saw it, anyhow. "I thought my life was as good to me as his was to him. I fired the shot, and he fell on the floor, and I fired the second shot. I knew that I would be a child in his hands if he got hold of me. I weigh just over 120 pounds, I think Allen weighs 170. I've had the pneumonia this past winter, and I don't think I was able to protect myself against him. I was told he had a gun and was looking for me. When he came in his right hand was in his pocket. He was about three feet inside of the door when I shot the first time, and he turned and fell. I did not see where his hands were when I shot the second time. I supposed he was going to get there if he could, for I thought he had come there to kill me. Of course I couldn't let him murder me, so I fired."

The entire hearing only took part of a day, which was no doubt a disappointment to the audience. Although there were sympathetic murmurs when John Henry told his story, there hadn't been all that much show as yet. But a quick decision from the Judge could mean that he saw no cause for a trial and was about to dismiss the case—and that would be the end of John Henry's jail days, once and for all. The disappointed citizens of Leadville would just have to find some other entertainment to amuse themselves.

But the Judge's decision didn't come quite as expected.

"I am binding this case over for trial," the Judge said, "so a jury can decide on the merits. I am also raising the defendant's bond eight-thousand dollars to secure his presence at the next session. Court dismissed."

If John Henry hadn't had five-thousand dollars, where in hell was he going to get eight?

Being remanded to jail again was more than uncomfortable; it was downright dangerous, considering the fact that Bill Allen was himself a former Leadville policeman and had most of the police force siding with him. Police protection took on a whole new meaning when it was the police protecting their own and taking revenge on their prisoner—or so went John Henry's thoughts as he languished in his little cell and waited for his friends to find another three-thousand dollars bond. His only consolation was that the papers were still supporting him, with the *Democrat* reporter personally delivering each day's edition to him in his cell and eager to print his comments on the same.

Holliday has been, without doubt, an abused individual. The manlier class of the community not only appreciate this, but have little criticism to make as to his action in connection with his trouble with Allen, for whatever the latter's intentions may have been, Holliday had reasons, whether or not they are good in law, for believing that past persecutions were to be concluded by a violent assault. Should Holliday be obliged to remain behind bars up to the day of his trial it would probably go very hard with him, as his constitution is badly broken and he has been really sick for a long time past.

The reporter's assessment of his physical condition wasn't just sensationalism. He had been sick a long time, and being confined to a cell was making him sicker. He couldn't sleep for fear of being ambushed; he couldn't eat for fear of being poisoned. And when the cough came back on him, tearing at his lungs, he wasn't even allowed a shot of whiskey to ease the pain. Still, he hated reading the newspaper accounts that made him out to be some kind of invalid. He still had his pride, after all.

But pride aside, the newspaper stories served a purpose. For when none of his friends could come up with the additional three-thousand dollars bond, the reports of his pathetic situation gained sympathy from the Judge, who lowered his bail back down to the original five-thousand and set him free until his court date in December. And all he had to do was keep himself out of trouble until then.

He couldn't leave town, but he could go off for a day—as he determined to do when the High Line Railroad opened with a free train ride to Breckenridge. The excursion was a publicity stunt for the new route between Leadville and Denver, advertised to shave 120 miles off the usual trip and turn twelve hours into ten, weather permitting. But the excursion train would only be gone for half that time, leaving Leadville at eight in the morning and arriving in the gold mining town of Breckenridge at noon for a gala celebration and picnic before turning around and coming home again. And though it would only be for the day, John Henry counted himself lucky to be getting even that far away, all things considered.

The excursion left from the station in Leadville on a chilly Sunday in October, on the third anniversary of the gunfight in Tombstone. It was a fittingly gloomy day, with a drizzling snow just as there had been that other October morning, and John Henry couldn't help but think how little his life had changed in the three years since then. He'd been dodging death back then and he was still dodging it now, being jostled in and out of jail, and with crowds of people watching to see what he'd do next. Or so it felt to him, anyhow, as the other passengers hushed and stepped aside when he mounted the platform, waiting to board the train. *"That's Doc Holliday!"* they whispered, as if he couldn't hear them talking behind his back. *"Do you think he's got that fancy pistol on him, the one he shot Bill Allen with? Do you think he means to murder someone here?"* He almost stopped to announce that the pistol in question had been stolen away by the police as evidence in the upcoming court case, leaving him less armed than most of the other men there—then thought better of it. Considering the state of things, it was probably better to have the crowds treat him like a dangerous man and leave him alone.

But once the train and its two locomotives pulled away from the station and steamed up the long grade toward the highpoint of the Continental Divide, 12,000 feet into the sky, nobody paid him much attention anymore. There were better things to look at than a solitary man sitting in the chair car and huddled in a heavy wool coat—the same coat he'd worn on that other October morning. Even his wardrobe hadn't changed much since the day the McLaury brothers and Billy Clanton died—men who'd been supposedly unarmed, like Bill Allen, but meant to kill him anyhow. And not wanting to remember, he tried to focus on the view outside the rail car instead. What's done is done, the rhythm of the rails seemed to say, what's gone is gone.

But Mattie wasn't gone, though he had thought he'd lost her forever. Mattie wasn't gone, and she would be pleased to hear how he'd taken the excursion train over the pass to Breckenridge and back. And thinking of Mattie, he started to compose a letter to her, telling her about the trip:

Mount Elbert, off to the west, is already crested with snow and Mount Massive towers into the clouds, white as snow themselves.

The mountains are like fortress walls around these valleys, and studded with pine trees. At Bird's Eye, near top of the line, the tracks come back around one-hundred-eighty degrees, giving the engineer a look back across the gulch at his own caboose. We see him looking back at us and he waves. There is rock cascading down the mountainside here, the roadbed just wide enough for the two lines of track together. Waterfalls plunge over the black rocks down to the East Fork of the Arkansas River, a sliver of silver meandering along the valley floor eight-hundred feet below. And past that, the mountains rise again, quilted with color: blue Spruce and Lodgepole pine and golden-haired aspen, slender and white-limbed and quivering at Autumn's touch. There is game here, deer and elk, squirrel, cottontail, snowshoe hare . . .

By the time they reached Breckenridge, he was feeling fine again.

Shooting Bill Allen had accomplished one thing at least: he wasn't laughed at anymore. Nor did he find himself challenged on every corner, as he had been after the gunfight in Tombstone. Instead, there seemed to be a sort of sympathy growing for him amongst the sporting class, along with a rising tide of animosity toward Johnny Tyler's whole Sloper gang. With any luck, the sea change would bring him a sympathetic jury, as well, come December.

But there were other dangers in Leadville as autumn darkened into winter—ice on the city streets, wolves in the hills, illnesses stalking. And John Henry took sick again with another bout of the pneumonia that had nearly killed him the year before. So when his court date was called for the weekend before Christmas, he had only enough strength to appear for the initial proceedings before requesting a continuance until the March session. The sympathies of Leadville, he hoped, would wait on him awhile longer.

He stayed close to Mannie's place those months, working when he could and resting when he wasn't working. He wrote long letters to Mattie. He spent long hours sitting in a rocking chair, staring out of his bedroom window at the mountains towering in the distance. Some days, the saloon cat found its way upstairs and came to sit on his lap, purring while he rocked. The cat was a comfort, until it wandered off one night and never returned, and John Henry had a dream that it had been eaten by wolves.

But slowly, he got better again—never all the way well, and never as well as he had been before the last course of the illness, but no longer feverish and bedridden, at least. So when an invitation came from the Leadville Miner's Union to attend the first annual Miner's Ball, he didn't decline. An event would give him something to look forward to, after having nothing but a trial to look forward to for all these months. And the truth was, he felt flattered to have been invited, seeing the invitation as a sign of acceptance by the better society of Leadville, miners being better than sporting men, socially speaking. Well, he was a gentleman, after all, even under bond and accused of a capital crime. And a gentleman ought to be invited to balls and socials, and ought to attend if he had the strength to go. Besides, it would give him something amusing to write to Mattie about, and he'd been sadly short on amusing stories of late.

But it was Kate he was thinking of when he arrived at the Miner's Union Ball held in the prettily decorated lobby of the Leadville City Hall. Kate had loved such affairs, and was at her most dazzling when attending them. And how she loved to dress for the party! Her costume plans took weeks of preparation beforehand, her toilette took all day and often made them late in arriving—especially when she tested her wiles on John Henry and seduced him into a session of lovemaking even before the party began. Yes, Kate would have loved being escorted to a Leadville dance, and he would have enjoyed taking her.

So where was she now? he wondered, now that her lover Johnny Ringo was dead and gone. Who was escorting her now? For it was certain that Kate wouldn't be living alone, wherever she was. She liked having an audience too much for that. She liked the theatricality of a love affair, even when it was going down in flames—or maybe especially then. There was more drama in the ruins, and Kate was nothing if not dramatic. And for the first time, it occurred to John Henry that he and Kate could never have been lastingly happy together, even without his feelings for Mattie, even if he'd had the patience and the loyalty of Job. For happiness wasn't exciting enough for Kate. And neither was he, in the end.

Wyatt's Josie would know where Kate was, if he really wanted to find her, seeing as they'd been friends back in Tombstone. But Wyatt and Josie were off in the Coeur d'Alene country of Idaho, chasing the gold rush, and likely hard to find themselves. And why disturb them, when they were so happily prospecting together? Wyatt had found his match, so it seemed, and Josie had found hers in him.

And John Henry was alone at the Miner's Union Ball, even in the crowd of a hundred and more guests. The string orchestra played waltzes and polkas and reels he was too tired to join; the supper committee presented a lavish repast he didn't have the appetite to eat. And he ended up spending the rest of the night as he spent every night: drinking the liquor and trying not to remember what he couldn't forget.

The trial was called to order on the third Saturday in March, then recessed over Sunday with nothing more accomplished than having empaneled a jury. Truth was, it had been hard to find twelve unbiased citizens, with all the newspaper stories that had been written since the shooting. So after three rounds of prospective jurors being questioned with no one completely ignorant of the case, the attorneys gave up and accepted twelve men who at least didn't claim to be siding with one party or the other. And then on Monday morning, the trial began.

The Lake County Courthouse was again crowded with spectators, as it had been for the hearing the summer before. But this time there was a real show to see, with a real jury whose verdict would decide John Henry's fate—whether freedom, or a life sentence of hard labor in the Colorado State Penitentiary in Cañon City. Not that the penal code demanded a life sentence for assault, but any length of time in prison would be a life sentence for him, sick as he'd been and continued to be. Even a week in the Leadville City jail had nearly broken him.

So he listened intently as the attorneys made their opening statements, and hoped the jury was listening intently, as well, weighing truth against lies. And that Blind Justice, teetering overhead, wouldn't come crashing down.

The lion's share of the day was taken up by the District Attorney, assisted by a team of windbag barristers who stated and restated the charges without saying much of anything new—except for the parts they made up or purposefully left out. "The testimony will show," said Alban Danford, Esquire, of the firm of Dunfield and Danford, "that William Allen, the prosecuting witness, on the nineteenth day of August last, went into Hyman's place on Harrison Avenue, and had no sooner got inside the door of the club room when a pistol was fired at him by Doc Holliday, the defendant. Until the time of the shooting on that day, Allen had not seen Holliday. After the shot was fired, Allen turned to run out the door of Hyman's place, when Holliday fired again, the bullet passing through Allen's arm. Holliday was endeavoring to fire a third shot when he was arrested. It will also be shown that on that day Holliday had made frequent threats to kill Allen."

Then he looked patronizingly toward the jury and paused a moment to educate them on the legal definition of the crime alleged.

"An assault is an unlawful attempt coupled with a present ability to commit a violent injury upon the person of another, and if you believe from the evidence beyond a reasonable doubt that the defendant pointed the revolver at Mr. Allen and discharged the same with malice afore-thought or with a reckless and total disregard for human life, and that the use of said weapon was likely to kill Mr. Allen, then you must find the defendant guilty of an assault with intent to commit murder. Murder, gentlemen of the jury. It is only because of the defendant's poor aim that Mr. Allen is yet alive today, and not murdered as Holliday intended. Remember that point as you listen to these witnesses bear testimony. And if it is shown by the evidence that William Allen went into the saloon in a quiet and peaceful manner, and that Holliday, before the shooting, had threatened to kill Allen, which evidence will be here thoroughly discovered, then you will be justified in bringing a verdict of guilty."

While the lecture went on, John Henry scribbled notes to his defense team, listing every inaccuracy and imagination. Bill Allen may not have seen him before the shooting took place, but he'd certainly come looking for him earlier that day. And the only threats John Henry made were in the cause of self-defense against Allen's weeks of threatenings. As for the affront to his marksmanship, that didn't even deserve a comment. If he'd meant to kill Bill Allen, he'd have done it. But his attorneys, a pair of public defenders with already heavy caseloads, took only a passing glance at his notes before they began their own opening statements.

"Your honor," said Mr. Ashton, the junior partner, "if the evidence disclosed such a state of affairs as pictured by the prosecution, then, of course, the jury would find the defendant guilty. But the testimony will not show any such state of affairs. It will, on the contrary, show that on account of a financial transaction, Mr. Allen had threatened to kill Dr. Holliday, and had hunted about the streets for him, carrying a deadly weapon. Dr. Holliday had called upon the city marshal and talked with him about the probable trouble with Allen, and the marshal's advice was simply to not have trouble with Allen. No offer of protection was made; no admonishment to Mr. Allen was given. Dr. Holliday was several times informed by his friends that Allen was looking for him, and would kill him on sight. If this state of facts is shown by the testimony, then the defendant would have been justified in taking a gun and killing Allen, and the jury must find him not guilty."

John Henry was less than impressed by the performance of his counsels, both of whom seemed eager to finish up the case and get back to more interesting matters, and made little effort to dazzle the jury as the prosecution had. And when the proceedings ran past supper time and the Judge said there would be a night session, Mr. Taylor, the senior partner, came to his feet and said that he was not able to finish the case at night as he had too much work on hand already. So the day ended with the witnesses being sworn in but no actual testimony given—and John Henry left the courthouse feeling more fitful than when he went in.

The prosecution occupied the next two days, bringing the same parade of witnesses that had appeared at the hearing—with the notable addition of Bill Allen himself, now healed enough to take the stand.

Allen had been well-coached by his lawyers, that was plain to see, as he arrived in court wearing a somber black suit and a plain boiled shirt and looking more like a preacher about to recite a Sunday sermon than a saloon bouncer—an oddly muscular preacher who might have wrestled with the Devil a time or two. His only accessory was a white sling that cradled his wounded right arm—the arm he rubbed now and then during his testimony, as if it still pained him, though that too could have been coached by his lawyers.

"Can you tell us, sir," his lawyers asked, being amusingly respectful, "where you were on the afternoon of the nineteenth of August last, where you went from there, and why?"

"I was in my room until about four o'clock in the afternoon. Then I came downtown and got some tickets for the theater before going to work at the Monarch, where I am a bartender."

"And you stayed there at the Monarch, working at the bar?"

Allen nodded. "Yessir, for a time. Then I went down to Hyman's saloon and had no sooner got inside than someone began shooting. I heard the first shot and turned to run out the door, and saw Holliday leaning over the cigar case with a revolver pointed at me. Before I got out the door, I slipped and fell, and a second shot struck me here," he said, rubbing his wounded arm.

"And what has been the effect of the wound?"

"The arteries in my arm were severed and I nearly died from blood loss. I was paralyzed for some time, and not able to work. For two weeks I was confined to my bed, and for two months I could do no work with the arm at all."

"And how did you escape the mêlée?"

"Holliday was about to shoot again when the barkeep caught him. I was then searched by Captain Bradbury, and afterwards placed in a wagon and taken to my room."

"And was any weapon found on you when you were thus searched?"

"No sir, not even a penknife."

"And what was it that made you go into Hyman's saloon that afternoon?"

Bill Allen shrugged. "I had no particular object in going there at that time."

"Did you know the defendant, Doc Holliday, was in that saloon at the time?"

"No sir, I did not."

John Henry could hardly write his notes fast enough, with all the errors in Allen's testimony. And as the prosecution went on with the questioning, the only thing that Allen seemed to remember correctly was the positions they were each in at the time of the shooting—a hard thing to falsify with so many witnesses in the saloon at the time and the first slug still lodged in the frame of the door. And even when the defense took over for the cross-examination, Bill Allen went on making up his story.

"Isn't it true," Mr. Ashton said, "that you demanded money from Dr. Holliday, and threatened to 'do him up' if you did not receive it?"

"I don't recall anything about any money," said Allen.

"And do you not recall threatening Dr. Holliday in front of a gambler named Edward Donner, saying you could 'do up the son of a bitch', and that you would be happy to take his pistol and put it in soak?"

"I don't remember such a thing."

"Do you remember coming out of the Monarch Saloon on the day of the shooting, and having the owner, Mr. Cy Allen, tell you not to go to Hyman's saloon as Holliday was there?"

"All I remember Cy telling me was that Holliday had a gun and was going to kill me, and I said that I would not have any trouble with anyone."

"Do you remember asking a certain Officer Charles Robinson, who was in the Monarch Saloon on the day of the shooting, to go and arrest Dr. Holliday and take his pistols away from him?"

"I don't remember anything like that."

"Do you remember saying in front of a man named Pat Sweeney that if Dr. Holliday did not pay you five dollars before such and such a date, you would 'beat out his brains'?"

"I don't remember that conversation taking place."

"You seem to be having trouble remembering anything about last August the nineteenth. Perhaps your memories are more clear about earlier events in your life. Do you remember shooting and killing a man in Illinois and being tried for the same?"

There was a shudder of excitement in the courtroom, and Bill Allen suddenly lost some of his composure, while John Henry gained a little more respect for his lackluster public defenders. Of course the prosecution objected, but the point had been made nonetheless.

So after the second day, John Henry left the courtroom feeling a little more optimistic than he'd been the day before. His court assigned attorneys might be capable enough, if they put their minds to the job.

By Wednesday, he was feeling the effects of the early court sessions. He wasn't used to being anywhere but in bed at nine o'clock in the morning, let alone dressed and shaved and sitting beside his attorneys at the defense counsel table. If the testimony weren't a matter of life and death to him, he might have been tempted to doze while the prosecution ran through their long list of witnesses.

There was Town Marshal Faucett who'd heard Holliday say that he would shoot Allen on sight; R.B. Williard, a sport who was playing cards at Hyman's earlier in the afternoon and heard Holliday ask someone to fetch his gun; George Ahrens, a miner who was outside the saloon at the first shot and came running in to find Holliday firing at Bill Allen; Captain Bradbury, the policeman who'd disarmed Holliday immediately after the shooting and said the pistol was still half-cocked when he took hold of it; William Taugherbaugh, the clerk at May's clothing store next door to Hyman's saloon who saw the victim being placed in an express wagon and taken away with blood streaming from his arm; George Libby, a gambler who'd watched the whole thing and claimed the victim had no gun on him at the time of the shooting; and Dr. D'Avignon, who'd treated Allen and said that the gunshot had cut the artery and stopped the circulation, nearly causing the loss of the arm. All of which was true, but not the whole story. It wasn't so much what he'd done as why he'd done it, and the prosecution seemed inclined to overlook that information.

So John Henry took notes on every testimony and passed the papers to Attorney Ashton, who read quickly through them before passing them to Attorney Taylor, who read them before beginning the cross-examinations. And John Henry was almost grateful, if one could call it gratitude, that his many legal troubles through the years had taught him something useful about the legal process. For without his help, his attorneys might not have been able to get the story straight at all—and with his help, they managed to refute almost all of Bill Allen's perjurious testimony.

But the trial wasn't over yet, and the defense would still have to prove that John Henry had acted in self-defense when he shot down an unarmed man.

On Thursday morning, the defense opened by calling Pat Sweeney to the stand. The gambler who had never done John Henry wrong in the past might just become the star witness now.

"I know Holliday and Allen," Sweeney said after laying his hand on the Bible, "have known them both for some time. Had a talk with Allen before the shooting in the Monarch Saloon. He said Doc owed him five dollars, and that if he didn't pay him by Tuesday, he would do him up. I told Doc about it. I then saw Doc and Allen both on the day of the shooting, saw Allen coming down the street toward Hyman's saloon. He was walking rapidly, with his hand in his coat pocket. He entered the saloon and looked around the gambling room as if he was hunting someone. I saw the butt of a revolver in his hand. After Allen went out I went to Doc Holliday's room to tell him that this man was looking for him. He asked me what to do, and I told him I didn't know. He asked me to go find Officer Bradbury or Marshal Faucett. I went, but I couldn't find either of them. I saw Allen standing by the stove in the Monarch saloon, and saw him talking to Cy Allen before Captain Bradbury called to him."

The prosecution couldn't wait to cross-examine.

"You seem to have a particularly close relationship with the defendant. Would you say this puts you in a compromising or prejudicial situation as a witness, Mr. Sweeney?"

He took the question placidly. "I know both Doc Holliday and Bill Allen, and am not on unfriendly terms with either one of them. When I met Allen the first time, he was on the police force here."

"And what was your relation to the parties in question at the time of the shooting?"

"I went to see Allen about four days before the shooting and he said that Holliday had taken a loan of five dollars from him, and he would give him until Tuesday to pay him."

"You are aware that Mr. Allen denies such a financial arrangement?"

"Then he's a damned liar. Everybody knows Bill gave Doc five dollars and was wanting it back."

"And why do you suppose, if everyone knew of this troubling financial situation, no one offered to rectify matters?" Attorney Danford smiled as he asked the question, as if he had just caught an annoying rodent in a trap.

"I guess everyone knew it wasn't the money Allen was after. That was just a pretext for doing Doc in."

Pat's testimony would have been even more persuasive, if he hadn't walked out of Hyman's saloon just as the shooting took place, missing the most important part of the story. And after him, the defense called only one more witness.

"Mr. Donnell," said Taylor, "can you tell us what your employment was at the time of the alleged shooting?"

"I was a dealer at the Monarch Saloon, in the game room. Don't work there anymore, however."

"And what can you tell us of the parties in question?"

"I knew both Holliday and Allen and had seen them at the Monarch some days before the shooting. They were in conversation, when Allen stepped from behind the bar with his hand in his pocket as if there were a gun there. He told Doc Holliday he had better get the money by Tuesday or he would do him up. I could see that Allen had something in his hand. I imagine it might have been a pistol."

"And what about the day of the shooting?"

"I was out of town at the time, and did not see it happen."

"Thank you," said Mr. Taylor, and turned the witness over to the prosecution, who declined to cross-examine.

"That's it?" John Henry whispered to his lawyers. "That's all you have for me? Where's the rest of my witnesses? You heard what Pat said: everybody knew Allen was comin' for me!"

"We've already established that there was a financial transaction involved," said Mr. Ashton, "and you can tell about the threats yourself when you take the stand. You're fully capable of speaking on your own behalf."

"But you can't leave it at my word against his! We need more witnesses! Hell, we need the whole town to testify! Surely, with all the saloons on Harrison Street and all the sports who knew about the situation between Allen and me . . ."

"You show me which sports," Mr. Taylor said, "and we'll try to get the sheriff to round them up for you. But gamblers have a way of disappearing whenever the law comes around, and I don't have all day to go chasing them."

"But we're runnin' out of time!" John Henry said. "You can't mean to end like this without even tryin' to win my case!"

Attorney Taylor was already packing up his things, getting ready for the lunch recess. "You're right, we are running out of time. But this isn't our only case. Mr. Ashton and I have a mining rights trial to handle next week, and an office full of paperwork waiting on us as well. So this, I am afraid, is the best we can do. We'll have to leave things until the jury instructions, and throw some precedent cases at the jurors. There's bound to be something about similar cases in a jurisdiction somewhere near here . . ."

But John Henry wasn't content to leave his life to the chance of a precedent case being found.

"All right, if you won't get me more witnesses, I will," he said, and Taylor raised an eyebrow in amusement.

"You want to subpoena your own witnesses? That's not something I am familiar with in criminal law."

"But it's not impossible?"

Taylor thought a moment, and turned to his partner. "I suppose not. What do you think, Mr. Ashton?"

And as soon as the lunch recess was called, John Henry was standing in the Judge's chambers, being sworn in as an officer of the court, with a handful of subpoenas to deliver to whomever he could find before the court was called back into session.

So now he was law and outlaw rolled into one, with one last hour left to save his life.

Lunch wasn't the busiest time in the saloons, with the mine workers still on the day shift and the sports still sleeping off their hangovers from the night before, but there were enough customers to act as trial witnesses, if you added all the saloons together. So he started at Hyman's place at the far end of Harrison and worked back from there toward the Court-house, stopping into every saloon and gaming hall along the way. At the Board of Trade and Gandolph & Company, at Saint Ann's Rest and the Texas House, at the Baer Brothers and Prendergast's and twenty places in between, he pushed through the doors and banged his cane on the bar and gave the same hoarsely shouted invitation:

"Free drinks for a month! Courtesy of the public defender's office, for every man who will stand up for me in court this afternoon!"

It didn't take long until he had his own parade of witnesses, following him back to the Lake County Courthouse like the Pied Piper's rats.

When court reassembled, the crowd overflowed the benches and filled the waiting area with standing-room only spectators, and the Judge had to ask where all the people had come from.

"These are our . . . witnesses, your Honor," said the public defender, looking around him in bewilderment at the dregs of Leadville society all crowded into the hallowed halls of law and order, for John Henry hadn't yet told him what had convinced every drinking man in Leadville to show up, eager to testify. That information could wait until he'd won the case.

"I do not intend to hold this trial beyond the end of the week, Mr. Taylor," the Judge replied. "There will simply not be enough time for all these men to take the stand."

But John Henry wasn't about to let his hard work be frustrated. He leaned over to Attorney Ashton and whispered a question, and Ashton tugged at the sleeve of Attorney Taylor, who listened and then said:

"Your honor, if I might approach the bench?"

So after a brief consultation, the Judge nodded, seeming a little non-plussed himself, and said to the crowd:

"Gentlemen, and I use that term loosely, I have agreed to take the unusual, but not necessarily inappropriate action, under the present cir-cumstances, of swearing you all in en masse and taking your testimony as a group, so to speak. Raise your right hands, please."

"But your Honor!" objected the law firm of Dunfield and Danford, speaking nearly in unison, "what about the Bible? You can't swear in these men without each one laying his hand on the Bible!"

"Counselors, I don't believe there are enough Bibles in Leadville for each of these men to hold one all at once," said the Judge. "And I doubt very much their holding one would make a substantial difference anyway. Gentlemen," he said again, addressing the crowd, "raise your right hand. Do you all, each and every one of you, swear to tell the truth, the whole truth, and nothing but the truth, so help you God?"

"I do!" said a chorus of voices, joined by a couple of "Amens!" and John Henry's witnesses were ready to testify.

They all said the same thing, of course, or a variation of it—and most of them even meant it. When the public defender asked them all, altogether, if they recalled Bill Allen making threats against the life of Dr. Holliday, they nodded and shouted and otherwise showed that they had indeed heard such threats. And when the public defender asked them if they considered Bill Allen, former policeman and fire department fitness trainer and current saloon bouncer, capable of "doing in" and killing someone of as slight a build as Dr. Holliday, the courtroom resounded in the affirmative.

The prosecution, disgusted with the entire proceeding, declined even a cursory cross-examination.

And then it was John Henry's turn to take the witness stand, telling the same story he'd told from the start, with his lawyers asking the same questions he'd been asked again and again. Yes, Allen had loaned him five dollars. No, he had not been able to repay the debt. Yes, Allen threatened to do him up or other such words if he did not pay by such and such a date. No, he did not consider that Allen was unarmed when he came into Hyman's saloon that afternoon.

"I considered that he had a pistol on him, as he had that mornin' when others of my acquaintance had seen him. I considered that if he had the pistol he meant to use it, as he had promised to do, and that my life was worth more than his five dollars. So I fired the first shot and missed, and fired again and struck him in the arm. I did not mean to kill him, or I would have done it. I only meant to stop him from drawin' the pistol I supposed he had in his right pocket, and I did so. I consider that I shot in my own self-defense, and not as an act of assault. And I challenge any man here to say otherwise, if he were in the same position as I. A man has a right to defend himself, and the law has an obligation to uphold that right."

"The law will decide what its obligations are," the Judge said sternly, before adjourning the court while he instructed the jury. And then came the final arguments.

It took two hours for the attorneys on both sides to restate their cases, but only fifteen minutes for the jury to decide John Henry's fate.

"We, the jury," said the foreman, reading the verdict out loud, "in the case of the People versus John Holliday, find the defendant *not guilty*."

The entire courtroom, packed with spectators and reporters and a hundred saloon patrons, let out a cheer.

There was nothing to keep him in Leadville, and plenty of reasons for him to leave—particularly his lawyers, who would soon discover that they owed hundreds of dollars in drinks at the saloons on Harrison Street. So John Henry wasted no time in packing his things and taking a twenty dollar loan from Mannie Hyman, with a promise to repay as soon as he could, then buying a ticket on the High Line Railroad. And this time, he wouldn't have to turn around at Breckenridge.

He arrived in Denver after a ten hour train ride, bought a paper from the newsboy at Union Station, and headed to the National Hotel for a long sleep. He had no idea what he would be doing after that, other than finding a way to turn Mannie Hyman's twenty dollars into a substantial amount more. But with only those twenty dollars to his name—less now, actually, after paying for the train and the hotel and a couple of meals—he'd have a hard time finding a high stakes table or favorable odds on a horse.

Throwing in Bill Allen's gold piece was the last thing he wanted to do, but when the rest of his cash went for drinks and penny ante games that didn't amount to much, he knew he had no choice. He was lucky to be getting into the poker game at all with some fancy sports at Ed Chase's Cricket Club who had an empty seat and thought it amusing to be playing alongside the infamous Doc Holliday. Without his fading notoriety, the five dollars wouldn't have bought him into a keno game.

He lasted a week at the Cricket Club before an unlucky hand lost him the gold piece and almost everything else he'd won along the way. The sports were sad to see him go, so they said, but glad to take his money. And once again he was nearly broke—and this time, he had no place to turn.

He knew he was going to have to ask for help from someone. But from whom? He couldn't ask Wyatt, who was off in the Coeur d'Alene gold-fields chasing his own elusive fortune. He couldn't ask Bat, who was sheriffing down in Trinidad and had already done more than enough for him. He couldn't even ask Barney Ford, the only rich man he knew in Denver, who'd already saved his life once and was finished repaying that debt. So where could he turn in his desperate situation?

The solution, when it came to him, was so obvious it almost made him laugh. It was ironic, really, that he had come to this after running from it for so long. But sick as he'd been and worn out as he was, he couldn't think of any other option. He was broke, he was alone, and weary, so weary of struggling along. So he bought himself a last bottle of whiskey and downed most of it, gathering his courage, before taking an unsteady walk to the Western Union office at the train station to send a wire to his father.

Henry Holliday's reply came quickly, but not in the way that John Henry had anticipated. He had hoped his father would send money, and leave it at that. He had hoped the distance between them, in miles and years and everything else, would somehow shield him from his father's displeasure. But instead of sending money or simply ignoring the request altogether, Henry sent him a train ticket and a letter explaining that he was himself on his way to New Orleans for a reunion of Mexican War veterans, and that John Henry should meet him there. It was a shrewd move on Henry's part, sending only the ticket and nothing more. If John Henry really wanted help, he'd have to come beg for it in person.

He almost didn't go, having to fight a temptation to throw the ticket away or cash it in and live on the remains. But then what would he do? And so he went, pausing just before he boarded the train at Union Station to buy a newspaper so he'd have something to read along the way. The newsboy, a fair-haired lad with polite manners and eyes of china blue, took his dime and tucked it neatly into a money purse, counting the total therein and making a note of the same on a torn piece of paper.

"You're careful with your money," John Henry said, almost admiringly. "I reckon your father's pleased with your economy." His own father was surely not pleased with his.

"I wouldn't know," the boy replied, "my father run off 'afore I was born."

"I am sorry to hear that."

"Nothin' to be sorry for. He wasn't much account, or so says my aunt. She raised me after my mother died. But I'm on my own now."

"On your own?" John Henry asked, surprised. The boy was barely out of knee pants. "You're how old? Nine years, maybe? Ten?"

"Eight, sir, nearly. But I'm smart for my age."

"I can see that." But he was also thin, as if he didn't eat enough, and sunburned across his high cheekbones as if he spent too much time outdoors. "Tell you what, if you promise to buy yourself some supper with it, not spend it on liquor or card games, I'll give you a half eagle for another copy of that paper."

"Fifty cents for one paper, Sir? You must be rich or crazy, one or the other."

"Let's say I like to read," John Henry replied, and tossed him the coin. And though his father would have called it foolishness to give away almost his last dollar, he knew that Mattie would be proud.

Chapter Fifteen

New Orleans, 1885

IT WAS LOVE AT FIRST SIGHT, THOUGH HE KNEW THERE WAS NO FUTURE in the affair. But how could he help being captivated, when she curved so sensuously around her crescent of river and flirted so seductively from under her filigreed balconies? She was a woman who knew her charms, and she wasn't too modest to use them. And from John Henry's first night with her, he was entranced.

He wasn't the first visitor to fall in love with New Orleans, for the city had been entertaining suitors for nearly two centuries, from French settlers to Spanish governors to the Americans who paid fifteen-million dollars for her and got the rest of the Louisiana Purchase as a bonus. All who came under her river delta spell left their love offerings of language and music and architecture. The accent of New Orleans—wide and slow as the Mississippi itself—was made of the memories left by all of these: Creole, Cajun, Indian, Southern plantation. The city smiled when she said her name—"N'Awlins!"

He arrived a day ahead of his father, checking into the Gregg House Hotel on Canal Street where the Mexican War veterans were headquartered. He could have used some sleep after his long journey, but he was too apprehensive of the coming reunion to relax. After all these years and all these miles away, he wasn't sure what they would have to say to one another, or if his father would pick up where he'd left off, cataloging his son's faults and finding him a disappointment.

Bourbon Street took the edge off his nerves, with its saloons and gaming halls and bordellos singing out into the night, and by midnight he was worn out with the sight and sound and sense of the place. In his healthier days, he would have romanced the city all night long and not gone to bed until dawn. But weary as he was, the best he could do was to refill his silver pocket flask and have a drink before falling into an exhausted sleep in his rented bed at the Gregg House.

It wasn't surprising that he dreamt of women, after having his senses so aroused by the city. There was Kate, dressed up like a Spanish senorita and riding a shining black horse down narrow cobbled streets where ladies' lingerie hung like banners from the iron balconies. There was Mattie, dressed in wedding white and waiting for him on the steps of the Cathedral of St. Louis, smiling sweetly and whispering something in French. There was his mother inside the church, kneeling before the idoled altar and praying the rosary for his Protestant soul. But even in his sleep, he knew the dream was wrong. His mother wasn't Catholic and would never have set foot in a Catholic cathedral, let alone prayed a Popish prayer at a candle-lit altar, and Mattie's wedding white was for Jesus, not him. Then from somewhere in his dreaming memory came things that seemed more real: his Mother's voice calling him to come sit beside her for evening prayers, his father's stern rebuke over some mismanaged chore.

And then he was a child again, standing proud the day his father had left Georgia for the War looking lean and handsome in a steel gray uniform with a silver-bladed sword at his side. His father was a hero, and he was a hero's son . . .

He woke with the late afternoon light slanting in through long shuttered windows, and knew at once that he was not alone. For even before he opened his eyes to see who his visitor was, he could smell the sweet odor of old tobacco—the kind that both his father and Wyatt smoked.

"Mornin', Pa," he said, his words coming out with a cough that tore at his chest.

"You' been drinkin' all night," Henry Holliday said, more a statement than a question.

He didn't bother denying it. He had been drinking some, after all, falling asleep with the whiskey flask still in his hand. But drinking never had been much of an issue with his father, being a man who drank some himself.

"Mind if I open the windows?" his father asked. "It's stuffy in here."

It was so like Henry to be all business and no sentimentality, even after their long absence from one another. His father hadn't changed at all.

But when Henry swung open the shutters, the sunlight showed that he had changed some. His face, once hard and tanned from years in the sun supervising his farms and orchards, had fallen into lines and furrows. Like a field gone fallow, John Henry thought, his father's face looked worn out. His hair, once handsomely shot through with steely streaks was now gone all gray, worn out as well. Yet he stood erect as ever, his posture resolute. Henry Holliday at sixty-six years of age had both changed and not changed, and somehow John Henry took comfort in that.

But it wasn't until he pulled himself from the bed and stood before the tall mirror over the dressing table that he realized how much he himself had changed. For gazing into the mirror, he could see both his own reflection and his father's behind him, and he recognized for the first time how much alike they looked, with the same square jaws, the same blue eyes, the same steel gray hair—

It was a shock to see that he looked near as old as his father, now that illness and hard living had taken their toll. His own face was ashen and thin, his shoulders stooped over his tortured lungs. The mirror reflected two old men, both past their prime, though he himself was only thirty-four years old.

He sighed, a rasping sound, and caught his father looking back at him in the mirror. Their eyes met, and in that moment John Henry saw not the angry disappointment he had remembered all those years, but sadness. And if he hadn't known his father better, he might even have imagined the shine of tears there, as well.

"I'll be fine, Pa," he said, "once I get some rest. It's just been a rough year or two, with the weather and the pneumonia and all . . ."

His father nodded and said nothing, then cleared his throat and flicked cigar ash onto the floor.

"The Veterans are meeting tomorrow mornin' to take a steamboat upriver to the Exposition," Henry said. "I've never sailed on a riverboat before."

"Neither have I," John Henry replied, and thought that there was so much that he still hadn't done in his life—and so much that he had. It would take more than this brief time in New Orleans to tell it all.

Henry Holliday had brought a traveling companion along with him, a lanky teenaged boy from Valdosta by the name of Zan Griffith, short for William Alexander, whose father owned the local livery stable. As a serving boy Zan's manners were rustic, but he was good at carrying bags and brushing down traveling clothes, and so had made Henry's long journey from Georgia more comfortable. He was also amusing in his enthusiastic excitement over the trip, having never before traveled farther from home than Thomasville at the terminus of the Atlantic and Gulf Line Railroad—and that was all of sixty miles from Valdosta. Now he was in New Orleans where everything seemed foreign and fascinating—especially the food, which Zan ate with incautious curiosity. On his first day in the City, he feasted on hot Café au Lait and warm fresh beignets, rich oyster Jambalaya and aromatic Filé Gumbo, spicy Crawfish Etouffée and a whole bagful of sugary Pralines, then slept as well as if he'd dined on his usual sweet potatoes and greens.

"The boy's got an iron stomach," Henry said with some admiration as they watched Zan eat his way through the day. "Used to be a time when I could eat like that, before three wars disrupted my digestion." Then he nodded his approval when Zan asked if he could order a second bowl of gumbo, an affirmation that was not lost on John Henry. In his own childhood, he'd been warned to temperance by his mother and berated by his father for taking as much supper as his young stomach craved. Now here was stern Henry not only allowing a lavish indulgence, but even encouraging it. But Zan was grateful enough for the generosity and said his thanks between every dish.

Zan's enthusiasm didn't stop when supper was over. He swallowed up New Orleans like he swallowed up his food, hardly stopping to chew before tasting something new. As they strolled along the cobblestone streets of the French Quarter, he raced ahead of them from one new sight to another: a river man shucking oysters from shell to bucket with swift blows of a knife blade, an Indian squaw sitting cross-legged in the street with her baskets of Sassafras bark and Filé spice, the Catholic cathedral crowded with black women in white turbans saying Mass in Frenchified African accents. It was all amazing to Zan Griffith, and even the cigar shop where Henry stopped to buy himself a box of the famed Creole cigars left him wide-eyed with wonder.

"Jean Delpit's is the finest tobacco in the world," Henry explained as they paused before entering the St. Louis Street mansion that served as both home and shop to the Delpit family. The residence was on the second floor of the pink brick building, shuttered Creole-style against the street with a balcony at the back facing a private courtyard. The tobacco shop occupied the ground floor, where high arched windows let in the light and let out the aroma of Louisiana Perique and Natchitoches cut tobaccos, ready for packing and rolling. "Won every award from here to Paris," Henry said with the reverential awe of an accomplished cigar smoker. "You can smell the quality from out here on the street."

But Zan Griffith didn't want to stand around on the street, smelling tobacco. He wanted to be inside, watching the tobacconist at work and pestering him with questions about how the tobacco was cut, how it was dried, how it was stored and rolled and packaged for shipping to other shops around the world. He even admired the tin cases and wooden boxes that contained the loose leaf for those who wanted to roll their own cigars and cigarettes.

"You plannin' on goin' into the tobacco business yourself?" Henry asked as Zan's questions piled up.

"Maybe," the boy replied with a grin. "Or maybe I'll take up cigar smokin' myself. They say you can tell a man's character by the way he takes his tobacco. My Pa just chews, but I like smoke better than spittle. I think I'd rather be a man of quality and smoke my leaf instead, like you, Major Sir."

Henry didn't say anything in acknowledgement of the compliment, but John Henry saw a trace of a smile line his mustached mouth. It was no wonder Henry liked having the boy around, with the way Zan made such eager obeisance. And without wanting it, the thought came to him that if he himself had shown more deference as a youth, perhaps his father would have enjoyed his company too, instead of constantly chastising him. But Zan Griffith wasn't Henry's son, firstborn of the firstborn and heir to the Holliday name, with the whole weight of the family's expectations hanging on him. Zan didn't have anything else to do but be respectful, and Henry didn't require anything else of him.

Like Francisco. The name came like a ghost out of the past. Henry had doted on Francisco too, the boy he had brought back with him from the Mexican War, and Francisco had returned the affection. Unrelated as they were, the soldier and his adopted son had shared a bond that seemed almost like father and child, enough to make Henry weep over Francisco's grave and vow to provide for his widowed wife and children, even if it meant taking away his own son's inheritance.

But the inheritance was long gone now and so was Francisco, and John Henry was foolish to let such memories trouble him. What did it matter if his father had preferred a Mexican orphan boy to himself? What did it matter now if Henry preferred the company of a guileless serving boy? John Henry had only come to New Orleans to collect a hand-out, anyhow, not to rebuild old bridges. What was done was done, and all he needed from his father now was enough money to get himself back to Colorado and settled once more. And once Henry had made that bequest, John Henry would leave and never look back again.

There was no convenient time to talk about money, however, with Henry's Mexican War reunion about to begin. His father would entertain talk about finances when his own business was finished, and not before, and John Henry knew him well enough to wait for the proper moment.

The reunion turned out to be a much bigger event than John Henry would have imagined it, if he had given it any thought at all. To him, the Mexican War was old history now, a faraway story from a faraway time, already long over before he was born. The war that he remembered was the one that had stormed through his own life, with Yankees marching across Georgia and bringing battles closer to home. But to the men of his father's generation, the Mexican War was the best fight of all, a swift and clean campaign that had brought about the Treaty of Guadalupe Hidalgo and doubled the size of the United States. The Mexican War was the first test of Manifest Destiny, and it had proved a complete success. Now, forty years after the Americans had routed the Mexicans from Texas and taken away all of their land north of the Rio Grande, the two nations were friends and business partners once again—a standard for the reunited United States to follow. And if there were any question as to the virtue of the cause and the valor of the men who fought for it, one had only to look at the list of the heroes of the Mexican War: Robert E. Lee, Stonewall Jackson, P.G.T. Beauregard, James Longstreet, Zachary Taylor, Winfield Scott, George McClellan, Ulysses S. Grant. The men who later commanded armies in the War Between the States were trained on the fields of the Mexican War.

That was the tenor of the crowd of veterans as they gathered that bright April morning at the Washington Artillery Hall for their march to the steamer at the head of Canal Street. They were a picturesque party, in the mismatched remainders of their old uniforms: regular army in pale-blue wool suits and dark-blue forage caps; volunteers in various costumes of their own devise, from the Texans who came in buckskin and home-spun to the Mississippi Rifles decked out in crimson shirts and straw hats. Even Henry Holliday was dressed for the day, trussed up tight in the blue wool jacket he'd had stored away since the end of the war. Though it had long since been outgrown and the brass buttons strained tight against their moorings, Henry looked as proud as if he were a new recruit just marching off to war. And he was rightly proud, for there had been so many men volunteering for that fight that half were turned away and only the fittest were accepted into the service. Being a soldier in the Mexican War was a sign of strength and courage. Being a veteran of it was a badge of honor—or so the men who gathered that morning all agreed, as they greeted each other with salutes and embraces and tears of reunion.

"Smells like a cedar closet around here," Zan observed, and John Henry had to agree.

"That's the way the wool smells when it's been put away," he explained, "like cedar wood and camphor balls. I reckon most of these men haven't worn their uniforms in forty years. I don't remember ever seein' my Father's uniform before. He was in Rebel gray in the war I knew."

"Must have been somethin' havin' a Major for a father," Zan said. "That's what everybody in Valdosta calls him, you know. *Major Sir*, even when he was Mayor. But most of the time I call him Mr. Holliday, like he tells me to. Like he told me to call you Dr. Holliday, not *Doc* like the paper did."

"What paper are you talkin' about, Zan?"

"The newspaper, Dr. Holliday, Sir. *The Valdosta Times*. They had a whole special edition about you after that gunfight in Arizona. *Doc Holliday* it called you, and gave the whole story of the trial. My mother kept it, and gave it to me to read before I came along with the Major. She said if I was to meet you in New Orleans, I'd be meetin' somebody mighty famous, and I ought to know somethin' about him beforehand. But I already heard about you, even without the paper. Why, there's not a soul in Valdosta who don't know about Doc Holliday and the gunfight in Tombstone!" He said it all in a rush of words, as though the story were as exciting as a day in New Orleans, as though John Henry's troubles had been something entertaining. Then he added with a look of chagrin, "But when I told the Major about my mother givin' me that paper about Doc Holliday, he scolded me for sayin' it. Said I should never call his son by that name, *Doc* like the paper called you, but always call you Dr. Holliday instead. 'My son is a better man than that story makes out,' he told me. 'My son is a professional man, graduated from the Pennsylvania College of Dental Surgery,' he said, 'and you will treat him with due respect.' I reckon he's mighty proud of you, Dr. Holliday, Sir. I guess you're pretty proud of him, too."

There were no words to answer the boy, and no need to try, as the Mexican Army band struck up in brassy clamor for the march to Canal Street. They'd be a noisy parade, wending their way along the narrow cobbled streets of the French Quarter, one last march for the men who were made heroes in that long-forgotten war. And as the old soldiers fell into step, it struck John Henry that maybe all it took to be a hero was to come out of a fight still alive on the other side—and his father had done that three times over.

The Mexican War veterans had chosen New Orleans as the site of their reunion to coincide with the World's Industrial and Cotton Centennial Exposition celebrating the one-hundredth anniversary of the first bale of cotton shipped out of a United States port. With an investment of nearly $2,000,000 the exposition buildings had risen like voodoo magic out of the swampy land north of the city, turning two-hundred acres of Exposition Park from imagination to reality in just twelve short months. Like all other world's fairs, the Cotton Exposition was having a hard time recouping its investors' money and would probably turn out to be a financial disaster, even with the expensive ticket price of one silver dollar a day for admission. But to the thousands of visitors who crowded the grassy paths between the Louisiana Live Oaks, it was a spectacular success.

There were three main entrances to the Exposition: two by land at Magazine Street and Saint Charles Avenue, and one by water coming up the river from the French Quarter. That was the route the veterans had chosen for their arrival, taking the hour-long steamboat ride up the Mississippi to the dock at the fairgrounds, six miles above the city. Though they could have made a faster arrival by streetcar or carriage through one of the land gates, they could not have made a showier one. Spectators along the shore said they could hear the music of the company even before they could see the boat coming around the crescent bend of the river, a thrilling symphony of marching band and steamboat calliope that set the tone for a grand day of celebration.

The fair was laid out in a long rectangle alongside the Mississippi, set in a tract of old bearded Live Oaks that shaded the grassy walks. Toward the river were the Horticulture, Furniture, Art, and Mexico pavilions. Toward the newly dredged lake were the Live Stock Arena, the Racecourse, and the United States Exhibit Hall. There was a grand fountain in an artificial pond with water jets that shot 120 feet into the air. There were electric lights strung from the trees that illuminated the spring evenings like strange daylight. There were public comfort stations and public telephones and an electric railway, and altogether it was a breathtaking vision of life in the late nineteenth-century, a modern world of electricity and power and progressive invention.

From the Exposition wharf, the Mexican War veterans made their way to the Main Hall—the largest on the fairgrounds and one of the largest buildings ever erected anywhere. With turrets and flagpoles and walls of glittering windows, it covered thirty-three acres of former plantation land and housed exhibits of machinery and manufactures from around the civilized world. The Music Hall at its center was equally immense, with a seating capacity of thirteen-thousand and a magnificent pipe organ at the back of the stage. Yet in spite of its enormity, the place was quiet as a church when the Mexican War Veterans entered and took their places on the stage and the meeting was called to order with a prayer.

It seemed to John Henry, sitting with Zan Griffith on the side aisle of the hall, that the entire mood of the meeting was reverential, beginning with the National Anthem played by Professor Borchert's Military Band and the reading of a lengthy epic poem that saluted "Attention, warriors! brave and true, Appearing here for Love's review!" and continuing through several speeches extolling the heroes of the War and its beneficial effects on the United States. But the oration that won the cheers of the crowd was that offered by the Honorable William M. Burwell, who called for the government to recognize the service of the Mexican War Veterans by paying them a pension, as it had those who served in the Revolution and the War Between the States.

"What reward has been granted them by the Federal Government?" he asked. "We see thousands, tens of thousands, aye, hundreds of thousands of soldiers who served in the civil war drawing from the treasury of a grateful country pensions to assist them in keeping the wolf from the door. Have the Mexican veterans been so rewarded? What recompense does the Government make them for having devoted years of their life to its assistance? I cannot believe the question decided. Let us unite. Let us demand a pension from our fostering government. Comrades, it rests with you!"

The speech brought cheers and tears, and if Washington were listening there might have been a promise for speedy recompense to be made. But John Henry knew better than to think passioned words would impress politicians for whom the War was as forgotten as ancient history. Washington hadn't wanted to put money into protecting its own borders down in the Arizona Territory; it wasn't likely the government would pay for something even less profitable.

"Let's leave them to their reminiscing," he whispered to Zan, as he gathered his hat and cane. "They're bound to be here for hours shakin' hands and congratulatin' themselves, and I'd rather see what there is to see here at the fair."

Zan agreed and came along eagerly, which John Henry appreciated. The truth was, the march through the cobbled streets of the French Quarter had about worn him out and left him aching and wheezy, and he was afraid that if he sat in the stuffy Music Hall much longer he'd embarrass himself and his father both by falling sound asleep. It had taken the last of his concentration to stay politely awake during the speeches—waiting while the Veterans spent the rest of the afternoon swapping old stories would be unbearable. But walking through the enormity of the Exposition would be difficult, as well, so he was glad to have Zan's company to lend an arm when the cane became a burden. He knew he must look like an old man, hobbling along and leaning on a boy for support, but he hardly cared what people thought of him in this foreign and faraway place. And once they were out of the Music Hall and exploring the rest of the fair, his interest overcame his discomfort. For though he'd seen electric lights in Colorado and a couple of telephones in Arizona, he'd never been anywhere with both in such abundance. Even the interiors of the great halls were lit by electricity, an otherworldly illumination that gave a yellow glare to the exhibits. And in that artificial daylight, the collections of native plants and minerals and taxidermied animals in the United States Hall seemed somehow artificial, too.

It was the exhibits presented by the states and territories that captured John Henry's attention, as he and Zan strolled the long promenades of the Government Building. They were laid out according to geography: southern states to the south of the building, northern and eastern states to the north and east, western territories to the west, so that standing in the center of the hall on the huge compass engraved on the floor was like standing in the middle of America itself.

"Let's start in Georgia," Zan said, "then go west like you did," and John Henry thought it a novel approach to a tour of mines and manufactures. So they started with the State of Georgia exhibit, viewing a cased display of native Georgia woods, samples of soft white fibers from the Savannah Cotton Exchange, glassware and plates from the Georgia China and Glass works, and a Confederate canon invented by a foundry worker from Webster County. It was all admirable in a workmanlike way, and as rustic as John Henry remembered his native state. But there was nothing about the exhibit to remind him of his own years there—of growing up in the wake of a war, of falling in love in a hot Southern summer, of trying to please an implacable father, of heartache and anger and a run for his life.

"You look sad," Zan commented, as they left Georgia and crossed over to the State of Texas displays.

"Just tired," John Henry replied, "it's been a long journey." As indeed it had.

The Texas exhibit was fittingly expansive, with separate sections for the many wonders of that wide state, from mountains of minerals and barrels of beach sand to the entire front of a locomotive representing the railroad town of Denison.

"I lived there once," John Henry remarked. "It didn't last long as a boomtown," he said, and turned away from the railroad town to the western frontier with its stuffed buffalos representing the great herds that had nearly disappeared in ten years' time and Indian headdresses in token of the lost nomads of the Llano Estacado. But there were no saloon displays or Faro layouts, no dance hall pianos or outpost supply stores, no iron-barred jail cells or stagecoach wheels worn from long miles crossing the windy Panhandle. And without all that, it didn't really seem like Texas.

They moved on: from Missouri to Colorado, from Kansas to New Mexico, every exhibit bringing back memories of his life. But interesting as the exhibits were, they were somehow empty of what it was that had made those places exciting to John Henry. Like the stuffed buffalo that stood for a whole decade of danger and adventure, the displays seemed glass-eyed and heartless, mere shadows of another world. And walking through the hall felt like walking through a mausoleum cemetery in New Orleans—a beautiful city of the dead without a soul.

Dead but not silent, as the sound of gunfire startled him out of this thoughts.

"What's that noise?" Zan asked. "Sounds like popguns, only louder."

"Sounds like blanks," John Henry corrected, hearing the familiar play of percussion, steel on steel. Then following the firing came a burst of applause.

"It's a gun show!" Zan said with glee. "Over there!" And with his usual eager enthusiasm, he grabbed John Henry's coat sleeve and turned him around, pointing toward the Arizona Territory exhibit. "How did we miss that one?" he asked, then took off at a canter, not waiting to hear the reply.

"We didn't miss it," John Henry said, as he followed along at the more sedate speed of his walking cane. "I just didn't think I'd bother relivin' those particular memories."

But there seemed little choice, as Zan pushed his way past the other onlookers and made them a space at the front of the crowd where they could see the cause of the commotion.

At the center of the Arizona Territory exhibit, between piles of silver ore and a wall-sized map of the desert country, was a live demonstration. At first, John Henry thought it was some kind of ballet going on, with a corps of male dancers in dark suits instead of ballerinas in satin shoes. It could have been a dance he was watching, the way the men turned gracefully to face one another, falling into two straight rows across the floor like an old-fashioned quadrille. But instead of bowing, they pulled pistols from beneath the folds of their long dark clothes and began shooting at each other.

"What is it, Dr. Holliday, Sir?" Zan whispered as they watched the choreographed spectacle.

But before he could find the words to answer, an announcer spoke for him. "Ladies and Gentlemen! I give you the Gunfight at the OK Corral! The famous street fight between Marshal Wyatt Earp and his posse of lawmen and a band of desperate desperados! See how the criminals fall, my good friends! See how the long arm of the law reaches out with hellfire and brimstone to subdue the wicked! See the brave heroes who made their legend in Arizona! Then come to see the Territory for yourself!"

It was all just a sales pitch, a pretty show to encourage adventurous tourists to visit the western desert, but to John Henry it was unnerving. For as the choreographed gunfight reached its graceful finale and Billy Clanton and the McLaury boys fell to the ground in a pretty and painless death, the man in the silver marshal's star stood grinning as though it were all done in a good day's work. And worse, one of his companions picked up his used shotgun, swung it over his head, and cheered.

"Is that what it was like, Dr. Holliday?" Zan asked too loudly. "Is that how you killed them?"

He would have said that it was nothing like that at all, that there was nothing proud about it, that it was the most desperate of moments, frightening, confusing, heart-racing, gut-spilling, smoke-covered, bloody, awful, awful . . .

"*Awful,*" he whispered, as he had the day it happened, and that was all he could say before the crowd converged upon him.

"Is it him? Is that him?" they all seemed to ask at once, "Is that Doc Holliday? Doc! Doc!"

Then the closeness of the crowd, the questions hitting him like gunshots, the electric glare, the airless room all overwhelmed him at once and he broke into a gasping cough that shook him to his knees, and all he could think of was the blood that foamed into his mouth and too late onto his white linen handkerchief.

The crowd hushed, then moved away with a wave of distaste, leaving him alone in a circle of onlookers.

"Ah, that's not him," a small boy's voice sounded, joined by others in a murmur of agreement. "That's not Doc Holliday! Why, that's just an old sick man!"

And one by one, his audience turned and left to discover other, more interesting sights.

"Zan," John Henry whispered as the boy came to his side and shouldered him to a stand, "go find my father . . ."

He hadn't expected Henry to give up the rest of his day at the fair; had only known that no one else could help him back to the city, sick as he was. But Henry came as soon as Zan told him his son was ailing, putting aside his plans to join the other veterans at a special evening showing of the Battle of Sedan cyclorama, the huge circular painting that depicted the entire French and German armies engaged in the most famous conflict of the century.

"What's a European battle to us, anyhow?" Henry said with a shrug, not adding what John Henry already knew by the advertisements: that the cyclorama was the largest painting ever displayed, that it was accompanied by stirring narration and live orchestral music, that it was lit at night by an amazing electrical light show. And that the Mexican War veterans were, on that night, the special guests of the presenters, being considered expert critics on the realistic depiction of military scenes.

Henry never mentioned any of that, but John Henry knew it, and was surprised by his father's sacrifice.

"I'll see it tomorrow evenin' instead," Henry commented as they took the street car back to Canal Street, "and take you and Zan along. And maybe we'll have time for Stonewall Jackson's sorrel, as well. Strange to think old Jackson's animal is still alive so long after his own passin'. Seems like horseflesh is stronger than human flesh, sometimes." Though there was nothing sentimental in his father's tone, John Henry could see the concern in his eyes as he took shaded glances at his son.

"And can we see the Cora, too?" Zan asked eagerly.

"What's the Cora?" John Henry asked, glad to change the direction of his thoughts.

"It's the world's biggest hot air balloon, Dr. Holliday, Sir. Came all the way from Canada just for the fair. The paper says it's eighty feet high and a hundred-sixty feet around. Imagine that!"

"Didn't I tell you not to believe what you read in the papers?" Henry said. "Reporters don't care about the truth, just about gettin' paid for a story. Next day, they're on to somethin' new, leavin' their lies behind to haunt you."

And as the streetcar clattered along toward the French Quarter, John Henry wondered just what it was those Valdosta papers had said about him.

His father left him to sleep awhile at the hotel while he took Zan to an early supper at a Creole restaurant around the corner from Canal Street. Then he came back to the room alone.

"Where's the boy?" John Henry asked as he coughed himself awake.

"I sent him down to the tobacconist to buy me a box of loose leaf," Henry replied. "He'll be there all night, likely, askin' questions." Then he reached into his vest pocket and pulled out a fine new Delpit cigar, examining it admiringly, and said, "I've sent for a doctor to come take a look at you while Zan's occupied."

"I don't need a doctor, Pa," John Henry said, pushing himself up to sit on the edge of the bed. "I just need to get out of this sultry air. It's hard to catch a breath with all this humidity off the river. I'll be fine, once I'm home in Colorado where it's dry."

"Colorado is not your home, John Henry. Georgia is."

"Georgia was, until you threw me out," he said without thinking, and immediately regretted the words. The last thing he wanted to do was rile his father before they'd come to some kind of financial agreement.

But Henry seemed dispassionate. "I only put you out of the house, not out of the whole damned state. You still had family there. You still do. It was your choice to run off."

"I didn't see as I had a choice, after what happened."

"And what happened was your choice too," Henry said. "Your Uncle Tom told me about you shootin' that darkie on the Withlacoochee. He reckoned rightly that I'd need to know, if the law came nosin' around, so I could put them off. Reconstruction was bad times to be makin' trouble with the coloreds."

John Henry had never spoken to his father about the shooting; had never spoken to him at all since that time. Until now. "And did the law come around?"

"They did. It took a lot of talkin', along with some cash, to send them off elsewhere. They never did find the shooter, so they said."

His father was probably expecting some words of gratitude, but he couldn't come up with any, considering how it was Henry's mistreatment of him that had led to the shooting in the first place. If his father hadn't thrown him out, if he hadn't been holed up at Tom McKey's place on the river, if he hadn't been drinking to assuage the pain and the loneliness . . .

"I want you to come home," Henry said, startling him out of his recollection.

"What?"

"I want you to come back to Valdosta with me, John Henry. Especially now that I see the condition you're in. You need someone to take care of you."

"I told you, I'll be fine," he said. Illness was weakness and he would not be weak.

"We'll let the doctor decide that."

"I've seen plenty of doctors! They all say the same thing—go find a mineral springs resort, soak in the water, breathe in the vapors. It's a miracle, so they say. A pricey miracle . . ."

His last comment was calculated to put his father to thinking about money, which was all he'd come to New Orleans for, after all. Not to be invited home. Not to find his father turned soft and sympathetic. An old man, dreaming dreams.

"I know the consumption, son, better than you do. I nursed your mother through it, before she died."

John Henry couldn't afford to get his father riled, but Henry shouldn't have mentioned his mother.

"You nursed her? Seems like you were hardly there. Seems like you spent most of your time down at the orchard, visitin' Rachel . . ."

In other times, his comment would have brought on a beating. In other times, his father had put him out for saying such a thing. But now, Henry said in measured tones: "You don't know everything you think you do, John Henry."

"I know what I saw!"

"You were a boy. You didn't see all that much. And you understood even less."

And though John Henry should have kept his calm, played with a poker face, he couldn't do it. "Well, I'm not a boy now, and I still don't understand it!"

Henry turned away from him, bit off the end of the cigar and tried to light it, but his hands were shaking. And when he turned back around to face his son, there was a struggle in his eyes.

"You think I didn't love your mother?" he said, his voice rough with emotion. "Well, let me tell you somethin', son. I loved your mother as much as any man ever loved a woman. Wanted her more than any man ought to want a woman, gave everything I had just to get her. And for awhile, we were happier than I knew two people could be. And then she took sick, and I had to watch her dyin', little by little, until there was nothin' of her left . . ."

"So you went to another woman for consolation."

Henry's jaw tightened. "I won't deny I thought about it. Lusted after her, even. What man wouldn't have done the same, in my position? Sick as your mother was, it had been a long time since she'd been a real wife to me. But I swear I didn't cuckold your mother with Rachel Martin."

"Then what about the orchard?"

There was a long silence before Henry replied, then he said quietly, "I reckon Adam was tempted too. I offered. But Rachel wouldn't have any of it. Said a woman's place was to help a man do his duty. Said she could never trust a man who would be unfaithful to his wife. Said she could never face your mother, when they met in the hereafter, if she'd stolen her husband away. So I waited."

"And married her before the mournin' was even over."

"What I did, I reckoned I did for all of us. I needed a wife; you needed a mother. And Rachel needed to have an honest life offered to her, after I'd suggested otherwise. A man doesn't run away from his responsibilities."

And though John Henry felt the sting of his father's judging words, Henry didn't belabor the point. Instead he went on with his own story, as if finally having it out were a relief. "But livin' with Rachel was harder than I expected it would be, once I'd got the hunger out of me. She suited me fine in the marriage bed, but she's different from what I was accustomed to. She's not from fine people, like your mother was. Still, she's a good woman, and I reckon I've had no real reason to complain. But don't you ever think that I didn't love your mother—" his voice broke on the words, and he went on with tears in his eyes, "that I don't love her still, God help me! And I don't want to lose what's left of her the same way I lost her. I want you to come home, John Henry, and let me take care of you."

He was moved by his father's story, and almost persuaded. But could they so easily put the past behind them? Was his father really changed so much? Was he himself changed enough to forgive and forget? And then Henry said something that drove away any other thoughts.

"And what about your own boy? You haven't said anything about him."

"My boy?" John Henry said, bewildered, as his mind ran back through the years. Kate had lost a baby at Sweetwater, a boy the doctor had said. But that child was stillborn, never taking a breath and buried in the dust of the Texas panhandle. And then forgotten, at least by him. And that

317

was all, as far as he knew. Had Kate had another child, somewhere along the way? Had she never told him?

"You don't know, do you?" Henry said, watching his face. "You don't even know everything that goes on in your own life, let alone mine."

"I don't know anything about a child," he confessed, and wasn't sure that he wanted to know.

But Henry went on anyhow. "There was a letter come for your Uncle Tom some years back, postmarked from Denver. From a girl there who claimed she'd had Tom McKey's baby boy and just wanted him to know about it. Wasn't askin' for money or anything else, just wanted him to know. Come as a shock to Tom, as you can imagine, as he's never been anywhere near Denver, never even left the state of Georgia, after the War. So we knew there had to be some sort of mistake. But then we heard that you'd been in Denver, and we started to put two and two together. It was you the girl was writin' to, using your Uncle Tom's name. It was your baby boy she was writin' about. But we didn't know where to find you, or if you'd even want to be found."

His mind was racing, his heart racing along with it. How could it be possible? Who could have written such a letter? The closest he'd come to marrying was Kate, and she was never in Denver with him. And he was never with any other woman long enough to have her make a point of writing to his family. There'd been no one, not that he could recall.

And then he remembered.

"What was her name?" he asked his father, trying to remember it himself.

"I don't recollect. It's been a long time, like I said, eight years maybe. Tom kept the letter awhile, in case we should hear of your whereabouts. But then he got nervous about Sadie findin' it and thinkin' ill of him without cause. So he burned it, for safety sake. I reckon he did the right thing."

There had been a girl in Denver, a pretty thing who'd twisted her ankle at the Admission Day parade that summer of '76. He'd taken her home, being a gentleman, and learned that she was something less than a lady. But she'd been sweet and companionable and he'd been content to keep visiting with her—living with her, really, for those lonely months when he'd been using his uncle's name. Tom McKey, he had called himself, and answered what questions he could. Did he even know her real name, or just the name the Madam had called her? Had he told her he was from Valdosta? Had he even said goodbye when he left town in a hurry after the run-in with Bud Ryan?

"I reckon it's possible," he said. "I just never thought . . . I just didn't think . . ."

"Men usually don't. And the woman gets left with the child as a souvenir."

"I didn't know," he said again. And wondered what he would have done differently, if he had. Would he have stayed and faced a prison sentence for the knifing of Bud Ryan, just to see his child? Would he have been a better father than his father had been to him? Or would the boy have hated him as he had despised Henry most of his years?

"I should like to have seen my grandson," Henry said sadly.

Oldest son of the oldest son of the oldest son, the boy would have been. The last of a long line of Hollidays.

When the doctor knocked on the door, he found two grown men crying.

Zan Griffith got to see the hot air balloon Cora the next day, along with the Battle of Sedan Cyclorama and Stonewall Jackson's sorrel, when Henry took him back to the Exposition grounds and John Henry stayed close to the French Quarter. He shouldn't have done all that walking in the thick air, the doctor said, with so little good lung tissue left. As for returning to Georgia, that was out of the question now, even though the atmosphere there was less humid than in Louisiana. The years of battling the consumption, the bleeding and healing and bleeding again, had left his lungs covered with scar tissue that didn't allow for proper respiration. The only hope in his advanced state, other than one of those miracle hot springs cures, was to move to a dryer climate where humidity wasn't a detriment, like Colorado or Arizona, perhaps. He didn't suggest what John Henry and his father already knew: in the end, it would be the dampness in the air that killed him, no matter how dry the climate was. Eventually his lungs would stop filtering water entirely and fill up with fluid, drowning him. But for now, he had to get out of New Orleans.

He could have taken the train west, but he had another trip in mind. He had never been on a riverboat before, other than the excursion ride to the Exposition grounds, and would likely never get the chance again. So he bought passage on the *Natchez*, headed up the Mississippi toward St. Louis, and looked forward to trying his hand at the legendary riverboat poker games, now that he had some money in his pockets again. For Henry had not come empty-handed to New Orleans, and gave his son enough for the trip back to Colorado and for some time after. And once John Henry got himself settled there, his father would be sending him something more—the proceeds of what was left of his inheritance.

"But I thought you sold it all," John Henry said in surprise when his father mentioned the property. "I thought you gave my McKey holdings away for Francisco's family." He was amazed to be able to say it without bitterness, though the knowledge had broken his heart once. But things had been different then, or were different now.

"I did, and was glad to do it. Francisco was like a son to me, his family the closest thing I will ever have to a posterity. But that was just your mother's money. I've done well myself, these past years. I have some property of my own to pass on."

He didn't have to say what he was thinking: he was likely to outlive his son, and would have no one to pass his property to if he didn't do it soon. His only daughter had died in infancy, his only son was ailing, and his second wife had never given him any children at all. And his only grandchild, his heir, was a boy lost to him years before.

"I'm grateful, Pa," John Henry said truthfully. "I'll try not to shame you anymore."

"I'm not ashamed of you, John Henry," his father said. "I stopped bein' ashamed the day the papers wrote about the trouble down in Tombstone."

"What do you mean?"

"I mean a man's got to take a stand for what he believes in. He's got to be willin' to die for what's right, or he's never really alive. Hell, you wouldn't be a Holliday if you weren't a fighter."

It was the greatest compliment his father could ever have given him.

CHAPTER FIFTEEN

The *Natchez* was readied at her moorings on the levee, loaded with cargo and crew and eager to board her passengers. Some, like John Henry, would have the luxury of sleeping in one of the forty-seven elegant staterooms, eating in the stained-glass dining cabin, and passing the time in the finely appointed gambling salon. Most would be sleeping on the deck, swatting away mosquitoes and sharing the two public privies.

"Be watchful of the lower class," Henry warned his son. "These boats are notorious for pickpockets and con men. Keep your money belt on you, and a pistol handy, just in case."

"I'll be careful, Pa," John Henry said, knowing too well already the dangers of such society. It had been his world for most of his grown life, after all. But it wasn't only for himself that he had to be watchful now, it was for Zan Griffith, as well, who was coming along with him as a traveling companion.

The boy was part of the financial deal between John Henry and his father. "Take him along, or don't take the money," Henry had said, leaving John Henry little choice. And in the end, he was glad to have the help, though it should have been the older man who had a valet attending him. But Henry was worried about his son's health on the long journey and wouldn't take no for an answer. "The boy will fetch and carry for you, and call for the doctor if need be. And eat up all your gamblin' winnin's, if you don't watch him close." And Zan, of course, was thrilled to be going along on the adventure.

Henry was enjoying the adventure some himself, as he escorted John Henry and Zan aboard the *Natchez* and took a tour around before the sailing. She was a beautiful ship, three decks tall from water line to pilot house and three-hundred feet long from bow to paddle wheel, painted gleaming white and trimmed out in gaudy scarlet red. She had eight steel boilers and thirteen engines to drive her through the water and two towering black stacks to breathe out her wood smoke, and as long as she didn't explode or run aground, as packets sometimes did, she'd make good speed on the river.

The *Natchez* took her name from the rowdy city on the banks of the Mississippi, but took her decorations from the Natchez Indians who lived there first. The main cabin was ornamented fore and aft with scenes of war-dancing, sun-worshipping braves and squaws. And though genteel ladies were welcomed into the grand salon, the painted natives adorning the walls were scandalously unclad. Zan was entranced.

"Best keep him away from the stage shows at night," Henry warned. "I hear the dancers are almost as naked as those Indians."

"They are?" Zan asked eagerly.

"Mind your manners," Henry scolded him, but there was a smile behind his stern words. He was fond of the boy, that was clear. "Now run and fetch a porter for these travelin' bags while I say my goodbyes to Dr. Holliday."

"Yessir, Major Sir," Zan said, and scurried away into the crowd.

"You'll miss his company," John Henry said.

"No doubt. But he'll enjoy the trip. He's never been away from home before, and now he's headed up the Mississippi. He'll be talkin' about it for years, and wantin' more. His folks may never forgive me. So how long from here to St. Louis?"

"Four days, more or less."

"And then by train to Colorado?"

John Henry nodded, and found himself suddenly wishing he were going east instead of west, back home to Georgia again. He still had family there, as his father had pointed out, aunts and uncles and cousins. And Mattie, hidden away in her convent in Savannah. Would Mattie welcome him if he came to see her? Would it only make him miss her more?

But the doctor had been clear in his instructions: a dryer climate might win him another five years if he were lucky, and he was too much of a gambling man not to play the odds. And who knew what another five years would bring, anyhow? Maybe they'd find a cure and he'd live forever. It was a hope worth hanging onto, at least.

He was about to say as much to Henry when the steam whistle blasted, signaling non-passengers to disembark.

"Where has Zan gotten off to?" Henry said. "We need these bags delivered to your cabin."

"I can handle the bags on my own, Pa. I always do."

"You shouldn't have to, that's what porters are for." Then he hailed an elderly black man in a ship's uniform and said, "Hey there, boy! There's a tip for you if you'll carry these bags."

The man nodded in acknowledgment and made his way toward them through the crowd.

"He's not a boy, Pa," John Henry said, "he's older than you are."

"Nonsense, son, all coloreds are boys! Have you forgotten your upbringin'?"

What he hadn't forgotten was Barney Ford. And that was when he knew that he could never go home, even if he found a cure and Mattie was somehow waiting for him with open arms. He could never go home because home hadn't changed much, and he had.

The old man gathered up the bags and took the coin Henry tossed his way, and John Henry watched him go, shuffling when he walked as though it pained him some.

"Goodbye, Pa," he said, turning to his father with outstretched hand. "I appreciate all you've done for me."

"Goodbye, son," Henry said, taking his offered hand and then pulling him into an embrace. His suit coat smelled of cedar wood and fine tobacco. "Take care of yourself," he said.

"You take care, too," John Henry replied, gentlemanly as he'd been taught.

And then, because it would have pleased his mother to hear it, he added, "I love you, Pa," and realized when he said the words that he meant them.

Henry may not have been the hero that his son had wanted him to be, but he'd probably been the best father that he could. And maybe that was all it took to be a hero, anyhow.

The Mississippi hadn't impressed him much, the last time he'd seen it. That was the summer he'd stayed in St. Louis with Jameson Fuches, when his first experience with the river was crossing over it on a ferry boat from Illinois. He'd expected something grander back then, after all he'd heard of it, something bigger than its one mile width.

Problem was, he'd been seeing it from the wrong direction. Crossing the Mississippi was one thing, traveling along it was something else entirely. From the deck of a riverboat pushing north against the current, the river seemed endless. It meandered more than two-thousand miles from the headwaters in Minnesota down to the Gulf of Mexico, passing ten states and watering twenty more, and in all that distance, the scenery seldom changed. The muddy water rolled along between tangled wooded banks, miles on end, with only now and then a clearing on a bluff where a city made a stand: Baton Rouge, Vicksburg, Memphis, Cape Girardeau. But mostly all there was to see was river, and islands in the river, and shore birds flying above the river.

Zan never tired of the view, spotting Blue Heron and black ducks, snowy Egrets and Canadian Geese, and pestering the crew with constant questions. "You planning on being a riverman one day?" a deck hand asked him, and John Henry listened and laughed.

When Zan wasn't cataloguing wildlife or learning the steamboat trade, he was eating his way through the entire dining room menu, unafraid of even the most unusual dish. And when he finally slept, he slept well.

John Henry admired Zan's spirit, but couldn't muster the same enthusiasm in himself. His own sleep was too short, as always, and he had to make up for the lack by spending his afternoons in a reclining chair on the promenade deck. He stretched out his long legs, tipped his hat over his face, folded his hands against his vest, and drifted off to sleep to the sound of the paddlewheel while Zan hung over the rail, watching the river going by.

There was a dream he had on one of those lazy riverboat afternoons, a dream that came and stayed with him. There was a boy on another river far away, a fair-haired boy who stood barefoot on the sandy bank, picking up stones and skimming them across the water. One jump, two jumps, sometimes three in a row if he tossed them just right. And sometimes, they made it all the way to the other side without sinking. "The best skimmin' stones are the smooth ones," the boy said, "the ones that been polished shiny by the wind and the weather." Then he turned and smiled and said to John Henry, "Ain't that right, Pa?"

It was all a confusion of course, brought on by the river and the rich food and the revelations of his visit to New Orleans. But as dusk came on and drifted across the water, John Henry began to wonder how you went about finding something you didn't even know you'd lost.

Chapter Sixteen

THE WESTERN TRAIL, 1885

HE HAD PLANNED TO SAIL AS FAR AS ST. LOUIS BEFORE HEADING WEST, but found he enjoyed riverboat travel so much that he decided to sail a little longer, and stay on the river all the way to Keokuk instead. Riverboat travel was so much easier than railroad travel, floating for days at a time instead of jolting along behind a locomotive and braking for every little whistle stop along the way. And sailing up to Iowa had the advantage of taking him close to the Earps' hometown, where he was looking forward to having another sort of reunion.

The Earps were long gone from Pella, of course, having left with a wagon train years before on the first of their many western adventures. But the town still had memories of them—the eighty-acre farm with its neatly planted fields of corn, the two-story house where the boys had been raised, the apple orchard where little Morgan had climbed a tree and fallen from it, taking his big brother Wyatt along with him.

It was easy enough to find the family homestead, just by asking around. Pella only had two-thousand residents or so and only one famous name to boast about, and everyone seemed to know Wyatt Earp. And whether or not the papers there had been any more accurate than they'd been elsewhere, Wyatt was becoming something of a legend already, so that when John Henry mentioned his own name by way of introduction, a local portrait painter offered to do a life sitting of him, free of charge.

But it was Morgan that he was coming to see mostly, trying to get close to his old friend again somehow and say the last goodbyes he'd been denied. And as he strolled around the tree-shaded streets of Pella, getting a feel for the place, it struck him that it was sad for a man not to go home in the end, back to the town that had raised him. Morgan should have been laid in the soft green earth of Iowa instead of the sun-baked dirt of California where his body had been sent after he died. Iowa was home, like Tara was home, the way Mattie's cousin had spoken of it once.

It surprised him to remember such a thing after all this time away, suddenly recalling Sarah Fitzgerald's long-ago words. He hadn't known what she'd been talking about, back then. But now, being in the place where Morgan should have been and wasn't, he thought he finally understood.

Railroad travel wasn't as easy as river travel, but the rails went everywhere, spreading out across the country like an iron spider's web, stringing together east and west, north and south, Gulf and river and everything in between. To get from one place to another it was only a matter of deciding how long you wanted to travel, and what you wanted to see along the way. Zan Griffith wanted to see it all and was happy that their journey back to Colorado would mean riding on a couple of railroads at least, passing through Iowa and part of Missouri before crossing over the Missouri River at Saint Joe and catching the Atchison, Topeka, & Santa Fe down into Kansas and across the wide open cattle country.

Except that the cattle country wasn't so wide open anymore. Where there had once been endless miles of unfenced grazing land, barbed wire now sliced across the landscape.

"I reckon that's what you call civilization," John Henry told Zan in answer to the boy's questions, "or greed, maybe, dividin' up the property."

But it was more than that, as they discovered when they arrived in Dodge City—a strangely quiet Dodge that welcomed them with empty streets and emptier cattle pens.

"Where's all the beeves?" John Henry asked Deacon Cox when they checked into the familiar old Dodge House Hotel. "Used to be there were thousands of head over on the other side of the Arkansas during cattle season. Now there's nothin' but mud."

"It's the quarantine against Texas fever," Deacon Cox answered with a sigh. "Those Texas cows have been makin' our local cattle sick, so the Western Cattle Trail's been shut down. No Texas beeves allowed in

Kansas or Colorado or Nebraska or Wyoming or New Mexico, even. So there's no more cattle drives for Dodge this year, and maybe never again. Which is mighty bad for business, I might add."

John Henry tried to imagine Dodge City without the summer influx of hundreds of herds and thousands of trail-weary cowboys, and couldn't.

"And that's just the half of it," Deacon Cox went on. "Now there's talk of an Act of Congress to make bankin' games illegal. Which means no Faro, nor Roulette, nor Blackjack, nor Stud Poker even."

"Poker's not a bankin' game," John Henry said. "It's not even much of a game of chance, after the first deal. Poker's more about probability and psychology."

"Tell that to the government. They want to shut down the Western Trail and the cowboys right along with it, seems like. But the Grangers have been here already, drivin' the gamblers out and tryin' to turn Dodge into a farm town. You won't find the saloons too lively, anymore."

"Which accounts for the quiet on the streets, I reckon," John Henry said. With no cowboys with fresh pay in their pockets, there'd naturally be fewer sporting men to take it away from them. And with no sport to speak of, there'd be no customers for the Front Street saloons. Which would leave Dodge City pretty much a ghost town, compared to what it had once been.

"What's a Granger?" Zan asked, still studying on the unfamiliar word.

"Granger's a group of local farmers," Deacon Cox replied, "workin' to advance the agricultural business. They never did like the cattle coming through here, nor the cowboys. So they're usin' the quarantine as an excuse to clean things out, as they see it. But they won't like Dodge City much without the cowboys, once the shops start closin' up. Business goes where there's customers, and there's not so many customers anymore. But I reckon there's one benefit to all this progress."

"And what might that be?" John Henry asked, wondering how a sporting man was supposed to make a living without his sport.

"At least now you can get a good night's sleep without all the racket," Deacon Cox said. "Plus, we got plenty of rooms available. Maybe we'll make ourselves into a vacation resort, and advertise the peaceful climate."

There was a time when Dodge had been labeled the *Beautiful, Bibulous Babylon of the West*—and had taken the insult as a compliment.

Now all at once she was nothing much more than a dusty layover on the rail line to Colorado. And as he and Zan boarded the morning train to Pueblo after spending a quiet night in Dodge City, John Henry paused on the platform, taking off his hat and looking back into town. He remembered meeting Morgan for the first time there, and Bat Masterson, as well. And saving Wyatt's life.

"What are you doin', Dr. Holliday, Sir?" Zan asked, wondering at his moment of silence.

"I reckon I'm mournin' the passin' of the Wild West," John Henry said. "We'll never see the like of it again."

Pueblo had more life to it, not being a cowtown, and they laid over there a few days before traveling on, taking in the shows and paying a visit to Clark's Magnetic Mineral Springs, which John Henry had missed before when he was occupied with more pressing matters. But he remembered how the young desk clerk at the Fariss House hotel had extolled the place, citing its curative powers and the odd magic of its chemical composition, and he was curious.

The place billed itself as the Best Resort in the West, most conveniently situated at the confluence of several railroad routes, and having the most agreeable weather anywhere—sixty-five degrees in the middle of May and air so rarified it seemed to sparkle. And the mineral water really did seem to have some kind of magical properties, including the ability to magnetize whatever was dropped into it, as the manager demonstrated on their arrival at the bathhouse.

"Just an everyday table knife," he said, fishing a piece of dining room flatware from a bucket of spring water kept handy for demonstration purposes. "But after soaking in Clark's Magnetic Mineral water, look how it attracts these iron filings!" Then he opened his other hand to show a pile of metal shavings, and as he did they flew toward the knife blade and clung there.

"Well, I'll be . . ." John Henry said. "Are you sure you're not pullin' some sleight-of-hand, for the boy's benefit?" He'd pulled too many fast cards himself to believe everything he saw.

But Zan believed every bit of it. "I seen somethin' like that back home, only with an iron nail. If you point one end of the nail to the north and hit the south end with a hammer, it turns magnetic too, for a spell. Doesn't work every time, but I seen it once or twice."

"And what good would a magnetic nail be?" John Henry asked with a laugh, and Zan answered him thoughtfully.

"Well, I reckon maybe a magnetic nail would be easier to pull out of a board, if you had a magnetic hammer to pull it with. And there's probably lots of other things it would be good for, as well . . ."

"And you'll be the one to figure it out!" John Henry said, amused at how Zan had to study on everything. "But what good is magnetic water, other than doin' tricks with a knife?"

"Ah, that's the real magic," the manager said proudly. "When you bathe in Clark's water or drink it—we bottle it and sell it all over the country—the magnetism pulls the impurities from the body, ridding the sufferer of all manner of illness and infirmity: constipation, dyspepsia, rheumatism, catarrh of the bladder, eczema, cancer, liver infections in all stages and forms . . ."

"But what happens after the bath?" Zan asked, looking worried. "I mean, if the knife gets magnetized, won't we turn magnetic too?"

The manager smiled and leaned close, saying in something like a conspiratorial tone: "Now that, lad, is the secret of the Springs. For it has been noted that when a gentleman has spent some time bathing in the magnetic water, he is more attractive than before to the ladies, and has far more success in romantic endeavors, if you follow my drift. Been reported in the papers, even."

"Oh!" said Zan, looking eager and embarrassed all at once, and John Henry let out a laugh.

"You can't believe everything you read in the papers," he said, echoing his father's words of warning. "So how much for a bath?"

"Two-bits each," the manager replied, "plus a nickel for the Turkish towel."

It seemed like a reasonable wager on the odds that, this time, the papers might just be right.

He didn't know whether it was the mineral content of the water, being manganese and magnesia and potassium and lime together with iron and impressive amounts of arsenic and sulphuric acid, or just the eighty degree warmth of it, but John Henry did feel better after a soak in springs. And after three days of return visits, he was feeling altogether relaxed and maybe even a little recovered. As for being a magnet to the opposite sex, he hadn't noticed that effect just yet.

"Maybe it takes more soaks," Zan said, observing how they could still walk down Union Avenue without drawing any undue attention, even when they passed dance halls full of women. "Or maybe we should be drinkin' more of it. We could buy a bottle or two, just to keep it handy."

"It doesn't take magic water to make a romance, Zan. Just the right two people comin' together. Takes luck, more than anything. Or the hand of God, maybe."

"Well, you know somethin' about luck, that's for sure. I ain't never seen a man win so many card hands in a row as you, Dr. Holliday, Sir."

It was true that he'd been on a streak since leaving New Orleans, proving the old gambler's adage that it took money to make money, for once he had some cash in his pockets he suddenly started getting more. There were the poker games he'd wagered on and won aboard the *Natchez* sailing up the Mississippi, and the games he wagered more on and won again on the railroads west across Iowa and Missouri and Kansas. And every time he won he thanked Zan Griffith for being his lucky charm, which seemed to please the boy and probably had some veracity to it. Without Zan's company, he might have stayed too long at the tables or wagered too much, not worrying about anybody but himself. With Zan along he felt a need to be more circumspect than usual, folding when he was only comfortably ahead rather than reinvesting all his profits as he might otherwise have done.

So although he might not have seemed the showiest gambler on the western circuit, by the time they arrived in Colorado he had nearly doubled the allowance his father had given him and had enough to spend on amusements like the Mineral Springs and the Varieties Theater. He even considered buying himself a fine saddle, though he didn't own a horse and rarely rode anymore. But Pueblo was known for its saddles, and it seemed a fitting souvenir, if a man did ride.

Zan had to see the saddle manufactory, of course, asking his endless questions.

"Is that really your name?" he said to the owner of the shop, who had introduced himself as a Mr. Gallup, which made Zan laugh when he should have been acting polite. "You mean, like the way a horse runs?"

"It's spelled a little differently," A.C. Gallup replied, "but I like to think a horse wouldn't run as well without one of our saddles. They're the best in the country, you know. Coveted by every cowboy who can scrape together the money. Even a ten dollar horse rides better with a forty dollar custom made Gallup saddle on him."

The saddle was special, John Henry had to agree. From the wide leather skirt to the deep riding seat to the high backed cantle, the Pueblo-style saddle looked like luxury for any horseman who could afford it.

"But it's not just for comfort," Gallup said. "See how the rigging rides under the fork instead of wrapping around the horn? Makes the saddle steadier when roping or even running. It's the best, as I said. And the finest leatherwork, as well, each one individually crafted. Works of art, that's what our saddles are. I don't anticipate the demand will go down, even with the close of the Cattle Trail. As long as men ride horseback, they'll be needing good saddles." Then he paused and said, "So what's the boy up to?"

He nodded toward Zan, who was hovering over a display of saddle strings, picking up one silver concha rosette after another. One by one, he placed the metal decorations on the back of his open hand, then turned the hand over fast, watching the concha slide off and catching it with his other hand before it fell to the ground. Then he'd try another one with the same result.

"Is he practicing for something?" Gallup asked, and John Henry answered with all the seriousness he could muster.

"No sir, I reckon he's just testin' his appeal. Seems the boy's turnin' magnetic. He just doesn't know that silver won't stick."

"Magnetic?" A.C. Gallup said, obviously impressed. "Is that right?"

It was all John Henry could do to keep a poker face, though he laughed about it for days afterwards. But he couldn't help admiring the boy's optimism. For hadn't he once believed in impossible things himself? And didn't he still?

From the railroad depot in Pueblo the tracks ran north to Denver, and south to Trinidad, and west toward Cañon City and onto Leadville, and all of those destinations had their draws and their drawbacks. But Cañon City had the attraction of being the entrance to the Royal Gorge of the Arkansas River, and that was worth seeing all by itself—especially since John Henry felt a sort of ownership of it, having been one of the gunfighters who'd defended its railroad right-of-way in the battle between the Santa Fe and the Denver & Rio Grande.

Zan was almost as impressed by the story of the Royal Gorge War as he was by the Royal Gorge itself, with its ten-mile long chasm cut through the solid granite of Fremont Peak.

"They call it the Grand Canyon of the Arkansas," John Henry told him, when Zan had caught his breath long enough to start asking questions. The grandeur of the place had a way of taking you off guard like that, even if you knew it was coming. The train left Cañon City and headed into the canyon and all at once you were caught between walls of granite rising a thousand feet up to the plateau above. "Took the river thirty million years, so they say, to carve down through the rock. Imagine one little stream doin' all that."

Except that the Arkansas wasn't exactly a little stream, with its white-water rapids churning dangerously close to the railroad tracks that shared the narrow canyon floor. At some points there wasn't enough room for the tracks and the river both, and the train had to give way and go over a hanging bridge suspended from the sheer rock walls.

"And how did the railroad war end, Dr. Holliday, Sir?" Zan asked, using the formal address that was becoming something familiar between them. "Was there a big gunbattle? Did anybody die?"

"One man," John Henry replied. "He got shot in the back by a drunk guard for the Denver & Rio Grande. But that wasn't really part of the battle. The only real war wound that I know of was a man who lost a couple of teeth defendin' the telegraph office. Mostly it was takin' a stand and makin' a show. And then the government came in and settled the whole thing, anyhow. Most wars are like that—the brave men do the fightin' and the cowards stay home and sign the treaties." But when Zan sighed, obviously disappointed in the unromantic ending of the war for the Royal Gorge, he added, "Did you know there's sea monsters buried in these rocks?"

The boy was full of questions all the way to Leadville.

It was amazing how much things could change in two short months. The last time he was in Leadville there'd been snow on the ground, and now the weather was almost balmy. The last time he was in Leadville he'd been sleeping in a borrowed room above a saloon, and now he was checking into the finest suite in the finest hotel in town.

The Tabor Grand Hotel had been under construction for the last two years, and John Henry had watched it rising from foundation to Mansard roof, taking up a whole city block on Harrison Avenue. And like everything else the Tabor money touched, the Grand Hotel really was grand. From the plushly carpeted lobby to the gable-windowed guest rooms to the Presidential Suite that occupied most of the fourth floor, Tabor's newest showplace was as elegant as his silver fortune could make it. And lucky for John Henry, the Grand Hotel had finally opened just in time for his return to Leadville.

The Presidential Suite had been designed for Horace Tabor's personal use, in deference to his dreams of one day buying himself the Presidency of the United States, but as Horace wasn't yet in town and the hotel wasn't yet full-up, the manager agreed to rent the suite to John Henry for one night—cash money up front, of course.

"No offense, Doc," the manager said, "but the last time you were in town you were short on finances, as I recall."

"No offense taken," John Henry replied, as he opened his money purse and pulled out enough for one night and a nice tip to go along with it. "Now where's the dinin' room? My valet and I have just come in from a long train ride, and we'd like somethin' to eat." Then he pulled out another handful of coins and added, "And we'd like a bottle of champagne, if you can find one."

The manager took the money warily, as if it might be tainted, then his greed got the better of him and he said, "Are you sure you just want one night? I could probably arrange for a couple more, if you're planning on staying around ..."

"That's very generous of you, but one night'll be fine. I'm only in town to do a little business. I plan to be done and on the train again by tomorrow evenin'. Now about that champagne . . ."

The manager, he knew, wouldn't take long in telling all of Leadville that Doc Holliday was back and spending money like he'd just discovered a silver mine.

The truth was he couldn't stay in Leadville for long. He was already feeling dizzy from the altitude and knew that by morning he'd be sick at his stomach and short of breath as well. But it would only take one day, if things went well, to do what he had to do, and then he and Zan would be on the High Line Railroad headed back down to the easier air of Denver. Until then, he planned to live as lavishly as his new-found inheritance and his newly-made gambling winnings would let him, starting with supper in the hotel dining room. Though he didn't have much appetite himself, Zan as usual had enough for the both of them, and happily ate his way through two steaks and three desserts and a whole basketful of warm breads while John Henry watched him enviously and sipped at a glass of French champagne. He would have preferred a tumbler or two of whiskey, but the champagne added to the impression he was hoping to make, while sipping at it gingerly would leave his head clearer, come morning. And he'd need his head clear, in case things didn't go well.

He had relied on the hotel manager to spread the word of his return and sudden wealth, and he wasn't disappointed in that regard. By the time he was bathed and dressed and breakfasting with Zan in the dining room, there was a reporter from the *Leadville Democrat*, asking for an interview. Where had he disappeared to so suddenly after his acquittal on the assault charge against Bill Allen? And what were his plans now that he had returned?

John Henry was guarded in his reply, saying only that he was suffering a bit from the effects of the altitude and not really in a mood for talking, then he allowed the reporter to follow him from the hotel to the Bank of Leadville building.

"It seems like you've come into some money," the reporter said, stating the obvious in hopes of getting an explanation.

"Let's say I've had a lucky streak," was all the answer that John Henry would give him. Then he tipped his hat and stepped into the bank, leaving the reporter without much of a story but with plenty to write about.

The bank manager had heard of his return, as well, and looked up eagerly at his arrival. It was amazing how money could change the way a man was welcomed.

"What can we do for you, Doc?" the manager said graciously. Fawning, even.

"Just a little financial transaction, if you don't mind. I have a sum of money I'd like delivered, if you can make a bank draft for the amount."

"Making a draft requires opening an account, of course. Be happy to help you with that myself. Where'd you like the delivery to go?"

"Just here in Leadville. To Mannie Hyman, down the street."

The manager looked confused. "Why, you could walk that there yourself, without the expense of opening an account. Not that I am trying to dissuade you from opening an account. We'd be honored to have your money here, Doc. But are you sure you want a delivery?"

"Dead sure," he said, and pulled out his money purse. He owed Mannie twenty dollars with interest, for starters, along with back rent for all those months he'd stayed above the saloon without working much. And though Mannie might never ask for the rent to be repaid, John Henry still had his pride.

The bank manager took the money and made out a draft to be delivered the next day, after John Henry was gone again. For while he wanted to repay his debt, he didn't think it prudent to stay around for a lot of discussion, as Mannie Hyman's place was one of the saloons where he'd promised free drinks for a month, courtesy of the Public Defender's office, and he didn't want to be obliged if they hadn't yet made good on the deal. He didn't mind taking care of his own debts, but he considered the free drinks to be part of his attorney's services, or should have been if they'd been doing their job better.

"And there's one more thing," he said, when the bank manager had finished up the transaction, taking his signature on the draft.

"Anything at all, Doc. Glad to have your business."

"I need a Liberty head gold piece, shiniest one you've got."

Zan was disappointed to learn that they wouldn't be visiting Tabor's Opera House during their short stay in Leadville, nor any of the other sights of the famous silver mining camp.

"But the Opera's just down the street," he pointed out to John Henry when they were done at the bank, as though that needed pointing out. They could see the Opera House from where they were standing on the brick sidewalk, and almost read the playbill posted beside the double-doored entrance. Surely there were minstrel shows and varieties acts along with the opera and other amusements.

"We don't have time," John Henry explained, without really explaining, as time had never been much of a concern in their travels thus far. "Besides, I have a special job for you to do today."

"A special job, Sir?" Zan asked eagerly, forgetting about the Opera House. He was a good boy, always wanting to please.

"I need you to take these travelin' bags over to the railroad depot and buy us a couple of tickets to Denver. Then wait for me there."

"That's it, just wait?" Zan said, crestfallen, and John Henry knew what he was thinking. Waiting at the train depot in a town like Leadville, full of adventures, seemed like a terrible waste. "For how long?"

"Until I get there. And if I don't show up by the time the train leaves, I want you to get on it and get yourself back to Georgia." Then he opened his money purse again and handed Zan fifty dollars—enough for train fare all the way back home, plus living expenses along the way.

"But Dr. Holliday, Sir! I'm supposed to be takin' care of you! I can't leave Leadville without you. What would the Major say?"

"You'll be leavin' me at some point anyhow, unless you plan on movin' to Colorado yourself. And I doubt your folks would appreciate that. But don't worry over much. I don't plan on missin' that train."

He sounded sure enough, but as he watched Zan gather the bags and trudge back toward the depot where they'd arrived just the day before, he slipped a hand into his pocket, making sure his pistol was there and ready, just in case.

The Monarch Saloon was crowded as always in mid-afternoon, halfway between the miners' hours and the gamblers' hours and with a good congregation of both, and that was just the way John Henry wanted it to be. An audience would be appropriate for what he had to do, along with offering a little protection if need be.

Through the crowd he could see Bill Allen standing behind the bar in his dingy barkeep's apron, pouring drinks. Though Bill's shooting arm wasn't in a sling anymore he wasn't using it either, and it hung bent-elbowed at his side while he served the customers with his left hand instead. If he had a gun under the bar, he'd have an awkward time using it.

But there were likely other guns in the saloon, in spite of the ordinance, and likely some of Johnny Tyler's slopers there, as well, though the leader himself was nowhere to be seen. Which was good news and bad news, depending on one's point of view.

And then Bill Allen looked up from behind the bar and caught sight of John Henry standing in the doorway.

"What the hell are you doing back in Leadville? I thought we run you out."

"Nobody ran me out, Bill. Nobody runs me anywhere. Thought you would have learned that already, the hard way. How's your shootin' arm these days?"

The crowd was already hushed, and now a murmur ran through it.

"Damn you to hell, Holliday," Bill said.

"Been there and back," John Henry replied. "And you're lookin' a little the worse for wear, yourself."

"You want something? Or do you just want to stand there talking smart? I got customers to take care of."

"As a matter of fact, I do want somethin', Bill," he said, moving toward the bar while the crowd made way. "I've been wantin' it for months now. Been dreamin' of it, even. Came all this way back to Leadville just to get it done." And as he reached into his pocket he heard the ominous sound of a saloon-full of pistol hammers being raised.

"You threatening me, Holliday?" Bill asked, reaching his left arm toward the bar, his hand shaking some and knocking over a bottle of whiskey on the way.

"Are you scared, Bill? Are you afraid I might shoot you again, and get the job done right this time? I didn't miss last time, you know. I was just bein' generous."

"You shoot me here, and you'll hang for it! I got a whole saloon full of witnesses watching your every move!"

"Oh, I had counted on that," John Henry said with a smile. Then he slowly slid his hand from his pocket, pulling out a shiny new gold piece. He rolled the coin over his fingers, letting it catch the light, then tossed it onto the bar. "There's your money back, Bill. Don't say I'm not a man to keep a promise. Hope your arm was worth it."

Then he turned and strolled out of the saloon with a dozen loaded pistols ready to shoot him in the back. It was, to his recollection, the bravest thing he had ever done.

Zan was waiting for him at the railroad depot, sitting on the luggage and looking bored. But he brightened when he saw John Henry turn the corner into the train yard and mount the wooden steps to the platform.

"Did you get your business done, Dr. Holliday, Sir?" he asked.

"I did. And that's the end of Leadville for me."

"Don't you like this town? Seems like a nice sort of place." Zan said it wistfully, looking back down toward the busy streets he hadn't been able to explore. "And I ain't never seen a real silver mine before."

"There's not all that much to see," John Henry replied. "A silver mine's mostly a hole in the ground filled with greedy men. And sometimes, in winter, the snow covers over the shafts and folks fall right in, and get swallowed up in silver fever. Sometimes, the town itself can swallow you up."

It was a pensive speech, and Zan was about to start wondering why and asking his too many questions, when John Henry changed the subject and said with a laugh:

"So you think the Leadville Opera House is impressive? Wait 'till you see the one Tabor built in Denver! Looks like a palace. Then there's Baron Von Richthofen's castle, and the Harness races, and the Gettysburg Cyclorama . . ."

By the time the Denver & Rio Grande had built up a head of steam and was rolling toward the Continental Divide, Zan had forgotten all about Leadville.

They saw it all, or as much of it as John Henry could manage. Though the mineral springs at Pueblo had refreshed him some, the brief layover in Leadville had worn him out again, partly from the altitude, partly from the strain. So mostly they stayed close to the Windsor Hotel and made short day trips around the city, taking in the sights.

Zan enjoyed the cultural exhibitions, especially the life-sized mural of the Battle of Gettysburg that was housed in a specially designed circular building and presented with narration and rousing music from a military band. In front of the painting, making a three-dimensional display, were artificial earthworks and stone walls, shattered trees and broken fences, leaving the audience feeling like they were right in the middle of Pickett's Charge across the Pennsylvania countryside. The Cyclorama was one of a set of four matching murals displayed around the country, so the curator said, and the only one anywhere in the west.

But what Zan most wanted to see was a real horse race, "the kind that gets called by an announcer," he said, "not by the riders, like at home. A saddle horse race."

John Henry knew what he was talking about, having come from the same hometown. In Valdosta, the local boys raced each other for wagers and called the winners themselves—often ending up in fistfights if the call didn't go the way they wanted. Horse racing was dangerous sport in the country. What Zan was hoping for was something more civilized, with a groomed track and a grandstand for the spectators, and John Henry knew just where to take him.

Jewell Park lay along the banks of the Platte River, south of the city, with a rail line connecting it to Larimer Street in the business district, which made getting there an easy half-hour ride. And actually, it was the rail line that had created the resort, in hopes that Jewell Park with its horse races and bandstand for summer concerts would attract riders to the train. It had been a serendipitous relationship, and both businesses were prospering.

Jewell Park was a prosperous venture for John Henry, as well, after he put money on a one-mile race and made $40 when his horse came in second place. Zan had picked the animal, a chestnut four-year old named Brevity, mostly because he liked its color, which seemed as good a reason as any for picking a horse. So although John Henry had never held much with horse racing, thinking it too chancy a sport without any real strategy on the part of the gambler, he was beginning to rethink his position. That $40 was the easiest money he had ever made, having nothing to do but stand there in the afternoon breeze and watch the race. And without any effort on his part, he got the same exhilaration all sporting games gave him.

"I reckon you're still my good luck charm!" he said to Zan over the cheers of the crowds. Then he collected his winnings at the ticket office and put them back onto another race, this time a two-year old on a three-quarter mile run.

Zan let out a whoop and a holler when their horse came in a winner again, sounding like a young rebel going off to war. But when John Henry took that money and put it on a third race, the boy's smile faded some.

"Shouldn't we keep part of the winnin's, Dr. Holliday, Sir? I mean, with the price of our hotel suite and all. I reckon with all those carpets and diamond-dust mirrors, it must be pretty pricey. I reckon it'll get expensive if we stay there much longer."

"I admire your economy," John Henry said, "but we won't be stayin' at the Windsor much longer."

"Are we movin' on again?"

"You are," he said, as kindly as he could, "but I'm not. It's near time for you to go on home, now that you've got me all the way to Denver. The Major will be pleased by how well you've taken care of things, but your folks are sure to be missin' you by now."

"But Dr. Holliday, Sir . . ." Zan said, ready to object.

"No buts about it, Zan. I can't keep you here with me, much as I'd enjoy havin' your company. My kind of life isn't . . ." he paused, trying to explain himself in easy words, and couldn't. "My life isn't healthy for a young man like yourself. It's late nights and bad meals, and too much drink. It's saloons and gamblin' dens and the worst kind of people. And sometimes, often, it's downright dangerous. You know what I was doin' in Leadville while you were waitin' at the depot? I was walkin' into a crowd of pistoleers who were one thought away from shootin' me down. Is that the kind of life you want for yourself?"

"But it doesn't have to be like that! You could change things, if you wanted to."

John Henry sighed heavily. "I wouldn't know where to begin. This is the only life I know, anymore. And I'm too tired to figure out another way. But you're young still, Zan, you've got your whole future ahead of you. This world is full of opportunity for a bright young man like yourself." And as he said the words, he remembered thinking them before, when he'd been the young man just starting out.

"Do you really think I'm bright, Sir?"

"I think you ask more questions than anybody I've ever known! And if you're listenin' to the answers, you must be learnin' something. Now go pick me another winnin' horse, and let's make ourselves some money. There's no use havin' my lucky charm along if I don't use it."

There was no question what Zan's farewell gift should be, after he'd made John Henry all that money at the races. The only question was how to get it back to Valdosta without taking a horse along with it. But in the end, they decided Zan would simply carry it with him, like he'd carried John Henry's traveling bags halfway across the country. Besides, a fine new Pueblo Saddle wasn't something to hide, even without a horse to put it on.

"There's plenty of ten dollar horses back home to wear it, anyhow," Zan said, recalling the saddle manufactory and the man with the serendipitous name.

"And you'll beat any rider around, with that new saddle under you. I'd lay odds on you being the best mounted horseman in three counties, or more. Maybe even all of Georgia."

As they stood together on the platform at Denver's Union Station, Zan's unusual baggage was gathering admiring glances. His new saddle was a fine piece of leather work, the prettiest one in Gallup & Company's Denver store, hand-tooled and decorated with fancy silver conchas on the saddle strings.

Zan noticed the admiring eyes and laughed, "I reckon they think I'm a cowboy!"

"I hope not," John Henry said. "A cattleman maybe, or a rancher. But not a cowboy, unless you like the law on your tail."

"But I thought you killed all the bad cowboys. That's what the newspaper said, anyhow."

"You can't believe everything you read in the newspapers, Zan."

"No Sir, Dr. Holliday, Sir."

And before John Henry could get philosophical, the conductor called out, "All a'board!" and herded the passengers toward the train.

"You remember your changes?" John Henry asked for the third time in an hour. He didn't like sending Zan clear across the country all on his own, but how else was the boy supposed to get home? "I wrote it all down for you: Denver & New Orleans Railroad to Pueblo, then the Santa Fe back through Dodge . . ."

"I remember, Sir. I'm gettin' good at travelin'. And if I lose my way, I'll just start askin' questions."

"That's an easy bet," John Henry said with a smile.

It was no wonder that Henry had been fond of the boy. John Henry had grown fond of him, as well.

There were fifty trains a day coming in and out of Union Station, with dozens of horse-drawn cabs and carriages crowding the open-air plaza that fronted onto Wynkoop Street and hundreds of riders making the hourly stop on the Denver Electric Railcar that came down 17th Street. And with all that traffic and all those passengers, Union Station was a natural spot for a newsy to bring his business. So it shouldn't have been a surprise for John Henry to run into the same newsboy he'd met as he left for New Orleans—at least, he thought it was the same boy. From across the plaza, with the sun glaring off the granite pavers, his eyes might have been playing tricks on him.

He studied the boy from a distance, taking his time to light up a smoke and consider things. Had the boy said his father was a gambler, or was John Henry just imagining that after the fact? Had he said anything of his mother at all, other than mentioning that she was dead? And though it was crazy, he found himself wondering if this boy might be his boy. Then he laughed at his own foolishness. There had to be hundreds of waifs on the streets of a big city like Denver. Just because he'd supposedly had a son who would have been about the same age as the orphaned newspaper boy didn't make them related.

Still, he was curious. And what would it hurt if he had another conversation with the boy while buying a copy of the *Rocky Mountain News*? It was innocent enough, and then he'd be satisfied and could put the whole sad story out of his mind. So he crossed the plaza and waved to get the boy's attention.

"Paper boy!"

The boy heard him and turned around, looking up for his customer. And John Henry, drawing close, looked down into the boy's face, seeing eyes of china blue behind sandy lashes. Like his own eyes, he knew. He had looked like this fair-haired boy, when he was young, only not so thin and weather-worn.

"Paper, Mr.?" the boy said. "Latest news hot off the presses!"

"Please," John Henry said, fishing for a coin and trying not to stare. And what if this were his son? What then?

"You sure you don't want two papers, like last time?"

"Pardon me?"

"Last time I seen you here, you bought two papers in a row. Paid me a half eagle for the second one."

"You remember that?"

"A half eagle for a newspaper's something to remember. I was hoping you'd come around this way again."

"You were hoping to see me again?" he said, as if that meant something, but the boy answered with a shrug.

"Sure. I could use the money."

He was a practical boy, at least. Not like John Henry had been, always dreaming. But why should he be anything like John Henry? The boy wasn't his son, only a street urchin who looked something like him. Yet he couldn't help pursuing the thought.

"How old did you say you are?"

"Eight years this summer, Sir. Same as last time you asked."

"You remember me asking that?"

"I have a good memory. Especially for numbers and such. But I remember people, too."

"And what did you say your name was?"

"I didn't say."

The boy was clever—or maybe just protecting himself from a stranger's unwelcome questions. Well, that was easily overcome; all they needed was a proper introduction. "My name is John Henry Holliday," he said to the boy, offering his hand, "and what's yours?"

The boy didn't answer straight off, looking him over as if he were sizing him up. Then he nodded and put out his hand.

"Pleased to meet you Mr. Holliday. My name's Tom."

Chapter Seventeen

DENVER, 1885

JOHN HENRY'S LAST MEETING WITH COLONEL J.T. DEWEESE HAD BEEN in the Denver City jail where he'd been locked up and awaiting an extradition order. Now he was paying a more formal visit, calling at the law offices of DeWeese and Naylor on Curtis Street, just around the corner from 16th Street—and conveniently close to his new home at the Metropolitan Hotel. As Zan had pointed out, the elegant Windsor Hotel had been expensive lodgings for a long stay, so John Henry had made a move to more moderate accommodations—at $1.25 a day the Metropolitan was a substantial savings over the $4.00 a day plus tips charged by the Windsor. And now that he had some legal business to pay for, he'd need the extra cash. But the Colonel wasn't so sure that John Henry's business was all that legal.

"You want to pay me to spy for you?" DeWeese said, affronted. "Our firm's expertise is criminal law, not domestic affairs. You need a detective, not a lawyer."

"I don't know anyone else personally," John Henry said, "and this is a delicate matter. And it's not spyin', exactly. I just want you to make some inquiries around, find out what you can. Surely there's someone who knows somethin' . . ."

"There's always someone who knows something," the Colonel replied, "but that doesn't mean the information is reliable. That's the whole purpose of our great court system, to weigh the evidence and decide the truth."

"And that's what I'm after," John Henry said. "I just want to know the truth, so I can get on with my life. It's this not knowin' that's weighin' on me."

"And what makes you so sure you're related to this boy? Just because you might have had a son who could possibly be the same age as this child doesn't mean anything, legally speaking."

"But his mother named him Tom, the same as I was called back then. Doesn't that mean anything?"

"Perhaps. But you said the boy doesn't know the father's identity, neither given name nor surname, is that right?"

"That's right. His mother died when he was very young, and the aunt who raised him never told him much. But the fact that he's called Tom . . ."

"Only means that he has a common name. There must be hundreds of young Toms in this city. Do you want us to check up on every one of them for you, just in case they might be related to you as well?"

"No, Sir. It's just that this boy . . . I know it sounds crazy, sounds crazy to me even, but this boy, he looks like me. That's got to mean somethin'."

"It means the child has blue eyes and yellowish hair, from what you tell me. Hardly enough to make a paternity claim."

He didn't press the point, but he could have said that the boy had the Hollidays' high cheekbones, the McKeys' fine chiseled nose, the bravery of being descended from generations of fighting men. For what could be braver than facing the world alone at such a tender age, of being proud of it, even? He slept in livery stables, he said, or in the back rooms of saloons if the weather was cold. He bought his own meals, got his own clothes, showed up every morning at the *Rocky Mountain News* to collect a pile of papers which he had to pay for himself if they didn't get sold. So it was no wonder that he had looked forward to a second meeting with the man who had given him a half eagle for one copy of the news—that money paid his way for a week, the way he lived. But it wasn't the way a boy should have to live, no matter whose child he was, and especially if he were John Henry's son.

"It's not just the look of him," he said. "There was the letter, as well, as I told you. The girl wrote to me in Valdosta—or the man she thought I was at the time, tellin' me she'd had a child. But I wasn't there when the letter came so I couldn't respond."

"A letter proves nothing," DeWeese said. "Do you know how many girls have written to accuse a man of fathering a child? How many of them are false attempts at gaining a profit?"

"But she wasn't like that!" John Henry said, feeling a need to defend his faded memory of her, in case she were the mother of his son. And hadn't she been sweet to him? Hadn't she been kind?

"She was a prostitute, Dr. Holliday," Colonel DeWeese said harshly. "But if she were the Queen of England and every word were true, that still doesn't prove this boy is your boy."

"Which is why I want you to investigate for me! Find out about the old aunt who raised him, see if you can learn anything of his mother. I can't do it myself, without drawin' attention and complicatin' matters more. But surely you have ways of lookin' into these things. You're a lawyer, you can find courthouse records, birth certificates, death notices . . . somethin'. There has to be some way to find out more about him."

DeWeese sighed. "And if we do find something, some evidence that links him to you. What then?"

"I don't know," he said. "I haven't figured that out yet."

And what would he do, if Tom were his? Explain to Mattie how he'd lived with a harlot and begat a child on her? And how would his family back home treat the boy? As Henry's rightful heir, or as an embarrassing evidence of John Henry's wastrel life?

A life, as he'd tried to explain to Zan, that wasn't fit for a child to share. His main occupation was gambling, when he was feeling well enough to gamble, in places where children weren't welcomed. And when he wasn't feeling well, he was coughing up his lungs and staining his bed linens and cursing the illness that was slowly wasting him away. It was a miserable existence for a man. It would be a cruel existence for a child.

But was living on the streets any better? At least John Henry had a real bed and a roof over his head, while the boy who looked like him and might be his son had no shelter from the storm.

And then the real storms began.

Denver's weather was often turbulent, as the warm air from the plains rose up and collided with the cooler air coming down from the mountains. And in the summer, when the hot air was hovering near ninety degrees, the collision was noisy with thunder and lit by lightning bolts that streaked from sky to ground and back again. Which was grand entertainment from inside a saloon, but bad for anyone caught outside.

John Henry was playing cards on the afternoon of the biggest storm of the season, holding his own but not making much headway, when the sky opened up all at once and thunder rattled the walls of the Cricket Club. There had already been a lot of rain that summer, and the dirt streets quickly turned to mud that flowed over onto the board sidewalks. And then the rain froze and turned to hailstones the size of hazelnuts.

"Damn if it isn't snowing!" one of the other sports said, looking toward the open door of the place, and John Henry followed his gaze to see the hail piling up like an icy snowdrift on the sidewalk outside. And suddenly the saloon was overcrowded with pedestrians escaping to safety, and one of them announced that Cherry Creek was flooding over the Larimer Bridge.

John Henry heard the words above the clatter of the hail, and dropped his cards in mid-play. For if Cherry Creek were flooding at Larimer Street, it would be doing worse downstream where it ran past Wynkoop and the livery stables for the horse-drawn cabs of Union Station. And that was where Tom the newsy liked to sleep on warm summer nights, with the horses for company and plenty of hay to make himself a bed.

If John Henry had been healthier, he would have stolen a horse the way he'd done once in St. Louis, and ridden off into the storm to rescue the boy. But his horse-stealing days were over, and he had to wait for the hail to pass before catching the Electric Railcar down to Union Station, then walking the two blocks back toward Cherry Creek.

He was drenched and winded by the time he got there, having to stop too often to catch his breath and straining to see his way through the steady rain. Ahead of him, the usually tame trickle of Cherry Creek was surging over its banks with white-capped waves and washing right up against the foundations of the closest buildings. The livery stables, built closest of all to the creek bed, were two feet deep in water.

"Tom!" he called against the rain, his voice too weak to carry far. "Tom!"

But the boy didn't answer, and John Henry shuddered at the sight of the angry creek carrying rail posts and timbers and bridge spans downstream along with it. What if Tom had been swept away as well?

He couldn't stop to wonder and paused only a moment before turning toward the stables and wading into the muddy overflow. The force of the water took him by surprise, nearly knocking him off his feet, and he called out to the boy again and still heard no reply. But where else could Tom be? He had no home, no one to care for him.

The livery doors were opened wide, the water lapping around them. But as John Henry peered into the wet darkness, he saw only flood and floating refuse, and said out loud to himself, "So where are the horses?"

A small voice answered him from somewhere overhead, like an angel hovering in the hayloft.

"The liveryman took the horses away. Horses are valuable."

"And why didn't the liveryman take you away as well?" John Henry asked, looking up to see the boy lying in the hay, arms folded beneath his chin.

"I'm not a horse," Tom said. "So now there's fish in the stable instead."

"Pardon me?"

"Down there. You're standing in 'em: Sunfish and Crayfish and little trout. They washed up with the creek, after the rain started coming hard. Did you ever see fish swimming in a livery before?"

"I can't say as I have."

"Maybe we should catch 'em and have ourselves some supper," Tom said. "I'm hungry."

"Maybe you should come down from there, and I'll buy us some supper instead."

Tom considered a moment. "Maybe we should catch us some fish and buy us some supper, both." He was a bargainer, this boy.

"Sounds good to me," John Henry said. "And then maybe we'll find you some place drier to spend the night. How does that sound?"

"Sounds good to me," Tom said, echoing his words as he shimmied down from the hayloft and splashed to the floor. "Nice to see you again, Mr. Holliday," he said, as if there were nothing unusual about meeting up in a flooded horse stable in the middle of a summer storm.

"Nice to see you again, as well, Tom," John Henry said.

The Metropolitan Hotel wasn't as elegant as the Windsor had been, with its diamond-dust mirrors and crystal chandeliers, but Tom thought it was grand, anyhow. He had never stayed in a real hotel before that he could remember, and had never had a housemaid come to make up his bed—even though his bed at the Metropolitan was just a pallet on the floor and not a proper mattress.

"You must be rich to live in a place like this!" he said to John Henry when the maid had curtsied and left the room.

"If I were rich I'd still be at the Windsor. But sometimes I am more flush than others, when my work is goin' well."

"So what do you do for work?"

John Henry thought a moment before answering. "You might say I'm a banker. I handle people's money."

"Maybe I should be a banker," Tom said, sitting cross-legged on his pallet on the floor, and not quite ready for sleep. "I'm good with money, too."

"So it seems!" John Henry said with a laugh, as he settled himself into an arm chair and opened the late edition of the newspaper. "Looks like it was quite a storm today. Paper says there were several people injured when their homes were struck by lightnin', and a telegraph pole was hit and shattered to pieces."

"Will you read it to me?"

John Henry looked at him quizzically over the top of the paper. "Don't you know how to read?"

Tom shrugged. "I read all right, I guess. But I like to hear the stories better."

Well, why wouldn't he like to hear a story? He was only eight years old, after all.

"All right," John Henry said, making space for Tom beside him and opening the paper wide so they both could see, then reading aloud: "*There is a tradition that when Count Murat and his party of permanent settlers first reached the mouth of Cherry Creek in the fall of 1858, friendly Indians warned them against camping in the bottoms on account of great floods which had come down the creek in times past . . .*"

It was the first time, in John Henry's recollection, that he had ever read a bedtime story to a child.

He went to see DeWeese the next day, finally knowing what he had to do, though the attorney thought it an expensive proposition.

"Why don't you just hire the boy as a valet instead?" DeWeese said. "Then he'd have a home and an income both, and be better off than he is now."

"I don't want him to work for me!" John Henry said. "And a hotel is hardly the right kind of home for a child, especially when I'm away until the wee hours of the mornin'. Tom needs a real home, with a mother to take care of him. And I can't offer him either."

"Then have you considered taking him to an orphanage? There are three good institutions here in Denver, and none would charge you."

"He's not an orphan. At least, we don't know that he is . . ."

"Nor do we know that he's your son. And you don't have any obligation to provide for someone else's child."

"But if he were my son, I would be obliged. And it's more than that—I want to provide for him. Hell, somebody needs to. Did you know that he lives in a livery stable? In that storm yesterday, the liveryman got the horses out to safety and left Tom there alone. He's worth less than a horse to anyone but me."

DeWeese pondered a moment, then said, "Well, it's your money to spend as you please. Just know that I advise against it. At some point, your inheritance will run out, and then both of you will be on the streets. And a man in your condition has to consider the future. Who will pay for the doctor when you can't work anymore? Who will pay for your hotel, your living expenses? If you give it all to this boy, you'll be back where you started, relying on your gambling income until you can't gamble anymore."

"And that's why I came to you. I want you to figure out some way for Tom to have what he needs, and hold back somethin' for me, as well. But first off, I need you to find him a home. There must be some family around here that would be willin' to take in a child if his expenses were paid. A good family that would care for him and not steal his money. He needs a family. I need him to have a family."

"I can make some inquiries," DeWeese said.

"And I want him to go to school, as well. A good school. A private school, if the public school isn't good enough. I want him to know what a gentleman needs to know . . ."

"Even if he turns out to be nothing special?"

John Henry paused before answering. "He already is somethin' special."

Tom was easier to convince than DeWeese had been. He didn't live on the streets because he liked it. He just hadn't known what else to do for himself. So when John Henry offered him not just a room in a hotel, but a home with a real family, Tom was more than willing. And the prospect of going to school instead of standing around Union Station all day selling newspapers was almost beyond his reckoning. He was, as he had told John Henry at their first meeting, smart for his age and eager to learn more.

To keep things uncomplicated, it was Attorney DeWeese who made all the arrangements for Tom's new living situation and who delivered him to his new home. But once he was settled there, John Henry saw no harm in paying a visit, as a friend of the boy's family as he told the lady of the house when she opened the door to him.

"And I hope you won't mind if I take him off with me, from time to time," he told the woman. "His father would have wanted him to explore the city a little, see the Cyclorama, perhaps. I'd be pleased to take him."

DeWeese had already told her, of course, that the boy had a benefactor who might like to take him on excursions, so John Henry's question was more politeness than anything. But the woman still took a long look at him before giving her permission.

"And what relation did you say you are?" she asked.

"A friend of the family," he replied, the answer that his lawyer had told him to give to anyone who asked.

"That's funny," she said, "I thought maybe you were kin. He looks just like you."

It was only decorum that kept her from asking any more questions, but John Henry could see the curiosity in her face. He'd have to be careful how he treated the boy when he made his visits, if he didn't want to add to the woman's suspicions. She hadn't yet discovered that the Mr. Holliday who came to visit Tom was the notorious Doc Holliday, and he didn't want her getting any the wiser. So he answered her comment with a benign smile, and said casually:

"It's the eyes, I reckon. His father's were the same color."

But it was good to know that someone else could see what he had always seen.

It was late autumn when a message arrived from DeWeese, asking him to come to the law office on a private matter, but John Henry was almost too apprehensive to go. He had gotten comfortable with things the way they were, with Tom living in a good home on a quiet Denver street, and having their visits together from time to time. And though he would have preferred to have seen the boy more often, he knew it was the best situation for both of them. Tom had the family and the schooling he needed, and John Henry had the quiet rest of his solitary life.

But DeWeese's message was urgent, "Come at once," he wrote in the note he sent by way of a courier, "information too confidential for the post."

So John Henry dressed carefully and had a long drink before setting out from the Metropolitan to the Curtis Street law offices. Would this be the day when his whole life changed? And how would he share the news with Tom? *"I know something about your parents . . ."* And would the boy be glad to learn that his benefactor was also his father? Or would he hate the man who had deserted his mother and left her with a broken heart?

"Come in, Dr. Holliday," Colonel DeWeese said, gesturing him into his private office. "I've received a letter that will interest you."

"About my boy?" he said, almost afraid to ask.

"No, actually," DeWeese said. "We're still exploring that matter. This is something else entirely."

"But you said you got a letter?"

"I did. Or rather, you did, but addressed to me as the last known contact for you after the trouble in Arizona. I suppose it was published that I was handling your case pending the extradition . . ."

"The extradition?" John Henry said, cutting him off short, his heartbeat quickening. "I thought that was settled. I thought Governor Pitkin found a flaw in the paperwork . . ."

"He did, and so declined to return you to the Territory. But that doesn't mean the Governor of Arizona has forgotten the case."

"So he's pursuing extradition again? He's resending the papers?"

"I don't know. I only know that someone has requested a meeting with you here in Denver to discuss the matter."

"Here? Who wants to meet with me?" His first inclination was to leave before hearing the answer, to run as fast as his feeble legs could carry him. But DeWeese's answer stopped him cold.

"Someone of note, interestingly enough, though I don't know why someone of his stature would be concerned with this case. It's Senator Thomas Fitch. He'll be waiting for you to call on him at the Windsor Hotel."

If it had been anyone other than Fitch asking to meet him, he would have packed his bags and been on the first train out of town. After all the trouble Tombstone had caused him, with cowboys trying to kill him and lawmen arresting him and governors wrangling over him, he had no desire to revisit the place or the people that had been part of it. Tombstone was over and done, as far as he was concerned, and he wanted nothing more to do with it. But if Senator Fitch had gone to all the effort to track him down and come to Denver to meet with him, there must be something important he needed to discuss. So although it seemed like a risky bet, John Henry sent a message to the Windsor agreeing to the meeting.

It wasn't hard to find the Senator, as he sat center stage in the gilded lobby of the Windsor, surrounded by an attentive audience. Fitch still knew how to draw a crowd. And as always, he was orating:

"Virginia City, ladies and gentlemen! The Comstock silver lode! And I was there to take part in it, giving my humble efforts to the editorship of one of the two newspapers in town—the leading paper, I am proud to say. Of course, our competitor wasn't any too happy to have me there, and challenged me to a fight. And not just a battle of words, mind you:

a pistol duel. The citizenry was thrilled by the prospect even though the duel didn't come to much, and I well remember what a young reporter said of it . . ."

John Henry already knew how the story ended, from the first time he had met Thomas Fitch, but he didn't interrupt the show as the Senator went on:

"Yes, I remember that reporter well. He called me an arrogant newspaper editor, and said that I was better suited to law or politics. In turn, I editorialized and told him he was better suited to something more full of lies, like novelizing, perhaps. Well, I took his advice and he took mine, so I suppose you could say that he is responsible for my career and I am responsible for his. And I dare say, without my advice he wouldn't have had nearly the success that has come his way. You may have heard of that reporter, or perhaps read something of his work. His name was Clemens back then, but now he calls himself Mark Twain."

There was an appreciative murmur from the crowd gathered around the Senator and even a smattering of applause, for if anyone had missed hearing about Mark Twain's bestseller *The Adventures of Tom Sawyer*, they surely could not have missed the recent publication of its sequel *Adventures of Huckleberry Finn*—a book banned in Boston for crude language and selling wildly everywhere else. And though the Senator's link to the success of either book was anecdotal at best, he didn't mind taking some of the credit. Of course he was happy to sign a few autographs as well. Fitch was still, as he had always been, a natural showman.

But John Henry wasn't interested in the same kind of attention, and he waited for the crowd to thin before speaking to the Senator.

"Looks like you haven't lost your touch for the dramatic," he said. "Does Mark Twain know you're tradin' on his name?"

"I'm sure he wouldn't mind. I get a good story and he gets some free publicity, thereby allowing us both to profit. A pleasure to see you again, Dr. Holliday," Fitch said, offering his hand. "So have you read Clemens' new book? They say it's ground-breaking, if you don't mind the vulgarity."

"I'm not much for novels," John Henry replied, "I get enough fiction from the newspapers. But I reckon you didn't call me here just to talk about literature."

"Indeed not," Fitch said in a lowered voice. "But I believe that particular conversation is better suited to a less public setting. Say, the Gentlemen's Reading Parlor?"

John Henry knew the place from his own stays at the Windsor. The parlor was just off the lobby but separated from it by a set of heavy double doors, and it was only euphemistically called a reading room. For although it did have a few good volumes in a small bookcase by the window, it was actually the men's smoking room where they could have a cigar or a cigarette without being bothered by the ladies. And it was generally empty during the late morning, as it was on this day.

Except for one man, sitting with his back to the door in a cloud of cigar smoke—a familiar aroma, a fine blend of Cuban tobaccos. And for a moment, John Henry thought that his father had come to visit, and was surprised to find it a pleasant thought.

"Pa?" he said out loud.

But when the man in the chair turned to look at him, it wasn't Henry Holliday who was sitting there enjoying a cigar, but Wyatt Earp.

"Long time no see, Doc," he said, as if he'd been expecting him, "have a seat."

"I thought you were in the Coeur d'Alene."

"The gold didn't pan out, so we went down to Texas instead. Now we're here in Colorado. We've got a dance hall and a saloon up in Aspen."

"We? You mean you and Josie? I've never known you to go into business with a woman before."

"Never met a woman smart as Josie," Wyatt said.

She was smart, all right, John Henry thought. Smart enough to leave Johnny Behan behind and hitch herself to a brighter star, even though it had meant breaking up two marriages to do it.

"We thought about visiting you in Leadville," Wyatt went on, "but I heard you'd left town."

"I took a vacation. I went down to New Orleans to visit my father."

"Your father? I never heard you mention him. I figured he was dead."

"He was, nearly. But things are better now." He had no intention of going into that story with Wyatt, or anyone else. "So what brings you to town, Wyatt?"

"Same as you, I figure. Got a letter from Fitch asking me to meet him here. Where did he find you?"

"Just up the street. I'm livin' here in Denver now. I didn't much like the climate in Leadville." He meant it two ways, but Wyatt only caught one of his meanings.

"You are looking some thinner, Doc."

"I'm all right. So what do you suppose Fitch has to tell us?"

Wyatt took a slow draw on his cigar, looking satisfied. "I figure it's the pardons finally coming through, like they promised. Be good to be a free man at last, stop having to watch my back everywhere I go."

Watch your back, Morgan had told him. Did Wyatt know he'd echoed his brother's last words? Did he even know himself what it was that was chasing him?

"I hope you're right, Wyatt," John Henry said, "I truly do. Especially considerin' the alternative."

And then Fitch made his entrance.

"Gentlemen," he said, opening the double doors with a flourish and then carefully closing them behind him. "I appreciate you both coming on such short notice. You are surely wondering why I asked for this meeting, and I hope you will be glad for the cause of it."

"I'll be glad to hear we're not goin' back to Arizona," John Henry said, "though Wyatt has his hopes up a little higher."

"We were promised pardons," Wyatt said. "We're still waiting for them."

"And I wish that I could deliver them to you. But those pardons were promised by the former administration. The new governor isn't bound to honor the promises of his predecessors."

"But it was Henry Hooker who told us," Wyatt said. "He had a letter . . ."

"I don't remember any letter, Marshal Earp, and neither should you. Whatever Colonel Hooker may or may not have said, whomever he may or may not have been representing is not pertinent information now. What matters is that Governor Trittle, who is the man currently in power, has agreed to let bygones be bygones."

"And which bygones are those?" John Henry asked.

"The governor has agreed to stop pursuing legal action to bring you back to trial, in spite of continued pressure from certain parties in Cochise County to secure your extradition."

"Behan," Wyatt said. "We should have killed him when we had the chance, there at the Sierra Bonita."

"Be glad you didn't," Fitch said. "There'd be no deal for you now if you'd killed a lawman, no matter how crooked."

"What kind of deal?" John Henry asked.

"Governor Trittle has agreed to ignore the wishes of those other parties on the condition that you don't draw any more attention to yourselves. Things in Arizona have changed since you both left, thanks in part to your work. The cowboy element is greatly decreased; the border troubles are cooling down. Now it's the economy and transportation that the governor is concerned about. He needs to attract more business to the Territory, more railroads and more settlers. And that's hard to do with images of street fights and vigilantes fresh in people's minds. So what he wants is for you to lay low and not remind the public about your previous difficulties. It's that simple."

"We put our lives on the line for the Territory!" Wyatt said angrily. "And now he wants us to be forgotten?"

"He is willing to forget, would be a better way to put it," Fitch replied.

"And how much did this absolution cost?" John Henry asked.

"I don't know what you mean, Dr. Holliday."

"There's always a price for redemption. Who's payin' it?"

Fitch paused a moment. "Henry Clay Hooker," he said. "He's agreed to make a rather substantial contribution, on behalf of the Cattlemen's Association, to the governor's next campaign fund. On condition that the governor would grant a favor in return and offer you his forbearance. That's politics, as well as religion."

"And all we have to do is lay low," Wyatt said with a tone of disgust. "And what if we don't? I don't much like the idea of turning into a shadow."

"If you find yourselves in legal trouble again or in the press, the deal is off."

"Meaning what exactly?" Wyatt said. "I like to know what I'm getting in for."

"Meaning that if you don't do as requested, the governor is free to seek extradition again. He'd feel obliged, in fact, to prove to the good people of Arizona that their government will take whatever measures are necessary to uphold law and order—even to the point of bringing you back to stand trial for murder."

"That's funny," John Henry said, "since it was the government's not takin' action that caused so much lawlessness and disorder in the first place."

"As I said, let bygones be bygones. All you have to do is keep yourselves out of the spotlight, live quiet lives from here on out, and there'll be no need for any further legal proceedings. And I, for one, will be grateful to be done with it all. For as interesting as your case was, gentlemen, it didn't do much for my own career. I'm not even allowed to mention it in my memoirs."

"Allowed by whom?" Wyatt said, suspicious.

"That is privileged information, as is this entire conversation. Which never happened, as far as I am concerned. If anyone asks about our meeting, I will say that it was a happy coincidence to run into you both here on my way through Denver. And I suggest that you say the same. And I'm sure we'll all be happier when the troubles in Tombstone have faded from memory."

They might all be happier, but Wyatt would never forget. And after the Senator had finished his little drama and left them to consider things, John Henry asked:

"So what happens now, Wyatt?"

"I suppose we have to do as he says. Although that might hamper my business plans some. Mining camps aren't known much for tranquility. I can't even remember all the mining partners who've sued me for one thing or another. And you've never been able to stay out of trouble for long."

"Oh, but I've changed," John Henry said. "I haven't used my pistol on anyone, not since I shot Bill Allen. Why, I'm practically a paragon of virtue now."

Wyatt almost laughed at that, but John Henry had meant every word. He really was trying to live a more circumspect life, now that he had more than just himself to consider. And though he was just about to tell Wyatt about Tom, he thought better of it. He still had no proof that the boy was his, after all. So instead he said:

"Have you ever thought about havin' a family, Wyatt?"

"I do have a family. I've got my brothers. I've got Josie—thinking of marrying her, even."

"That's noble of you. And what about children? What about havin' someone to remember you when you're gone?"

"We're not supposed to be remembered, Doc. You heard what Fitch said. We're supposed to ride off into the sunset and be forgotten. As I suppose we will be. And I suppose we'll need to stay scarce of each other, as well. Seems like there's always reporters around whenever we get together." Then he took one more draw on his cigar and put it out, watching the last of the smoke rise and disappear. "Well, it's time I took Josie to lunch. She'll be out in the lobby by now, waiting. Care to join us?"

"I don't have much appetite, these days. But I don't mind stoppin' by to say hello on my way out."

Josephine Marcus was just as he had remembered her: beautiful dark eyes and hair and a figure that men admired and women envied. And she seemed to be unabashedly in love with Wyatt, clinging onto his arm when he came close and gazing up at him like he was some kind of hero. Well, maybe he was, to her.

"Good-bye, old friend," John Henry said, taking Wyatt's hand after making his pleasantries with Josie. "I reckon it'll be a long time before we see each other again, things as they are."

"Things as they are," Wyatt repeated. "But it's strange, isn't it? If it weren't for you standing up for me back in Dodge, I wouldn't be alive today. Yet you must be the one to go first."

"But I'm not gone just yet," John Henry said, letting go of his handshake and giving Wyatt a quick embrace. Then, tears in his eyes, he walked away on suddenly unsteady legs. It would only take him a short streetcar ride to be at the house where his boy lived, and he'd need to be done crying by then.

It wasn't just the Arizona Territory that was trying to become more civilized. The whole country seemed to be in a race to forget its frontier days. From the closing of the Western Cattle Trail to the passage of the Congressional Act against banking games to Denver's new campaign to regulate the red light district, the world of the sporting men seemed to be changing on every hand—which made it harder than ever for a sporting man to stay out of trouble.

But trouble was what Fitch had told them to avoid, and John Henry did his best to comply. And the truth was, he didn't have the energy he'd once had and laying low was about all he wanted to do, anyhow. So he spent his time visiting with Tom, or playing cards in the quieter establishments in town, or resting in his hotel room reading the paper. And writing to Mattie, letting himself forget that she was a nun and speaking his mind to her as freely as he ever had. A man needed a woman who understood his soul, after all, even if he could never have the pleasure of being married to her.

She wrote regularly in return, telling him of the small pleasures of her own life: reading, teaching, caring for the elderly and ailing. It was, in many ways, much as her life had always been, only more serene—or so she said in almost every letter. And he began to realize that serenity was probably what she had wanted all along, and the one thing he could never have given her. His life had never been settled and wasn't still, as he waited for the changing world around him to deal another unlucky hand. And soon enough, it did.

The Denver newspapers had been mostly occupied, through that winter, with the falling price of silver and the failure of President Grover Cleveland's administration to do anything about it. But once that story grew stale, they started looking for something more exciting to write about—and found it in a new campaign against the gamblers.

We have ordinances! the headlines shouted, *Why can't we enforce them?* And the police, urged on by the papers, had no choice but to do the enforcing.

John Henry wasn't working the night the raids began, as the police made a sweep through the sporting clubs and arrested whole saloons at once, but he took it all as fair warning of what was to come. And not daring to chance an arrest, he decided to leave town for awhile, at least until things cooled down some in Denver. But he didn't plan to stay gone for too long. He had his boy to think of, after all.

Pueblo was friendlier to the sporting community, with plenty of entertainment in the saloons and gaming rooms along Union Avenue and only occasional interference from the police. And Pueblo had the added attraction of Clarke's Magnetic Mineral Springs, which was a comfortable retreat after the cold winter in Denver, whether the waters had any real healing powers or not.

He wasn't the only sport who liked to take the mineral water, of course—gamblers were always willing to wager on a miracle—so it didn't surprise him to see some familiar faces there. But when one particular gent showed up there and everywhere else he went, he began to be wary. He'd been followed in Pueblo before, and he didn't need the same kind of attention coming his way again. But until the man did something more than visit his same haunts at the same time he visited them, there wasn't really any reason for concern. How many Perry Mallens could there be in the world, anyhow?

Then one night he came out of the Comique Theater and found the man lingering there as if he'd been waiting for him.

"You're Doc Holliday, aren't you?"

"I've been called that," John Henry answered warily.

"I heard you murdered a man named Frank Stillwell, down in the Arizona Territory."

"Is that right?"

"I heard there's still a warrant out for your arrest, any time the governor wants to make good on it."

"Is there a point to this conversation?"

The man gave a satisfied smile. "Just wanted to make sure I had the right man, that's all." Then he tipped his hat and walked off into the night.

John Henry didn't wait around to find out what the man was after. By noon the next day, he was back aboard the Denver & Rio Grande, leaving Pueblo behind in a cloud of coal smoke and headed on toward the San Juan Mountains.

Chapter Eighteen

SILVERTON, 1886

DECIDING ON A DESTINATION HAD BEEN EASY ENOUGH. THE SAN JUANS were full of mining camps that opened up every spring after a long winter of being buried in the snow, and the richest camp in all those mountains was Silverton. So when John Henry heard about a gang of gamblers headed that direction, he thought it fortuitous timing at the very least and gladly joined them for the journey, knowing he was safer traveling in a crowd than traveling alone—especially if he had a bounty hunter on his trail.

But what started out as a getaway turned into something of a pleasure trip when the train left the wide valley of the Arkansas River and turned west toward the high desert and headed up into the San Juan Mountains. The railbed was narrow gauge from Durango to Silverton, the right-of-way through the Animas Gorge barely wide enough to accommodate the railcars, with a tumble of cold river to one side and a tumble of rocks and fir trees to the other. The views were spectacular, the five river crossings splendid, and at the end of the line was Silverton, sitting so close against the mountains that a landslide could have covered the whole town.

From first appearances, Silverton was nothing but brothels and dance halls and one-girl cribs lining both sides of Blair Street, with a scattering of saloons thrown in to make it seem a little more respectable. A man could get off the train and back on again without having to walk more than a block to lose his bankroll and his frustrations both. But John Henry hadn't come for the soiled doves, only to play a little poker and Faro and whatever other games Silverton had to offer and to help those

363

eager miners out of some of their hard-earned pay. And as he heard it, there was plenty of money to go around, with the mines paying off on the first of May for a whole winter's work and the miners being instructed to go to town and not come back until they were soused, satisfied, and $300 in debt. With that kind of economy, it was no wonder the sporting fraternity made Silverton their spring headquarters.

John Henry opted to make his own headquarters discreetly outside the Red Light District, at the Grand Imperial Hotel on Greene Street, and looked forward to a good sleep after the long train journey, but soon discovered that Silverton didn't sleep much. The town was roaring at all hours of the day and night, as the miners and the gamblers tried to make up for lost time and fit a whole year's amusement into a few short summer weeks. Although the Grand Imperial was the best hotel in town, even its heavy velvet draperies and fancy wallpapers couldn't keep out the Silverton street noise, and John Henry spent more time tossing and turning in his bed than truly resting. So it was no surprise that when he awakened late the next morning after his arrival, if one could call it waking after having been awake most of the night already, he had a bad headache and a worse disposition, and then he cut himself on his straight razor while shaving and his day was looking sorry before it even got started. But there were still the games to be played and money to be made, so he finished dressing and went downstairs to the hotel dining room, intent on having a peaceful breakfast before commencing to work.

He hadn't even been seated yet when he caught sight of the bounty hunter who had followed him all over Pueblo. The man was sitting on the far side of the room with a steaming cup of coffee in front of him and a notebook laid open on the table, intently scribbling away. Composing a wire to the authorities in Arizona, perhaps, bragging that he'd got the drop on Doc Holliday? Well, he wouldn't be getting the drop this morning, as John Henry kept a wary eye on him and backed slowly out of the dining room. The man hadn't noticed him coming in, he was certain, but it was only a matter of time before their paths crossed again. But how had the man found him so quickly? Had he been riding on the same train, while John Henry had been incautiously distracted by the view? Whatever the answers, he needed to be on guard and armed, even if carrying a weapon went against some Silverton ordinance. So he hurried back to his hotel room and took his Colt's from his traveling valise and slid it into the pocket of his frock coat, ready for however the day might stack up.

By the time he got back downstairs, however, the man had disappeared and John Henry began to wonder if he were imagining up a phantom, a fantasy of his travel-weary mind. Had his meeting the man been imaginary too, a mix of magnetic mineral water and bad memories and nothing more substantial than that? Or maybe he'd just had too much whiskey and too little sleep and was having some kind of waking nightmare. Maybe he should just go back to bed and sleep the whole thing off.

But if the man were real, he'd be back again soon enough—and if he knew where John Henry was staying, then the hotel room was just as dangerous as the rowdy streets of Silverton, and maybe more so. At least out in the crowds, there was a chance of hiding and making another getaway; holed up in his hotel room, he was nothing but a sitting duck. So he took another shot of whiskey to settle his nerves, then headed across the street to the Arlington Saloon, where Wyatt had run the gaming tables during another sporting summer—and where there might be friendly faces to back him up, if need be.

It was amazing how a little gambling could make a man forget his worries. And by late afternoon, when he'd played a couple of hands of poker and won on the Faro layout, he'd almost forgotten about phantoms and other such fantasies—until he glanced up toward the bar and saw the man sitting there having a drink and watching him in the reflection of the long plate glass mirror.

"Do you see that fellow at the bar lookin' this way?" he asked the dealer, nodding guardedly in that direction.

"I don't see no one in particular," the dealer replied. But at least he hadn't said he saw no one at all, which would tend to confirm John Henry's phantom delusions.

"The man with the notebook in his hand," he said pointedly. "Do you know him?"

"Can't say as much. No, I don't believe I've ever seen him around here before. But there's lots of folks in town I haven't seen before."

"But you do see him?" John Henry asked, and the dealer gave him a narrow look.

"I don't need eyeglasses, if that's what you're getting at. And I'm reading these cards just fine, if you're calling me a cheat."

Calling a man a cheat, even unintentionally, was a dangerous thing to do, and John Henry quickly rescinded his words. "No Sir, I am not sayin' anything of the sort. You are a straight-arrow dealer, from what I can see. It was more my own eyesight I was questionin', havin' spent so long starin' at these cards. In fact, I believe I've stared at these cards for too long, and ought to bow out of this game now. If you'll excuse me."

And as he laid down his cards and pocketed his winnings, he glanced toward the bar and saw the man wave toward the barkeep, ready to settle up his bill. He was being followed, all right, and high time for it to end.

He was waiting just outside the door, pistol hand in his pocket, when the man stepped out of the saloon and onto the board sidewalk, and fell in close behind him.

"Why are you trailin' me?" he whispered, drawing his Colt's and pushing it into the man's back.

"Is that you, Doc?" the man said over his shoulder while he threw up his hands.

"Who the hell else would it be? Put your arms down. This isn't a holdup."

"You've got a gun at my back! How am I supposed to act?"

"You're not supposed to make a scene, for one thing. You're a sorry bounty hunter, not knowin' the rules of your own game!"

"Who said I was a bounty hunter?"

John Henry eased up on the pistol a bit but still kept it close. "If you're not after a bounty, why are you followin' me? I saw you in Pueblo before this. Don't tell me you're only here by coincidence."

"It's true I'm following you, but I'm no bounty hunter. I'm just doing my job, I swear."

"Then what are you? A summons server? The angel of death, comin' to make an early call? I'm not ready to give up the ghost just yet."

"Nothing so poetic as that!" the man said with the start of a laugh, until he felt the pistol shoved at his back again. "Can you please put that thing away? I'm not armed. Check me to see."

John Henry hesitated a moment, then used his free hand to pat down the man's suit coat. There was, indeed, no weapon there—only the little notebook he had seen him use before.

"Satisfied?" the man said.

John Henry pocketed his pistol but kept his hand on it as a precaution. He didn't want to make any trouble in Silverton, but he wasn't about to be taken in, either. "So if you're not a bounty hunter, why are you followin' me? Did I lose a game to you somewhere and forget to pay up? Did I shoot some kin of yours and you're out for revenge?"

The man laughed again, easier this time, and turned around to face him. "Nothing of the kind! I'm just a reporter looking for a story. When I saw you in Pueblo I figured I'd found one. Then you left town before I got a chance for an interview, so I followed you here. That's all."

"You travel a lot for a reporter. What paper do you write for?"

"The *New York Sun*. I'm the Colorado correspondent. I do stories about the mines, mostly, business pieces for east coast investors. Dry stuff. But every now and then I stumble over something interesting, something that might make the front page. Like you. A real Wild West legend in his sundown days."

"If you're tryin' to sweet talk me, that won't do it." He might well be in his sundown days, but he didn't need an over-eager newspaper man to point that out.

"Actually, I was hoping you might let me follow you around for a bit, watch how a gambler plies his trade, maybe catch a shoot-out or two."

John Henry almost laughed in the man's face. "I wouldn't get much gamblin' done with a reporter lookin' over my shoulder. As for shoot-outs, I haven't been in one since I left the Arizona Territory, and I don't intend to have one for the benefit of the readin' public. Sorry, but I don't do interviews."

There had been a time, of course, when he'd used the newspaper to his advantage, a skill taught him by Bat Masterson. But things had changed some since Senator Fitch offered a deal on behalf of the Governor of Arizona: no legal trouble, no press. There had been no equivocation in the terms. But as he stepped out into the street, ready to be done with the conversation, the newspaper man said:

"You can walk away from an interview, but you can't get away from a story."

"Meanin' what?"

The man shrugged. "Meaning I'm going to write about you, one way or another. Like that incident in Leadville when you killed the bartender over a bad drink. Our readers love that kind of blood and thunder."

"I never killed anyone in Leadville!"

"But you were in a shooting there. I checked it out. If you don't want to give me the particulars, I'll just have to make up the rest."

"You'd purposefully lie, just for a story?"

"I don't consider it lying. I consider it creative writing. So what do you say, Doc? Will you grant me an interview? Or shall I just use my imagination?"

"You give journalism a bad name," John Henry said with disdain. Then he added: "But give me a day to ponder on it."

"Done!" the newspaper man said cheerily. "Though if you're thinking of leaving town on a sudden again, just remember that I'll be right behind you. 'Cause I don't mind following you all over the state of Colorado if I have to. It'll just make the story more interesting."

He thought about it the rest of that day, as promised, and all through the night, as well. And when he left his hotel room early the next afternoon he was looking his dapper best in his black derby hat and freshly pressed suit. If he had to make a showing in the *New York Sun*, he might as well give the newspaper's Colorado correspondent something worth writing about. But making a showing was all he was planning to do. He still had no intention of actually answering questions if he could get around it.

The reporter was waiting for him in the hotel lobby, notebook in hand and looking a little too confident.

"I figured you'd show up," he said. "Got a table waiting for us in the dining room, so we can have a nice chat."

"I don't have much appetite," John Henry said, "but you can walk along with me, if you'd like."

"Walk? To where?"

"To the Arlington Saloon across the street. I thought you wanted to see a sporting man about his business."

"It'll be hard to ask questions while you're playing a card game."

"You never said anything about makin' it easy for you. You only asked me for an interview. Well, I'm givin' you one. I suggest you start writin'."

"But don't you want some privacy?" the man asked, still trying to wrangle an exclusive conversation.

"What for? You're plannin' to put me all over the front page of the paper, anyhow." And without waiting for the man to reply, he headed out onto noisy Greene Street.

The reporter let out a sigh of frustration as he pulled out his well-sharpened pencil and trotted along behind, throwing out questions that John Henry pretended not to hear. It was an easy pretense, with the crowd and the commotion as bad as ever. And as they walked, the man in the derby hat whistling to himself and the man with the notebook shouting at him with no reply, the crowd closest around took curious notice and fell into step, until they all reached the Arlington together like a street preacher and his eager congregation.

But John Henry wasn't interested in leading them any farther, and he stopped at the door of the saloon and turned toward the assemblage, tipping his hat and saying, "If y'all will excuse me now . . ."

"You can't just walk off!" the newspaperman said. "What about our interview?"

"What about it?"

"Do you expect me to just wait around until you feel like talking?"

"I expect you to go away and leave me alone. You asked for an interview, and I gave you one. It's not my doin' that the streets of Silverton are so noisy. And now I'm gonna spend the rest of the afternoon and most of the evenin' playin' cards. You can follow me again, if you don't mind the bouncer throwin' you back out for bein' bothersome. You wanted to see what a sporting man's life is like? Well, this is it."

And with that he turned his back and walked into the saloon where he ordered a whiskey at the bar and joined into a game of poker.

But it was hard to settle himself, with a crowd of onlookers peering in through the plate glass windows of the place and raising a ruckus outside. For the newspaperman, instead of giving up and going away, seemed to be encouraging the rabble by asking questions and scribbling down answers, as if he were interviewing the whole crowd. And John Henry had a good idea who the questions and answers were about, as now and then one or another of the men nodded and pointed toward the saloon where he was sitting at cards. They were talking about him, he was sure, or what little they knew of him, anyhow.

"You playing poker or just admiring the view?" one of the other players commented when John Henry missed a turn. And when he lost a bet he should have won, he decided it was time to put an end to the distraction. Being followed was irritating; being interrupted at his work was costing him money.

He closed his hand and stepped out onto the board sidewalk—and into the middle of a gory story about himself and an adventure he didn't remember having.

"That's him!" someone said, "That's the Doc!" and a general cheer went up, as if he were an actor stepping out before an audience.

"Hey, Doc! Tell us about the time you robbed the bank in Dodge City!" a man in the crowd called out, and was joined by another saying, "That's right! Tell us how you shot the sheriff and made off with the loot!" And then another voice, louder, added, "And how 'bout the time you robbed that stage out of Santa Fe?"

"To hell with stage robbery! Tell us how you ran across that bunch of dirty greasers down on the border and started a graveyard!"

"You can run away from an interview," the newspaperman said with relish, "but you can't get away from the story!"

"But that's not my story," John Henry objected. "I was a friend to the law, most of the time."

"The law's not nearly as interesting as the outlaws who break it. And you were an outlaw—still are, in the Arizona Territory. I'm sure our readers would love to hear what these gentlemen here have to say about you."

He couldn't have the papers telling fanciful tales about him and bringing trouble he didn't deserve. He had enough trouble of his own, already. And though he still didn't like the idea of being interviewed, he thought he ought to be able to defend himself, at least. So he turned to the crowd and said in the loudest voice he could muster, though it wasn't much more than a hoarse stage whisper:

"When any of you fellows have been hunted from one end of the country to the other, as I have been, you'll understand what a bad man's reputation is built on. I've had credit for more killin's than I ever dreamt of. Now, I'll tell you of one little thing that happened down in Tombstone in the early days. There was a hard crowd there, of course, and I thought I saw a chance to make a little money, and so I opened a gamblin' game. Things went on all right for awhile, but at length some of the boys got an idea that they were not winnin' enough, so they put up a job to kill me . . ."

There was more to the story of Johnny Tyler and the Slopers, but it was enough to say that Johnny and Milt Joyce and the rest of the gang had wanted him gone and he had stood his ground—and still was, with Leadville being the proof of it. The newspaperman, he noticed, was writing it all down.

"I heard what they thought of me, and I made them a little speech, said that sort of thing couldn't go on in a well-regulated community, and then, just to restore order, I gave it to a couple of them, and that settled the whole trouble. I was in Tombstone six months after that and never had another difficulty with them. It has been that way wherever I have been. I never shoot, unless I have to."

"That's right, Doc!" a voice in the crowd shouted, "Never shoot unless you have to, and then you give 'em hell!" bringing cheers from the rest of the men.

It wasn't quite the message John Henry was trying to deliver, but at least everyone was listening, and he went on.

"Down on the border I had a couple of little scrapes, but they didn't amount to much. And if I did have to fix one or two trouble-makers along the way, it had to be done in the interest of peace. I claim to have been a benefactor to the country. But it seems like every crime that occurs in a new settlement is always laid out to one or two men, and I've found time and again that I've been charged with murders and robberies when I hadn't been anywhere near the place."

Kate, of course, was the one who had brought most of those charges, when she was liquored up and miserable over their failed romance. But he'd always been exonerated in the end.

"Tell us about that gunfight at the OK Corral, Doc! Tell us how you poured lead into that Clanton gang!"

"Blood and thunder!" the newspaperman said. "That's what the people want!"

But there was more to the story than the newspaperman knew, more than anyone would ever know. There was truth behind it all, if only he could explain himself.

"The way I see it, some few of us pioneers deserve credit for what we have done, bein' the fore-runners of government. As soon as law and order were established anywhere we never had any trouble. If it hadn't been for me and a few like me, there never would have been any government in some of these towns. When I have done any shootin', it has always been with this end in view."

And having used up all the voice he had left, he paused a moment and waited for the crowd to react. But instead of applause or a round of cheers for the work he'd done in the interest of civilization, there was silence. Then one of the men at the front of the crowd gave him a look of disgust and spat into the street.

"Nah! He's not gonna tell! He's keepin' all the good parts to hisself!"

And as the man's words passed along through the crowd, his audience moved slowly away in disappointment, leaving him alone with the newspaperman.

"They don't want your explanations," the man said at last. "They've got enough excuses in their own lives. They want the man who might turn loose with a shotgun again and kill a crowd of cowboys. They want the legend!"

"But that's not me," he said.

"You're Doc Holliday, aren't you?"

"Meanin' what?"

"Meaning you may not be the legend, but the legend is you. And you'll never get away from the story."

He could run from a bounty hunter but he couldn't run from his own reputation, and Silverton turned out to be not much of refuge after all. So once he'd made back his traveling expenses and a fair amount more, he bought a train ticket to Pueblo and from there north to Denver. He was missing the boy who might or might not be his, missing the feeling of family he had when he was with him even if he might be only imagining the relationship. But mostly, he was tired of traveling and ready to be settled again.

He was tired a lot these days, a bone-deep weariness that whiskey didn't soothe. He felt old, though he was only thirty-five years that summer, and knew that he looked old as well. His fair hair was turned gray too early, his body had grown gaunt. His face, when he examined it in his silver-framed shaving mirror, was drawn and ashen. Only his eyes were still the same, china blue like his boy's eyes, or so said the woman who took care of Tom when he went to visit after his long trip away.

"You sure do look like kin," she said to John Henry. "What did you say your relation was?"

"I didn't say," John Henry replied, dodging an answer, and saw a glimmer of consternation pass across the woman's face. She was surely frustrated to know so little about the child she was mothering, but what more information could he give her? Tom himself didn't know his father's surname, and Colonel DeWeese hadn't yet turned up any leads to discovering it. So if the boy's eyes looked remarkably like those of the man who came to visit him and left her to wonder, she wasn't the only one who was wondering.

Then Tom came to the door and John Henry stopped worrying about what the woman thought.

"Mr. Holliday! You've been gone so long—sixteen Sunday papers, almost!"

John Henry smiled at the boy's peculiar mathematics, counting time by editions of the newspaper. Well, the paper had been his life, after all.

"It was too long," he agreed, "but I had a business trip to make."

"Banking business?" the boy asked.

"You could call it that."

"Mr. Holliday is a banker," Tom said to the woman, as if he were introducing them for the first time. "That means he handles people's money."

"I know what it means," she said. "And which bank do you work for, Mr. Holliday?"

"Actually you could say I'm more of an investment banker. I go wherever the deals are."

"And where'd you go to this time?" Tom asked.

"Down south," John Henry said, "Pueblo first for awhile, then to a little mining town called Silverton. The town's nothing to remark on, but the scenery is grand."

And as he described the journey, Tom's eyes were alight. "I'd like to see those mountains," he said, "and ride on that train, too! I've never been anywhere on a train."

"Never?" John Henry said in surprise, though he shouldn't have been surprised. Where would Tom have gone to on a train, anyhow, all alone as he'd been, and how would he have paid to get there? There was so much the boy hadn't experienced in life, so much life he still had to see. And no telling how long John Henry had left to show it to him. "Tell you what," he said, "how 'bout we take a train ride together, one of these days soon? Go see some sights together?"

"And where did you have a mind to take him?" the woman asked, taking a step closer to Tom as if to protect him.

"Wherever he'd like to go," John Henry replied. "I remember when I was his age, watchin' the trains come and go and wonderin' what the world was like somewhere else."

"Wondering and doing are two different things. You'll fill the boy with wanderlust, making him such offers. He belongs here at home, not traipsing around the countryside on some wild adventure."

"And who are you to decide where he needs to be?" John Henry said with irritation.

"I'm his mother," the woman answered quickly, putting a hand on Tom's shoulder. "And who are you to him?"

He paused before answering, holding himself back from saying what he wanted to say, holding back the hoped for truth that he was Tom's natural father with more right than anyone to decide what the boy would do. But he couldn't say it yet, not without some real proof. So he forced himself to politeness and said coolly:

"I'm just a friend of the family, Ma'am, lookin' out for his needs."

It wasn't any more information than the woman already knew, and clearly not enough to satisfy her, but she responded as politely as he had done, saying she was glad the boy had such a kind benefactor and that perhaps a train ride might be acceptable at some future date. Then she asked as if an afterthought, "Silverton, was it?"

"Pardon me?"

"Where you had some business. You said it was a town called Silverton?"

"That's right," he replied.

"It sounds lovely."

He had taken up his old room at the Metropolitan Hotel but only some of his old life, as Denver was continuing the campaign against gambling and the sporting clubs were still under siege from the city police. But even without a daily income from gaming he could live comfortably enough for awhile, having returned flush from his recent travels to the San Juans. And when that cash ran out, he'd just make another business trip.

It would have been a fine plan, if the Academy of Music hadn't burned to the ground. The blaze was started by a patron who left a cigarette smoldering in one of the velvet upholstered theater seats, or so the fire department said later. But how they could tell, John Henry couldn't imagine, as there was nothing much left of the theater or its red velvet seats. What he did know was that the first warning he had of the fire was his hotel room filling with smoke and waking him with a choking heat.

The Academy was across the street from the Metropolitan Hotel and down a few doors, and by the time the volunteer firemen arrived with their shiny new pumping car, the whole block was ablaze. The Academy went first, followed by the stores on either side, then the St. Cloud Restaurant and the Western Union Station before the flames jumped the street in search of something more to devour, and found the wood-frame walls of the Board of Trade Saloon and Charpiot's Restaurant. And when that didn't satisfy, the fire moved on toward the German National Bank, bursting all the windows in the fine brick façade and sending cinders and smoke swirling into the Metropolitan Hotel next door.

"Fire!" a man's voice shouted, "everyone out!"

John Henry threw himself out of bed and fumbled with the door lock, then yanked open the door to find the hallway filled with hotel guests in their nightclothes, not bothering about propriety as they pushed toward the stairs to the main floor and escape. What did a suit of clothes matter if a man burned to death in a hotel fire?

Then he remembered that it wasn't just clothes he was leaving behind, but all his personal possessions, as well—and years of Mattie's letters tucked into a leather satchel. They'd gone with him everywhere, even chasing across the desert after the troubles in Tombstone, and he wasn't about to leave without them now. So he turned around and headed back toward his room while the smoke billowed up thick as fog.

He felt for the letters more than looked for them, stumbling around the smoky room and struggling to get one good breath after another, and somehow he found the precious package and clung onto it while he made his way back toward the door. But where was the door? Ahead of him? Behind? The smoke blinded him, left him disoriented, gasping for air, and dizzy, so dizzy . . .

The firemen found him there some time later, collapsed on his bed and barely breathing. "Smoke inhalation," they called it, like being smothered with a layer of ash and soot drawn into the lungs, and they covered him in a blanket in spite of the heat and carried him out of his room and down the stairs, depositing him in a horse-drawn cab for a ride to the Denver City Hospital.

The doctors pronounced the same diagnosis and prescribed daily exposure to fresh cold air for his lungs and honey poultices for his throat, and said that a healthy man could recover fairly quickly. But for a man in his physical condition, with his lungs already compromised by the consumption, recovery would be harder. Still, with any hope . . .

He had lived on hope for years already. He reckoned he could live on it a little longer.

He was four days in the hospital with a week of doctor's house calls after that, and running out of cash fast. There'd been the medical bills to pay, the new clothes and accessories to buy to replace the ones ruined by smoke, the move to the pricier Windsor Hotel while the Metropolitan was scrubbed and restored. But he was in no fit state to make another business trip looking for some gambling winnings. He might get to his destination in one piece, but once he arrived he wouldn't have the stamina to sit up all night at a poker table or even to deal the Faro cards with a steady hand. What he needed was easier money, the kind that came without much work on his part. What he needed was a lucky horse race, like the kind he'd bet on when Zan Griffith had been traveling with him. But without Zan along as his good luck charm, he'd have to do the horse picking himself, and a little good advice would help. And according to the bartender at the Bon Ton Saloon, the man to talk to was J.S. Smythe, the night watchman at Jewell Park.

"He knows all the horses, knows the riders and the rigs as well. Knows which horses carry the biggest bets. Knows which ones will likely lose, or can be made to lose. 'Course, he can't guarantee you a winner, but he can educate you so you can make your own bets."

"And how much does he ask for this learnin' opportunity?"

"Nothing, unless your horse wins. Then he takes a cut, as you'd expect. There's nothing illegal about it. The racing's on the up and up, for the most part, and Smythe ain't got no special power over the horses. But if there's anything going on between the riders and the promoters—well, he's in a position to know something about that. And he's generous enough to share the information, wishing you well and asking nothing but his fair share."

"And what share do you ask, for bein' his broker?"

"That's between him and me. But if he don't lead you straight, we'd both be out of business. He'll be along by here later this evening, if you're interested in meeting with him. And no money out for you, if you don't like what he has to say."

It seemed a reasonable enough arrangement—a little inside information for a percentage of the proceeds, and nothing paid at all if the information didn't pan out. What could be simpler?

He met Smythe that same night, being introduced by the barkeep who said he thought they might have something in common as they both shared an admiration for good horseflesh, and Smythe said that it was nice to meet a fellow horse fancier. Then they took their conversation out onto the street and around the corner, where the other saloon-goers wouldn't overhear them. Smythe couldn't share his information with everyone, of course, or the bets wouldn't pay out to proper advantage, so he was choosey about whom he brought into the business. But on that hot August night it would have been better for both of them if they'd kept their business indoors.

The Denver City Police had started another sweep of the gambling district, this time armed with the Vagrancy Law, which was broad enough to put a net around the entire sporting community. If a man was not regularly employed he was deemed a vagrant and was subject to arrest and a fat fine—or an invitation to leave town permanently, whichever would get rid of him quicker. It was guilty until proven innocent, with the burden of proof lying on the vagrant to show some reason why he shouldn't be sent away. And rumor had it, there was a bonus for every officer who made an arrest. So when the night policeman patrolling 16th Street came across a couple of men having a discussion in the shadows behind the Bon Ton, he didn't even bother asking questions before arresting them both.

It seemed distinctly unfair to John Henry to find himself behind bars again when he was only trying to make a little honest money, and even worse to find himself written up in the newspaper again. As far as he was concerned, the only crime he'd committed was being too sick to travel and make his living elsewhere. But the newspaper made him out to be a menace.

The notorious Doc Holliday was arrested last evening by the police for vagrancy. He was standing on 16th Street when Officer

Norkott called up the patrol wagon and gathered in the suspects. The intention is to keep them in jail until this morning and then arraign them in one of the Justice Courts.

Doc Holliday has the reputation of being a killer. He gained his notoriety as an Arizona rustler in 1881-83. He was a member of the noted Earp Brothers gang, who are reported to have killed a dozen or more men in those bloody days of Arizona's history. Holliday is credited with doing his full share of the killing. The country finally became too hot for Holliday and he came to Colorado, where he was joined by Wyatt Earp, the most noted of the Earp Brothers. Within a few months of his arrival here, Holliday was arrested on 16th Street by an Arizona officer. The prisoner protested against being taken back to Arizona, saying that he would surely be lynched. After two weeks parleying the Governor refused to sign the extradition warrant, and Holliday was released. He then went to Leadville, and soon engaged in two shooting scrapes, which he got out of by leaving town. He then came to Denver, and since that time has been living here. His only means of living is gambling in its worst form and confidence work.

The *New York Sun* reporter had been right: he might not be the legend, but the legend was him, and it seemed he could never get away from the story. And if he'd been in a better mood, he might have laughed at the irony that his second Denver arrest had happened in nearly the same location as his first, on a sidewalk along 16th Street. Sixteen, it seemed, was not his lucky number.

When the Justice Court convened the next day, Smythe's case was sent on to trial which he would no doubt win as he had a regular job as a night watchman, while John Henry's case was continued indefinitely. He was, after all, a known gambler by trade with no other legal occupation, and a notorious one besides. He was, the Judge said, exactly the kind of character that Denver did not want, and a fine example of why the Vagrancy Law had been enacted, and he would do well to leave the city and never come back—or spend a very long time in jail.

"So you're runnin' me out of town, Your Honor?" he asked incredulously, as he stood at the docket in his rumpled attire and unshaven face, looking every bit the vagrant after two nights in the city lockup. If he'd been allowed to go back to his hotel for a bath and a change of clothes he could have made a better presentation of himself.

"Let's say I am giving you the opportunity to leave rather than face imprisonment," the Judge decreed. "You and your kind are a pariah and a blight on the good character of this community. You so-called 'sporting men' live off the labors of others and provide no goods or services to aid the economy, and the law requires that you be removed from among us, one way or another. So in the crude parlance of your own sporting community: Go to hell, Dr. Holliday. We don't want you here anymore. Next case!" And with a gavel swing, John Henry was no longer a legal resident of Denver City.

So where was he supposed to go, now that he wasn't allowed to live in Denver? And how was he supposed to stay close to his boy, if he couldn't live nearby? And how could he travel, when he was still recovering from the smoke inhalation and having a hard time even getting through the day?

It was his doctor who gave him an answer to the last question, when he laid a stethoscope on John Henry's chest and listened to his respirations.

"I think a visit to a mineral springs would do you some good, at least to clear up the damage done by the smoke, perhaps filter out the remaining impurities. There's a resort in the mountains where I send my patients, and where some have had quite remarkable results. The baths there are close to one-hundred fifty degrees, highly charged with lime and magnesia. It's a bit of a travel, something over three-hundred miles, but the Denver and Rio Grande has a station there so the trip won't be too unpleasant. And the outdoor sport is famous, when you're feeling up to a little recreation. They say there's no place in Colorado for better fly-fishing."

Chapter Nineteen

WAGON WHEEL GAP, 1886

THE PLACE WAS NAMED FOR A THOUSAND-FOOT DEEP GASH IN THE RED sandstone mountains of the Rio Grande del Norte, where the river cut between the cliffs and left only enough room for a narrow wagon road alongside. Story had it that an old wagon wheel had been found in the gap, left over from the first explorers to the area. But what made Wagon Wheel Gap famous was the mineral water that bubbled up from the broken earth. *Little Medicine*, the Indians called the springs, and red men and white men both came from miles around for the healing waters.

The *Little Medicine* was now surrounded by a first class spa built by railroad tycoon General William Palmer, with a fine hotel and comfortable bathhouses adjacent to the thirty pools of bubbling water and a saloon and gaming hall where resort-goers could while away their evenings after spending their days soaking in the pools. But soaking was only part of the regimen ordered by the staff of doctors at the springs. There were also spring water poultices and spring water enemas and spring water injections, all designed to flood the body with healing minerals and flush out disease and dissolution. And if the patient were a little more dissolute in the morning after a night of liquor and tobacco in the hotel saloon, there was always another treatment available for an additional charge.

John Henry had been compelled to ask DeWeese for a draw in order to pay for the trip, but the Colonel hadn't questioned the disbursement. He was easier in giving his approbation for the inheritance money to pay for health care than to pay for the orphan boy his client had stubbornly insisted on supporting. So John Henry had arrived at Wagon Wheel Gap with enough money to pay for his trip and sufficient left over to stake himself at the games as his physical condition permitted. And what other choice had there been but to dip into his inheritance, once Denver had thrown him out?

He didn't tell Mattie about his unexpected exile, when he wrote to her from Wagon Wheel Gap. She'd been worried enough to learn about the fire in his hotel room without the added bad news of his ridiculous arrest. So he left out that part of the story, and told her instead about the beauties of the Rio Grande Forest country and how the doctor in Denver had given him high hope for a miracle cure there. And why not expect a miracle from such a place, where the Rio Grande River was born and the mineral springs came up both icy cold and boiling hot, like the forces of life itself? Like heaven and hell, and all mankind hanging somewhere in between.

And then, for the first time, he told her about the homeless boy he'd met in Denver, whose mother was dead and whose father's identity was still in question, and how he'd taken an interest in the child's welfare. He told her how he'd asked his lawyer to find the boy a home, and how he'd put money into a trust fund to help support him. He told her what a smart boy Tom was, brave enough to live on his own but with a sensible side as well. Then, without mentioning his own possible paternity, he added: "He's the sort of boy we might have had together, if we had married." And the thought occupied him for pleasant hours while he took the water cure, imagining Mattie as Tom's mother, imagining the three of them living a long and happy life together. The kind of life he should have had, if luck had dealt him differently.

The tourist season at Wagon Wheel Gap ran from late May until mid-October, when the winter settled down on the mountains and stayed until the early summer melted it away again, and the season was already half over by the time John Henry arrived. Now, with the last warm days of Autumn waning and an early snow drifting into the high passes, most of the resort guests were packing up and making plans to go back to wherever it was they called home. But John Henry, not having a home anymore, would stay as long as the manager allowed, taking the baths and still hoping for a swift recuperation. Though he'd been soaked and poulticed, prodded and pricked and nearly drowned with the healing waters, he had yet to heal. His lungs, already scarred by the consumptive cough, seemed unwilling to give up the smoke and soot they'd taken in with the fire, and he'd seen no sign of the remarkable cure his doctor had suggested. But as long as the baths stayed open, he would keep on bathing. What other option did he have?

It was toward the end of one of those Autumn days, just as he was about to take a long hopeful soak, that a visitor came to call.

"Excuse me, Dr. Holliday," the bellboy said when he knocked on the door to John Henry's bathhouse dressing room and found him robed in a heavy Turkish towel. "There's someone here to see you. He says it's urgent and can't wait until you're done with your bath. He says he must speak with you right away."

"Did he give you his name?"

"No Sir. I'm sorry, Sir, I should have asked. But he gave me this for you to read, said it would explain why he was here," and he handed John Henry a page from a recent edition of the *Rocky Mountain News*, with an article circled in heavy black ink. It was a long interview with the infamous Doc Holliday, below a byline which read *Silverton, Colorado*.

So the *New York Sun* reporter's story had come back to haunt him after all, being reprinted in the Denver paper. But what more did the reporter want of him now, to follow him all the way to Wagon Wheel Gap? Hadn't he done enough damage already? Did he want an autograph to go along with the interview? Did he want a photograph of the two of them together, as a souvenir?

"Did the reporter say what he needed to see me about?"

"Reporter, Sir?" the bellboy said, looking puzzled. "He's not a reporter. He's a lawyer. He said to tell you he's an Attorney, and he has news about someone important to you. Was that what was in the paper, Sir?"

"No," John Henry said, his mind racing. He didn't know what the newspaper article had to do with anything, but if there were a lawyer come to see him with news of someone important, it could only be Colonel DeWeese with news of his boy. What other lawyer knew of his whereabouts? The only people he'd told about his trip were DeWeese and his doctor. And Tom, of course. He couldn't just go off again without letting Tom know where he was going and when he'd be back. The boy missed him so when he was gone, counting the Sundays until his return. Did DeWeese have some news about his boy, at last? Why else would he make the long trip to Wagon Wheel Gap instead of sending a letter over the wire?

"Tell him I'll be right there," John Henry said, "as soon as I'm presentable. Tell him to wait for me in the Hotel Lobby. No, tell him to wait in my room. You know which one I'm in?"

"Yes, Sir."

"And after you've shown him there, go to the bar and buy a bottle of your best champagne and take it to my room as well."

If DeWeese had come so far to see him, it must be news worthy of a celebration.

He dressed as fast as his shaking hands would let him—shaking not only from sickness but from exhilaration. Certainly, DeWeese had news about his boy, good news that would put all his wondering to rest. And the next time Tom's foster mother asked what right he had to say what the boy should do, he'd be able to put her in her place. If a father's rights superseded a mother's rights, they were surely far superior to those of a woman who was merely acting like a mother. Still, he was grateful for her caring for his son, and he would tell her so, perhaps even making her a nice bequest by way of thanks. And then he would take his boy and they would travel together, maybe even back to Georgia so Henry Holliday could finally meet his only grandchild—oldest son of the oldest son of the oldest son.

But it wasn't Colonel DeWeese who was waiting for him in his hotel room, but a man he'd never seen before, a narrow man with shaded eyes and slick pomaded hair and an odor of bad cologne about him. Was this Naylor of the firm of DeWeese and Naylor, Attorneys at Law? He couldn't remember if he'd ever met DeWeese's partner. But before he could ask for an introduction, the man said:

"So you're him. You're the infamous Doc Holliday!"

"Pardon me?"

"I wouldn't have guessed as much, from what the stories say. I wouldn't have guessed you for an invalid."

"I am not an invalid," John Henry said, defending himself against the rudeness. "I'm here to heal from an injury. I was in a fire this past summer. Surely DeWeese mentioned that . . ."

"Yes, I know about the fire," the man said. "I've seen your room at the Metropolitan Hotel. A shame you had to lose so many belongings to the smoke. I hear your entire wardrobe had to be replaced."

It surprised him to hear that DeWeese had examined the results of the fire, but perhaps that was part of his oversight of John Henry's finances. "It was costly, all right. But I had enough to cover it, even without the disbursement. There's still plenty left. It was a generous inheritance."

"A generous inheritance," the man said, repeating his words with a smile. "Yes, of course." But there was something about the smile that made John Henry wary.

"You said you had news for me? Have you found something?"

"Oh yes, indeed. Perhaps even more than I was looking for. Do you mind if I have a seat?"

John Henry motioned him toward the chair set between the two long windows, but stayed standing himself, too nervous to sit. "So? What do you have for me?"

"It's more a question of what you have for me," the lawyer said. "But let's start by saying that I am a reasonable man. I only want what's fair."

"Fair? What are you talking about?"

"Come now! Let's not play games with one another! Surely you knew you couldn't keep up the charade forever. Surely you knew some clever soul would see through your ruse and call you on it."

John Henry took a step backwards, feeling for the door.

"Who are you?" he said. "You're not Mr. Naylor . . ."

"Thankfully not!" the man said with a laugh. "Naylor's been dead these past five years! DeWeese just keeps the name for convenience."

"Then you work for him?"

The man shrugged. "I did, times past, until we had a parting of the ways. He didn't agree with my greater ambitions for the firm. But I keep in touch. There's a secretary there, a lovely girl who takes dictation and types letters—you've met her perhaps? No? A shame, she's quite charming. And quite incapable of keeping a confidence. So when she mentioned that my former partner had been doing some legal work for a certain noted citizen of our city—she is quite taken with celebrity, poor thing—of course I had to look into the matter further. And guess what I found? The notorious Doc Holliday, infamous in every Western State and Territory and still wanted for murder in Arizona, has been making regular money advances to a certain married lady living in Denver. Scandalous, to say the least. So I went to visit her."

"You did what?" he gasped.

"And found, instead of the sporting man's paramour I was suspecting, only a rather plain looking housewife, and not at all the kind of woman one would accuse of playing the adulteress. Nor did she seem to know anything of Doc Holliday, although she's had several conversations with a Mr. Holliday, a reclusive banker who visits with the family. That wasn't what I had expected to find, and I thought that perhaps DeWeese's secretary had got the story wrong, and that it was this Mr. Holliday for whom the firm was doing work instead of Doc Holliday. An easy mistake, surely. I was, in fact, about to let the investigation go, when the woman mentioned that her Mr. Holliday had recently returned from a business trip to a town called Silverton. Well, that caught my attention, as I had just read an article in the *Rocky Mountain News* about Doc Holliday visiting the town of Silverton. What an amazing coincidence! And when she mentioned that her Mr. Holliday had been the victim of an unfortunate hotel fire, as had Doc Holliday . . ."

"There's lots of hotels, and lots of fires. Someday the whole city may burn down."

"No doubt, but there's only one Metropolitan Hotel where Mr. Holliday was known to have stayed and where Doc Holliday had his residence until the Academy of Music fire."

"Lots of people live in hotel rooms."

"In the same hotel room? At the same time? And what of the coincidence of Mr. Holliday making a trip to Wagon Wheel Gap, as the woman also mentioned, at the selfsame time that I find Doc Holliday visiting here? Come now," the man said with a triumphant smile, "you can't pretend I haven't found you out!"

He seemed to be wanting applause for his detective work, but John Henry answered carefully: "So what if I'm known as Mr. Holliday to some folks? It's just a title they're lackin'. And why shouldn't I do a little good in the world, and share my fortune where I please? I'm not the Devil some folks make me out to be."

"It's not your identity that intrigues me," the man said, "but the fact that you're trying to hide it. Not that I care about your reasons. I'm a lawyer, not a preacher. But if you're so intent on keeping your anonymity, I imagine you'll be willing to pay something for it as well."

"Are you're tryin' to blackmail me?" John Henry asked in amazement. The man had daring, if nothing else.

"I prefer to call it a business agreement. Say ten-thousand dollars for my silence?"

John Henry wanted to hurt the man, slam a fist against his smiling face and send him sprawling. But he was too weak to be making a fist fight and too wary to pull a gun—indoors, at least.

"I'll give you my answer tomorrow," he said.

"That'll be fine," the lawyer replied. "I don't mind spending a day or two in such a swank place as this. On your tab, of course. Now which way is the dining room?"

The blackmailer's greed was his one saving grace, for once he'd discovered that he was trailing Doc Holliday, he stopped searching for any more answers and hadn't yet learned anything about the boy who was at the center of the intrigue. If he'd found out about Tom and tried to do him harm in any way, John Henry would have been obliged to silence him permanently. As it was, all the man needed was a good scare to show him the foolishness of his ways. And for once, John Henry was glad to shoulder the legend of Doc Holliday.

The man had put himself up for the night in one of the resort's empty guest cottages, adding it to John Henry's tab as he'd promised to do, and having his own celebration with a bottle of wine he had delivered from the bar. But he seemed sober enough when John Henry went to collect him late the next morning in a two-seater horse and buggy borrowed from the hotel livery.

"Are we going somewhere?" the man asked.

"You are, as soon as we've finished our business. I'm takin' you back to the depot to make sure you get on the first train to Denver. And then I hope to never see you again."

"Fair enough," the man said, as he collected his overnight case and climbed up onto the seat. "You know, I was worried that this might all be more difficult. But you've been quite the gentleman thus far."

"I was raised well," John Henry said. What he didn't say was that in his world politeness wasn't always kindness, and a man who offered you a ride wasn't necessarily doing you a favor.

The resort property lay a half-mile north of the town and the railroad depot, but John Henry turned the buggy to the west instead of the south, and counted on the convolutions of the trail to keep the lawyer from discovering that they were going the wrong way. He'd been on that trail himself a time or two, when the resort staff had arranged for expeditions to the scenic overlooks high above the gap, and he thought he could find his way back again all right. But by the time the blackmailing lawyer figured out that they were nowhere near the railroad, they'd be too far off in the red sandstone cliffs for anyone to hear his cries for help.

"Are you a trout man?" John Henry asked, talking to keep the lawyer distracted as the horses found their way upwards along the trail.

"A trout man?"

"These headwaters are famous for trout fishin'. There's browns, rainbows, cutthroats. Best fly-fishin' in Colorado, so they say. You'll see the lay of the river soon, once we come around this bend."

The trail kept rising, passing through stands of tall spruce and aspen and into a tumble of red rocks hanging high above the valley floor.

"I didn't guess you for a fisherman," the lawyer said.

"I'm not. But the staff at the hotel like to brag a bit, so I've heard somethin' about it. Maybe you'd like to do some anglin' on the way to the train?"

"What are you talking about?" the man said with a laugh. "I don't have any fishing gear."

"Well, that shouldn't be a problem for a man as rich as you. You can buy yourself some fine gear with all that blackmail money you'll be takin' home with you. Assumin' you ever find your way home."

And before the man could ask what he meant, John Henry had reined the horses to a stop and commanded: "Get out!"

"What?"

"I said get out."

"Here?" the man said, looking around at the trees, the rocks, the river a thousand feet below. "We're not to town yet."

"Then I reckon you're gonna have a long walk."

"You can't mean to leave me here!"

"This says I can," John Henry replied, as he slid his hand into his coat pocket and pulled out his Colt's, cocking it and taking aim at the blackmailing lawyer. "Now get out of this rig before this pistol makes you get."

The man scrambled down from the buggy seat and stood looking bewildered, and John Henry had to hold back a laugh. Revenge was amusing.

"Throw me your coat," he said, covering the man with his revolver.

"What do want with my coat?"

"Nothin'. But it's in the way of you takin' off your trousers."

"What?"

"You heard me. Take off your trousers."

The man kept frightened eyes on the pistol and did as he was told, revealing long black stockings held up by red knee garters. It was funny how much less intimidating a man looked when he was wearing nothing but his knee socks.

"Now take off your vest and your shirt, and toss them up here with your trousers."

"You can't be serious! It's freezing out here!"

"Sow the wind, reap the whirlwind! Don't dawdle, I haven't got all day. And don't forget your boots, please."

"You're going to leave me my underclothes, at least?"

"Of course. I am a gentleman, remember? We wouldn't want to frighten the ladies when you finally get to town."

"But what about our agreement? What about my money?" The man looked almost pathetic, pleading for his treasure while standing in his shorts and undershirt on a cold Colorado mountaintop.

Almost. He was a blackmailer, after all.

"Would you care for another suit?" John Henry said.

"Another suit?"

"A cut of the cards, which of course I always carry with me, bein' a sporting man. You pick a suit and if I draw it, you win the money and your clothes back, as well."

"And what if you win?" the man asked, shivering.

"Then you lose the money, and I keep your clothes. Simple enough. Are you game?"

"If I win it's the whole ten-thousand dollars?"

"If you lose, it's nothin' and a long walk home."

"Then I guess I'm game," the man said, his greed getting the better of him. If he'd given up on the money and vowed never to try blackmail again, John Henry might have called it even and left him with his clothes, at least.

"All right," John Henry said, laying the loaded pistol aside but close at hand and pulling a well-worn deck of playing cards from his coat pocket. "Your call."

"You didn't s-s-shuffle," the man said, stammering with the chill.

"Ah! You're a clever one!" John Henry said, snapping the cards together again and cutting the deck in two, then arching them until they slipped back into place, one after another like a cascade of dominoes. Years of practice such a display took, knowing the cards like he knew his own hands. "Name your suit."

"Ten-thousand dollars?" the man asked.

"Ten-thousand dollars," John Henry replied.

The man hesitated, looked toward heaven as if God cared about the turn of a card, then closed his eyes and whispered: "Hearts!"

It was the simplest of card games, like the Spanish Monte he'd learned as a child from Francisco, and the hardest to win. For whatever

390

card the player called, the dealer would deal something else, unless he was encouraging a bet. Then the game might go on all night, letting the player win just enough to think he wasn't going to lose. It was all about avarice and nothing about luck. But the air was cold on that mountaintop, and John Henry was shivering himself and worn out from holding the lines on the buggy, and he was ready to get the game over with. So he paused a moment for effect, then slowly drew a card from the deck.

"Diamonds!"

It was always diamonds, unless that was the suit the player called, then he drew something else instead, knowing the feel of every one of the marked cards in his personal deck. A blind man could play the game, if he practiced it long enough.

"Never try to out-deal a dealer!" he chastised the man. Then he picked up his Colt's and waved the barrel off toward the southeast, showing the way. "Better start walkin'. Night comes along early in these mountains."

"But we can work this out! We can make some other deal!"

"We just did," John Henry said with a smile. "And I won."

He had no remorse about leaving the man undressed and defenseless like that, alone in the wilds. It was better than he deserved, and might even be instructional. And he wasn't so far from town, really, just a few miles, once he got headed in the right direction. As for the cold, that was harder on John Henry than it would be on the healthy but hard-hearted lawyer.

In truth, the buggy ride and the chill October day had taken their toll, and he felt worse than he had when he'd arrived at the springs, in spite of the weeks of baths and constant dosing with mineral water. Even holding his eight-pound pistol steady had been an effort. And by the time the resort closed for the season, the staff doctor had to acknowledge that he had not been one of their miracles.

"It's the scar tissue from the consumption," the doctor said with a professional but apologetic voice, "aggravated by the smoke damage, of course. The scarring keeps the waters from circulating properly. It's a matter of mechanics, really. If the water can't infiltrate the tissues, the mineral balance can't be restored. And with the consumption and the smoke inhalation both . . ." A long pause, a death sentence of silence. "But there is one other treatment, if you think you can tolerate another trip."

He could tolerate anything, if it would give him his life back.

"A sulfur vapor can sometimes go where the water molecules can't permeate. You breathe in the vapor and it fills the lungs, forcing out the disease. It's been used medicinally for hundreds of years."

"Then why haven't you suggested it before?"

"It's Indian medicine. The vapor caves were owned by the Utes until very recently. They thought the place was sacred, an entrance to the underworld. A *Palace in Hell*, they called it, best as the translation will allow. But it might be the miracle you've been looking for."

He'd been to hell a time or two already. He reckoned he could go there again if he had to. "So how do I get to these vapor caves?"

"You don't. At least not until springtime. The caves are at the foot of Glenwood Canyon, and the only road to get there goes through Independence Pass, and that's snowed in from October until May, sometimes longer."

It was a cruelty, surely, to offer a miracle then take it away again.

"So what do I do until then?"

"Until then," the doctor said with something like sympathy, "you live."

He wasn't supposed to show up in Denver again, according to the Judge of the Justice Court, but since that was the connecting point for all the railroads running through Colorado, he didn't see as he had much choice. Besides, he had something important to take care of in the city, something that was worth daring a little more trouble with the police.

But the police couldn't bother him if they didn't know he was around. So he stayed far away from the bad luck and saloons of 16th Street and found a hotel in another part of town, then used an assumed name when he signed the guest register. And as soon as he was rested up from his journey, he made his way to the house where Tom lived.

The woman met him at the door, her eyes full of questions. But before she could begin asking them, Tom came tumbling past her, throwing his arms around John Henry.

"Mr. Holliday! I'm so glad to see you!"

John Henry laughed, then stood back to take a look at the boy. "You've grown stocky while I was away, Tom! What have they been doin' to you?"

The boy wasn't really stocky, just filled-out where he used to be scrawny, but he didn't look like a street waif anymore, either.

"We've been feeding him," the woman observed, "though it's hard to keep him filled up. He eats twice what our other boys eat but he's still the thin one in the family. I think he means to be a tall man someday."

"Mama's a good cook," Tom said, and the woman smiled at him fondly.

There was such an obvious affection between them that John Henry had to hold himself back from being envious. He'd wanted to find a mother for Tom, after all. How could he be offended now that his plan had been successful? Still, it was hard to see his boy becoming part of someone else's family—if Tom were indeed his boy.

But he had a purpose in this visit and couldn't let himself be distracted by such doubts. There was something he wanted Tom to see, something that he hoped would help explain things to the boy, and little enough time left to see it.

"Go get your coat," he told Tom. "Feels like there's snow comin'."

He was right about the weather, and by the time they'd walked to the electric streetcar line that carried them downtown, then walked from the stop on Larimer Street to the great circular auditorium that housed the Gettysburg Cyclorama, the icy clouds had opened up and the sky was littered with snowflakes.

"Did you know that every snowflake is different?" Tom asked, as he held out a small hand and tried to catch one in midair.

"And how can you tell?" John Henry replied. "They melt before you can get a good look at 'em."

"The Snowflake Man makes pictures of them," the boy said earnestly.

"The Snowflake Man?"

"He's a kind of scientist. He lives in Vermont and studies snow. They have a lot of snow in Vermont, you know."

"I reckon they do. So how does this scientist make pictures of snow-flakes?"

"He photographs them," Tom said.

"Is that right?"

"He uses a special camera with a microscope, and he works outside where it's too cold for the snow to melt. And every photograph of every snowflake is different. He says it's because of the way the ice crystals grow."

"And where did you hear this fantastic story? I've never read about it in the papers."

"Our schoolteacher told us. She used to live in the same town with the Snowflake Man, so she knows about him. They call him that on account of his photographs."

"That makes sense."

Tom turned his head toward the sky and let the snowflakes fall onto his face, dusting his sandy eyelashes and melting as they met his warm skin. "The Snowflake Man says his photographs are important because snowflakes don't last. *Earthly beauty is fleeting*, that's what my teacher says." Then he gave John Henry a pensive look. "That's sad, isn't it?"

But John Henry could only nod a reply as he looked down wistfully at the boy, hands full of snow and fingertips turning red from the cold. For there was likely nothing as beautiful or as fleeting as childhood, and soon enough Tom wouldn't care about catching snowflakes anymore. He'd join the rest of the grownup world, complaining about the cold and the inconvenience, instead of considering the snow with childlike wonder.

But wasn't that why he'd brought the boy here to the Gettysburg building, because life was fleeting? For the creators of the Cyclorama, like the Snowflake Man with his miraculous photographs, knew the importance of making a memorial before the memory faded. And today, there were memories John Henry wanted to pass on to Tom before he himself faded away.

Although the Gettysburg Cyclorama was essentially a giant painting in the round, viewing it was nothing like looking at a picture. The audience was ushered into the darkened theater for a "showing," where they stood on a raised platform in the center of the room and were surrounded by the sights and sounds of the most famous battle of the War. With electric lights illuminating sections of the canvas and the air smoky with stage explosives, the experience was as much like reality as paint and set pieces and rousing music could make it.

The subject of the panorama was the tragic third day of the fight at Gettysburg, when General Robert E. Lee ordered a brave charge across the open countryside and thousands of good Southern boys died carrying out his orders. And though one might watch the showing and wonder at the strategy that sent foot soldiers to fight against Yankee artillery, one couldn't help but be impressed by the daring of it. What if Pickett's Charge had succeeded? Would it really have turned the tide of the War, as Lee had promised it would? Would there be two American nations now instead of one, if the Rebels had prevailed on that day? And how might the Fourth of July be remembered if it had signaled the end of the United States on the day after the Battle of Gettysburg?

Those were the questions the Cyclorama asked but didn't answer, as the showing began with the call of a bugle and a narration spoken from out of the shadows:

> "It is dawn at Gettysburg, July 3rd, 1863 . . . You are standing on the western slope of Cemetery Ridge, just behind the center of the Union lines. Through two days of desperate fighting, neither side has been able to gain the advantage . . . Today, General Lee believes his army can deliver a crushing blow. . .he will risk a frontal assault against the Union center at Cemetery Ridge . . . At one o'clock the Confederate canon open fire, the Yankee guns thunder back. The massive bombardment continues for nearly two hours . . . It is one grand raging clashing sound so incessant that the ear cannot distinguish the individual explosions . . ."

Then came a tympani of canon fire and a percussion of pistol shots and muskets, and an old man in the audience began to weep out loud.

"It was just like that, all right!" he said. "I was there!" and he pointed toward a panel of the painting where a fence ran along a country road, and leaned close as if to find himself in the mass of life-sized figures. "I was right there, at that fight, I was there . . ."

The painting had that effect on people, especially those who had been in the battle themselves or knew someone close who'd been there. Some folks cried, some folks cheered, but no one saw it and came away unmoved. And Tom, young and impressionable as he was, seemed awestruck by the spectacle, watching wide-eyed and breathless.

"My family fought in that War," John Henry said quietly after the finale, when the theater lights came up and the audience lingered almost reverently. "My father and his brothers, and all my mother's brothers. They were all brave men, all willing to serve. But my cousin Mattie's father was the only one at Gettysburg."

"Was he killed?" Tom asked in a whisper.

John Henry shook his head. "He wasn't in the fight proper. He was Captain Quartermaster, watchin' over the supplies, which meant that he had to stay back to cover the retreat. But he was close enough to see it all, and wished he hadn't."

"Which side was he on?"

John Henry almost laughed at the question, since the answer was so obvious to him, but it was a reasonable enough one to ask. There had been plenty of families with split loyalties during the War, part Rebel, part Yankee, brother against brother, father against son. But to his knowledge there wasn't a trace of Northern blood in his veins, not since his first Irish ancestors had landed in the New World and made their way quickly south. And no one had ever confused him for a Yankee.

"My Uncle served in the Seventh Georgia Regiment," he replied proudly, then recited Uncle Rob's chain of command as he had learned it in his own long-ago childhood. "Anderson's Brigade, Hood's Division, Longstreet's Corps, General Robert E. Lee's Army of Northern Virginia."

"Good," Tom said with something like relief. "I like the Rebels best."

"And why is that?"

"Because they didn't hide, and they didn't give up."

It was so simple, seeing the fight the way a child saw it, without all the rhetoric of states' rights and abolition, of upholding the Constitution or saving the Union. Through a child's eyes, there was no great Cause to be defended, only the defense itself.

"And do you know why they didn't give up?" John Henry asked.

Tom thought about the question for a long moment before answering, then he gave John Henry a solemn, blue-eyed gaze. "Because if you give up, then you'll never win."

So wise he was, for one so young—but then he'd had more challenges than most children his age. "That's right. And it's right about the rest of life, as well. If you give up, you've already lost. General Lee's army knew that, and so did my Uncle Rob. So they fought on, against all the odds. And if God had been willin', they would have won that war."

"And what about all those men who died?" Tom asked, turning back to the painting with its endless struggle.

"What do you mean?"

"Did they go to heaven, for trying so hard? Or did they go to hell, because they killed people?"

The question came as a surprise and John Henry had to consider it before answering. "Well, I reckon some of them are still there, waitin' to find out. Folks say that's the most haunted ground in the whole country. Seems reasonable enough to me, with so many men sufferin' and dyin' there. And I reckon there's some who still haven't given up, even though the fight's been over for twenty years now."

"Mama says there's no such thing as haunted ground, or haunted houses, or ghosts. She says that's just silly superstition."

"Does she?" He could have argued the point and told the boy how he'd been raised on stories of haints and bogeymen and spirits that looked back at the world through uncovered glass. How the whole South seemed like haunted land, with shadows of dead soldiers still marching along the dark roads and echoes of Indian war chants in the names on the rivers and hills: Etowa, Kennesaw, Oconee, Chattahoochee. There'd been ghosts all around, when he was growing up.

But that wasn't what he'd come here to tell the boy, so he left the thought behind and knelt down to look at Tom face to face.

"You said you liked the Rebels best because they didn't give up?"

"Yes."

"Well there's somethin' I have to do that's a lot like that. There's a fight I have to make, and I don't know how it's gonna come out. But I know that if I give up, I'll never win."

"What kind of fight?" Tom asked, his voice quavering. "Are you going to a war?"

"In a manner of speakin'. I am goin' away again, Tom, back up to the mountains. There's a place there for people like me, people with illnesses that can't be cured any other way. It won't be easy gettin' there and it won't be pleasant once I do, but I have to go, I have to try to get better. I have to keep on fightin'. . . ."

"When will you come back?"

"I don't know. But I want you to know that I am only leavin' you because of this fight I have to make. Like my Uncle Rob, when he went away to join up with General Lee's Army. He left his whole family behind, not because he wanted to leave them, but because of the fight. You understand that, don't you? You understand that sometimes a man has to go, even though his heart doesn't want him to leave?"

Tom nodded, and John Henry went on.

"I want you to know, if I don't come back . . ." He hesitated, not wanting to say too much, afraid of saying too little.

"I want you to know that I am proud of you, Tom, so proud! That I never knew a boy so fine as you are, or so smart. And I am sorry, so very sorry for all the hard things that you've had to bear . . ." His voice broke on the words. For the boy's life wouldn't have been so hard if his mother had lived, if his father hadn't deserted them. If his father, whoever he was, had been a father . . .

And emotion overwhelming him, John Henry pulled the boy into his arms and said with tears in his eyes, "I love you, Tom! I want you to know that. I love you always!"

"I love you, too!" the boy replied easily, as only a child could say the words. As if the words were light as snowflakes, and love were an easy thing.

It was nearly dark by the time they got back to the house where Tom lived, the snow piling up along the sidewalk and covering the steps that led to the front door. From inside the house, a golden glow warmed the windows, while outside the streetlamps gave off a smaller light.

"You'll come in, won't you?" the woman asked, as Tom ran ahead of John Henry into the house, hungry for supper and happy to be at home again.

"Not tonight, thank you, Ma'am. It's been a long day already." But the truth was, having already said his goodbye to Tom, he didn't think he could bring himself to stay and have to say it all over again.

"Of course," the woman replied, then pulled her shawl close as she stepped out onto the porch and said in a hushed voice, as though keeping her words from anyone inside the house: "There was a man here, awhile back, asking questions. I think he may have been some kind of investigator. I'm not sure what it was he wanted. But I don't think I told him anything that shouldn't have been known."

"You did fine," John Henry said, trying to smile reassurance.

And what could she have told the man, really? That a lonely orphan child had found a friend in a cold and careless world? That a kindly family had given him a home? That Doc Holliday had finally done some good with his life?

"He hasn't come back," the woman said. "I expect he's given up on finding whatever it was he was looking for."

"I reckon you're right."

And though the woman's eyes were still full of questions, she didn't press him for answers. Instead, she said with a brighter voice, meant for the rest of the family to hear: "So will we be seeing you again soon? Christmas is coming. I'm sure Tom would be happy if you joined us."

"You're kind to think of me," he said, politely as his mother had taught him. "But I'm afraid I'll be away for some time again. There's another health resort up in the mountains that the doctors have suggested . . ."

He let his words run out, unwilling to say what didn't need saying. For it had to be obvious to the woman, as it would have been to anyone who looked at him, that his health was failing him. His custom-made clothes now hung on his bony frame, his high cheekbones cut a sharp angle in his face, his blue eyes were shadowed and sunken under his sandy lashes.

"He'll miss you," the woman said softly, giving a glance back into the house, where Tom's laughter had joined that of her own boys—a house filled with light and laughter, the way a home should be.

"I'll miss him, too," John Henry said, and felt the woman's eyes on him, studying him as she always did, and seeing too much. Then she took a step closer and laid a gentle hand on his arm, saying:

"Is there anything you'd like me to tell him, while you're away? Anything at all you've wanted to say?"

But what more could he say, without knowing for sure?

"No," he said sadly. "There's nothin'."

And before her sympathy could make things even harder, he turned up the collar of his overcoat, nodded a silent farewell, and stepped out into the snowy, lonely night.

He left Denver two days later, before the police discovered his presence there, before his presence could bring any trouble to the boy. And having no place else to go that he really wanted to be, he wandered while he waited for the road through Independence Pass to open up again. It was a long wait, through the coldest December in a dozen years, the snowiest January, the most bitter February, the bleakest March. Wherever he went, from Denver to Pueblo to Trinidad to the Black Canyon of the Gunnison River, the weather was the same and it seemed that spring would never come.

The newspapers blamed the long winter, the worst in memory, on the eruption of the island called Krakatao, the far-away volcano that had caused the extraordinary sunsets of three years before. The explosion had blown two-hundred million tons of rock and smoke and ash into the atmosphere, darkening the skies and slowly lowering temperatures all over the globe. *Volcanic Winter*, the scientists called it, bringing droughts to Europe and deadly floods to the Far East, hurricanes to South America and blizzards to North America. On the Great Plains, thousands of head of cattle froze to death where they stood, decimating what was left of the western herds. And John Henry, huddled in his heavy overcoat and finding no warmth anywhere, could only hope his luck would hold and the weather wouldn't outlast him.

Leadville was the coldest city in Colorado, in that or any other year, and he would have avoided it altogether, if it weren't also the last railroad stop on the way to Independence Pass. So when May finally came with the first temperatures above freezing and the coach road through the pass sure to reopen soon, he made his way back to the Cloud City. But as always, the altitude took its toll on him and by the time he arrived at the front desk of the new Hotel Delaware, he was breathless and dizzy.

"Room's up the grand staircase," the manager said, "second floor. Shall I have the bellboy carry your bags?"

John Henry could only nod an answer and wish the bellboy could carry him, as well. It took all the energy he could muster to make it across the lobby and up to the first landing, pausing and panting, then dragging himself up the second set of stairs to the long gas-lighted hallway and his room. He'd appreciate the fine accommodations later, when he was well enough to admire the printed wallpapers, the heavy carpeting, the shiny mahogany bedroom suite, the delicate lace curtains at the window. But for now, all he wanted to do was sleep until all the snow in Colorado melted away.

He had as many friends as he had enemies in Leadville, but no one in particular on whom he needed to pay a visit, so he kept himself to himself for the whole of his two weeks' layover there, his only occupation being preparing for the coming ordeal of crossing the Continental Divide. For if Leadville's altitude were enough to make him weak and sickly, the twelve-thousand foot summit of Independence Pass would surely be worse. As for the road itself, it was a narrow ribbon that twisted and looped along the edge of the Sawatch Range, rising toward the tundra at the top of the Rocky Mountains, and so precipitous that a wrong step by the horses could send a stage coach careening over the cliffs. But there were spectacular panoramas for those who were brave enough to ponder on them and didn't mind the bruising eighteen-hour ride. And there was no other way to get to the vapor caves.

John Henry was brave enough, and desperate enough, as well, despite warnings that the rough ride could set off the bleeding in his lungs again. But what other choice did he have, anyhow? It was either make the crossing and try the Indian medicine, or give up and die.

And Leadville was not where he wanted to play his last hand. So as soon as the road was opened he bought a ticket on the Carson Stage and a bottle of Laudanum to ease the pain, and set out on the ride of, and for, his life.

Chapter Twenty

Glenwood Springs, 1887

Yampah, the Indians called the caves, *Big Medicine*. They lay at the confluence of the Roaring Fork and the Grand Rivers, protected by ragged mountain ranges and narrow canyon walls, and the Utes had fought bloody battles to keep them. But what the Comanche and the Arapahoe couldn't win in war, the white men had simply surveyed away: prospectors, explorers, farmers, squatters—they took over the Ute hunting grounds and built a town they called Fort Defiance.

Defiant it was, sometimes buried in snow sixteen feet deep and sometimes surrounded by flood waters as the snow melted off and overflowed the two rivers. But against the odds, or maybe because of them, the town continued to grow. For wherever there was a glimmer of hope that the mountains might be hiding a fortune in silver or gold or anything else that sparkled, there were men eager to endure any hardship to find it. But it was something less glamorous than silver and gold that turned the town of Defiance into a real city. It was coal, a black ridge of it running through the narrow valleys of the Roaring Fork and the Grand, coal that fired the smelters that pulled the silver from the raw ore of mines from Aspen to Leadville, coal that brought bankers and businesses and talk of a railroad someday soon. If silver were king in those mountains, coal was his consort and queen, and Fort Defiance looked to have a regal future.

The same geology that gave coal to the mountain valleys gave them the vapor caves and the hot springs, and the springs gave Fort Defiance its new and more welcoming name: Glenwood Springs. And with coal to pay the way and the natural wonder of the caves to draw tourists, Glenwood Springs was about to boom, once the railroads arrived.

As for the Indians who had first inhabited the place, they still returned every summer, gathering like ghosts to their sacred caves and sending prayers to the great Manitou. If they were praying for the white men to leave and give them back their land, their God didn't seem to be listening.

John Henry learned about the town from the other passengers on the stage run through Independence Pass, but he learned about the Indians on his own soon after arriving. The stage stop was right in the middle of town in front of the new Hotel Glenwood, and he was happy he didn't have to travel any farther than up a flight of stairs to his room overlooking Grand Avenue. While Glenwood Springs was lower in altitude than Leadville, only five-thousand feet or so, he was still short of breath after his harrowing ride and suffering some from the effects of the Laudanum he'd taken to ease the journey. He was dizzy and drowsy and feeling confused—all symptoms, he knew, of the powdered opium that was mixed with alcohol to make the Laudanum tonic. But better to be drugged than in pain, and the road had been as rough as all the warnings. So when he got to his hotel room and dropped to sleep without even closing the heavy drapes at the window, then had a dream of Indian drums echoing through the night, he blamed it on the Laudanum—until he woke early the next afternoon and heard the same drums again.

He pulled himself from the soft feather mattress of the bed and went to the window, taking his first good view of Glenwood Springs. From that second-story vantage point he could see the wide dirt street that ran through the middle of town, lined with a tumble of buildings, from wood-frame shanties to fine brick houses. He could see how the town stretched out past the main road with narrower streets and smaller structures, and here and there a lumber yard or a horse lot and livery, before it gave out and turned back into sage and buck brush. And he could see at the far end of Grand Avenue, where the road stopped at the river and the river ran between the canyon walls, the unexpected and unsettling sight of a circle of Indian teepees and the smoke of a dozen Indian campfires.

He rubbed a hand across his eyes and took another look, then pulled the bell cord and called for the bellboy.

"Yessir?" the boy asked when he knocked on the hotel room door only a few moments later.

"You're quick," John Henry said.

"Thank you, Sir," the boy, a teenager really, replied. "Can I help you, Sir?"

"What's that out there?" he said, nodding toward the window, "along-side the river?" And though he half expected the bellboy to tell him there was nothing there and he was only imagining things, the boy replied:

"Why, that's the Ute camp, Sir. The tribes are here for the summer, like always."

"Tribes?"

"Yessir. This is sacred ground to the Ute, especially the Uncompahgre. They come up from the reservation to visit the vapor caves, but they don't bother the town. They're harmless, most of the time."

"I thought I heard drums last night."

"That was them, getting ready for the Sun Dance. They're practicing, maybe."

"What's the Sun Dance?"

The bellboy shrugged. "It's a kind of religious ceremony, best as I can figure. Lasts the better part of a week. They build a lodge, then they dance around it all day and night. Supposed to be, they're asking the Great Spirit to give them visions and powers—healing powers, mostly. Maybe that's why the vapor caves heal people the way they do."

"Indian Medicine," John Henry said, recalling the words of the doctor at Wagon Wheel Gap. There had been a note of disdain in the doctor's voice, but he'd offered the suggestion anyway.

"I guess so," the bellboy said. "But sometimes it works. There's three caves altogether, the natural one the Indians use and the two new ones the Defiance Land Company carved out of Lookout Mountain. They're planning a whole resort around them. There's going to be an Italian-style hotel and the biggest hot water swimming pool in the world, along with bathhouses and pleasure gardens and picnic pavilions and outdoor concerts."

"Sounds ambitious."

"But for now, there's just the dressing rooms at Cave Two and Three, so you can trade your street clothes for a bedsheet before you go inside. You won't want to wear much more than that, as it's something like a hundred and twenty degrees in there."

"And what about Cave Number One?" he asked, his mind for numbers noticing something missing.

"Oh, you won't want to bother with Number One. That's the Indian cave. It's mostly just a hole in the ground near where the hot springs come up. The Indians use it when they come for the Sun Dance, for healing. They lower a body down into it and leave him until he's better or dead, whichever comes first. Then they do a big dance to the Manitou—that's the spirit that's supposed to live down there. So will there be anything else, Sir?"

"I'd like a tumbler of whiskey, if you can manage it."

"Yessir. Right away."

"And I'd like another tomorrow morning, as soon as I wake up. I'd appreciate you having it ready for me."

"You just ring the bell, Sir, and I'll bring it right up."

"That'll be fine. What's your name, son?"

"Art, Sir. Art Kendrick. Best bellboy at the Hotel Glenwood, or any other hotel in town."

"I'll remember that. So do you have a newspaper in this town, Art?"

"Sure do, two of them: The *Ute Chief* and the *Glenwood Echo*."

"Then I'd like a copy of both every day, as well," he said, and tossed the boy a half dollar. "Here's a tip in advance. And there'll be another everyday if you don't forget my liquor and my paper."

Art Kendrick caught the shining coin and grinned. "Will you be staying with us long, Sir?" he said hopefully.

John Henry turned back to the window, looking off toward the end of Grand Avenue and the Ute encampment with its columns of smoke.

"I reckon that depends on the Indians," he said.

Art Kendrick, the best bellboy in Glenwood Springs, was too polite to ask him to explain.

The attentive service was what one would expect of a fine establishment like the Hotel Glenwood, the newest and nicest hotel in Glenwood Springs and second only to the Windsor in Denver for luxury accommodations, according to the hotel's newspaper advertisement. But although there wasn't a diamond dust mirror or European crystal chandelier in sight, the Hotel Glenwood had something not even the Windsor could boast: electric lights in every room, courtesy of the country's first hydroelectric plant. The power came from the two rivers that ran between the narrow canyon walls, the same rivers that supplied the cold running water pumped into every private bath while hot water was pumped from the nearby hot springs. A guest could walk into his hotel room, pull on a light, and draw a warm bath without even calling on the staff for help. Of course there were the other usual amenities, like a well-appointed dining room, parlors for smoking and for billiards, a gentleman's barber shop, a guest laundry. But there was something more at the Hotel Glenwood that truly set it apart: a trained nurse on staff for the benefit of the invalids who came to use the hot springs and the vapor caves.

There were also twenty-one saloons within easy walking distance, according to the hotel manager, when John Henry had dressed himself for the evening's entertainment and asked advice on where to find the best sporting palaces. No palaces yet, the manager had informed him, but plenty of bars and gambling houses, and he was sure to find something to satisfy him. And once the railroad arrived after blasting its way through the solid rock of the mountains to lay a roadbed, there would be even more in the way of pastimes. Maybe even an Opera House, the manager said hopefully, for the more diversions there were in a town, the more patrons there were who needed a place to sleep. And that made for good business.

It was business that took John Henry on a tour through the best of those twenty-one saloons, scouting out opportunities. For though he'd come to the mountains for his health, he could use a little work as well to help pay for things. As Colonel DeWeese had pointed out, his inheritance money wouldn't last forever and some well-played card games could make it stretch awhile longer. And unlike Denver which didn't want him anymore, Glenwood Springs seemed pleased to have a noted sport at its gaming tables. "Damn, if it isn't Doc Holliday!" he heard more than once that night, from bartenders who offered him a free drink on the house, hoping he'd share some of the more lurid details of his history.

"Was it you that shot a bullet into Big Nose Kate's buttocks?" "Did those Earp boys really run a stage robbing racket?" "Is it true that you snuck back into Arizona to murder Johnny Ringo?" His legend seemed to have a life of its own and was growing larger all the time.

But his well-mannered refusal to reply only brought him more free drinks and a bigger audience, until he had to move on to the next saloon in town. And so it went for most of that first evening, until he was sure that when he felt like making some big bets, there'd be plenty of sports eager to challenge him. As far as business went, infamy was even better than fame, most of the time.

It was well past midnight when he stepped out of the last of the downtown saloons, but the sky seemed as bright as day. And full of free liquor as he was, it took him a long moment to focus his eyes and realize that it wasn't daylight he was seeing at all, but streetlamps. There were dozens of them, courtesy of the hydroelectric plant, lining Grand Avenue from one end to the other, electric streetlamps that outshone the moon and the stars and all but did away with the darkness. He'd seen electric city lights before, of course, like the string of single bulbs that had dazzled Leadville, but that was like candles compared to this. With so many streetlights blazing all at once, there seemed to be no night at all in Glenwood Springs, only endless day.

But as he stood there trying to decide whether to ignore the artificial daylight and go on to bed or stay awake and start drinking all over again, the blaze of lights suddenly dimmed and disappeared, and the street was plunged into darkness that seemed even deeper than natural. And though it was no doubt just the streetlamps going out for the night, the unexpected end to the light gave him a shiver of memory. He'd seen an eclipse long ago, when the moon had moved in front of the sun and left his father's field hands moaning as if the end of the world had come.

Whether it was the Laudanum or the liquor or both of them together, all at once he felt like he was back in those fields again, running from the darkness to his mother's sickbed, afraid that it was the Angel of Death passing over. And when he reached her, she was still as stone, as white as the sheet that lay over her, and he fell to his knees weeping.

But she wasn't dead yet, only sleeping, and she awoke and told him not to be afraid—

He closed his eyes and pushed the memory away, and when he opened them again the darkness was less deep, the moon making its usual cool shadows. The moon and something else, and he lifted his head to see the Indian campfires along the river, gold and glowing against the canyon walls, above the caves they called *Yampah*.

It had been a long time since he'd gone undressed in a public place, since his days of skinny-dipping in the Withlacoochee River and nude bathing on the sand beach in Galveston. And never had he felt as naked and unprotected as he did on his first visit to the vapor caves, without a pistol or even a pocket watch at his side, his only weapon being a pail of water and a wet rag given to him by the gatekeeper so he could cover his face when the heat got to be too much for him.

"Even so, ten minutes is as long as you'll want to stay down there, first visit," the gatekeeper advised. "There's an hourglass in the cave to help you watch the time. You might be able to last a bit longer if you step out to cool off every little while. Some folks get good at the steam baths and can go an hour or more, in stages. 'Course if the caves aren't to your liking, there's always the hot springs. We've got ten porcelain tubs, and they're only a quarter dollar for a good long soak, if you'd rather."

"I've had a good long soak," John Henry said. "I've been nearly drowned in mineral water already: poulticed, pricked, enemaed even. The vapor caves are all I've got left."

"Well, good luck to you then," the gatekeeper said. "It's a hell of a place."

A Palace in Hell, the doctor at Wagon Wheel Gap had called it, and that was a fair description: a palace on account of the sparkle of electric lights that lit the stone ceilings and lined the stone staircase, and hell on account of the way those stairs descended into a sweltering catacomb filled with yellow fog and smelling of sulfur. The Prince of Darkness himself would have felt at home there.

But there were no demons waiting at the bottom of the stairs to welcome the lost souls in their bedsheet shrouds, only two attendants who motioned the way through the long corridor and guarded the entrance at the main chamber of the cave. And as the door slowly opened, John Henry found himself stunned by the strange beauty of the sight before him. The vapor shimmered and shifted in the incandescent light, the way a heat wave shimmered on a distant desert horizon, though this mirage wasn't distant. It was moving toward him, floating wraithlike through the open doorway. Beyond the door he saw other apparitions in the vapor: pale figures leaning against stone walls or stretched out on marble slabs like corpses in an undertaker's parlor.

But the specters weren't dead men yet, only other cave visitors resting themselves while the heat and the vapor enveloped them. Rest was all one could do, in such an atmosphere, and rest was what John Henry needed, rest and the sulfurous vapor permeating the scarred tissue of his lungs. And as he gathered his shroud about him and entered in, he almost laughed at the irony that had made this hell his last hope for salvation.

It was a full week after that before he could write to Mattie about his arrival in Glenwood Springs and his visit to the famous vapor caves, after he'd dragged himself from the depths and slept off the after-effects. And even then, he couldn't bring himself to tell her everything. He didn't tell her how, after spending so many careful years in a dry climate, he'd felt like a drowning man in the steam saturated air, how he'd gasped and choked, how he'd had to use the pail of water meant to cool his skin to catch his bloody vomit instead. As for the ten-minute time limit for a session in the caves, he came nowhere near it before escaping to the cooler air of the antechamber and collapsing on the stone floor of Cave Number Three.

But he learned how to take the heat and the vapor, or at least how to tolerate it the way the other patrons did, by taking shallow breaths and cooling himself with the wet cloth while he lay stone-still on a marble slab, looking like one of those vapor cave corpses. Some days, he went back in two or three times more, with a soak in the mineral springs in between. Some days, one session was all he could manage before giving up and going back to his hotel to rest, worn out by the heat and the humidity. And that was pretty much his routine in Glenwood Springs:

steam as long as he could, soak as long as could, sleep as long as he could. Though even sleep was hard to come by, as the night sweats soaked his bed linens and woke him, chilled and feverish at the same time, and more tired than when he'd laid himself down. And it was that part, in particular, that he didn't tell Mattie: that in spite of the daily soakings and steamings, he didn't seem to be getting any better.

He wrote to Tom, as well, carefully cheerful letters about the hot springs and the vapor caves and the magnificent mountain scenery, the cattle drive that came through the middle of town and turned Grand Avenue into a dust storm, the railroad that was grading and laying track that would soon link Glenwood Springs with Aspen and the rest of the state. And it pleased him when Tom wrote back thanking him for the stories and asking for more, even though the letter's pretty penmanship showed it was really the boy's adopted mother doing the writing. But the boyish questions were all Tom's: Were there real cowboys riding with the cattle herd? Were there still Indians hiding in the mountains? Would he be coming back to Denver soon?

John Henry's reply was longer, answering every question the best he could—all except for the one about his returning to Denver. And how could he answer that, when he didn't know for sure, himself? Instead, he told the boy how the Indians had been sent far away from their green mountain passes to live on arid reservations to the south and the west, but still returned to their Yampah caves for the midsummer's Sun Dance. They came in small groups and family bands, the men riding on painted horses while the women walked behind with the long-poled travois that carried the heavy canvas teepees. Then the women made camp along the river and set up the shelters while the men talked and smoked and beat their drums long into the night. And other than that, they were as quiet as moccasins on soft earth, keeping to themselves and staying away from the town.

But the town didn't stay away from them as the time for the Sun Dance grew close. While the Indians were gathering for their sacred ceremony, the people of Glenwood Springs were gathering out of curiosity. First it was bathers at the hot springs, taking the long way back to town in hopes of catching a glimpse of the Indians in their encampment. Then it was sightseers, taking a picnic lunch and watching from the opposite bank of the river as if the Indians were a scenic attraction. Then it was hawkers, setting up stands just beyond the ring of teepees and selling food and trinkets as if the Utes were a carnival side show.

"They're odd looking Indians," he wrote to Tom, *"and not much like the lean and sinewy redmen I imagined when I was growing up. There weren't any Indians left in Georgia, in those days, but there were plenty of stories about them, and I liked to think that they were still hiding somewhere in those piney woods, running swift-footed as the deer. These Utes are squarely built, short of stature and swarthy, and seem better suited to farming than to hunting after game. Which is, no doubt, what the Indian Bureau hopes they'll do, turning domestic and peaceful on their government reservations. But they don't look too domesticated to me, dressed as they are in their buckskin and their beads, with their eagle feather headpieces and their carved bone breastplates. They look fierce as the Apache that infested the Arizona Territory before the ranchers moved in. I wouldn't put it past them to scalp one or two of these tourists before the summer's over."*

He didn't really expect the Indians to go on the warpath, of course, but he knew that Tom would like the story better if it had more adventure to it. For what the Indians seemed to be doing, mostly, was cutting down trees for the Sun Dance lodge that stood in the middle of their camp. It had one sturdy cottonwood for a center pole with twelve slender pines for the palisade that surrounded it and boughs of cedar laid over it all for a roof. But there were no walls, leaving the lodge open to the summer air and the spectators who got as close outside the circle of teepees as they dared, considering the safety of their scalps.

It pleased him to write to Tom, like it pleased him to write to Mattie, taking his mind off his illness and thinking about something more interesting for as long as he had pen to paper. But other than that, his only escape from himself was the whiskey that started and ended his days.

There was no mistaking the beginning of the Sun Dance. It came with another night of Indian drums followed by a morning of the same, and ruining what was left of his already troubled sleep. After a bout of heavy coughing at bedtime, he'd been awakened twice before dawn with a sudden pain like a knife in his side, and now he was in a foul mood.

"It'll be like this for the better part of a week," Art Kendrick said apologetically, when he arrived with John Henry's morning whiskey and papers. "Once they start dancing, they don't hardly stop, except to sleep. They don't even take food or water, for the first two days straight. It's part of the sacrifice."

"At least they get a choice," John Henry said, taking the whiskey slowly, and hoping the pain in his side was the result of his intemperate drinking of the night before. There'd been a new saloon opened up and a big party to celebrate, and he'd spent longer there than he should have done. As for his own lack of eating, that came from being wary of food on account of nausea and indigestion. If the Indians chose to do without dinner for a few days for some religious ceremony, he couldn't feel too sorry for them.

"Don't know about they're having much choice in the matter," Art replied. "They don't exactly choose the Sun Dance. More like it chooses them. They come to it because they've had a dream or a vision, calling them. It's an honor to be called. It blesses the whole tribe."

"And how can starving bless anyone?"

"They say it brings them closer to God. Makes them appreciate how the Great Spirit gives them life."

"Or takes it away," John Henry muttered. "Is that all the whiskey you brought?"

"It's your usual, Sir," Art replied. "But I can get you more, if you need it."

"What I need is more sleep," he said irritably. "But that doesn't look likely, with all this damned drumming. Sounds like a giant heartbeat, echoing off the canyon walls." The pounding was relentless. The very air seemed to vibrate with it.

"That's just what it's supposed to be," Art said, "the heartbeat of the tribe. But you'll understand that if you go see the dancing. It's better at night, though, with the campfire light. I can call you a cab for later, if you're not feeling well enough to walk that far."

John Henry was about to make some smart reply and say that he didn't need a cab to get around a city as provincial as Glenwood Springs, that it was less than a mile from the hotel to the Indian camp and the weather was fine for walking. And when had he ever not walked to get himself from where he was to somewhere else? He'd walked all over Atlanta and Philadelphia and Dallas and Denver, and everywhere else in between. He'd even walked halfway from Tucson to Tombstone, before catching the Benson freight on a night that was better forgotten. And when he'd had too far to go on foot, he'd hire a horse and ride.

But Art was right about his current condition, though he hated having to admit it, even to himself. He was feeling more poorly than ever, and after a night of pain and nausea and a morning of pounding drums and headache, he could probably use a lift to the Indian camp, though in his healthier days he wouldn't have wasted the money.

"All right," he said, feeling something between anger and resignation, though it wasn't Art's fault that he was sick and getting sicker. The boy was only trying to do his job. He was, after all, the best bellboy in Glenwood Springs, and he knew how to earn his pay. Well then, let him earn it.

"Now go and get me another shot of whiskey," John Henry ordered. "This one's not makin' a damn dent."

He waited until Art had taken the serving tray and disappeared into the hallway, then he cursed and hurled the empty whiskey glass against the back of the closed door. But weak as he was, he didn't even get the satisfaction of seeing it break.

Even Buffalo Bill Cody's Indian and Wild West Show couldn't have hoped for a better audience, as the whole of Glenwood Springs turned out for the first night of the Ute Sun Dance. Outside the circle of teepees and the sacred ceremonial ground there was a standing-room only crowd with everyone straining to see over everyone else to catch a glimpse of the goings on.

The cab driver had somehow managed to find John Henry a place at the front of the crowd, though that still meant seeing the dance from something of a distance. For eager as they all were to watch, no one was foolish enough to trespass into the Indian camp when all the braves were in attendance. Sun Dancing or not, the Indians still had their knives and their pistols, and could have made a massacre if they'd been provoked. At least, that was the word that went through the crowd, only adding to the excitement of the evening.

But the Indians seemed mostly to be ignoring the spectators, intent as they were on their drumming and their chanting and their dancing—if you could call it that—stamping their bare feet on the dusty ground in time to the drums and moving toward the center pole of the lodge and back out, over and over again, and the whole time blowing on eagle bone whistles that hung from long leather cords around their necks.

It was the shrill whistling that impressed John Henry, who had a hard enough time just walking and getting his breath without trying to make music at the same time. But it wasn't really music they were making, according to a man standing next to him in the crowd. It was a kind of continual prayer.

"They whistle it instead of saying it, and the sound rises up to heaven," the man said. "Like the smoke that rises up from the campfire and blesses the whole camp."

"Sounds superstitious," John Henry commented.

"Perhaps. But isn't that what the Israelites believed, when they made their sacrificial fires in the days of Moses? As it reads in the King James: *"It is a continual burnt offering, ordained in mount Sinai for a sweet savour, a sacrifice made by fire unto the Lord."*

John Henry studied the barefoot Indian dancers in their long skirts and their bone breastplates, their brown skins glistening with sweat in the campfire light, and laughed.

"I don't see as how you can compare these savages to the Children of Israel. They're not even prayin' to the same God."

"Aren't they?" the man said. "They worship the God of Creation, as did the Israelites. Whether that's Sunawav, as they call him, or Jehovah, it's all the same, isn't it?"

"I know folks who would call that blasphemy."

The man laughed and paused to pull a flask from his pocket, and it shined a reflection of the Indian campfire. "I've been called worse than blasphemer, in my days. Care for a drink?"

John Henry replied by reaching into his coat pocket for his own flask, raising it for a toast, and for a congenial moment they both enjoyed their liquor. There was something friendly about sharing a drink in the dark like that, with only the glow of the campfire for light. Then the man said thoughtfully:

"And who's to say they aren't Israelites, or something even older?"

"What do you mean?"

"There's a legend they tell about how they first came to these mountains. It was in the beginning of time, when Sunawav held all the peoples of the earth together in a bag. He gave the bag to Coyote and told him to carry it over the far hills to the valleys beyond. But Coyote was curious about what was in the bag, so he opened it up and the people fell out, scattering to the four winds and taking their different languages with them."

John Henry considered the story, finding an odd familiarity to it.

"It sounds something like the Tower of Babel," he said, "when God scattered the people and gave them all different languages."

"I thought so too, when I first heard it," the man said. "According to the legend, that's how the Ute came to these mountains, and here they've been ever since, at least until the government moved them out. But they were the first people on this land even before the other Indians appeared. They're ancient, according to the legend."

"But you can't really believe these Indians are kin to people in the Bible. How is that possible?"

The man shrugged. "It's their legend, not mine. But I suppose with God all things are possible."

"That's mighty believin' for a blasphemer."

The man laughed again, an easy, generous laugh. "I've been accused of being a believer a time or two, as well!" And as he turned to smile at John Henry, the campfire light rested on something else—a white collar band tucked between the lapels of his black suit coat.

"You're a man of the cloth?" John Henry asked in surprise.

"I'm a man of God," he replied, "I just wear the cloth. I'm Ed Downey, priest of the Catholic parish here."

"Well, I reckon that explains the Bible stories."

"And you're Doc Holliday."

He was accustomed to being known in sporting circles and by a few too many reporters, as well, but having a Catholic priest know him by name was something new. The last time a Catholic priest had addressed him by name was in Atlanta, when he'd been with Mattie at Mass—an unexpected and bittersweet memory.

"And how do you know about me?" he asked warily.

"I have my sources," the priest said, casting his gaze heavenward. Then after a reverent moment he added with a smile, "And of course, Art tells me everything."

"Art Kendrick? My bellboy?"

"The best in Glenwood Springs, so he says. But he does seem to know everything that's going on."

"I thought priests were supposed to keep confession private!"

"Oh, Art's not Catholic. He just likes to talk. And I find it useful in my line of work to be a good listener."

Except for the clerical collar, Ed Downey might have been a friendly bartender, bantering with a customer. And by long habit, John Henry sized him up: average height and weight, a little soft from a life spent indoors, a hairline receding but not yet gray, an intelligent but harmless face. Like a sheep among wolves, and nothing to be wary of.

"So just what is it that Art's told you about me?" he said, thinking that he'd have to skip the boy's tip, next morning, for sharing confidences.

"Not much. Mostly about your being here for the vapor cure, like lots of others."

"And did he tell you it's not workin'?" It was the first time he'd said as much out loud, and hearing the words made them seem painfully real.

"I'm sorry to hear that," Ed Downey said, with something like real sympathy in his voice. Like a good bartender, or a good priest—and the sympathy encouraged John Henry to keep on talking.

"The doctor at Wagon Wheel Gap sent me here. He said it might be my miracle. But all I've got so far is bedsheets and steam baths and a turn in the porcelain tubs. I haven't seen any of this *Yampah* yet."

"To get Indian medicine," Ed Downey said, "you have to go to the Indian cave."

"I don't follow."

"You've been visiting the new caves, the ones the white men made. Maybe you need to try the old cave."

"But that's just a hole in the ground, according to Art."

"It is, but the Indians use it for a sweat lodge. They don't stay in the heat for a mere ten minutes at a time, like the white men do. They stay until the heat kills off the disease, assuming the patient can outlast it. It's a life or death treatment, but if it's Big Medicine you're looking for, that's where you'll find it."

"And do you believe in this Big Medicine?"

The priest answered thoughtfully. "I think there may be something to this place that we don't understand. It's sacred ground to the Ute, anyway, the reason they come back to these mountains year after year. But they're willing to take white man's money, if you want to try it. And it's only fair, I suppose."

"What's only fair?"

"For them to make what they can off the cave, before the Denver & Rio Grande comes through this fall. The railroad's grading a right of way through the canyon, and the only spot wide enough to hold the tracks is right over the Indian cave. So the D&RG is sealing up the cave and building on top of it."

"But how can they do that? You just said it was sacred ground to the Indians."

"Since when did sacred ground ever stop the railroads?" the priest replied.

John Henry had to concede the point. Georgia had been sacred ground too, before the white men and their railroads had come, before the Indians had been sent west on the Trail of Tears. And only their names remained.

In all his childhood imaginings of Indians, he had never imagined trusting his life to one, but after considering Father Downey's words he reckoned that he didn't have much to lose. The Palace in Hell hadn't done anything for him as of yet, and he was running out of time and treatments both. So while the rest of the town stayed close around the Ute encampment for the following days of the Sun Dance ceremony, John Henry arranged for a ride to where Cave Number One opened up in the side of the mountain—and that was where he finally came face to face with the Indians, though it was only one lone brave who was guarding the entrance, standing still as a totem pole. He had eagle feathers in his long plaited hair, buckskin leggings and a necklace of bone, and he made no comment as John Henry dropped a silver dollar into a basket at his moccasined feet. Then, wordlessly, the Indian stretched forth one arm and pulled aside the woven blanket that covered the entrance to the cave, and nodded.

There was no electricity to light Cave Number One, only the dim glow of a railroad lantern set on a small stool, and there were no modest bedsheets handed out by polite attendants to cover his nakedness. There was only the warm darkness of the cave, and the woven basket-like stretcher waiting on the stone floor near a ragged opening in the rock—the *Yampah,* John Henry reckoned, the hole in the ground where the Manitou lived, and he couldn't help the feeling of panic rising up inside of himself. Soon another Indian or two would appear, and he'd be strapped to that stretcher and lowered down into the earth, buried alive to sweat out his disease or die. Or, God be willing, to be resurrected healthy and whole at last. And as he considered saying a prayer to his own God or any other one that might be listening, he remembered one of the Bible verses he'd learned long ago at his mother's side:

"Naked came I out of my mother's womb," he said, reciting the words as he stripped off his clothes, *"and naked shall I return thither: the Lord gave, and the Lord hath taken away. Blessed be the name of the Lord . . ."*

When the Indians entered, they found him lying on the stretcher, eyes closed and hands folded over his heart like a dead man already.

He'd had to close his eyes, for fear of cowardice getting the better of him. He'd had to count his breaths to keep them coming evenly as the Indians slid the stretcher over the edge of the crevasse, as he felt himself hovering in midair for a long moment before swinging out and down toward the hard floor of the cave. How far he descended, he didn't know, and didn't want to know. And before he could let himself calculate the time and the distance, the heat overwhelmed him. The cave was a cauldron, boiling over, burning his skin and singeing his lungs. The cave was a furnace, burning him up like stubble, the way hell burned up the sin and the sinner both. *And there shall be wailing and gnashing of teeth*, he thought before he stopped thinking altogether.

He should have pulled on the ropes that guided the stretcher to signal he'd had enough, but the heat had sent him into a deep and dreamy sleep and a place where an ancient altar was attended by a holy man in eagle feathers readying a sacrifice. There was the altar, and there was the fire, but where was the sacrifice? And then he felt himself being lifted up and knew that he was the one being offered. Yet the hands that carried him were gentle, reverent even, honoring the life that was about to leave him. But instead of fire, he felt air and water, instead of burning he was cool as his life ebbed away and the gentle angels lifted him to heaven at last.

He woke in his own bed, wishing he were still dead. The angelic dreams were gone, replaced by a spasm of coughing and a mouthful of vomit as a reminder of his return to a painful mortality.

"Welcome back," a familiar voice said, and John Henry saw Father Ed Downey sitting in his shirt sleeves on a side chair, a newspaper laid open in his lap.

"What are you doin' here?" John Henry whispered hoarsely.

"You'd be better served by asking what *you* are doing here," the priest replied. "I walked over from my house when Art told me you were ailing. You were carried here by the Indians, after they rescued you from the cave."

"Rescued?"

"It seems you fell asleep in the sweat lodge, or went unconscious. They got nervous when you didn't ask to be brought up, so they went down to get you."

"The angel hands . . ." John Henry said, remembering his trip to heaven, his sins burned away like stubble and forgiven. All a dream? "I thought I had died," he said sadly.

"Not yet," the priest said. "But very nearly. The doctor at the hotel here says another ten minutes would have done you in for sure."

"Which would make you my murderer," John Henry observed, as he tried to sit up and found himself too weak to do it. "As I recall, it was your suggestion that I go to the Indian cave."

"As I recall, it was your doctor's suggestion. I just pointed out that you weren't at the right cave yet."

"So what are you doin' here?" John Henry asked irritably. "I'm not dead, and I'm not Catholic. Doesn't look like there's any prayin' for you to do."

"I suppose Art thought you might need someone to talk to, once you came around. Which it looks like you do. He thought by the address on the envelopes that you might be from a Catholic family."

"What address? On what envelopes?" But before the priest could answer, he remembered: Mattie's letters, written from Saint Vincent's Convent in Savannah and neatly stacked on his dressing table.

"So why does a man who wants to live so much that he is willing to try Indian Medicine suddenly wish he were dead, instead?" the priest asked curiously. "What happened down there in that cave?"

John Henry put a hand to his head, trying to remember. There were angels, that much he knew, there was a feeling of lightness as he was lifted up toward heaven.

"I thought I was forgiven," he said, looking up at the priest, "though I don't remember repentin'. All I remember was the hellfire, burnin' me up. But I reckon it was just the heat and the Indians."

"Hellfire is one way to be made clean," Father Downey said. "But there's more pleasant ways to go about it. When you're ready to try again, come talk to me."

"I told you I'm not Catholic. I don't need Confession."

"Everybody needs confession," the priest said with a smile, "even if you keep it between yourself and God. Though considering the fact that He already knows what you're confessing to, He's mostly just letting you get it off your chest."

"You don't sound like any priest I ever knew."

"Maybe it's been too long since you've known a priest," Ed Downey said. Then he folded the newspaper and picked up his coat, and nodded toward the dressing table with its stack of letters from the convent. "But I'm glad to see you have a worthy correspondent."

"My cousin," John Henry said. "She took her vows a few years back. But we were close before that."

"That's not what one would expect, considering the legend of Doc Holliday."

"I'm not the legend," John Henry replied, "and there's a lot about me you wouldn't expect."

Ed Downey smiled. "I look forward to hearing more about it. And for the record, if you were meant to die today, the Indian cave would have done it."

"Meanin' what?"

"Meaning, I suppose, that God has a reason to let you keep on living. Maybe I can help you find out what it is."

As it turned out, he had more to thank the Indians for than just pulling him out of the cave before it killed him. According to Art Kendrick, the Indians had tied his basket stretcher to one of their travois and dragged him behind a painted pony all the way back to town—then left him at the foot of the Grand River bridge, not knowing what else to do with him or even who he was. But some of the townsfolk recognized him, and when word got back to the Hotel Glenwood that Doc Holliday was stretched out drunk or unconscious alongside the river, the bellboy was sent to go collect his guest. There might have been an uprising against the Indians for the supposed torture of a white man, if the hotel doctor hadn't quickly confirmed that the only marks on the victim's body were those of disease—along with some old bullet wounds from his well-known and bloody past.

The other thing the doctor noted was that his consumption seemed to have taken a sudden turn for the worse in the weeks since his last house call. The patient's respirations were shallower and more frequent, his chest percussions revealed more scarring and less breathable lung tissue, the pain in his side signaled new pockets of infection as the disease spread toward his other organs. The only good news was that a doctor in Prussia had at last discovered the cause of the disease: a contagious tube-shaped organism he called *Mycobacterium tuberculosis*. But as for a cure, there was no hope on the horizon yet.

John Henry didn't need a doctor's diagnosis to tell him that the Indian cave had taken its toll. He'd gone in feeling poorly and come out feeling worse, in body and in spirit. For having passed through the veil toward that happier world once, as he remembered it, he didn't think it was fair to have to do it again—and maybe with unhappier consequences the next time. What if God weren't as forgiving as the Indian fires? What if he really did end up in hell?

He'd spent so much time trying to live that he hadn't given much thought to dying, but the thought began to haunt him now, waking him at night with ghostly memories of the too many men whose lives he'd taken: the faceless boy on the Withlacoochee River, the laughing Buffalo Soldier in Fort Griffin, the drunken and dangerous Mike Gordon in Las Vegas, the Mexican Federales in Guadalupe Canyon, the McLaury brothers and Billy Clanton at the OK Corral.

Those killings all troubled his conscience, though he could explain them away on account of being sick or drunk or defending himself or someone else. But there was one that troubled him more than the rest. The murder of Frank Stillwell in the train yard in Tucson was revenge, pure and simple, and vengeance, he knew, was the Lord's. True, Stillwell had been hunting them down, along with Ike Clanton, and had a loaded pistol on him when he died, but the only man he was aiming for at the time was Wyatt Earp, and Wyatt could have finished him off just fine all by himself. There'd been no need for John Henry to join in the affray, making target practice of Stillwell. But John Henry had chosen to stand by his friend, saving Wyatt and the rest of them from any personal responsibility for the killing—who could tell which of all those bullets had ended Frank's life? So all of them, if asked, could deny the deed—in a court of law, at least, and that was as far as John Henry's thinking had gone at the time. Now he was thinking about a bigger law and a Judgment Bar that likely didn't quibble over whose bullet had hit a man first if the final intent was murder. Now he was thinking of his own eternal life, and wondering where he'd spend the rest of it.

So although he wasn't a Catholic and didn't plan on becoming one anytime soon, he didn't think it would hurt to have a few more words with Ed Downey, hedging his bets. For sick as he was, he was still a sporting man at heart and he didn't like to lose a hand.

He didn't fight, this time, when Art Kendrick offered to call him a cab for the short ride to Saint Stephen's Catholic Church. He was having enough trouble trying not to cough his way through a conversation without adding any exercise, and there seemed little point, anymore, in pretending that he wasn't what he really was: an invalid. For he had pains everywhere now—throat, shoulders, lungs, stomach, hips, back. He had pains just sitting down on the leather seat of the cab, and worse when he stepped down to the street again. And without his daily dose of whiskey, morning and night and oftentimes in between, he'd have had to take the Laudanum the hotel doctor prescribed for him. But he wasn't ready just yet to give up fighting and he wanted his wits about him, at least.

So he took the cab to Saint Stephen's and arrived just as afternoon Mass was ending, and carefully settled himself on a hard wooden pew while he waited for Father Downey—who looked more like a priest now in his vestments and his rosaries, giving blessings to his sparse congregation. Saint Stephen's was small for a Catholic Church, a modest one-story frame building with two rooms and a wooden altar, and nothing like the splendid Church of the Immaculate Conception in Atlanta with its soaring stained-glass towers. There wasn't even a steeple on Saint Stephen's shingled roof or a bell to call the parishioners to prayer.

"Miners need their rest," the priest explained when John Henry pointed out the missing bell tower. "I won't have a lot of clanging ruining their sleep. They'll come to services when they're ready, and I'll be here for them as often as I can be."

"And where else would you be? Do you have another occupation?"

"No, but I have another congregation. Three of them, actually: Aspen, Rifle, and Red Cliff. I make a monthly circuit of the churches, saying Mass wherever I happen to be. But we're growing in these mountains. There'll be a full-time priest here soon. But I don't suppose you came here to talk about Parish business."

John Henry took his time replying, and Father Downey waited on him patiently, taking a seat in the pew just ahead of him. Then in the quiet of the empty sanctuary, John Henry began, his voice a painful, ragged whisper:

"I was raised on fire and brimstone; my mother trained it into me." He paused, taking a shallow breath. "She was born a Baptist before she married my father and joined up with the Presbyterians and the Methodists. She wasn't always pleased with their teachings but she made sure I knew the Good Book. I haven't always lived by it, but I'm truly afraid of dyin' by it."

"It's good to fear God," Father Downey said, "if the fear turns you toward Him."

"So what am I supposed to do?"

"Well, if you were Catholic, I'd hear your confession and offer you penance. And then it would be up to the saints and the angels to do their best for you. Short of that, I can listen to what you want to say, and offer my best advice."

"You know I've killed some men in my time."

"I've heard tell of it."

"Not as many as people say, but more than I wished I had. One man in particular. He haunts me. Not like a ghost exactly, more like a regret. And I'm afraid I'll get fire and brimstone for it."

The priest was quiet, considering. Then he turned toward the altar with its candles and its crucifix. "I can't tell you that you won't suffer for what you've done. Even our Lord suffered, and he was innocent. And I can't tell you it doesn't matter anymore, as long as you regret it. A life is a sacred thing, no matter whose. We don't have the right to take it away, and we don't have the power to give it back again, once it's gone."

"So there's no hope for me?"

"There's hope. But there'll be a sacrifice required."

"An eye for an eye," John Henry said, "a life for a life?" *The sacrifice was me*, he thought, remembering his dream in the Indian cave. "Am I supposed to kill myself, to make amends? Or let the law do it for me?"

"I think what you need to do is save a life," the priest said, "in exchange for having taken one."

"And how am I supposed to do that? I can hardly walk anymore. It's not likely I'll be ridin' out with a posse ever again."

"I don't know how you're going to do it. That'll be between you and God. But I think it's your best bet for salvation, in the parlance of the sporting world."

"You're not like any priest I've ever known," he said for the second time.

"And you're not like any outlaw I've ever known."

John Henry sighed heavily. "I'd like to be done with that life, once and for all."

Father Downey's gaze turned back to the altar, then up toward the raftered ceiling with its electrified brass chandelier. "Do you know who this Church is named for? Saint Stephen the Martyr who was killed for his testimony of Christ. And do you know who killed him?"

John Henry wasn't practiced on saints, not being raised a Catholic, and he shook his head and said, "I don't recall just now."

"He was killed by a mob, while a man named Saul stood by and held his robe, watching the martyrdom. Saul killed the saints, before God called him to repentance on the road to Damascus. Before he became Saint Paul."

"Meanin' what?"

"Meaning everyone can change, even Saul. And even you."

Summer ended early in those mountains and September came with cold mornings and a frightening new sign of his disease, as the pain in his side finally came up through the skin, opening into an ugly, pus-filled ulcer that reached from his waist to his ribs. And it was that, even more than the weakness and the wheezing, that confined him to his hotel room, as the ulcer oozed through three changes of cotton bandages a day and ruined whatever clothing he put over it.

It was a tubercular lesion, the doctor said, like the ones that had been destroying his lungs for years, and there would likely be more of them as the tuberculosis spread—though the name consumption still seemed more fitting. The disease was eating him alive from the inside out, consuming him like Job's worms. But he couldn't find it in himself to have the patience of Job in his afflictions. He was miserable, short-tempered, demanding, even though Art Kendrick was quick to answer his every request. But what he really wanted, he couldn't have: his health, his life.

So he slept most of September away, sleep and whiskey being his only escape from the inescapable truth that he was dying. Dying slowly, painfully, his body wasting away while his mind stayed too aware. And though he still wrote letters to Mattie and to Tom, sometimes Art had to do the writing for him while he dictated his thoughts, his hands too weak to hold pen to paper. And sometimes, Art had to read him their replies, as well, when the light pained him too much to see.

And while he was suffering, the world kept going on around him. There were stage coaches pulling to a stop in front of the hotel and parties in the public rooms down below. There were hotel guests chattering as they passed by his door, and gunshots in the distance from the saloons that stayed open all night. There was life outside his room, and in his dreams he imagined himself still there among the living.

On the fifth of October the railroad finally came to town, and Glenwood Springs celebrated with the biggest party the mountains had ever seen. It had taken two years for the Denver & Rio Grande to grade and lay track all the way from Aspen to the valley of the Grande River, so it was fitting that the celebration went on for two whole days, in honor of it.

If John Henry had been healthier, he might have attended the banquet that was held in the main dining room of the Hotel Glenwood, attended by local business leaders and railroad dignitaries, and he would have enjoyed the fireworks display set off down by the river. But sick as he was, all he got to see was the parade that wound its noisy way past the hotel, when Art pushed him in a wheeled chair out onto the balcony of his room. If anyone in the cheering crowd recognized the bent-shouldered figure blanketed against the autumn chill as the infamous Doc Holliday, they didn't care enough to point him out.

It was a week later that the D&RG brought him a visitor, come all the way from Denver via the new Aspen to Glenwood Springs rail line—though the visitor had to wait awhile longer still to see him, while Art got him washed and shaved and changed into a fresh nightshirt. There was no thought of putting him in his street clothes and making him too worn out for company. Even lifting him from the bed to the chair beside it had left him panting and dizzy. Truth was, he probably wouldn't be in a suit again until he was laid out in his coffin. Which got him to thinking about something he'd meant to do.

"Art," he whispered hoarsely, "when I'm gone, I want you to have my things sent back to Georgia. You can use that address on the envelopes there."

"To the convent, Sir?"

He nodded, out of breath already.

"What'll a nun do with your belongings?"

"She'll know," was all he could manage to say. Maybe she'd give his clothes to charity. Maybe she'd send his diamond stickpin to Uncle John, who'd given it to him in the first place. But the letters he hoped she'd keep and put together with the ones he had written to her, and let them be a combined witness to the love that had been between them—a love that was mostly words and nothing much more, yet had always been so very much more.

"So who is this Colonel DeWeese, that's come all the way up here from Denver to see you?" Art asked.

"My lawyer. I sent him a wire," he paused, catching his breath—never enough—"awhile back, telling him he ought to settle up my affairs." And DeWeese, being a smart attorney, had come as soon as the rail line was open. "Easier to do business with a livin' client, than a dead one," John Henry whispered.

But Art didn't seem to catch the humor. "Yes, Sir. Shall I bring him up now?"

There was no disguising the shock on Colonel DeWeese's face when he was ushered into the room and found what was left of John Henry Holliday huddled in a chair and looking up at him with sunken blue eyes.

"Nice to see you, too," John Henry whispered in response to DeWeese's stunned silence.

"I'm sorry," DeWeese said, finding his voice again, "I had hoped the mountain air would have done you some good . . ."

"That was the plan."

"Well," DeWeese said, pausing as if considering his next comment. Then he put on a more professional air and went on. "I've brought some papers for you to sign: Power of Attorney and such, the usual trust documents. But I suppose I could have mailed them . . ."

"I don't mind a visit," John Henry said, and he meant the words. Confined to his room as he was, his usual company was Art Kendrick or one of the other bellboys, along with the hotel doctor and the trained nurse—not the kind of cheery society he'd been accustomed to in his sporting life.

Not that Colonel DeWeese was particularly jolly company. He'd been appropriately somber in all their previous meetings, and sometimes disapproving, as well, when his client had insisted on squandering his inheritance on a lonely orphan boy. Even now he was businesslike, glancing at Art Kendrick and saying pointedly: "Would you excuse us?"

Art nodded and quickly left the room, while DeWeese took an appraising look around the place, his glance lingering on the stack of Mattie's letters that covered the top of the dressing table. Times past, John Henry would have kept them hidden away, savoring their privacy. Now he let Art leave them out in plain sight, a comforting presence. As long as Mattie's words were there, he never felt completely alone.

"You have a correspondent," DeWeese observed.

"I do," John Henry replied. "My cousin's a nun. She's been instructin' me about the journey ahead."

"Journey? Are you going somewhere?"

John Henry smiled weakly at DeWeese's lack of imagination. "I'm gonna die," he reminded the Colonel. "She's been offerin' her advice on how to do it well."

"I see," DeWeese said, before an awkward pause, then he cleared his throat and went on. "As I said, I could have mailed the papers, but that wouldn't have served my business. I came here myself because I've brought someone to meet you. Someone you've been trying to find."

It took a moment for DeWeese's words to register, and even then John Henry wasn't sure he'd heard him properly.

"My—son?" he said unsteadily. Was he dreaming again, or too full of whiskey? But DeWeese seemed real enough, his suit rumpled from the long ride and smelling of stale tobacco. Surely, he wouldn't dream such details.

"So it appears," DeWeese answered. "We found someone who knew of the parlor house first, where the girl worked, and through that the name of the family that had put her out, and through that the name of a sister who lives in Chicago, who had some old letters telling of a child . . ."

"My son?" John Henry said again, still disbelieving.

"Yes, though the family knew the father as Tom McKey. But the evidence is probably strong enough to make a case in probate court."

And then John Henry realized what else DeWeese had said. "You brought him—here?"

"I realize now it may have been a rash thing to do, considering your health. But I thought you ought to meet your heir, as there is still some substance left of your inheritance, and this boy will be next in line to receive it. That is, if you choose to make a will naming him as your offspring. Another matter that needs to be settled before . . ."

"Does he know? Did you tell him—that I am—that I'm his father?"

"No. I thought you should meet him first, decide if you want to reveal the relationship. If not, no one else need know. I have kept my own files private on this matter, in deference to the families involved. And there is no law requiring the passage of property to an illegitimate child . . ."

John Henry's heart was racing, his head spinning. "Open the window!" he said hoarsely, "I need some air . . ." Though he knew that opening the window wouldn't help. He needed to breathe and couldn't. He needed time to prepare himself, but there was too little time left.

"Would you like me to bring him back later?" DeWeese asked. We're here for a day or two . . ."

"No!" John Henry said. If he did have a son, even a stranger whom he'd never seen before, he needed to know. The only son of the only son of the oldest son, the child would be; the primary heir of the Holliday name. But would he even look like a Holliday? And wishing things had turned out differently, he thought of Tom, who had looked so much like him. Tom, whom he'd loved like a son even if there'd been no relationship at all between them. And suddenly, a wave of sadness washed over him, and he was crying.

"We'll come back later," DeWeese said uncomfortably, "when you're feeling better."

"I'll never be feelin' better!" John Henry said, too sick to be ashamed of the tears. "I could die this very night and never know . . ."

DeWeese pulled a handkerchief from his coat pocket and gave it to John Henry. "All right then," he said, and went to the door. "He'll see you now," he announced to someone in the hallway, then he stood aside as a small figure entered the room. "Dr. Holliday, I'd like you to meet Tom McKey."

And there stood his boy.

He was ten years old now, taller than John Henry had remembered, and sturdier as well. But he still had the same fair hair, the same sandy lashes and china blue eyes, the same high cheekbones that bespoke his heritage. He was a Holliday, all right, though he wore the McKey name now—and was pleased to have it at last.

"This man, Colonel DeWeese, he came to visit and told Mama what my real name was. He said my father was named Tom McKey, too, like me."

"And what do you think of your new name?" John Henry asked.

"It's all right, I guess. It's nice to know who I am." Then he shrugged his narrow shoulders. "Wish I knew more about my father than just his name, though."

Colonel DeWeese, who'd stayed standing at the door, cleared his throat again. "I believe I'll excuse myself for a few minutes. There's some business I need to attend to . . ." and he stepped out of the room, leaving John Henry alone with his son.

"I knew your father," John Henry said. "I knew your mother, too, a long time ago."

"You never told me that!"

"I—wasn't sure. I had Colonel DeWeese do some searchin' for me. But I don't reckon our meetin' there at Union Station was just a coincidence. I think maybe it was Providence."

"What's Providence?" Tom asked, and John Henry was reminded of how much learning the boy had missed in his lean childhood, how much he still had to experience. But at least he'd had the promised adventure of a train ride, though not in the way John Henry had hoped it would be . . .

But there wasn't time for melancholy, not when he finally had his boy beside him. "Providence is somethin' like a plan," he said, "like somethin' that's meant to be. That's the way my mother explained it to me, anyhow."

"What was my mother like?" Tom asked. "My real mother, I mean."

John Henry closed his eyes, trying to remember. It was so long ago, in a time he'd tried to forget. "She was young," he said, "and very pretty. I met her on the day of the Centennial Parade, when all of Denver was celebratin' the statehood. She'd twisted her ankle, as I recall . . ."

There were other things he recalled, as well: how he'd seen her home after her small accident, how he was surprised to find where she lived and what she did for a living, how he'd spent the most comfortable hours of his fugitive life in her company . . .

"She was a very sweet lady," he said, summing her up in too few words. "I think you have that from her. You have her good heart." And what more could he say about her, anyhow? He'd never even known her real name.

"And what about my father?" Tom asked, as John Henry knew that he would. "Was he really a bad man, like they say? Was he really a no-account?"

There was worry in Tom's blue eyes, a fear that he might be no-account too. And he was indeed the son of a no-account, at least at the time of his conception, with a father who'd been running from the law and had more running still to do, a father who hadn't looked back long enough to even learn that he'd had a son. But things were different now.

"Tom, there's—somethin' I need to tell you . . ."

But his words ran out with his breath. What was he going to say, anyhow? If it were a burden being the son of a wastrel, was it any better being the son of a legend? For half of his own life he'd been a legend's son, Henry Holliday's boy, with a world of expectations because of it. What would it be like to be Doc Holliday's son? What would the world expect of his child?

And at that moment, he knew what he had to do. *Make a sacrifice,* Father Downey had said, *save a life in exchange for taking a life.* And he knew whose life he had to save.

He took a ragged breath, praying for the right words to say.

"I knew your father, Tom. I knew him his whole life, from Georgia to Denver and everywhere else in between."

He paused, took another breath, then spoke in shorter, easier sentences.

"And this much I can tell you: he was worth more than he knew himself. We all are. Every life is precious. And every breath is worth takin'. And whatever he may have done wrong in his life, he made up for in you. You're the best part of him. You're worth everything to him."

"How do you know that?" the boy asked.

"Because he loves you, Tom. With all his heart."

And before the boy could think too much about the words and realize John Henry had spoken them from his own heart, he put DeWeese's handkerchief to his mouth and pretended to cover a cough. But it was tears he was hiding, for joy and for sorrow both.

Tom watched him sadly and said: "Will I ever see you again, Mr. Holliday?"

"Not in this life, Tom. I've used up my ticket here. But if there's a God in heaven, I will see you again there!"

And without being asked, Tom knelt down beside him and laid his head on John Henry's knee.

"I don't care about my father!" the boy said. "You're my hero, Mr. Holliday!"

"There's no such thing as a hero, Tom. Just a man who's tryin' to do the right thing."

My son, John Henry said to himself, savoring the words as he ran his fingers through Tom's sandy hair. *My son!*

He didn't make a will, but signed the rest of his inheritance over to DeWeese to administer until Tom's coming of age, with regular draws for his maintenance until then. With careful management, there would be enough money to send the boy to college one day and help get him started in the world. He was a gentleman's son, after all, and could have a fine professional career ahead of him—though Tom was more inclined to be a rancher than a doctor or a lawyer. The reason he'd lived in the stables in Denver, he said, was because he loved being with the horses. But that, too, was something in his blood.

Colonel DeWeese took Tom away two days later, going back to Denver but carrying a few reminders of his visit to Glenwood Springs with him: a small portrait of John Henry done by a local photographer soon after his arrival in town; a folded Confederate flag that had laid at the bottom of his traveling trunk for nearly fifteen years; the walnut-handled Colt's Navy revolver that he'd received on his twenty-first birthday. Being young, Tom didn't inquire about the history of the souvenirs and John Henry didn't tell him. Maybe one day, he'd find out for himself.

And then he was gone, and winter settled in.

John Henry was never out of bed after that, and never had the strength to write another letter himself, and even dictating one took him days. His breathing was so labored that he couldn't talk for more than moments at a time, the lack of air leaving him dizzy, his pains so severe that any movement caused him agonies. But soon he'd be done with his sufferings, Father Downey promised when he made his daily visits, and death would free him of his mortal temple. And it was a blessing when he went to sleep one afternoon and didn't wake up again, dreaming endlessly.

It was amazing how real the dreams were, filled with people he'd known and places he'd been. It was amazing how easy it was to talk to them when he wasn't having to catch his breath and wait for the words to come. And most amazing of all, he spent whole days visiting with Mattie, riding out together over the green rolling hills of Georgia. They were children together again, and happy, with all the world ahead of them still—a world that hardly seemed to matter anymore.

He woke from his unconsciousness with a mouth as dry as a western desert.

"I need . . . a drink," he whispered against cracked lips.

Someone raised a cup to his lips—whiskey, to wet his mouth and wash away the pain. But though the liquor burned its way down with familiar warmth, it didn't chase away the chill that was stealing over him.

Then he heard the voice, calling to him.

"John Henry!"

It was musical, like the strains of a song long forgotten. He lifted his heavy eyes to follow the sound, and saw someone standing at the foot of his bed—a woman, seeming to glow in the pale November light.

"John Henry!" Alice Jane McKey Holliday said with a smile.

"Well, I'll be damned . . ."

He hadn't recognized her at first, it had been so long since he'd last seen her, since she'd died when he was still a boy. But it was indeed his own dear mother, real as the room in which she stood, wearing a gown of brilliant white in place of the black mourning costume that had been her attire for most of the years he'd spent with her. Years that seemed ages ago and present all at once.

"It's time for you to come home now," she said gently. "I've come to fetch you."

An angel, he thought. *My mother is an angel now, though I've been a devil most of my life.*

His whispered voice came even softer now, "This is funny . . ."

"Come along, dear," she said, and reached a hand to him.

It seemed to take all the strength he had, bringing his own hand up to meet hers, but once their fingers touched the strength came back to him again, like warmth and light filling his soul. Then, like the well-mannered son she had always taught him to be, he rose from his sickbed and followed her.

The time was just past ten o'clock on a snowy mountain morning, and the day was going to be glorious.

435

Chapter Twenty-One

In March the first Southern blizzard in history swept through Georgia. It began in the evening as a persistent cold rain and by dawn the colder winds came, turning the rain to snow and dusting the dirt streets and winter-brown fields. The snow kept coming, piling around doors and window sills, sheeting onto frozen panes of glass. It kept coming, blown by the wind into drifts that covered yards and walks and porches, weighing down the limbs of the shaggy pines. It kept coming, a roaring mass of white filled with lightning that flashed like artillery fire and thunder that rolled like cannonade, laying siege to the city and all the countryside around and leaving a changed landscape behind: no lane or road to be seen, only fields of snow and frosted houses huddling against the cold.

After the storm, the stillness lay heavy as the snow. And gazing out into that strange and silent world, Mattie thought of John Henry in the colder mountains of Colorado, and it chilled her more than ice and snow. It had been too long since she'd last heard from him, since before her move from Savannah to the convent of the Sisters of Our Lady of Mercy in Atlanta, and though she'd waited for weeks and months, through Advent and Christmas, through the Feast of the Circumcision and Epiphany, through the Feast of Saint Joseph, there was still no word. Had he never received her letter at all? Was he too ill to reply, or worse?

The Sisters of Mercy were not cloistered nuns, hiding from the world. They ran schools, founded hospitals, spent their days serving the needy women and children of their communities. It was their service that had attracted her to the order, once she had decided to devote her life to God after giving up the only other love she had ever known. For unhallowed or not, her heart had always been with John Henry, from the time they had both been old enough to feel the bond between them. Her heart had been with him even when she had sent him away, knowing they could not be together as they longed to be. Her heart had been with him wherever else he had gone, their correspondence keeping them close through the years. But now, with no letters to speak for him, there was only a silence as strange and unnatural as the snow.

She had not hid herself from the world by taking orders and making teaching her vocation, nor had she hid herself from John Henry's troubled life. She knew of his illness, his weakness for gambling, his pride and his recklessness. She knew he'd been hunted by the authorities for a shooting in Texas and a street fight in Tombstone, and she knew that if he'd confessed those things to her, there were doubtless other sins he needed to confess, as well. She even knew that he'd spent some time living with a woman named Kate Elder—a relationship revealed in one of the newspaper clippings collected by an old family friend and brought home to Atlanta. The friend, a businessman named Lee Smith, had made a trip to the West and visited with John Henry there, then shared his experiences with the family and a reporter from the *Atlanta Constitution*. No, there was no hiding from John Henry's misadventures, not even behind convent walls. Yet although she knew, perhaps, too much about his troubled life, her love for him never wavered. He was still, as he would always be, her own dear cousin. So she sent prayers to heaven on his behalf for a miracle and a remission of his disease, said the rosary for him, lit vigil candles in the chapel of the Church of the Immaculate Conception.

But now her prayers were for herself, as well, that she might somehow know what had become of him. With no word in all those months, she feared that it was too late for her petitions, that he had died in those mountains without the sacraments. She knew that baptism by authority was essential for salvation, and she couldn't bear the thought that he might never be saved, never go to Paradise, never be where she might someday see him again. And so she added a novena to her vigil candles and rosaries, offering nine days of prayer for the souls in Purgatory, and begging the Holy Mother that there might be some condescension made so that John Henry could yet be saved, even after his death. For in the silence of the snow, in the strange stillness that made her think of the colder stillness of Colorado, she knew somehow that he was gone.

As the world warmed and the snow melted, spring seemed to come on all at once, bursting into bloom with white-blossomed pears, winding purple wisteria, yellow tulips on the shady hillsides. In the convent garden, the vegetable patch shared space with a showy pink azalea, the practical and the ornamental growing side-by-side beneath a flowering Dogwood tree, the way saints and sinners both lived beneath the watchful eye of God. There was a legend about the Dogwood that the Sisters liked to share with their students, telling how the wood was used to make Christ's cross, and how the creamy flowers still made the sign of the cross and the crown of thorns. The Dogwood and the other Eastertime blossoms seemed a beautiful reminder of resurrection, of life renewed after a long dark sleep, of hope that love could also be renewed and live again. And without hope, how could there be faith?

She was there in the garden, spending an hour in prayer and contemplation between classes at the convent day school, when the delivery dray arrived on its usual stop. There would be cloth for sewing or sheeting for beds, bags of flour for breadmaking and slabs of meat for meals, and mail for the sisters if the driver happened to stop by the post office along his way. But on this day, there was something more than mail and supplies, as the driver unloaded all the usual goods, then asked if there might be a Sister Holliday at that place, as he had a trunk that belonged to her.

"To me?" she asked, looking up in surprise. "I have no trunk, only the few things I've brought to Atlanta from Savannah. We sisters live simply."

"Ah well, it's you then," he said with a shrug. "Got sent to Savannah first, then on to here from there. Likely left awhile in a train station somewhere, I reckon, with the wrong address and all, not to mention the weather. Did you ever see such weather as we've had this year? Snow's unusual enough, but a blizzard? The world's turning topsy turvy. Where would you like me to put your trunk, then? Been around some, by the look of it. Worn out, nearly. Label here says it came from Colorado. That's a long ways."

She stared at the driver, then at the wagon where there was, indeed, a traveling trunk, and for a moment hope and faith rose together inside of her. Could it be John Henry's traveling trunk? But why would it come here, to her?

"That'll be fine, Sir," she said with a calm she did not feel. "Please bring it along to the front door, and we'll see that it's attended to."

And what would she do with it then? Nuns had few personal belongings, their needs supplied by the shared resources of the convent. She'd had to pay a dowry to enter the novitiate, pledging her worldly riches and taking vows of poverty along with chastity, obedience, and service. But as she gathered her flowing black habit about her and hurried back inside the stately building that served as both school and housing for the Sisters, she wasn't thinking like a nun any longer; she was thinking like the girl she'd been so long ago, when she'd stood in the stained glass light of the Church of the Immaculate Conception and let her sweetheart go. And now here he was again.

Mother Superior was surprised to have a trunk delivered to her office, but allowed it to be taken to the Sister's room for a private opening. She understood that it had belonged to a dear family member who had recently passed on, and that it likely contained items of a personal nature. But the trunk could not be kept there permanently, of course, as the convent was not a storage facility and the Sisters were not guardians of material belongings. After its contents had been examined, it would have to be sent elsewhere. But for the night, at least, it could remain.

Mattie bowed her head obediently and thanked Sister Ignatius for her kindness, then went back to her teaching duties. The trunk, with whatever mysteries it held, would have to wait until school was over for the day and the other obligations of convent life were fulfilled. So it was not until vespers and supper and compline were done and she had retired to her room for the evening that she could finally be alone with John Henry's things. And even then, she hesitated. Unopened, his traveling trunk held all sorts of promise and possibilities, like a gift waiting to be unwrapped. Once the buckles had been unfastened and the lid raised, there would be no possibilities left.

She knelt to offer a prayer, then crossed herself and unhooked the beaded rosary from her waist, kissing it reverently before laying it on her dressing table. Next, she unpinned the black veil and unfastened the white coif and wimple, laying them beside the rosary and leaving her head and face uncovered, her neck and shoulders bare. Last came the modest habit of heavy black serge, its tunic and double sleeves and its two underskirts unbuttoned and laid beside the veil and the coif, and she was just herself at last. And standing there in her simple white shift, with her auburn hair cropped short and her feet bare on the hardwood floor, she felt suddenly young again, like the girl she'd been when John Henry had gone west, as she touched the smooth-worn leather of his traveling trunk, her fingers tracing the gold-embossed initials *JHH*.

The trunk opened with a smell of whiskey and stale tobacco, of damp wool and dirty linen—a smell so surprisingly human that it seemed John Henry had come into the room as well. She closed her eyes and breathed in the scent of him, almost expecting to see him standing there when she opened her eyes again. But what she saw instead was an envelope, addressed in an unknown hand and laid in the trunk atop a pile of folded cloth. Inside the envelope was a letter with the heading Saint Stephens Catholic Church, Glenwood Springs, Colorado:

Dear Sister Holliday,

I have the sad duty of sending news of the passing of your cousin, Dr. John Henry Holliday, who died at this city on the 8th of November, 1887. As you were his regular correspondent, he asked me to write to you when he passed—an event that he anticipated for all of his time here and for which he tried to prepare himself, both materially and spiritually. While he was not raised as a Catholic, he felt to seek my counsel in his preparations, and I was honored to be able to advise him. In our conversations, he expressed to me his gratitude for the preparation which you offered him, as well, saying that your letters had long been a comfort and blessing to him. I believe that he took your admonitions to heart, as he pondered on the state of his soul in the world to come and tried to find forgiveness for his earthly failings before leaving this life. In the end, he seemed to have made some peace with God, and had he lived longer, I think he might have sought the blessings of holy Church.

The contents of this trunk are your cousin's last possessions, and he asked for them to be sent on to you there in Savannah. I hope that you will find some good use for the clothes and other things, perhaps donating them to the poor served by your convent. There is not much left that is of great value. Whatever other belongings he had were already given away before his death.

As for his last days, he spent much of the time sleeping or in a state of delirium in which he seemed to be senseless of pain or discomfort, a tender mercy. I hope you may be comforted in your own time of grief to know that he was well cared for during his stay here, that he was warmly thought of by all who knew him, and that his life will be remembered well. Please accept my own condolences on your loss.

Yours sincerely,
Reverend Edward M. Downey, Parish of St. Stephens

She held the letter with trembling hands, her tears falling and smearing the ink. She'd known he was gone before his trunk had arrived, but seeing it written was somehow worse, somehow more final. But she wasn't ready yet to let him go, so she put the letter aside and began to unfold his things from the trunk: shirts of white linen and pale pastel, vests of gray brocade and brown wool, sets of linsey stockings and a pair of soft leather boots, trousers and suspenders, lawn handkerchiefs bearing his monogram and marked with rusty red stains, a suitcoat, a stickpin without a stone. She pulled the coat from the trunk and shook it out, then threw it around herself and slipped her arms inside. She'd never worn a man's coat before; never wanted to wear one, but she suddenly wanted very much to wear his, to feel him wrapped around her. Fifteen years, it had been, since she'd been this close to him.

Beneath the clothes there were other less personal items: a leather case holding a Sheffield razor, a small pocket knife, a pack of playing cards. But there was nothing that she could keep for herself, and she had to wonder why he had wanted the trunk to be sent to her at all, why he hadn't just asked the priest to dispose of his last belongings.

And then she found the letters, piles of them tied together with leather cords a dozen at a time, hundreds of letters altogether, envelopes yellowed and worn from years of handling, stained from years of traveling—her letters that she had written to John Henry through the years. He'd kept them all, cherished them all, and sent them back home at last in his stead. This was what he had wanted her to have: her words that he had loved as she had loved his. This was their life together, their only legacy. And spreading the letters out on the floor around her, she wept again.

But there was one letter left apart from the rest, alone at the bottom of the trunk, and as she pulled it toward the light she recognized with surprise the handwriting on it and her own name on the envelope, penned in John Henry's familiar script. He hadn't written in his own hand since early in the fall, since he'd begun dictating his letters to a bellboy at the hotel where he was staying. But his hand had surely touched this, his breath had breathed on these words—and with sudden emotion she held the letter against her cheek, as though she could somehow feel him there. Why had this letter been saved for last, after he'd sent all the others? Then she slid her finger under the seal and felt something tumble out of the envelope and onto her lap, something small that caught the light and gleamed like gold.

It was her little Claddagh ring, the one her Grandmother Fitzgerald had brought over the ocean from Ireland, the one her mother had given to her as a family keepsake, the one she had given to John Henry the day he had left . . .

She held it up to the light, noting how it had gained some scratches since she'd last seen it, how it needed cleaning to be beautiful again. Like John Henry, she thought: world worn, yet still precious. Then she slipped it onto the ring finger of her right hand, her left hand already wearing the plain band that was symbolic of her marriage to Christ and the Church.

When at last she unfolded the letter and began to read, she saw sentences slanted awkwardly across the pages, words unsteady as if his hand had trembled over them:

My dearest Cousin Mattie,

This will, perhaps, be the last thing I ever write to you myself, as this awful illness does its work on me. My body aches, my hands shake, my eyesight that has always been keen is turning dim. I have trouble even reading these words as I write them. I am bent like an old man, I am coming to pieces. You'd hardly recognize me anymore. Yet you will recognize this about me: my heart is still, as it has always been, as it will always be, yours. And so I return to you now the ring that you once gave to me, that I have worn these many years as a token of the bond that was between us: two hands for friendship, a crown for loyalty, a heart for love. It has been like a wedding ring to me, and I have, in my heart, been true to it and you, and I cannot bear to leave it for someone to steal when I am gone. If only I could, like this ring, come home to you now—

My friend Morgan Earp who was murdered in Tombstone during those dark days after the street fight never got to go home. His brother Wyatt sent his body to California where the family had taken up residence and had him buried there. He should have been sent to Iowa instead where he had grown up, to be buried in home ground, in his "Tara" as your cousin Sarah would have called it. I thought her talk of Irish legends and the burial place of kings sentimental nonsense once, but I find I have grown more sentimental myself through the years. I should like to have been buried in Tara too, in my own home ground, instead of in this far and frozen place. They have to break through the ice to do their burying here in the wintertime. I don't like the thought of it.

My thoughts are turning morbid, when I only meant to tell you how much I wish I could come home to you at last. I never meant to stay away forever. I never should have gone away at all—

And yet, had I stayed, what would have changed between us? Would you have left your faith to marry me? Would I have been able to see you married to someone else, and not have gone mad? How different might our lives have been, if I had been able to stay? There was no answer to it then; there is no answer still. But perhaps, in some eternal world, there will be answers we have yet to find. Dear Mattie, will you look for me there?

I love you. I always have. I always will.

John Henry Holliday

When the night bell rang for last lights she was still kneeling on the floor holding the letter, having read it over and over again until she'd committed every word to memory: *dearest Mattie, my heart is yours, I never meant to stay away.* With careful hands she folded the precious pages back into the envelope and slid it down into the pocket of John Henry's coat. Then, putting out the lamp, she slipped into bed wearing his coat for a blanket, wearing the ring that was the only worldly belonging they had ever shared.

Tomorrow she would pack his clothes and things back into the trunk and decide where to send them. Tomorrow she would put her letters together with the ones he'd written to her over the years, order them by date and place, and pack them away, as well. Tomorrow she would put on the habit and the veil and become a nun again, vowed to chastity and poverty, to obedience and service. But for this night, for this one night at least, she would dream of being with John Henry again, and always.

As eternity had no end, as God was love and lived forever, then surely love would live forever, too.

Postscript

PEGGY MITCHELL MARSH WAS AT A LOSS FOR WORDS, AND IT COULD not have come at a worse time. Gerald was dead, killed by a fall from his horse, and there needed to be a proper eulogy spoken, but Peggy couldn't think of anything to say. The mourners were gathered around the grave, their faces strained with emotion and flushed with the heat of the June sun, waiting for the words of comfort that only she could give. No one knew Gerald better than Peggy or understood what his loss would mean to them all—more than the death of a man; the end of an era, as well.

Suellen and Careen, Gerald's two younger daughters, stood sobbing quietly, leaning on Melanie's fragile shoulder, and Melanie was crying too. She had loved Gerald like a father though she was no real relation to him. Only Scarlett stood dry-eyed, alone and apart. She was Gerald's eldest, the most like him, and the one most shattered by his death. But she had cried herself out last night and couldn't cry anymore.

Beside the grave, Ashley Wilkes stood with the Book of Prayer laid open in his hands. Scarlett watched him out of cat-green eyes and was glad that it was Ashley who would speak the service. His melodious drawl would be a comfort to her on this most awful of all days. Ashley raised his eyes and for a moment Scarlett thought he might look her way, but he gazed past her and nodded to Will, the new foreman who had taken over at Fontenoy Hall when the Yankee Wilkerson had been fired. Will nodded back to him, and Ashley cleared his throat and looked up at the waiting crowd . . .

Peggy tapped her foot in anticipation, eager for Ashley to say something, anything. Surely, with all that poetry and philosophy of his Ashley would know what to say at a time like this. But he was as silent today as he had been for the last four months, waiting for Peggy to put words into his mouth.

"Well, go on waitin' then. Wait 'till he rots in his grave!"

She yanked the paper from her typewriter and threw it on the floor, where it settled down on top of all the other pages she'd thrown away. She had come at this scene from every angle and still it eluded her. She'd faced it full on, sidled up to it, snuck up on it from behind, and still there were no words to say. The family waited, patient and poised to go on with their lives and blissfully unaware of the struggle that she was going through on their behalf. Well, they'd just have to wait.

She was caught in the middle of "the humbles," the awful insecurity that overwhelmed her when she thought of her weakness as a writer. She didn't dare call herself an author. Authors were artists who could turn words into magic, the way Stephen Vincent Benet had done in his epic poem *John Brown's Body*. Peggy had never read finer writing about the War Between the States, and in the four months since she'd cried over the beauty of those words, she hadn't been able to finish a single sentence of her own. No matter that she wore the same old overalls and green eyeshade that she'd worn through all those hundreds of pages already done. She was out of words, and out of story, too.

The story—it was a headlong, desperate thing that had driven her the past year, spending her days bent over the Remington on her sewing table, typing as fast as her fingers could go, following her characters along as they lived their troubled lives. They were all real to her, like friends she'd always known, their faces and their voices clear in her mind: Scarlett and her foolish infatuation with Ashley that blinded her to the real love Rhett offered her, and Ashley's equal foolishness in holding onto a dream that was gone. She felt sorry for them, and saddened by them. And every night, as she crawled into bed next to John and fell into an exhausted sleep, she looked forward to being with them again in the morning.

Now it had all come to an end, no words, no story to tell, no imaginary friends to share her days. Just a stack of brown manila envelopes that held the pages of the chapters of a book she would never finish. What a waste these months had been.

On a blustery day in late November, Peggy took the car south to Fayetteville for Sarah Fitzgerald's funeral. Past the Atlanta City limits the paved road turned to dirt, and Peggy followed it through rolling hills and fields into rural Fayette County. This was the land of her ancestors, the place her Irish immigrant great-grandfather Phillip Fitzgerald had first called home, and the family still gathered here to bury the Fitzgerald kin in the old Catholic family plot in the Fayetteville Cemetery.

Fayetteville was one of those small Southern towns that had been on the verge of prosperity once, before the War and the generation-long depression that followed. Now it was just a quiet country crossroads with a scattering of old homes around the Courthouse Square. Peggy knew the place well from childhood pilgrimages with her grandmother Annie Fitzgerald Stephens to lay flowers on the family graves. Now the flowers were for Great Aunt Sarah Fitzgerald, and the family was gathering again.

Sarah Fitzgerald was Grandmother Stephens' younger sister, one of the seven daughters of Phillip Fitzgerald and his wife, Eleanor McGahan. Sarah had never married, but stayed on at the family farm to help put it back together after the Yankees had torn it apart. Peggy remembered well the stories Aunt Sarah had told of the Battle of Jonesboro, when the Yankee troops tore up the rail lines and burned the town and everything around it. Phillip Fitzgerald's home was four miles outside of Jonesboro, on the line between Fayette County and Clayton County, and the Yankees had made it their headquarters during the battle. Then, as a thank-you for the old man's hospitality, the Yanks had looted the house and burned the cotton fields that surrounded it. When the smoke had settled, all that was left of the family farm was the old white house with Miss Eleanor's green velvet drapes hanging bravely in the parlor windows.

They called the farm Rural Home, and Peggy had spent happy summers there visiting with her spinster aunts, and never tired of hearing them discuss the War and its aftermath in great, gory detail. And by the time she was old enough to join in grownup conversations, she could tell the stories as if she'd lived them herself.

In a way, Peggy had always lived in the past. The ghosts of those long-ago times walked and talked in her mind, and she felt she could see the world through their eyes, and during the summer of her eleventh year she had lived their life, as well, staying at the farm to pick cotton with the field hands. In the heat of the long Georgia summer, heavy and thick and humid, she had worked until her back ached and her hands bled, and she felt a part of her people who had gone before. Now Aunt Sarah was gone too, and with her the memories of the early days in Georgia. The final links with the Old South were coming undone, one by one.

The Fayetteville Cemetery was laid out along a low ridge that backed up to a line of shaggy pines, but other than that there were no trees—a shadeless and windswept final resting place for a people who loved the deep green woods and rivers. The wind was coming up over the hill and blowing across the cemetery, scattering the sparrows into the winter sky, and Peggy shivered as she listened to the Priest speak the funeral service. Although it had been a long time since she'd been a church-going Catholic, since before her mother had died, she recognized the Latin words dedicating the grave and Aunt Sarah to eternal rest: "*In manus tuas, domine, commendo spiritum meum . . .*"

Then from the back of the group of mourners a small figure in a nun's habit stepped forward to lay flowers on the casket before it was lowered into the grave—Sister Mary Melanie, her somber black gown billowing in the wind. She was Sarah Fitzgerald's first cousin, nearly as old as Aunt Sarah, a nun since before anyone could remember. Peggy watched as the old woman's paper white hands reached forward and trembled, letting the flowers go. But as Sister Melanie bent down, Peggy thought she saw something soft go across the wrinkled old face.

Why, she's smiling! Peggy thought with surprise. No tears; only that trace of a last, loving smile as Sister Melanie backed away from the graveside and lowered her hands beneath her habit. Peggy looked at her standing in the midst of the crowd: part of them all, somehow apart from them, too. Peggy had known her from childhood and had always been fond of her, gentle and loving Melanie, spiritual heart of the family—and the heroine and heart of the book she was writing. Had been writing. Might never finish writing.

But it wasn't only Melanie's name and spirit that Peggy had borrowed for the unfinished manuscript that was hiding under her sewing table—the thing was full of half-disguised relatives. Phillip Fitzgerald became Gerald O'Hara. Phillip's wife Eleanor became Ellen O'Hara. Eleanor's green velvet drapes became Miss Ellen's green velvet curtains that turned into Scarlett's green velvet gown. And everyone in the family would recognize feisty Grandmother Annie Fitzgerald Stephens as the stubborn Scarlett O'Hara. The book was so crowded with family characters that Peggy was afraid to show it to anyone in the family. Her father, an earnest and cautious lawyer, had raised her with a fear of lawsuits, and she knew that her story could likely get her sued. Though there would be no lawsuits if she never finished the story . . .

She was still lamenting over her lost muse as the service ended and the mourners moved away from the graveside, gathering to talk and reminisce: first cousins and second cousins and third-cousins-once-removed. But Peggy lingered alone near the grassy square of Fitzgerald graves—or thought she was alone until a voice spoke, interrupting her thoughts.

"There's not much room left in Tara now," old Sister Melanie said. "I'll have to find some other spot when my time comes."

"Tara—" Peggy repeated. "Isn't that the Irish legend?"

"Indeed, it is: the seat of the high kings in Ireland, and the place where they were buried as well. Sarah used to say that this cemetery was our own little Tara, our sacred family ground."

There was a rustling of leaves behind them and footsteps along the gravel path—another elderly woman, wrapped in fur and shivering in the wind.

"Are you ready to go yet, Sister?" the woman said, a note of impatience in her voice. "The roads will be bad if it starts to rain."

"Not just yet, Marie. Cousin Peggy and I were just havin' a little talk, and we're not quite finished. Why don't you go ask how Edward is doin'? I hear his arthritis has been actin' up again."

The old woman pursed her pale lips and turned away, irritated.

Sister Melanie sighed. "My baby sister thinks I need her to take care of me in my old age, and I do try to humor her. But she's not so young herself, as you can see. We're both of us old ladies. Now be a good child, Peggy, and let me lean on your arm. I'd like to go sit on that bench awhile. My arthritis is actin' up a bit, as well, in this damp air."

From that seat at the crest of the hill there was a sweeping view back toward town: neat gardens around old frame homes, the courthouse with its arched clock tower, the twin-chimneys of the white-columned mansion facing the Jonesboro Road.

"It looks the same as it always has," Peggy said. "I guess some things never change."

"Some things," agreed Sister Melanie, "and some people too. And those are the ones who end up like this little town, forgotten by the rest of the world. There's a lot of folks like that in this family, never could get past the old ways and move on. Sarah used to say that there are only two kinds of people in the world: wheat people and buckwheat people. When wheat is ripe a strong wind will lay it flat on the ground and it will never rise again. But buckwheat bends into the wind, then rises up again as straight as ever. Wheat people can't stand a wind, but buckwheat people can."

"I'll miss her," Peggy said, "and all of her stories."

"And do you still like to hear the old stories? Or have you outgrown the past?"

Peggy thought back to her childhood, when the family stories the old folks told were like fairy tales to her. She still remembered fondly sitting on the soft muslin laps of fat old aunts and the bony cavalry knees of old uncles, listening to their tales.

"I think I may like the past better than the present. Sometimes I wish I could go back in time, just long enough to see some of it for myself."

"Then I'm glad we're here together today," Sister Melanie said. "For I've a story to tell myself, one that I don't believe you've ever heard, about somethin' that happened durin' the War, and after. There's not too many in the family now that even remember it, but I do. And I'd like to pass it on before I die."

"I would love to hear your story!" Peggy said, forgetting the cold bite of the wind on her cheeks, the rain that was hovering in the clouds overhead. It would be pleasant to disappear into the past for awhile again and forget her writer's block.

But Sister Melanie paused a moment, as if gathering her thoughts. "Have you ever heard of Cousin John Henry?"

Peggy thought back through the pages of family history she had studied in Aunt Sarah's parlor, the piles of old family photographs that had filled the drawers of the mahogany hunt board. But she couldn't recall anyone by that name, and she shook her head.

"No, I don't reckon you have," Sister Melanie said with a sigh. "But once we all knew him, one way or another. He was as much a part of this family as Sarah was, a part of our story. But it's been so long now, long forgotten." Then she put her chin up, straightened her small shoulders, and went on: "Well, it's high time we all remembered him. I have never forgotten."

And so began a family story that Peggy had never heard, not even in whispers, though she'd spent her life listening for such tales—how Cousin John Henry had first idolized and then despised his father, how he'd lost not just his hero but his sweetheart, as well, how his pain and pride had nearly destroyed his life, how he'd gone west to right himself and found instead that he was dying, how in trying to run from death he'd finally learned to live. And how he'd discovered in the end that people loved were never really lost, and that love could make any man a hero.

"But why haven't I heard his story before?" Peggy asked as Sister Melanie finally finished her long tale. "Why doesn't anyone talk about him, if we're related? Doc Holliday—he's famous!"

"He was called infamous, back then," Sister Melanie said, "which made him a disgrace to the family, of course. The Hollidays were fine folks, not the kind to have an outlaw as a relation. So after he died and the reporters finally stopped writin' about him, the family simply chose to forget about him, pretend he'd never been one of us. Then the aunts and the uncles and the cousins passed away, one after another, and the story passed away, as well. Now it's buried here, with them," she said, casting her gaze over the rows of headstones, the Hollidays and the Fitzgeralds and their kin. "Here in our little Tara, as Sarah called it. There's no Irish kings, but it's our own sacred ground."

"It's sad he never got to come home," Peggy said, imagining John Henry's grave in the cold Colorado mountains. His exploits would have made a good story for the Atlanta Journal, if she'd been working there still.

"Oh, but he did come home, dear," Sister Melanie replied. "His father brought him back."

"But I thought you said he died in Colorado?" *Old people*, Peggy thought. Their stories often wandered like their minds.

But Sister Melanie wasn't senile yet, only full of secrets. "He did die there, and was buried there, as well, in a cemetery on a bluff overlookin' the town. It was a lovely spot, so they said, with a view of the mountains all around. But it wasn't home."

"So what happened?"

"Walk with me down to the road, and I'll tell you, if you're not too squeamish to hear the tale."

"What do you mean?"

"When Henry Holliday got word of his son's death he determined to bring him home to be buried properly, in Georgia. So he took the train all the way to Colorado and had John Henry disinterred."

"Dug up?" Peggy said, indeed feeling a bit squeamish.

"They'd been diggin' up lots of graves in Glenwood Springs, movin' them from the middle of town to the new cemetery on the bluff. It was just another job for the undertaker. Henry had a second coffin special made for the train ride back home, then shipped John Henry like freight. It wasn't such an unusual thing to do, back then, but expensive, and the family thought it ill-advised. I suppose they didn't really want John Henry around, even dead. But Henry wouldn't hear otherwise, and there were heated words. 'I made my own money,' he said, 'and I reckon I can squander it anyway I want. And I want my boy back home.' He was a hard-minded man, all right, but there's no doubt he loved his son."

"So where is he?" Peggy asked, pausing for a last look around for a marker with the name *John Henry Holliday* engraven on it, and not seeing one.

"When Henry said he wanted his boy back home, he meant in Griffin, where John Henry was born. Henry wanted to lay him in Rest Haven beside his sister, little Martha Eleanora, where Alice Jane had liked to visit. But that part of the cemetery was filled up, so he found a spot in a new section across the road instead. It's a pretty location, good high ground with a view of the countryside. I visited there with Henry, before he died, and a time or two after. But they'll be no more visitors after I'm gone."

"Why not?"

"Because there's no one but me now who knows where John Henry is. Henry had him buried without a marker, to keep his gravesite quiet. He thought John Henry deserved a peaceful rest, after what the newspapers had done to him, makin' him out to be somethin' he never was. So there's only a red brick vault and a cement capstone, and grass growin' over it all. I think he did right."

"You could tell me where he is," Peggy offered, "and I could go visit him."

But Sister Melanie seemed to sense what she was thinking, and said with a knowing smile: "You used to be a reporter, yourself. I'm afraid you might be tempted to sell the story to the newspapers, and that would defeat Henry's purpose in keepin' things quiet, wouldn't it? I don't want John Henry to be forgotten, but I'd like him to be remembered properly. Let his poor body rest in peace, now that his spirit has passed on."

"Ashes to ashes, dust to dust," Peggy said disappointedly, having found a famous relative only to lose him again too soon.

"And here we are, back to the modern world!" Sister Melanie said cheerily as they came to the black Model T, its engine rumbling in anticipation of the journey. "We'll be home before bedtime! Why, I remember when a ride from Fayetteville to Atlanta took two days in the back of a spring wagon. No one ever took buggies such a distance on these bad roads." Then she turned back to Peggy, laying a hand on her arm, and added softly:

"I remember when John Henry made the ride to Atlanta in one night in the middle of an ice storm, riskin' his own life to save someone else's soul. That's the man I'd like folks to remember. That's the man I have never forgotten."

Peggy looked at her a moment, questioning, then feeling a gentle pressure on her arm, she looked down—and noticed for the first time the glint of gold on Sister Melanie's right hand, a little Irish ring like the one

Mattie had given to John Henry and he had sent back to her: two hands for friendship, a crown for loyalty, a heart for love . . .

"Mattie?" Peggy whispered, as the driver helped the old woman into the car, settling her for the long drive back to Atlanta. "You're Mattie?"

"Yes, dear. Or at least I was, long ago. I've been Mary Melanie for forty years now, longer than I ever was Mattie Holliday. It seems like another life, almost."

"But you knew him. You loved him!"

"I still do love him," Sister Melanie said, her voice tender, her brown eyes misty in her heart-shaped face. "I always have, and I always will."

Peggy stared at her in speechless amazement, trying to put it all together, her writer's mind connecting all the characters: saintly Sister Melanie who was the model for sweet Melanie in her book, Melanie who was really Mattie Holliday, Mattie who loved her cousin John Henry, John Henry who was the legendary Doc Holliday. Peggy couldn't have invented a better fiction, yet it was all true. And all family, her relatives, her story.

"Go on and finish that book you're writin'," Sister Melanie said. "And then maybe someday you can write our story, too. Then everyone will remember what I have never forgotten."

Back home in Atlanta, in her apartment overlooking Peachtree Street, Peggy put on her long overalls and pulled the green reporter's eyeshade down over her forehead, her favorite writing attire, and uncovered the Remington typewriter on her little sewing table. It had been too long since she'd had her hands on the familiar keys, too long since she'd been with the people who filled her mind and her days, but now she was finally back where she belonged.

She picked up the brown paper envelope marked *O'Hara Funeral*, the last thing she'd been working on, and slid the unfinished page back into her typewriter. Aunt Sarah Fitzgerald's funeral played through her mind and played itself out again as Gerald O'Hara's funeral, and the words that had eluded her for somany months now flowed and she knew that she was done with the humbles at last.

But there was something that bothered her as stared at the words *Fontenoy Hall*, thinking that they looked all wrong. Fontenoy wasn't a proper name for the O'Hara plantation. It didn't mean anything, and the name of the family home should be something special, something worth remembering, something worth coming home to—

And thinking of Cousin John Henry Holliday who had finally come home at last, she suddenly knew the only name that would do. With her blue editor's pencil she crossed out the words *Fontenoy Hall*, and in the space above the line she wrote *Tara*.

Author's Note

A REPORTER ONCE ASKED ME WHY I CHOSE TO TELL THE STORY OF Tombstone and the O.K. Corral from the secondary character's point of view: Doc Holliday rather than Wyatt Earp. The answer is that I didn't plan to tell the story of Tombstone at all; I only wanted to save some Georgia history. But as Founding Director of the Holliday-Dorsey-Fife House Museum, the antebellum home of the Holliday family, I had discovered untold stories of Georgia's most famous Western legend and his family connections to *Gone with the Wind*, and as a writer I knew those stories needed to be told. And what better way to combine the facts of his life and those sometimes unprovable family stories than through historical fiction? So my book—I thought it would be just one when I started writing—would be something like "*Gone with the Wind* meets *Lonesome Dove*," the story of how a Southern boy became a Western legend. I imagined the project taking a couple of years to finish, as I tied those Georgia stories together with a dramatized version of the known history of Doc Holliday. But when I got into the writing, I realized that the "known" history was mostly fiction, as well, and that if I were going to write about the real Doc Holliday, I'd have to find him first. Thus began not just a couple of years of writing, but eighteen years of research and writing as I followed the trail of Doc Holliday from Georgia to Tombstone and everywhere in between.

As I researched his adventures, I found events that could be tied together to form a plot and discovered what I thought was a theme of his life: his belief in heroes. But my plotting had to be flexible, because I kept finding new information about him and having to revise my plan. Although this was to be a work of historical fiction, I never wanted to bend or ignore the history for the sake of the story—and sometimes the history was even better than fiction.

By the time Doc Holliday arrived in the Arizona Territory, he was mostly done practicing dentistry, making his living in the gambling halls of the West. But though he was working as a sporting man, he still considered himself a professional man, as evidenced by the way he signed the 1880 Federal Census in Prescott, Arizona: *J.H. Holliday, Dentist*. And as a professional man, he took up appropriate lodgings there, sharing boarding house space with John Jay Gosper, Secretary of the Arizona Territory and Acting Governor in the long absence of the appointed governor, John Frémont. Since a man's associates often tell us something about the man himself, I dug into Governor Gosper's Territorial correspondence and discovered a war of words between Mexico and Washington that threatened to become a real war. Down on the southern border of the Territory near Tombstone, American cowboys were crossing the border into Sonora, stealing Mexican cattle and rebranding them to sell to U.S. military bases, and sometimes killing Mexican citizens. Mexico demanded an end to the depredations and the Federal Government ordered Arizona to take action—which Governor Gosper did, alluding in his correspondence to a plan to end the trouble which may have involved a private militia. Soon, the Earps and their associates were chasing rustlers and stage robbers and bringing threats from the cowboys. And Doc Holliday was perfectly positioned as the middle man in what looked very much like a covert government operation—and a new way of looking at the story behind the O.K. Corral gunfight. The fact that another famous Prescott character, the former Senator Thomas Fitch, became the lead counsel in the O.K. Corral hearing following the gunfight added fuel to my conspiracy fire.

Another surprise about Doc's time in Arizona came from the deed books in Cochise County. I had a hunch that Holliday was a partner in a Tombstone silver mine, so I contacted the county clerk who said she had never heard of any such thing. Surely, after all these years, if Doc had been invested in the mining industry, some historian would have mentioned it. But she did a search of the records anyway and discovered to her amazement (and my satisfaction) that Holliday did indeed have ownership in a mine—together with Wyatt Earp. They also owned water rights, indicating that they meant to develop the mine, as water was necessary to the stamping process that extracted silver ore from the mineral-laden rock. But just as the story plays out in *Dead Man's Hand*, Doc and Wyatt soon sold their shares of the mine to Marcus Smith, attorney for the McLaurys who were suspected of being in league with the cattle rustlers. The fact that they sold their shares in what might have been a fortune-making mine for the small sum of $10 makes one wonder what they got in return.

To tell the story of the month-long O.K. Corral hearing, I studied the newspaper reports of witness testimony and relied for analysis on attorney and law professor Steven Lubet's excellent *Murder in Tombstone*. As Lubet points out, Wyatt Earp's testimony at the hearing, read from a written statement instead of being given in the standard oral format, is a perfect legal defense against the charges being made and may actually have been crafted by legal counsel Thomas Fitch himself. It's intriguing that Doc Holliday was never called as a witness by either side, though most everyone else in town testified. Did Holliday's Prescott associations make him a dangerous witness who knew too much? Like all conspiracy theories, this one will likely never be proven, but it made for a great and unexpected turn in the plot.

The story of Wyatt Earp's steel shirt and Doc's split from him in New Mexico comes from Kate Elder. The story of bounty hunter Perry Mallon comes from the newspapers in Colorado which followed Doc's Denver arrest and legal entanglements in great detail. And it's another nod to my conspiracy theory that two governors worked together to keep Doc Holliday from being returned to the crooked justice of Tombstone.

With all of Doc's time in court he had plenty of opportunity to learn how the legal system worked, and in Leadville, Colorado, he worked the system to his own benefit in a surprising way. The legal record of the Bill Allen shooting there is complete with daily testimonies and court filings—including Holliday's appointment as an officer of the court allowing him to subpoena his own witnesses, surely an unusual situation in any trial. And his witnesses really did all appear in court on one afternoon, a crowd of gamblers and saloon workers come to testify that Doc Holliday was innocent of the charges against him. I had to admire his cleverness and his courage in defending himself.

The story of his meeting with his father in New Orleans comes out of his hometown of Valdosta, where Zan Griffith returned with his souvenir saddle. Zan told about having gone with Major Holliday on the trip, and how the Major met his son there and begged him to come home with him to Georgia. When Doc declined, Henry sent Zan along with him to Colorado as a valet for the trip. It's the saddle that gives the most credence to Zan's story of his travels with Doc Holliday, for in the 1880's Colorado was famous as the home of the A.C. Gallup Company's "Pueblo Saddle," and there wouldn't have been a more appropriate parting gift for a young man. Zan kept that special saddle until the 1920's, when the old hotel where he lived was destroyed by fire—sadly, along with the saddle. But family and friends remembered Zan's story of accompanying Major Holliday to New Orleans and meeting there with the Major's famous son, Doc Holliday. If he'd been making up the story, the local folks would surely have known and challenged his facts.

With all of the facts that were included in my story, there were some things I chose not to detail because doing so would have slowed things down—like the makeup of Wyatt Earp's posse during the troubled days in Tombstone. Although Dan Tipton, Sherman McMaster, Vermillion Jack, and Turkey Creek Jack Johnson were real men with interesting histories, their backgrounds had nothing to do with Holliday's story. They were, in essence, Wyatt's hired guns and I left them at that. The narrative flow is also the reason I didn't spend much time with the Earp wives: Wyatt's Celia Blaylock and Josephine Marcus, Virgil's Allie, and Morgan's Louisa, whom the reader only briefly meets in *The Saga of Doc Holliday*. They are part of the Earps' story, not Holliday's, and other writers are welcome to tell about their lives—for further reading I recommend the excellent *Mrs. Earp* by Sherry Monahan, along with *Wyatt Earp: The Life Behind the Legend* by Casey Tefertiller, and *Doc Holliday: The Life and Legend* by Dr. Gary L. Roberts.

As for the boy whom Holliday befriends in Denver, this is where historical fiction takes center stage. There are several sources for Holliday's secret son, all of them anecdotal and unproven, but all sharing the same theme: the orphaned newspaper boy whom Doc meets and then supports. One story has Doc sending for the boy to come see him in Glenwood Springs when the train first arrived there from Denver. The boy didn't know the true identity of his benefactor but attributed his own success in life to the kind Southern man with the gentlemanly manners whose legacy paid for his college education. There are people who claim to be descended from Doc Holliday's child, but no proof as yet. So I took all those stories and put them together with the facts we do know to create Tom McKey, the boy who looked like Holliday and might have been his son. But it's easier to imagine Doc having a child than to answer the question of why the Earps never had any—in those days of many children and no family planning, neither Wyatt, nor Virgil, nor Morgan had any descendants. I like to believe that Doc Holliday did.

The year that Holliday died was indeed unusually cold, the work of the Volcanic Winter caused by the eruption of Mount Krakatau. That cold brought the first blizzard in history to Atlanta a few months later and seemed a perfect setting for Mattie to learn of her beloved cousin's death—and as I wrote that scene, the second blizzard in Georgia history swept through Atlanta, making it all very real for me. The story of Doc Holliday's traveling trunk being sent to Mattie's convent comes from the family, as does their reminiscence that the personal items were given to relatives while the trunk and the letters were kept by Mattie as her own mementoes. When she passed away, the trunk and letters were inherited by her younger sister Marie (the old woman in the cemetery in the Postscript of *Dead Man's Hand*), and then later burned by her. Perhaps Marie felt the letters were too personal to chance falling into public hands, being the private correspondence between her sister the nun and the infamous Doc Holliday. But for a time, the family read and shared the letters and they are remembered as being wonderfully written, full of adventurous stories of railroads and silver mines and the Wild West—a first-person account of some of the most famous events in American history.

Did Marie Holliday really burn the letters, or are there still a few in existence somewhere? Until Doc Holliday's own words in those letters or some other yet undiscovered sources are found, we will have to picture his life through history and movies and novels—and our own imaginations.

My life has been filled with his story, and my story through *The Saga of Doc Holliday* has become part of his legacy.

But maybe that was my destiny. For there was another fascinating bit of history I discovered along the way: Doc Holliday died on November 8th, the same date that I was born. It was also the date that Margaret Mitchell was born, which takes us back to the start of this long note, and to the start of my story, as well. I didn't set out to write about Doc Holliday, only to save some Georgia history, and my book didn't originally begin with John Henry, but with Margaret Mitchell writing *Gone with the Wind*, who really did have writers' block toward the end of her story and almost gave up until she attended Sarah Fitzgerald's funeral in Fayetteville. So what is now the Postscript to *Dead Man's Hand* began as a Prologue and Epilogue framing the story of Doc Holliday as told by Mattie to her younger cousin Margaret Mitchell. But when Doc's history grew far beyond the legend, my story had to change to make space for it, and the *Gone with the Wind* connection became just an afterthought. For in answer to the reporter's question as to why I would choose to write about the secondary character in the Tombstone story: John Henry "Doc" Holliday was never secondary in his own life. He was the star of the story.

My long list of acknowledgments begins in *Southern Son* and *Dance with the Devil*, the first two books in the Doc Holliday trilogy, and continues here, with thanks to: Robert Fisher, Arizona Historical Society; Christine McNab Rhodes, Cochise County Recorder, Arizona; Gary McClelland, Tombstone, Arizona; John Denious, Silverton, Colorado; Nancy Manley at the Mountain History Collection of the Lake County Public Library and Mary Billings-McVicar, Leadville, Colorado; Lois Ann McCollum of the Frontier Historical Society in Glenwood Springs, Colorado; and Dr. Arthur W. Bork, Prescott, Arizona, who knew and interviewed Kate Elder and shared his recollections with me. And especially to Erin Turner, Editorial Director of TwoDot Books, for believing that Doc's story should be told in just this way.

Love and thanks, as well, to the friends and family who were my first readers and staunch supporters: Patricia Petersen, Mack Peirson, Daniel Mikat, Michael Spain, Melinda Talley, VelDean Fincher, and Dr. Dorothy Mikat. Special thanks to Laura Pilcher, copyeditor extraordinaire, and to Dan and Sally Mikat for giving me long quiet weeks to write at their home on Mackinac Island, Michigan

And last but never least, to my husband Dr. Ronald Wilcox and our family who loved and supported me through twenty years of Doc Holliday. When I started this project we had young children. Now we have grown children and a daughter- and sons-in-law and grandchildren. And so to them all—Jennifer, Heather, Ashley, Ross, Sterling, Sam, Sarai, Ethan, Elise, Alexis, James, Cole, Nora and anyone else who comes to join us—remember that family is first and forever. In Doc Holliday's time, and our own.

—Victoria Wilcox
Peachtree City, Georgia

About the Author

Victoria Wilcox is Founding Director of Georgia's Holliday-Dorsey-Fife House Museum (the antebellum home of the family of Doc Holliday, now a site on the National Register of Historic Places), where she learned the family's untold stories of their legendary cousin. Her work with the museum led to two decades of original research, making her a nationally recognized authority on the life of Doc Holliday. She is the author of the documentary film *In Search of Doc Holliday* and the award-winning historical novel trilogy *The Saga of Doc Holliday*, for which she twice received Georgia Author of the Year honors and in 2016 was named Best Historical Western Novelist by *True West Magazine*. She has lectured across the country, appeared in local and regional media, guested on NPR affiliates, and was featured in the Fox Network series *Legends & Lies: The Real West*. She is a member of the Western Writers of America, the Wild West History Association, Women Writing the West, and the Writer's Guild of the Booth Museum of Western Art and has been a featured contributor to *True West Magazine*. In the summer of 2017, she joined actor Val Kilmer (*Tombstone*) as guest historian at the inaugural "Doc HolliDays" in Tombstone, Arizona, site of the legendary OK Corral gunfight.